I0545147

Killing Instinct

By
Douglas Brain

This is for my Mum, Christine Brain;

sorry about all the inaccurate psychology…

Preface

In order to really appreciate this book, a basic understanding of part of Freud's theory would certainly help, feel free to skip if you want to though.

Whether you agree with Freud or dislike his ideas, you will find they still endure today. One lasting concept is that the human psyche, our personality, is made up of more than one part. Freud (1923) saw the psyche as structured into three parts he called the tripartite; the id, ego and superego. Freud theorised that each conceptual, not physical, part, develops during our early stages of life and stays with us forever after.

The id (or 'it')

The id is the primitive and instinctive components of the personality. It consists of those parts of personality that are inherited from birth. The id is impulsive and entirely unconscious. It responds directly to our instincts. It has no idea, and cares nothing, about anything outside of what it wants.

The id operates on the pleasure principle (Freud, 1920). Freud said that it is the idea that every wishful impulse should be satisfied immediately, regardless of the consequences. When the id achieves its demands, we experience pleasure when it is denied we experience 'unpleasure' or tension.

The ego (or 'I')

The ego quickly develops as the baby becomes a child and mediation is required between the unrealistic id and the real world. The ego is reason and logic, counteracting the chaotic and unreasonable id. It is the decision-making part of the personality.

The ego is 'that part of the id which has been modified by the direct influence of the external world.' (Freud [1923], 1961, p. 25)

The ego operates via the reality principle, working out realistic ways of satisfying the id's demands, often compromising or postponing satisfaction to avoid breaking society's rules. Like the id, the ego also seeks pleasure through reduction of tension and avoidance of pain, but unlike the id, the ego is concerned with the outside world. However, the ego is not moral, it has no concept of right or wrong; something is good simply if it achieves its end of satisfying without causing harm to itself or the id. The ego is usually considered weaker than the id, the ego has to satisfy the id but fundamentally has to play along with what the id wants.

The ego is 'like a man on horseback, who has to hold in check the superior strength of the horse.' (Freud, 1923, p.15)

The superego (or 'above I')

The superego is developed between the ages of three and five. It is the moral component of the psyche. It is generally learned from our parents and other authority figures in society.

The superego's function is to control the id, especially its desires that are forbidden in society. It also has the function of persuading the ego to turn to moralistic goals rather than simply realistic ones and to strive for perfection.

The ego, whilst working within the real world to satisfy the id's desires, has to maintain balance between those desires and the conscience that is the superego. Some people see this as the angel on one shoulder and the devil on the other, with the ego in between. As long as the ego maintains balance, there is a balanced personality.

*

Don't worry if this doesn't all make perfect sense because the book doesn't use them completely correctly anyway. Essentially the id is the animal inside you wanting sex and food; pleasure. The superego is your conscience, coming from society, trying to make you a good person and making you feel guilty for not being perfect. The ego is the mediator, your guardian; trying to get pleasure whilst not breaking society's rules.

The id wants to eat the burger, the ego decides to pay for it first. The superego makes you feel bad for eating all that fat and not recycling the wrapper.

Freud, S. (1920). Beyond the pleasure principle. SE, 18: 1-64.

Freud, S. (1923). The ego and the id. SE, 19: 1-66.

Chapter One

I woke in the new dawn of a sunny morning. Sweat covered me from head to toe. My eyes took in the familiar surroundings, sunlight was creeping into the room around the edges of the curtains, eerily lighting the scene. I was in bed, sat upright, breathing hard. Gradually I contemplated my situation, calming myself. Clearly, I was at home. I was in bed. I was alone. These reassuring thoughts slowed my breathing and stopped my panicking glances about the room. I took one final deep breath and wiped the beads of sweat from my forehead. Calmly, I told myself; "It was a dream. Just a dream." Believing this mantra, I climbed from bed and pulled back the curtains. Standing in the burgeoning sunshine, I breathed in again, repeating the words out loud, "just a dream." Eventually believing them, I climbed back into bed and tried to banish the lingering feelings of terror that would not go away. I decided to replay the content of the nightmare from which I had awoken. My mind flashed through the images as they had come to me in the dark; every detail, every movement, every feeling of fear and disgust. The sunlight warming me through the window did little to allay my feeling of dread.

I closed my eyes and immediately I was back in the alley of my nightmare. It was dark. The high walls around me and the concrete on the ground were damp from the rain. The sodden black grime of the city mixed with the smell of the rain, making my flesh crawl. I remembered taking a deep breath through my nostrils, revelling in the taste of it despite my deep loathing of the odour. I allowed the particles that hung mid-air to be sucked in to my lungs, the action forced me to feel the essence of the place. It was a dark place. It was an evil place; a place of bad deeds. No decent person had need nor reason to be there, but there I was. As was someone else.

He stood in the shadows in front of me, not hiding but not making himself visible either. I strained my eyes to make him out but I could not. It was as if he was part of the night itself, a shadow lurking just beyond my capacity to see him. Someone had crossed through the entrance of the alley, his silhouette standing starkly against the yellow flare of distant streetlights. As he entered, I wanted to warn him, to warn him, to cry out at him to run but fear held me silent. I stood in the dark; unable to speak or move. I knew the man that stood in the shadows was dangerous. I held my breath as the other man entered. He

3

walked directly past us both and I relaxed; it seemed as if the evil I was afraid of was not to occur that night after all. I even smiled as, finally deep into the alleyway, I heard the sound of him unzipping his fly and the gentle tinkle of falling water commenced, accompanied by a soft sigh of relief.

Suddenly I was the other side of the alley, just to the left of the man in the shadows, looking over his shoulder. I have no memory of how I got there but I could tell that minutes had passed. Still he didn't move, instead he shouted into the night, the sound of his voice rolled down the sides of the alleyway like thunder down a canyon. "Come out! I can see you are there." His voice was confident, loud, threatening. It left little room for debate. "Your shadow betrays you, fool. Cowering behind the bins like the pathetic creature you are. Come out and meet your inevitable destiny." His booming voice echoed back, emphasising specific words that were given a metallic edge from the detritus of the city from which it reverberated. "Betrays... Cowering... Pathetic... Inevitable..."

The man slowly emerged from behind the bin where he had been relieving himself. He paused; standing in the centre of the narrow passage. A dim light emerged through the clouded city sky, illuminating the red brick of the walls. The reflected glow made him little more than a red shape before my eyes. He stood some distance from me, arms down but not against his body. His fists were clenched, his body tense. I saw a trembling movement in the outline of his clothing. He wore a leather jacket that quietly creaked as he shook. He flexed his muscles and tensed his legs, shifting his weight from side to side. I took his shaking as a sign of his preparedness to fight. Adrenaline was coursing through his body, amping him up for an encounter. He looked far from the pathetic creature the shadow had claimed he was. Instead, he looked like a predator waiting to pounce.

The shadowy man though, the shouting accuser, was not impressed by the preparedness of his prey. He laughed. Genuinely and with glee, he actually laughed. Not a forced exclamation of disdain but, as if he honestly found humour in the situation. This greatly deflated the other, who was still trying to show his best fighting stance.

"I'm not afraid of you," the now quaking man responded. His voice was remarkably calm, yet somewhere behind the bravado I could detect his fear building.

"Oh, but you are," the shadow called, confirming my understanding of the situation. "However, your fear makes you far more intelligent than I had initially thought; because you should be." The accuser was still finding humour in the moment as he loudly spoke his words to anyone who might be listening.

"I can handle myself..." the man called out now in a soft trembling voice. His fear made his retort sound like a question rather than a statement.

The shadow, removing all previous lightness from his voice, shouted now; "You cannot and will not cause any damage to me. Quite the contrary. I am about to destroy you. It will be as if you never existed as a human being." He paused, the tension was unbearable. Still in his loud confident baritone, he added, "do you know what it is to be disembowelled?"

The man who had entered our dark canyon to relieve himself had relaxed his stance during this exchange, perhaps believing that this was only to be a verbal confrontation. He obviously hoped that this would be a battle of insults, nothing more than a story to tell later with embellishments of his bravery. However, I could see that this was never to be the case. For, just as he started to open his mouth, no doubt to prepare another retort, the accusing man leapt forward in an instant release of energy. There was no preparation in his movement, but I knew that it was coming. He didn't lean back or tense his muscles, he simply moved forward. Suddenly, with the speed of an Olympic sprinter, his shadowy figure charged down the alley. The other man was about ten metres from him as he had spoken his last words. The attacker covered this distance in just six massive strides. I was there too, right beside him; his confident rush forward leaving his target standing dumbfounded in the dark.

As he struck him, it was with a punch I could not have imagined before I had witnessed it. He had been pumping his arms in his explosive sprint and his arrival at his prey was timed perfectly. He clenched his fist at waist height and threw it upwards in a graceful arc towards the chin of the standing man. The attacker's muscular limb was now connected with the jaw of his target. As the fist struck, his open mouth snapped shut with a high-pitched crack that sounded toothshatteringly painful. Then came the true power of the blow. Behind the clenched fist was the momentum of a man at full sprint. He used his whole body to drive home the power in a fluid movement that was almost beautiful in its purity.

Every part of the attacker's body was employed in driving his fist up into the cloudy night sky; taking his target's chin and head with it. Such force was uncontainable and the target's head snapped back in an unnatural movement I would have only thought possible in a car crash. The force of the strike proceeded to lift the victim from his feet and throw him deeper into the alley, head first, falling backwards.

The sound of the strike was devastating. I was expecting a loud bang, a slap maybe. What greeted my ears, however, was a sequence of noises that each sickened me to my stomach. The snap of his jaw closing was uncomfortable enough. Far worse was the loud click as his head snapped back causing me to picture some vital part of his spine cracking. Then there was silence. The flight of the body arching through the air made no noise as I watched, rooted to the spot. The peace of the scene was finally ended as the wet smack of an inert body struck pavement. His ass hit the ground first like the slap of raw meat on a kitchen counter. His arms and legs were next. They rattled and clattered like firewood falling on the hearth. Then the worst noise, the coup de grâce, the hollow pop of the back of his head making contact with the ground. I winced with each sound, empathically feeling the pain of each impact. My stomach agreed with the conclusions of my ears and complained greatly, causing me to wretch. Then, again; silence and stillness. The prey on the ground not moving. The attacker not moving; instead smiling, grinning while surveying the results of his gruesome art.

Slowly the attacker rose, animal-like, a hunter moving over to inspect the kill. I was there already, at the head of the victim who lay on the wet, filthy ground. The smile on the attacker's face was victorious. The sparse lighting revealed only his gruesome grin, the majority of his face remained in shadow, hidden from me. He loomed over the still form of the collapsed man. Amazingly, slowly, and with great effort, the figure beneath him took in a shaking breath. As the injured man breathed out, he groaned. I could just make out the colour of his eyes as he painfully ratcheted them open. They were a striking cobalt blue, they seemed lit from within and the image startled me. They were my eyes. As completely as if someone had pulled them from my head and placed them in this stranger. He looked deep into my soul, pleading for help.

Suddenly, a simple look of acceptance came over his face. The attacker nodded and knelt beside him. A flash of reflected light from the city sky shone back at me; the glint of an edge beaconing its deadly presence in the dark. With a lightning swipe of movement, the attacker slashed across the belly of the helpless man. The black leather jacket fell open to reveal pale flesh beneath; remarkably the skin of the man was unharmed. The attacker soon remedied this with another cut from the opposite direction. Just as the leather of the jacket had opened to him, so did the belly of his prey.

Blood seeped out from the cut, a lake of black in the already dark night. The sight and smell of impending death, intermingled with the stench of the alley assaulted my nostrils. My mind was overwhelmed at this fresh attack on my senses and thankfully finally rebelled at the situation. I had seen enough, too much. The walls of the alley closed in as my sight diminished to a pin-prick, then blackness.

Chapter Two

Forcing myself to recall my dream as I sat in bed hadn't calmed me. Rather than blurring into the usual random collection of unconnected thoughts and memories, this dream maintained its narrative in the dawn of the morning light. It was this clear, consistent memory more than any of the content of the dream that disturbed me as I rose from bed once more. I closed my eyes and bathed in the warming sun, trying to dispel the feeling of dread that remained like a bad smell.

That was it, I realised, my dread remained because there was indeed a bad smell in my apartment. Shaking my head in realisation that here was probably the source of my nightmare, I made my way to the bathroom to shower. It was truly a repugnant odour, but I couldn't quite place it. It lay somewhere between rotting meat and excrement. I checked myself, suddenly worried I had soiled myself in the night, I breathed out a deep sigh as I found nothing. However, the smell lingered, just as pungent as I left the bedroom and entered my small bathroom.

Making the shower extra hot, I forced myself beneath its powerful jets and ignored the tingling pain the water immediately caused me as it sprayed across my shoulders. I hoped the scalding water would blast the feelings from my mind as I raised my head to the jets and let it scour my face. I opened my mouth and let the hot water fill it. I gargled a little before facing down to spit it to the shower floor. I started to feel human once more as I opened my eyes.

Looking to the water circling down the drain I saw a strange sight, rather than clean clear water, it was a muddy reddish-brown colour. I glanced over my body to trace the cause, but I couldn't find it. Looking down again I saw that the water was as clear as I had expected it to be. I breathed fresh air through my nose, the odour was gone. This was not as comforting as it might have been because I still hadn't determined the cause. It looked like I had just washed whatever it was down the drain. I tried to shake the feeling but again failed, it remained as a shadow, reminding me of the darkness of my dream. I shut off the shower and vigorously dried myself instead. Resolving to simply dress and go to work, I hoped that routine would drive the last vestiges of the nightmare from my mind.

As I pulled a clean shirt from my wardrobe, I looked to the one in the hamper; it was stained the same colour of the reddish-brown fluid I had just washed from myself. I reached for the once-white shirt and pulled it from where I had balled it up and shoved it into the wicker basket. It was flecked with a dried substance that stank of the odour I had once again released into my apartment, having disturbed it from its resting place. It was so powerful I almost vomited as I ran and threw it into the washing machine. Slamming shut the door of the machine, I ran to the balcony and threw open the sliding doors, sucking in lungfuls of the cold Canadian morning air. I forced myself to take in my immediate surroundings, to focus on something other than my fear.

The clean, ordered city of Calgary lay spread out before me as it always had been. From the balcony, I could see the structures of steel and glass I was greeted with every morning. There was a long freight train slowly moving through the structures, its grimy presence offending the gleaming high-rises either side of the tracks. I looked back to the order of the new towers stretching to the sky. I copied them, reaching my arms to the sky and stretching the stiffness from my back. I took another deep breath and the cooling air immediately had the desired effect as my stomach once again settled. As it did, however, so did a thought in my mind. The dream of the dark alleyway, the blood and viscera of the man killed; that was the smell, the material on my shirt. As the thought became clear, I realised that it could not have been a dream. I looked back to the washing machine, the evidence lurking within. I dry swallowed and tried to think. The memory remained clear but it retained the substance of a dream. A vivid, detailed and terrifying nightmare, but just a dream nonetheless.

I dressed myself and turned the washing machine to the maximum setting. Pouring half a bottle of detergent into the drawer and pressing the start button. The smell was gone, shut away behind the thick transparent plastic of the door; the sound of water flooding the offending shirt was the final sign of its demise. The memory lingered, however. The stain was real, the fluid in the shower, real. Somehow, the dream too must be real. I ran to the bathroom and looked to myself in the mirror, my familiar blue eyes looking back at me. Contained now in the lined skin of a middle-aged man, they maintained the intensity that drew people to them. 'Honest eyes,' that is what my wife had called them. I looked to them now, looking for the truth I needed. All I saw were the eyes of the dying man, the dead man, looking back at me.

I sighed, rubbing my eyes, making my vision blur. The victim could not have had my eyes. This I knew; they are unique, unmistakable. No other could have them. The victim, therefore, was not real. I reminded myself of how I had moved in the alley. Standing next to the attacker, moving with him, looking over his shoulder. This too was not possible. The stain might be real but the dream could not be.

I left my flat without turning back. "It was a dream", I told myself with a forced smile as I set to work, "just a bad dream." I walked to the lift and tried to think of a reason for the smell. It wasn't blood, I decided. It was something nasty that had unknowingly spilled on me during the day, festering and rotting overnight. The truth hit me like a welcome slap in the face: my dream had been caused by the smell, not the other way around. "You are a logical person," I told myself, "you have a degree in psychology and a post-graduate degree in engineering. You are an informed, educated scientist, a man of logic. There is no other explanation." I let the words settle in my mind as I walked.

I calmly made my way to the bus stop, taking in the world around me to reject the discomfort of my introspection. I looked to the people, they too were walking to work or driving cars down the wide streets to parking lots beneath their offices. The memory of the dream started to fade, to drift to the swirling winds that whistled through the tall apartment building I had just left. "The dream belongs behind me," I told myself, "you are Edward Gooch, software engineer. Time to go to work." Each step was a step away from the memory of the nightmare, each one made me feel better, so I quickened my pace, breathing hard the cool morning air.

Chapter Three

"You are Detective Montgomery Beech. You are a confident, powerful, police detective," I told the blurry reflection in the metal elevator. It was something I did every morning, trying to prepare myself for another day as the youngest detective in the precinct. The doors juddered as they reluctantly slid open and I sighed as I stepped through them. "Minty..." the call rang out. It echoed against the glass partitions of the detective's office I was trying to surreptitiously enter. Sighing, I carried on walking to my desk. "Minty-fresh..." the caller renewed in his familiar mocking tone. I waved and tried to smile at the welcome. I dropped my bag on the floor and kicked it underneath my desk. Sliding out the chair and dropping into it, I closed my eyes and took in a deep breath. I tried to sink low into my chair. Feeling the soft material of my hoody against the back of my neck, I turned my head a little from side-to-side to allow it to comfort me. I took another deep breath and tried to collect myself. This was the part of the day I dreaded most, the new insult I expected but never appreciated was about to arrive.

I looked across to Detective 'Mike' Booth and sighed. He was sitting at his desk, chatting to one of his cronies, laughing at a shared joke that was probably at my expense. I didn't know what people saw in him but he was the centre of attention around the Precinct. He was large, tall really at a few inches over six feet. He was big too. Fat, I liked to think, but I suppose it would be fair to say that it was probably mostly muscle. His hair was long, not too long, but it blew in the wind and he liked to brush it from his eyes when it did. He was probably over forty now but to be fair he didn't look it. It was his relaxed attitude that people liked. He always seemed to be enjoying himself and the people around him. At the same time, he was an excellent detective, his arrest rate was one of the highest in the area and he knew it. He was a ladies' man too. Code, I thought, for him being divorced having had an affair with Jill from Human Resources. I winced as I saw him rise, knowing that he was going to walk over to resume his mocking of me.

Thankfully, however, I could see that he was heading to the elevator instead. It seemed that the loud announcement of my nickname was enough for today. I could hear him chuckling as he walked past and I ground my teeth in response. I knew it was pathetic of me, but his insistence on using that stupid nickname really ticked me off.

Thankfully, my mood lifted just as quickly as it had dropped as I saw Grace walk in. Catching her eye as she mimed drinking from a mug, I rose to meet her in the break-room.

"When's that dumb nickname going to go away?" I asked her as I pulled a mug down from the cupboard, handing it to her.

"You know it isn't, don't you?" she replied as she poured herself a coffee.

"I know, I suppose... But at least everyone else has dropped the 'fresh' part, why can't Booth? I'm not the new boy anymore." I was whining, I could hear it in my voice but, try as I might, I couldn't remove the childish tone from my words.

"Come on, Minty. You know the rules. The last to arrive is always the new boy," Grace responded with the happy smile she always greeted my complaints with.

"I've been here two years and had twenty convictions, I'm not minty-fresh anymore," I asserted in what I hoped was a confident manner.

"I wouldn't brag about that number, Minty. Twenty isn't very many, you know," her face crinkled slightly with her honest assessment of my performance as a detective.

"I know," I replied, "but I don't get any good cases, do I? The new boy gets the rubbish that don't deserve investigating."

"Minty, please... I came here for coffee and a rest, not another moan about your working situation," she said, sighing.

I recognised the noise: she was bored of hearing this from me, "sorry, it just gets on my nerves is all. I'll try to get over myself." I replied apologetically shaking my head. Trying to shake my bad mood away, I smiled and changed subject. "Anyway... How are you, Grace? Amazing as always."

"Totally," the change of topic quickly bringing back her good mood, "solving crime despite the inept policing that goes on around here." She beamed her glowing smile back at my half-hearted attempt at one.

Grace is one of our Crime Scene Investigator technicians

attached to the precinct and probably my best friend in the world. I spent my favourite five minutes of the day asking her about her cases and how she was 'solving them single-handed' while she avoided asking about mine. Eventually, however, I think she felt guilty about cutting me off as she broached the sensitive subject of my career.

"So how is work, Minty? Any good cases yet?" She asked sympathetically and hopefully.

"Nope. Nada. I've an arsonist who sets fire to waste bins and no-one cares. I'm trying to find a vandal whose damage to property is apparently called street art now. And... and I can see the Captain trying to attract my attention to give me some new rubbish..."

"Go on, Minty. You never know. Maybe he wants you to find out who murdered all the doughnuts?" She smiled as she picked at some crumbs from the empty doughnut box.

Coffee still in hand, I trudged reluctantly over to the Captain's office. He had a file in one hand and was beckoning to me with the other. He guided me into his office and sat me down with a comforting pat on my shoulder.

"Detective Beech." He greeted me with my proper title. At least he didn't call me 'Minty', I thought. Even though he still refused to call me Montgomery despite my asking him repeatedly to do so. That is where my nickname originally came from, just a simple shortening of Montgomery that I welcomed with good humour. It was Booth, I remember, cursing him again, who added the 'fresh'. It was him who sentenced me to being identified constantly as the new boy. Again, I had to shake the negativity from my mind as I tried to sit more upright opposite Captain Horton. He liked to tell me off for slouching so I shifted in my chair and tried to look professional while I waited for him to explain my new 'case'.

He was going to make me wait a while, I knew, as he dropped his head to read some paperwork laid out on his desk. I caught my reflection in his window and lamented the sight before me. I was tall enough. Close enough to six feet tall to tell people that was how tall I was, yet I somehow still looked little. I blamed my pale complexion and slight frame. I tended to wear larger clothes, hence the hoody this morning, to make myself look bigger but on reflection they probably just showed how puny I actually was. I had become a police officer soon after my twentieth birthday and quickly rose through the ranks. I was bright, and successive Captains recognised it until I was recommended to Police College to train as a detective. I remember my excitement on being assigned to the Calgary Police Force and Captain Horton; I thought it was going to be my time. That was two years ago and since then I had done little of value in my opinion. What was it about me? I wondered. Why did I look the perpetual child, why couldn't I shake this nerd off me? *I am a police detective*, I thought, sitting up straight again. Try and look like it, I told myself.

As the new arrival at the Station, even after two years, I was still getting the cases that no-one else wanted. I was assigned all the trivial investigations that wouldn't matter if they were never solved. Either that, or cases so simple they were just exercises in paperwork. But this morning, the Captain amazed me by gesturing to a man waiting at reception. He informed me that his name was Mr Gooch and he wanted to report a murder. I tried and failed to contain my excitement; an actual murder investigation. I wanted to leap up and run at the witness, the investigation was already playing out in my mind. Step one: interview the witness and establish the facts. I would have to get CSI to the scene immediately, I would of course request Grace lead the team there…

"Don't get too excited, Montgomery." The Captain firmly stated, sensing my anticipation building. "He wants to report a murder that we have no record of. Just a 'mole', I'm afraid."

That killed my excitement as quickly as it had started. A 'mole' is precinct code for a walk-in confession or witness of a crime with no basis in fact. A polite way of saying the witness is 'crazy', or a 'whack-job'. This quickly morphed into calling them 'whack-a-mole', to just being 'moles'. Just one part of the police humour to which you have to adjust as a new detective.

"And try not to look so miserable, Minty," he told me as I reached across his desk for the file. "And wear a bloody shirt, you look like a damn student in that hoody." He added for good measure.

Taking the file from the Captain, I tried to smile. The result was not convincing as he furrowed his brow in response. As I turned and left his office, my attempted smile immediately fell from my face. I tried to build some enthusiasm and confidence as I went. The witness was sat on the bench by the elevator doors. I briskly walked towards him across the office floor, his thin file flapping in my hand. He seemed to sense my approach because he looked up as I came near. He was tall, I registered as he rose to meet me, strong too. He wasn't thin as I was, nor big like Booth, just well proportioned. He looked athletic but not overly so, perhaps he used to be physical, no longer now that he was older. He was in his forties, I guessed, taking in the lines of his face, the grey in his blonde hair. He smiled and I was immediately disarmed. He looked at me with sparkling blue eyes and his face opened up to me. I couldn't help returning the smile. Finally reaching him, I shook his outstretched hand and introduced myself. His grip was firm and I took in his tidy demeanour and not inexpensive suit. He looked together and very professional, my assumption that he was going to be an alcoholic or mentally ill flew out of the window.

Chapter Four

I sat waiting in the police precinct, trying to decide what I was going to say to the officer when one was finally assigned to take my statement. I hadn't fully accepted that I was going to say anything at all until I had reluctantly walked through those large open double doors at the top of the five concrete steps from the street. Those steps, those doors, I had travelled past them every day on the bus to work but it was today of all days I had truly noticed them. I had been sat on an uncomfortable bus bench, head drooped, avoiding eye-contact with the usual commuters as I always did. Walking had helped me to dismiss the dream but, sitting passively on the vibrating, shaking bus, anxious thoughts had quickly begun to intrude upon any temporary peace I had fostered. I was trying to find comfort in routine but my mind insisted on returning to the dream and that stench. I had thought that reconstructing my evening prior to the dream would finally put my fears to bed but it had just made things worse.

I remembered that I had been walking the streets of the city last night, as I had been doing most evenings since my separation and subsequent divorce. That felt real, not a part of the dream, of that I was as sure as I could be. My wife had complained for years about my detachment, my analytical way of thinking, and to be honest I think I had mostly ignored her. I remembered how the suggestion that we separate had come like a bolt from the blue. However, the divorce papers quickly followed and before I knew it I was single. At first I was upset, of course, but I quickly settled into a new routine. That was my problem now. If I thought about it, I could distinctly remember taking an evening walk and getting something to eat from the food-court at the mall. However, if I analysed further, I could convince myself that the memory was indeed just that; a memory of memories, pieced together into a narrative that could have been any night of my recent life.

My life had become routine. I moved in a fog of familiarity through which I could only glimpse real life. The life I glimpsed was that of others. People around me lived, I observed. My wife would have liked that realisation, she would have agreed with it. My ex-wife of course, I corrected myself out loud to no-one in particular as the bus arrived.

So, I sat on the bus, contemplating the dream. I thought for a while about the possibility that it had been a psychic vision. I dismissed this hypothesis out of hand. I believed in psychics less than I believed in Santa Claus. However, I knew that many crimes had been solved with far less clear visions than mine. I firmly believed that these visions were people subconsciously recalling something they had seen or heard previously without realising it. The more I thought about it, the more that it seemed a likely explanation. I pondered the idea that I had indeed walked the city that night, wandering in a daze as I often did. Perhaps my eyes saw something, something my conscious mind paid no attention to, but my subconscious logged for later analysis. That later resolution of information in the form of a dream was what I had experienced.

I looked around me on the bus at the people all about, swaying back and forth with our movement through the busy city streets. My theory was starting to settle me, for it also explained the substance on my shirt. I had obviously come into contact with the material currently being washed from my shirt back at home. That smell, combined with my more open-minded state of sleep, was what had triggered the dream. Just as I was formulating my theory, I happened to glance out of the window. That was when my subconscious reared its ugly head once more. A pang of guilt surged through my throat and made me swallow the feeling. As the bus pulled to a stop to allow more passengers on, my civic duty rose to my mind and caused me to rise from my seat. I knew something, I heard myself tell my legs. *I had to tell someone*.

That is how I found myself sitting for over an hour on a hard wooden bench in the detective's office of the downtown Calgary police station. I watched as a scruffy young man in a grey hooded sweatshirt reluctantly approached me. He walked with what looked like a swagger but on closer inspection seemed forced. It was as if he thought he should walk with confidence but wasn't quite sure how that was supposed to look. Looking around me, he somehow stood out from the other detectives. He looked different. Young and naïve. His police badge was loosely hanging from a metal chain around his neck. He grabbed it with clumsy hands and pressed it towards me, accidentally showing me the back of his identification and not noticing. I rose and shook his hand, following him to the desk as he gestured that I sit. I still hadn't decided what to tell him or how to explain my dream and his look of boredom in anticipation of the interview wasn't helping matters.

I sat on the creaking wooden chair and tried to shrug his youthful disdain from my mind.

Chapter Five

Edward Gooch was an interesting witness. He started dictating his statement by telling me that he didn't believe he had seen anything he was about to describe. Immediately he sensed my confusion and explained his theory. It certainly was a new approach for a 'mole' to take. I let him talk, telling him the usual phrase that any information from a concerned member of public was of interest and value to the police. It was rubbish, of course. I would write it all down, have him sign it, file it accordingly and never read it again, no one would. It was the way of the police; if it was written down, it was dealt with.

I had expected it to be tedious in its pointlessness. Instead, the graphic nature of his dream and the narrative detail made it entertaining and actually quite interesting. Mr Edward Timothy Gooch had witnessed a murder in an alleyway last night. It was such a shame that it was all a fantasy. I had already checked the crime board as I did every morning. There had been no murder last night and something so violent and bloody would have been discovered by now. I discreetly pressed refresh on the department homepage on my computer just to reconfirm this. I didn't like his subconscious theory either. From the content and recall of his dream, it was obvious that he was an observant man. It seemed impossible that he could have witnessed something without realising it at the time. It was a dream, I knew that from the start: I think he did too really. I felt sorry for him; he obviously didn't have anyone to talk to. He was nice enough and I had, sadly, nothing better to do. So, I dutifully wrote it all down, feigning interest and concern, allaying his fears, being his sounding board, his therapist for the time being.

"He was sick!" I jumped at the sudden increase in volume as he shouted across the office that was now humming with people. "I watched as he sliced that man open--"

"And where were you standing at this point, sir?" I quietly asked, attempting to calm him down. People were looking and it was starting to get embarrassing. The interview had been going on long enough and I was starting to get bored.

"I... well I... I guess that I was standing in front of him... I can remember seeing the knife..."

"In front of him, sir?"

I could see his confidence dip, he was unsure again, like he was when he first sat at my desk. I only hoped that when he realised how stupid he was being, he didn't get violent. The last thing I wanted was an episode like last month; the abuse I suffered from Booth the last time a witness statement got out of hand went on for months. As if a male prostitute in an evening dress punching me in the face was anything out of the ordinary in a police station. As I watched Mr Gooch's face, I could see the light dawning on him and slowly reached under my desk for the baton I keep there.

"Maybe you've made a mistake, Mr Gooch?"

"Well, I guess... it felt like a dream, but more, more real..."

"You've someone you could talk to, sir? A doctor?"

His demeanour remained calm so I relaxed a little. His response was adamant but in no way violent.

"I am not mad, Detective."

"No sir, I didn't think that. I just thought, if you had someone who could help--"

"I'm not a psychiatric patient, Detective. I'm a respected engineer."

"I don't mean to suggest anything, Mr Gooch. It's just that we get a lot of cases like this, where the witness is mistaken. Could you be mistaken?"

Sitting back in my chair, thinking that he wasn't going to punch me after all, I watched as he tried to reconcile the truth with what he thought he had experienced. I let him think, not responding as he thought it through. Finally, he seemed to settle upon a reality he could be satisfied with.

"I suppose it must have been a dream... I did wake up in bed. I don't know how I got home... It was just so real. There must be some basis in fact..."

"I understand, Mr Gooch," I gently told him. He looked lost, wounded. I wondered if he might start to cry, "these things are unsettling. The mind is very powerful, it can create memories that feel very real indeed." He looked up at me, those bright blue eyes glistening with tears: he needed reassurance.

"Am I in trouble? For filing an incorrect report, I mean."

I smiled, I couldn't not. This strong, capable man needed something from me. It made me feel strangely close to him: I wanted to reassure him, to make him feel better. Besides, he had done nothing wrong, he was being very conscientious in fact. "Don't worry about it. I'll file it as 'no further action to be taken'. You haven't committed a crime, you were confused, that's all. As long as you're satisfied with that, of course."

He smiled now, his eyes twinkling and his shoulders relaxing in relief. It was as if a huge weight had been lifted. "That's fine, Detective. Thank you very much. I am so sorry about all of this." He quickly rose and reached to shake my hand; I accepted his warm grip as he placed his other hand around mine.

"You did the right thing," I reassured him. I paused, considering my new resolution to total professionalism, "just to be clear though. You haven't seen anything? Witnessed any crime?"

He smiled sheepishly, "no. No I haven't. I am sorry detective."

He continued to apologise as I began to usher him from the building. I filed the report, tagging it as 'withdrawn', and went downstairs to find Grace. As I walked into the basement office of the CSI techs that were attached to our department, I found her packing a case of equipment.

"What's up?" I asked as she snapped the lid of the case shut and shrugged into her blue windbreaker.

"Case downtown, stabbing," she informed me brusquely.

"I'm coming." I announced and spun around to race upstairs. Giving her no time to complain, I grabbed my own windbreaker, shouted in the vague direction of the Captain's office that I was heading out, and ran to meet Grace. I found her in her van outside the main door of the precinct, the engine idling. Mildly surprised to find her waiting for me, I climbed into the passenger side and she pulled off down the street.

21

We drove in silence. I knew her, and I knew that she didn't want to question me on the validity of my being there. I had no authority to jump on any case I wanted and she knew it. She also knew that she couldn't have talked me out of it at that point either. As she calmly drove through the wide city streets towards downtown, I tried to look at her through the corner of my eye. Catching sight of her familiar green eyes flicking between mirrors, checking for obstructions and traffic, I marvelled at her beauty. Her soft features, lit by the morning sun, showed her kindness and patience in a look created by time and experience. At thirty years old, she was most certainly a woman. Time had been kind, however, and having seen old photos of her, I believed she was more beautiful than ever. Sighing, I lamented for the hundredth time how I could never tell her that. She was my best friend and my regular confidante in times of crisis, something I could never risk with a clumsy advance.

I tortured myself further by risking a glance at her cleavage, rising and falling as she breathed deeply. She suddenly spun the wheel hard over in my direction, giving me a better glimpse of flesh revealed by her low-cut shirt. I quickly averted my gaze, pretending to look at the car she had just weaved around. I enjoyed my glances of her beauty, but they were starting to make me feel guilty. She was my best friend and a hugely capable woman; reducing her to a sex object like that didn't feel right. Still, I couldn't help myself as she turned back to face the road ahead. But now, now I had to concentrate as she pulled into an alley and parked just short of the police tape. I had come here for a reason, it was time to end the petty crimes I was forced to investigate. This was my chance; I intended to take it no matter what.

Silent since we left the station, Grace exited the vehicle. She dropped down from the high seat and strode towards the police guard. Flashing her badge, she ducked under the tape and disappeared into the alley to find the body. I got out of the van myself now, somewhat less confidently. I looked to the buildings either side of me, their closeness creating a brick canyon filled with air-conditioning equipment and dumpsters overflowing with rotting garbage. Mr Gooch's description of his dream filled my mind, his vivid description echoing in my ears as I glanced around the scene. I shook the déjà vu from my head by turning behind me and reminding myself that every alley in this part of the city looked just like this one.

I stepped over a puddle of suspicious grime and approached the crime scene. It was easy to see where the victim was as three bright portable lights backlit a low fabric screen. The rest of the alley was dirty and dimly lit despite the beautiful sunshine just behind me. I caught sight of the detective in charge just as he turned to look at me. He was talking to a uniformed officer, no doubt the responding unit, but dismissed him with a casual wave of his hand as he strode in my direction. I had just reached the police tape as he met me the other side, the plastic barrier separating us as effectively as the Berlin Wall at its most solid.

"What do you want, Detective?" He asked in a clipped tone; already I had annoyed him.

"This is in my jurisdiction," I pointed out, "so I wondered what was going on. Some problem, Detective?"

"I don't know who told you about this, but this is an Organised Crime case."

He glanced over to where Grace was under the floodlights, clearly aware of who had informed me. I tried to read his expression. I had only met him a couple of times, but Detective Will Force, cliché name aside, was a good guy and wouldn't single out a CSI for spreading a little gossip. Me on the other hand. Me he could crush. He could end my career if I just dared to duck under that tape. Organised Crime had become an important task-force in recent years, which meant they had seniority over any case they saw fit to take. That explained why it had not been reported to our precinct; they had jumped on it early for themselves.

"Come on, Will. You know me. I won't get in the way, I just want a peek."

"Fine, but no touching, and you will not tell anyone, understood?"

"Understood," I nodded with a smile as he raised the tape to let me enter.

As he turned back to the responding officer, I carefully walked towards the white lights of the scene.

"What've we got here then, Grace?"

"He let you in then?"

"Unofficial, but here, yeah. So, what's the picture?"

She pressed her latex gloves into a more comfortable fit and considered her response. Her demeanour had changed since the car and she looked very efficient and professional, as she always was when she was working. This is what had first attracted me to her, the dichotomy of her personality. One second she would be all girly and soft, the next cold and hard, describing how someone had been butchered for the price of a cup of coffee. She was a true professional, a brilliant CSI, yet somehow maintaining who she was underneath.

She gestured to the body beneath the sheet, "brutal one, nasty. The guy's been sliced up pretty bad. Half of what was inside is now outside, laid out all over the floor. I can see why Organised was called, some kind of message, no doubt."

"Knife?" I asked as I slipped some gum into my mouth and started chewing. The smell of the body wasn't helping my stomach. Desperate to not throw up, I concentrated on her instead.

"Yeah, but not your normal showy thing. This was a work of precision, something really sharp, professional, expensive."

"You know, my 'mole' this morning said he'd witnessed a murder with a knife in an alley."

"Forget it, Detective Beech," Will barked in my ear, "if you think you're taking my case because of some weirdo who predicted a knifing in an alley, you really are Minty-fresh."

I hadn't noticed him standing behind me and I was annoyed that he had heard me talking about Mr Gooch. "But he did predict it, Will." I said, half-heartedly.

"Yeah, well did he describe this?" Will asked as he whipped the sheet from the body with a flourish. I could see what Grace had been talking about, his intestines were spread out on his stomach, carefully arranged and still attached. I gagged, forcing the bile back and hoping they hadn't noticed. "You know as well as I do that they aren't ever specific enough. 'I see a man. A man in an alley. A knife.' I just predicted a dozen more. You know how common these attacks are, they're a psychic's wet-dream."

"I know," I replied, knowing that the statement didn't contain anything that I could specifically link to this scene. My shoulders drooped with the disappointing realisation that Will was going to keep this case and I was going back to taking pictures of graffiti for evidence of a crime no-one cared about. "Look, I'm tired of being Minty-fresh. I just want a real case," I found myself admitting to him.

"You don't want this one, believe me. Alley like this, body like that. Zero leads, zero evidence; there's no chance of closure."

"What about the display of his organs, maybe a signature?" I desperately pointed out to him, trying to get involved, trying to make myself a part of something.

"Nope. That's new, nothing to tie to anyone or any organisation we know of. This one's definitely a back-burner. The only hope we have is to catch the guy on something else and attach this to him later with a confession and a deal. Trust me, you don't want this one. Tell him, Grace."

"He's right, Minty," she agreed, "I have to finish my work here, but I'm predicting zero physical evidence. It was just too quick and clean, and this alley's got so many contaminants... this is going nowhere."

"Come on guys, where is your enthusiasm?" They both just looked at me. I knew where their enthusiasm was. Grace had been a CSI for eight years now and had seen it all; she knew when a scene would yield some evidence and she knew this one would not. Will too. A top-ranking detective in a high-profile task-force, he could see this going nowhere fast. "Will, look. This is a back-burner for you. You said it yourself, so let me be your ring." I winced at the unfortunate pun and tried to look imploring, desperate. He bit his lower lip and took a deep breath.

"Fine." My face lit up. "But the second you find something, you have to let me know. And if I find something, it's my case again in a heartbeat. Understand?"

"I understand completely," I nodded, trying and failing to prevent the grin that was quickly spreading across my face.

"I'll inform your Captain it's yours... I suggest you interview the attending officer yourself. I was never here, you beat me to it, okay?"

"Okay. And thanks, Will."

"Don't thank me, Minty. You just attached an unsolvable murder to your precinct's crime statistics. Don't expect any thanks from anyone soon for that." He shook his head with a wry smile and left the scene, ducking under the tape and walking to his car. Grace shook her head and returned to gathering evidence from the body. I was the only happy one, I thought, as I pulled out my notebook and started to sketch the scene.

We stayed in silence for a while, me making notes and Grace studying the area around the body. She made me jump a little when she finally spoke.

"A psychic witness, Minty?" She asked without turning around or looking up from where she was crouched.

"Well, it was worth a try," I conceded, trying to note the position of the body relative to the rest of the objects in the alley.

"Have you considered he might actually be a proper witness?" She asked.

"Not really," I said, still concentrating on my notebook, "like Will said, he didn't mention the guts thing. He could have been talking about any alley."

"Still…" Grace insisted.

That made me stop writing. She wanted to say something: experience had taught me to listen.

"The absence of knowledge does not disprove a theory," she said, placing whatever was at the tip of her tweezers in a plastic bag.

"You don't think he would have noticed the killer pull his innards out?"

"That's not what I'm saying," she insisted, an appropriate retort to my flippant question, "he might have repressed it, or run away before it happened."

"But Grace, you didn't hear him. It was a dream, there were gaps in his memory, he actually looked directly at the killer. There's no way he wouldn't have been killed too."

"He couldn't be the killer? Or an accomplice?" She asked, finally looking at me, gesturing to borrow my pen as hers had run out.

I passed her the pen, "Well, it did cross my mind but I dismissed it pretty quickly. After all, he came to me." I thought out loud.

"Remember your training though, particularly the history of dissociative killers. If he was behind or in front of the killer, watching the murder happen, he could have been watching himself do it."

"I suppose he might see the actions of a separate personality committing a murder as a dream," I admitted, looking in my pocket for another pen.

"I know it's unlikely. I'm just saying that you probably shouldn't rule it out on the basis of a missing portion of information from his statement."

She had a point. I needed to either rule out Mr Gooch, or investigate him to the end. I had ignored his statement because there had been no killing. Now there was, everything had changed. "What would you suggest?" I asked the back of Grace, who was looking for more evidence to collect.

"Do I have to do your job now, too?" She asked, "I am busy you know."

I sighed. I knew I was distracting her.

"What was in the statement?" She asked resignedly before I could leave, which was my instinct.

"Just a description of the alley," I said, looking around. "Could be any alley."

"Come on..." she coaxed, "there must have been something, some detail we could prove or disprove."

I looked around again, my eyes coming to rest on a dumpster. "He said the victim relieved himself behind the dumpster before he was killed, could you test--"

She cut me off, "if you think I'm testing for his urine in this place you can forget it. The contamination of all this filth means I could

27

never say if it was his or not, and can you honestly find me one dumpster in an alley round here that hasn't been peed against?"

"You've got a point," I conceded, looking around again. "I'll have to check the file."

"Come on, you wrote that less than an hour ago, you have to be able to remember it."

She was right, I was trying to improve my observational and recollection skills as a detective. I should be able to recall every detail. I looked again to the dumpster, remembering how Mr Gooch had told me about the victim there, "the victim," I repeated to myself. I snapped my fingers, "that's it," I remembered. "He said that he had bright blue eyes, just like his. He specifically remembered because it upset him."

"Well, there you go then." Grace said.

"Can you check the body," I excitedly asked her.

"You know better than that, the medical examiner has yet to release it," she reminded me.

I must have looked very dejected as she tilted her head and looked at me sympathetically.

"I can tell you however," she informed me with a smile, "that his driver's licence lists his eye colour as..." she paused for effect, "brown."

Chapter Six

"Last night I did not witness a murder."

This was my repeating thought as I once again sat on the bus, finally on my way to work. Staring out of the window, made almost opaque with the scratchings of childish graffiti, I stared at the alleyways passing by. There was no dead body in a dark place. There was no shadowy figure, no mutilated corpse.

"There is no killer."

I told myself. Over and over, trying to embed the mantra in my mind, just as the dream had become embedded. I was on my regular bus, completing my regular route, as I should have been doing hours ago. I shouldn't have gone to the police, that was embarrassing. I should have gone to work and forgotten all about it. The bus pulled to a stop outside my office without me noticing its arrival and I leapt to my feet. I jumped from the step to the sidewalk, only just alighting before the doors snapped shut with a bang. Glancing at the clouds that hovered over the distant mountains, I casually wondered when the rain would again fall. Lingering to look at the familiar horizon that created the distinctive line of dramatic angles, I smiled. *This was a safe place, I was safe, it was just a dream*. Turning from the reassuring sight of the distant wilderness, I trudged across the concrete square and into the tall grey building.

I breathed in the heavily conditioned air of the lobby and, waving my badge at the familiar-looking security guard, tried to walk casually to the elevator. I needed to shake these feelings of guilt and responsibility. I felt as if something was very wrong, something evil was stalking me. The shadow of my dream followed me. Shaking my head as the elevator doors opened, I smiled a greeting to the woman already in the small steel enclosure. Stepping in, pressing the button to my floor, I leaned back against the wall and let the feeling of acceleration carry me to work. Arriving at my floor, the woman said something to which I grunted and I stepped into my workplace. On the nineteenth floor of a generic Canadian downtown office building it was a typical software house. Open-plan desks were filled with large monitors and laptop computers. Toys and colourful knick-knacks were scattered around the grey furnishings and the quiet hum of people at work permeated the space. Specifically, nerds; headphones on, tapping pencils on desks or chatting quietly amongst themselves.

At forty years old, I was no longer just another computer nerd. I was management, so I made my way to my desk by the window and threw my bag under it. The view was my reward for seniority. Instead of looking in toward the grey fabric dividers and cream walls, I got to look out. It often occurred to me that rather than a reward, it may well be a punishment. The view to those distant mountains called me, the green and blue luring my eye. The contrast to the dull office was a constant reminder of the drabness of my life. Sighing, I pulled my chair from under the wood-effect desk. The only distinguishing feature of my area was that I had a larger, more comfortable, chair. Rather than denoting my status as a team-leader, the chair singled me out as being older than most of my colleagues. This is simply because when you reach a certain age in the industry, a small complaint about back-pain immediately gets you an upgrade.

Settling in, I pulled out my laptop. Making a show of starting to check my email, my attention was actually going into scanning around the room, looking for an opportunity for a chat and a coffee. While I was looking around, my computer made a beep. Checking the corner of my screen I noticed a message from my friend, Mark. Opening the application, I saw he had sent an emoji of a steaming coffee cup. Replying with a simple one-letter message of 'K', I grabbed my mug from my desk and walked to the break-room. From the corner of my eye I saw him rise from his desk and head in the same direction.

We met at the sink as I was furiously scrubbing at my mug, trying to erase some of the weekend's remaining grime from the bottom.

"Hey, Mr Gooch. Late in today?"

"Yeah, I had to go somewhere this morning."

"Finally seeing the doctor about that mole on your dick?"

"Yeah, last time I have sex with a mole." The morning pleasantries dealt with, I sighed.

"What's up, Edward? You don't seem your usual convivial self," Mark asked me with a concerned tone of voice.

"Rough night, I suppose," I muttered back.

"Yeah? Some hot young thing finally teaching you that the true meaning of divorce is loads of wild sex?"

"I wish," I replied, finally smiling slightly.

This was fairly standard banter with Mark. A good friend of mine, maybe my best friend, he had taken me under his wing ever since I had told him I was divorcing my wife. At thirty-three and single, he considered it his hobby to introduce me to singles life in the city. We had been out a number of times with him as my 'wingman' to 'pick up chicks' and it had always ended the same. I spent the evening lamenting the loss of my wife to some poor woman while Mark went off with her friend. I am sure the fact that I was a great distraction with my sad tales of lost love was the real reason he kept inviting me out. I didn't mind though, he was a good friend and I enjoyed his company. Especially because he was the next oldest in the office. Besides him were the proper management behind their real walls, and a room full of twenty-somethings fresh out of university. We had each other at work, and that seemed to work well.

"Come on, Edward. When are you going to get yourself out of this funk? You're a catch, good looking and loaded, you could have women all over you."

He was right, I thought to myself; I was a catch to someone. I had a good job with a good wage and a nice apartment in a desirable new downtown skyscraper. I was, admittedly, a little overweight, but I still looked good with it hidden in jeans and a shirt. I remained strong, and being tall certainly helped. Thankfully I still had all my hair, although a substantial portion of it was turning grey. I pondered my situation for a few seconds and arrived at a simple truth. I was happier alone. With no one around that I had to make conversation with, no one making demands of me, no one to think of, life was simple. I liked the simple life, it was easy and I had settled in to the routine of being single well before my divorce, I realised. *"Maybe my wife had a point,"* I thought to myself.

My short burst of self-analysis over, I returned to the real problem that was making me so contemplative: the dream. I decided to tell Mark about it, maybe talking to him would unburden me.

"It's not that, Mark. I had a weird dream last night and I just can't shake it."

"Is it safe for me to ask what it was about?" He quickly asked with a raised eyebrow.

"Yeah, it wasn't sexual or embarrassing," I reassured him with a smile, "just really real. You know what I mean?"

He poured himself a coffee as I sat on the kitchen counter and steeped a teabag in my mug. I sat there, high on the counter, swinging my legs, dipping the bag in and out. Watching the brown water drip from the bag each time, I debated how much to tell Mark.

"Can I tell you about it?"

"Of course, Edward. I always like a good dream. The weirder the better."

"No, Mark. Seriously, this isn't fun for me, it's serious."

"Then seriously, tell me. You can trust me."

I looked closely at him, checking his face. His look of friendly concern finally convinced me to open up to him. I checked around the break-room for anyone that might overhear and started to tell him about my dream. I told him everything, from start to finish, omitting no detail. He listened with interest and concentration, understanding how important it was to me. I told him about the fear of the victim. The smell of the alley, the dirt, the feel of the murder. I explained about the satisfaction of the hunter as he cut the man on the ground. Once I had finished the story and my tea, he considered it for a few seconds before responding.

"Okay, Edward. Well, it sounds like it's just a nightmare. Albeit a vivid one, but still just a nightmare. You've just been watching too much telly is all. Too many late-night binges on Netflix."

"Sorry, Mark but it feels like more than that. You know when you wake up from a dream and it's the most scary thing you've ever felt? But it quickly fades, reality intrudes and it feels vague, confusing, unreal. This hasn't lost any of the realness and it's been four hours."

Mark considered this for a moment. "Yeah, but... counter argument: I've had dreams when I don't remember even dreaming them. I think they're real. So, I think I've bought milk when I haven't. Or parked the car somewhere it isn't. Stuff like that. Haven't you?"

"Yes. But that stuff is always so trivial. That's just a dream lost in the detail of real life, so it's easy to confuse with real life. This isn't real, it can't be. So why does it feel as though it actually happened?"

"Hmm, I don't know..." he admitted finally, "You could maybe see someone, you know."

"What, a therapist? I had enough of those during the divorce."

"Yeah, I know they didn't work, but that was different. Your marriage was doomed..."

"Mark..."

"Sorry, forget that. Therapy can work though, it has for me."

"You?"

"Yeah, not to get into it but I had some personal stuff in the past and I saw a shrink through work. You should consider it. This has obviously shaken you up and even though I think there's nothing in it, you do. My experience is that if something affects you, it's probably trying to tell you something."

"I don't know..."

"Look, it's probably Freudian or something. You know... the hunter is you, the victim is your youth. Or better still, you're hunting your single life. The knife is your penis and you want to slice people up with it."

"Yeah right, okay. The victim was a man, Mark."

"Ahh, well then. There we are, your latent sexuality coming to the fore after forty years. Clear as day, problem solved, leave fifty dollars at the door."

Smiling at Mark, at the release he provided with his humour, I already felt better. We had a second drink each and relaxed, chatting about more normal things. The talk of promotions desired, technical issues arising, inept management; it helped me relax again. The music of life helped me feel more normal and as I walked back to my desk I was starting to forget the dream. Dreams are just random memories being activated in the brain, I told myself. Perhaps Mark was right and I had just binged on too much media content.

Chapter Seven

A murder case. I couldn't believe it. I, Detective Montgomery Beech, was investigating a murder. Despite the horrors of the crime scene and almost vomiting all over Grace when she revealed the mutilated corpse to me, I was pumped. That feeling lasted all the way up to the point at which I stepped back into the precinct detectives' office. Still smiling as I exited the elevator, confidently walking across the entrance, I caught the eye of the Captain. The look on his face immediately converted my mood from ecstatic joy to one of pure dread. I tried to maintain my walk of confidence as he beckoned me to his office. Passing Booth's desk, I noticed him draw his finger across his throat with a grin while humming a few bars from the funeral march. Ignoring him, I marched into the Captain's office and closed the door.

"Detective Beech... Minty... Sit down..."

"Sir."

I sat and remained still; I wanted to see what the deal was before complaining. I was determined to keep this case. Not only that, I was going to solve it.

"Minty, what were you thinking?" He barked at me.

"Sir?"

"First you visit a scene that was already assigned to Organised Crime, you know better than that. Then you take the case from them, then you start to investigate without telling me..."

"I thought I should strike while the memories and evidence were fresh, sir."

"Don't give me that. You know I would have bounced it right back to them. You're not ready for a murder case. I know you think you are, but I know you're not."

"Sir, I can do this. I know what I'm doing. Besides, how much damage can I do? Will from Organised was there and he told me they weren't even going to investigate. So, whatever I do will be more than nothing."

"They wouldn't have investigated anything because there is

nothing to investigate, Minty. Or did you find a lead? If you do find a lead, you know you'll have to hand it back, don't you?"

"Yes, sir. Unless it's a lead they're not interested in investigating."

"And what might that be, Detective? Tell me, how are you going to break this case wide open? Or have you realised that you just attached an unsolvable case to my precinct?"

I searched my brain for a reason to keep this case, something to justify my actions. I didn't think he could make my workload any more boring but I didn't want to take that chance. I had to keep this case, at least for a little while. Then it came to me; I had a witness to the murder. Pushing my doubts down, the fact that his testimony didn't exactly tally with the facts, I forged ahead.

"Sir, I believe I have interviewed a potential witness to this crime. He described to me the details of the crime scene and I believe he may have some information of value to this case."

"A witness. And Organised aren't interested in that?"

"Well, you see, sir…"

"Spit it out, Minty."

I prepared my words carefully and muttered them to the Captain's glare; "it was Mr Gooch. The witness you had me interview this morning." I braced myself for the explosion.

"The mole? The nut-job who somehow saw a murder and the murderer did nothing about it?" The Captain asked incredulously.

"Sir, the number of cases solved by psychic visions in this country--"

"Oh great. It gets better. He's a psychic now?" The Captain slumped back in his chair and placed his hand on his brow, closing his eyes in the process.

"No, he didn't say that. In fact, he thinks it was a dream."

"A dream. Some lunatic dreams about a stabbing and you think he's a useful witness."

He was leaning forward again now, and for a second I thought he was going to launch himself across his cluttered desk and attack me. I showed him my open hands and started to implore him, "I know it's thin. I know it's probably nothing. But please, I've been here two years. Two years of interviewing weirdos, solving vandalism cases, doing school visits. I've done my share, I've paid my dues. Please let me just investigate this. I know there's probably no evidence but let me find that out. I will do all the paperwork, document and log all the physical evidence, canvas the neighbourhood. I know it won't turn anything up but at least I will be doing actual police-work for a while." I had been planning to come at the Captain with confidence. Somehow, instead, I had ended up sat in his office, arms out, pleading with the man. I sat back in my chair and tried to regain some level of decorum.

"Okay," he said quietly, his hand back over his forehead again.

"Okay, sir?" I couldn't believe he was agreeing with me.

"Yes, you heard me," he replied with a deep sigh, "I suppose it will be good practice." Sitting more upright now, he quickly gave me his orders, "I want a full report on your findings by the end of the week and it had better be perfect. If you can tick all the boxes and run a perfect investigation on this dead-end case, maybe I'll assign you something juicier. Something with a chance of being solved."

I couldn't believe it, I had managed to secure myself a murder case. "Sir. Thank you, sir," I stammered.

"Minty. You're on your own on this one. I don't want you tying up any more resources on this exercise than necessary."

"No sir, of course not," I readily agreed.

"And, Minty. If you do find a lead, report it to me immediately. You might be ready for an academic murder case, but you are still not ready for an active solo. Understood?"

"Understood, sir," I replied, beaming from ear to ear.

"Good, now get out of here," he barked at me, returning to some paperwork in front of him.

I practically danced out of his office. A swagger in my step and a grin of confidence on my face. I looked to Booth, daring him to say something. He turned away to his computer and started typing as I returned to my desk. A murder investigation. A solo murder investigation. Detective Beech, here we go...

Chapter Eight

Taking a break from the effort of trying to get a team of arrogant young engineers to agree with me, I was hiding at work; sitting on the toilet. Not a pleasant image, I know, but there it is. My trousers and underwear were bunched up around my ankles and I was resting my elbows on my bare knees. I did need to be there, but I was also taking a time-out to regain my patience. I had just found a complicated problem in one of my team's code and it had taken me forty-five minutes to explain to him why his code wasn't a work of genius. It had taken a lot of tact to explain how it was in fact a dangerous and problematic load of rubbish, not that I used those words of course. Sat on the toilet following this 'chat', I took another deep breath and tried to remember again what it was to be straight out of university. I too thought I knew better than my elders; software is for the young after all, or so people think. Telling myself that it takes experience to appreciate experience, I tried again to forget the annoyance I was feeling and have another go at fully evacuating my lunch. This was a regular exercise for me, trying to expel my annoyance alongside my bodily waste. I found the physical sensation that accompanied the emotional effort really underlined the achievement.

As I completed my movement this day, however, something else happened. With my final push, I suddenly felt the walls of the tiny cubicle closing in on me. The fringes of my vision were fading as if I were driving down a dark tunnel. I bent forward to try to get my head between my knees, to recover from the feeling that I was about to faint, but it didn't help. I took a few deep breaths, but this failed to bring me back from the tunnel. With a thud, I fell forward against the bathroom door and slipped unconscious to the floor.

I awoke, but I wasn't awake. I was not in my body. The head of my body was on the cold tile of the bathroom floor, poking out from under the toilet door. I felt my detached being slide from the floor and pull itself upright. It was acting completely on its own as it pulled my underwear up from my ankles. As it moved its hips to perform the manoeuvre, I could feel the remains of my waste between my buttocks. I sensed a hand go back, no doubt to retrieve some paper to clean myself, when instead it bypassed the roll. As the right-hand of my body proceeded to pick the remains of my waste from between my ass cheeks, taking time to pull stubborn pieces from the hairs, flicking them down the toilet bowl, I tried to fight the nauseous feeling that was building. It turned out that this was not difficult to achieve because I had no control over my digestive system either. I felt sick. I felt like I wanted to be sick, but I had no body with which to respond. Once my hand had completed cleaning my waste, it opened the door and exited the bathroom without washing itself.

It was like being in a computer game in a story section. I had been playing the game, controlling my character, but now it was taking me unbidden to a specific location. I felt possessed but I had no fear, no trepidation. I should have been terrified, losing the control I had always taken for granted, but I just felt numb. It was easy, I let it take me. It was walking me to Johnny, the engineer with whom I had just had my most recent discussion. People were speaking but I could not hear properly, everything was muffled and somehow distant. My vision too, was not as it should have been, it was like a camera zoomed in on a target. As well as this, everything around me was dull and grey. In contrast, Johnny was in full technicolour, glowing and vibrant. As I approached him, my eyes zoomed closer, so that he completely filled my view. He turned to face me in his chair, detecting my approach in the reflection of his monitor. He dropped his headphones, which fell around his neck, and tilted his head quizzically. I saw my hands appear in front of me. My right hand was, no doubt about it, covered in shit. Wet, smelly, excrement was smeared all over my fingers. A little of the dark brown substance dripped to the plain blue carpet tiles of the office as I approached him.

Johnny's eyebrows formed a furrow as he detected that something was wrong with his boss. As I approached him, arms outstretched, one hand covered in shit, something was indeed wrong with me. I felt a smile form on my face and Johnny smiled in response. All teeth and parted mouth, his smug expression seemingly thinking I was on my way to correct my previous opinion of him. He thought I was going to tell him that he was the genius he thought he was after all. He thought I was going to place my hands on his shoulders and congratulate him for his insights. He sat back, ready to receive his much-deserved praise. I watched as I bent down and placed my left hand on his right shoulder. Then, knowing it was coming, but unable to prevent it, I watched my right hand as it thrust into his smile. My shit-laden fingers were pressed into his teeth, forcing open his mouth. They pressed deep into his maw, all the way to the knuckles. My left hand moved to the back of his head to prevent him pulling away as the fingers of my right hand started wiggling around the inside of his mouth. I was cleaning the shit from me on the inside of his cheeks, the surface of his tongue, tickling his tonsils with my fingers and their coating of excrement. My left hand moved again, forcing his chin up, closing his lips around my hand. I withdrew it from his mouth, ensuring his lips sucked the last of it from me. I saw my hand emerge, clean but for a little remaining under my nails, finally releasing Johnny from my grip.

As I stepped back, he turned and fell from his chair to his knees. Placing his head in his waste bin, he proceeded to spit the contents of his mouth into the receptacle. It wasn't long before he was vomiting into the metal can, the plastic bag inside crackling wetly in complaint. I turned and walked from the office. As my body entered the lift, I pressed the button for the ground floor. I realised, as my finger pulled back, shit still under the nail, that I had consciously pressed it. Suddenly I was back in control of that part of me at least. Experimenting, I tried to move my other arm. Little by little I realised that I was in command once again. Too late, I was in charge of my actions, as I walked across the lobby and exited the building. I was fired, that I knew, beyond that I had no idea what I had done or what I was to do now. So, I ran. I ran as fast as I could, faster than I have ever run in my life. I ran like a child would, without care or abandon I moved as fast as my legs were capable down the wide busy street.

The downtown streets of Calgary flew past as I sprinted down the smooth concrete of their construction. Glass frontages to coffee shops and offices in equal number were just blurs in the corners of my eyes as I stared directly ahead. Traffic was light as it always was halfway through the morning and the four-lane road offered no obstacle to my flight. I ignored the red lights that hung from wires above me, running through the wide intersection as a horn blared from a massive pick-up truck. Still I ran, stamina seemingly not a problem as I sprinted like a maniac. Traffic was building now as I approached the shopping district. Coffee and offices gave way to high-end shops with brand-names lit from behind in well-chosen colours.

I ran across a large pedestrian expanse, splashing through the fountain set in the concrete beneath my feet. I had travelled about six blocks as I turned hard left and raced down a side road and into the park beyond. Still running, sprinting, feet pounding the path through the park. Geese and ducks scattered before me as I made for the river I knew lay before me like a blue ribbon through the city. Upon reaching the bank, I leaped, sailing through the air, feet tucked into my chest. I hit the frigid water in the foetal position. Closing my eyes, I let the ice-cold water encompass me. Soaking my clothes, filling my shoes. I sunk to the bottom and hit the rocks. Relaxing my body, I let the cold take me, the glacial water sucking all feeling from me, bad and good. I screwed my eyes closed and let the powerful current take me away.

Chapter Nine

'No actionable evidence'. That was the phrase at the bottom of the CSI report I was reading for the tenth time. I had laid out the paperwork on my desk to see it all at once, but nothing was helping. A single sentence at the bottom of the last page kept attracting my attention. 'No actionable evidence'. They were right. Will was right, Grace was right, the Captain was right. This case had nowhere to go. Nothing to investigate. I shuddered as I thought, *"Booth was right. I am Minty-fresh after all."* I banged my knuckles on the desk, raging against the phrase.

I dropped the CSI report and instead recovered the autopsy one more time to search for inspiration. Remembering the first time I held those sheets in my hands gave me a shot of confidence. The lettering at the top spelt out my name. I ran my fingers over them, expecting to feel the importance of the information. This was my case, I told myself. Quickly I felt my shoulders droop however, as I turned over the cover. I knew that the contents inside weren't going to be any different this time around. Still, I poured over all the details, the medical words I had looked up and added explanations for in pencil, the diagram where I had highlighted the wound marks. I read again how the victim, one Armand Vincent, had died from blood loss. He had been unconscious at the time, I remembered this from the CSI report; he had not disturbed his blood pool so it was unlikely that he was awake for his demise. *"Lucky guy,"* I thought as I pictured the scene. Lay on the ground of a dirty dark alley, blood slowly flowing from you until you are no more.

I shook the morbid thoughts from my mind, trying to stay detached and professional. I turned to the last page of the autopsy report to read again the description of the weapon used. It was a very sharp short ceramic blade wielded with precision. For a while I had thought this would be significant, the breakthrough evidence I needed. I had grabbed at the phone with urgency to call Grace. I had wanted records of the sale of all knives with ceramic blades in the area for the last six months. With all credit to her, she hadn't actually laughed, but I had heard the smile behind the earpiece. "This isn't a movie, Minty," she explained patiently but with a tone that was a little condescending. Apparently, there is no register of knife sales, no database to access, no-one to ask who might own such a knife. The pathologist had thought the knife rare, where in actual fact they were sold in virtually every fishing store in the country. Hunters and fishermen used them to cut scales and delicate pelts from their trophies. Rare in the world of violence and murder, common as muck in the sporting community of this city.

That was where I had started my investigation; with the knife. However, I quickly discovered that sporting goods shop owners were very reluctant to allow the police a 'quick-look' at their receipts. Asking the Captain for a warrant for the records of one shop in particular only resulted in a disappointed frown and a gesture that I should leave. That was embarrassing; I should have known that wanting to find one knife in a sea of millions didn't justify a warrant for their records. Still, I was desperate; the knife was all I had. Remembering those missteps, I resolved to try harder and re-read the entire coroner's report word for word, looking up the complicated medical phrases once again to check I had understood them correctly. With a sigh, all I managed to do was confirm what I already knew. All the phrases and diagrams all added up to one thing; the man was punched, stabbed and killed.

Fighting the despondence I could feel approaching, I reminded myself of the facts. This was, from the start, an unsolvable case. I was just doing the paperwork, the due-diligence required of any murder in this city. I was just a lone police officer in a force of thousands; doing my job didn't mean solving every crime in this city of more than a million people. But, true as that was, I still wanted to solve this case. I didn't want my first real investigation to remain unsolved. I was going to crack this case. It was just the 'how' that was escaping me at this particular moment in time.

I had canvassed the area, such as it was. Being a dirty alley at the back of a restaurant there were few people to ask and I had found no witnesses. Neither Grace nor the coroner had found anything out of place on or around the mutilated body of the victim. Research into the victim himself had revealed nothing of interest; no enemies, no ties to organised crime, nothing. I had even researched Mr Gooch to see if he had any connection to the victim, but that too turned up nothing. Fighting the urge to scatter it all to the floor, I gathered up the paperwork and slotted it all back neatly into its folder. I placed the file into my tray and powered down my computer.

Standing to leave my desk, to call it a night, I happened to notice the much thinner file underneath my real case. The witness statement from Mr Gooch sticking out at an angle. It was like it was calling to me, telling me to investigate. There was nothing else to do, so why not be thorough? The Captain had said that he wanted the paperwork to be perfect. Ignoring a potential lead, a witness no-less, was not professional. It was my duty to find and interview Mr Gooch again. I had to find out what, if anything, he knew. I knew I was grasping at straws: he had no ties to the victim and no record of violence, not even a parking ticket to his name. Then there was the statement itself, just a generic description of what was becoming a very common occurrence in our dark alleyways each night. I knew the cause of this increase as we all did: with the decline of the oil industry there were fewer legitimate ways to make money, so mugging in these places was rife, as was selling drugs and guns. Such things didn't tally with Mr Gooch either, I had checked; he was a successful, well-paid engineer with substantial savings. Then, sitting like a stone in the middle of the report, was his insistence that the victim had bright blue eyes, how they had stared back at him as he had died. I pulled out the photograph of the man before he had been killed so viciously. They were not bright, they were a dark, unremarkable, brown. I sighed, it was a futile endeavour, but I would still interview my witness; the thought that I had something to do tomorrow made my leaving for the evening that much easier.

Leaving the precinct, I saw that Grace was waiting for me, leaning against the door of my car. Trying my best to meet her eyes instead of surveying her body like I wanted to, I approached her with a smile. No matter what was going on in my life, seeing Grace always seemed to make it better.

"I thought you would take me for a drink," she stated with a smile as I remotely unlocked the car and she climbed into the passenger seat.

"Yes, ma'am," I replied, firing up the engine of my old Toyota and pulling out of the precinct. There was a comfortable silence between us as I drove straight to the parking lot of a Country and Western bar that we had been to many times before. I felt the presence of her next to me and I let it calm me. I couldn't help smiling as I pulled into our usual spot at the local bar. It was our regular spot simply because it was a walkable distance to both of our apartments which meant that we could avoid a taxi fare when we counted up the bottles of beers we left behind after a particularly difficult day. Tonight felt like one of those nights as we walked into the bar. We skipped the queue by showing our badges and she took my arm in hers as we made our way to a booth away from the speakers. Her simple friendly touch lifted my spirits and I was smiling again as we slid across the benches of the booth to position ourselves opposite each other. The waitress dropped a couple of napkins on the table and placed two beers on top without asking. As she walked away, Grace started the conversation with a question.

"Why don't you ever check out the waitress's ass?"

"What?"

"You never look. Darlene has a great ass and you never look. Did you know that?"

"No..." leaning out of the booth to look at Darlene's ass, I had to agree with Grace.

"Hmm. You're right. I don't think I ever noticed."

"Too distracted by her cleavage no doubt."

"What?"

"Calm down, Minty. I'm teasing. You don't look at them either. Men do, you know. Look, I mean. Men look at me too, sometimes. I'm worth looking at perhaps?"

"Totally... You're totally worth looking at." I tried to bring it down a notch. I was feeling that my enthusiasm was too high and it was in danger of making things weird for us. I was wondering where this conversation was taking us when it ended as abruptly as it had started.

"So, solved your murder yet? You got my report, right?"

"Yeah, 'no actionable evidence'. Thanks for that."

"You're welcome, but I did warn you."

"I know, and I didn't listen. But the Captain said that if I go through the motions and do the investigation and all the paperwork perfectly he would give me a real case."

"He said that?"

"He certainly did."

"Well that is worth celebrating," she raised her bottle and gave a toast, "here's to the unsolvable murder. Let's hope it leads to the beginning of the greatest Detective's career in history."

We touched the necks of our bottles and drank the cold liquid down as the music started again. People migrated to the dance floor to commence their night's two-step moves. Dressed as cowboys with metal tips on their shirt collars or cowgirls with tight denim shorts, they soon started moving in synchrony, stomping boots to the beat of the music. This is the second reason we came so much, not to dance, but to watch and amuse ourselves with the display. The regimented movement, the timed stamping of leather-clad heels, the whoops and hollers. It was an amazing choreographed effort for a room full of complete strangers. The thing I liked to watch for was the complex mating rituals that went on at the same time. Somehow, in the midst of the formation, concentrating on where to go and what to do, people would pair up. Somehow, hands on hips and a spin of a bent knee, meant, "I like you." We loved watching this display; drinking beers, eating the cheap hot-wings, laughing and guessing at who would pair up each evening. In the corner, closer to the bar, a large man in a red checked shirt started shoving another man, who I could have sworn was wearing spurs.

"Time to go..." Grace downed the last of her beer and grabbed her purse from the corner of the booth. I followed suit with my beer and we rushed to the door. The nightly fight was starting early and we had to get out before I became the officer responsible. The local rule for bar fights was that the first police officer to arrive had to process the incident; if you were there, it was yours. We barrelled out of the front door as I heard the unmistakable sound of a man hitting the ground, taking a collection of glasses with him. Giggling, staggering sideways slightly from the drink, Grace scuttled down the stairs to the underpass. I helped her remain upright as we moved as quickly as we could under the railway line. Just as we made it out of sight, hidden by the tracks above us, a Police Cruiser arrived. Lights flashing, the car rocked from side to side as two uniformed officers exited and ran into the club. Just as we peeked through a gap in the underpass to check the coast was clear and we had made it away unseen, the earth started to shake. The early evening freight train was passing directly overhead and the vibration and noise knocked us off our balance. I was still holding on to Grace's arm. My efforts to support her failed and quickly she was supporting me instead. Together, we almost fell with the surprise arrival of the train and grasped at each other to prevent us hitting the ground.

We each let out a loud laugh at our escape and surprise at what was the very predictable occurrence of the train. We were looking directly into each other's eyes as the passing train made the lights of the city flicker and flash in the underpass. I watched points of light wink off and on, reflected in her wide pupils. Her red lips twinkled with moisture. Another engine, driving the massive train forwards from the centre, passed overhead. The noise was immense, the vibration knocked concrete dust onto our heads and into Grace's eyes. She blinked and turned away to shake the dust from her. When she looked back, the moment was gone.

"See you, Minty."

"Good night, Grace."

We let go of each other and slowly went our separate ways. Her to the north, to the nicer side of the tracks, me to the south. *"It's for the best, Minty,"* I told myself. Turning to watch her walk away, sadness washing though me, rinsing the hot excitement of the moment away.

Chapter Ten

I awoke with my face against a pile of rocks. I was on the bank of the river, sodden with icy water and shivering violently in the morning sunshine of a new day. I remembered my actions back in the office; something had happened to me, I had been possessed. Something or someone had taken control, made me do their bidding. Removing my jacket and shirt, I wrung the water from my clothes and tried to absorb some heat from the burgeoning sun. Recognising the healing warmth of the light, I stripped naked with aggressive actions, throwing my clothes from me. Pounding them on the rocks, I twisted and mangled each item as if it had offended me. I stood upright, arched my back and faced the sky. Screaming, expelling all the air from my belly, I cried out, "I am Edward Timothy Gooch and I am in charge of my own being!" Feeling that I had exorcised my demons, at least for the time being, I lay back on a patch of sun-warmed rocks and breathed deeply from my exertions.

As I lay on my back, staring at the blue sky, dotted with light white clouds; the thought occurred to me that I didn't know where I was. I sat up, scanning around me for any recognisable landmarks. I saw nothing. That is, nothing but the river, rocks and tall evergreen trees stretching far into the distance. It seemed that overnight the river had swept me from the city and into the surrounding countryside. None the wiser as to my location, but my concerns being discovered while naked allayed, I lay back and tried to calm myself. After an hour or so, lying in the September morning sun, I was finally dry. The cold breeze from the river was chilling me, causing my hairs to stand on end, so I pulled my clothes back on. They weren't dripping wet anymore, but they were still damp, and I shivered as I dressed. My phone was in my pocket, but it wouldn't turn on. Ruined by the water or a flat battery; it didn't matter, it was useless. Looking around, I surveyed my surroundings. I could only see a few hundred metres both up and down the river and there was nothing in either direction. The bank on which I now sat rose up from the river in a gentle hillside, thickly covered with rich green trees and vegetation. The other side was much steeper, forming a vertical grey cliff of stone.

I was lost, some way outside the city. I knew I couldn't be far from civilisation but the direction in which that lay remained uncertain. Walking into the woods behind me didn't seem to be an option; it looked impenetrable and I would be hopelessly lost in minutes. The other side of the river was out of the question, I had no hope of climbing the cliffs. So, the choice was fifty-fifty. Upstream back home to the city. Downstream to some other, unknown destination. I stood on the bank of the river, torn. I recalled what I had done yesterday, what my body had done anyway. It felt strange, I should be upset or at least concerned. Instead I felt numb, just as I had when it was happening. It wasn't me, Edward Gooch hadn't done anything. Nor did the loss of control worry me. Intellectually, it concerned me, but emotionally I felt nothing. I had always been very good at suppressing my anxiety, but this was a new level of denial: another cause for concern. I knew that at some point in the future, it would hit me. Until then I was happy to leave it where it was, somewhere in the back of my mind. I hadn't done anything seriously wrong, I thought, pondering the repercussions of my actions. I would be fired of course, and maybe a charge of assault was in my future but there would be little punishment for that, it being my first offence.

A cool breeze picked up from the water and it felt as if my demon was making his presence known as a shiver washed down my spine. His actions in the office might not be causing me anxiety, but my dream of murder still tortured me. What he did to Johnny felt trivial. It almost amused me, even pleasing me on some visceral level, but it was a million miles from murder. I realised with a shudder why the dream didn't feel like my own. It was his, the demon had been the killer, showing me what he truly desired. Yesterday, in the office, I had distinctly felt him inside me, controlling me, overpowering my will. Was Johnny just a prelude? A sudden panic flushed me with heat, countering the breeze previously felt. What if he took me again, this time committing the deadly violence he so clearly desired?

I didn't like the questions I was asking myself and feared the answers even more. I had let him take me, I realised. I had been happy to do it, a willing slave to his commands. My eyes closed and my hands fell to my sides; I was tired. That was why I had let him take me; it was more than a physical fatigue, I was tired of my life. The efforts it took to remain in control of the world were little but continuous; for forty years I had lived this way and I was fed up. Looking upstream to the city, all I could see was a future with more of the same, and suddenly it felt too much. I shook my head; if my passive attitude to life had meant that he could take me so easily, then I had to leave that life behind. I turned away, away from the monster, away from my life.

As I walked, I slowly started to feel better. Lighter, the weight slewing from me as I stepped across the loose rocks at the edge of the river. With every footstep I could feel the distance growing. I could leave my troubles in that clinical city of steel and glass. The city could have the demon, the people there could exorcise him. I nodded as grey rocks tumbled and knocked together beneath my feet. The detective was paid to handle him, I would simply leave, leave it all behind and start again.

As I awkwardly navigated the tight bend in the river, however, I was confronted by a more immediate problem. Directly ahead, moving slowly to the water's edge, was a very large bear. Stopping my movement, standing still, I studied it. I had lived in Canada all my life so I knew what to do and my mind searched itself, recalling the advice. First, I tried to identify the bear. As it gently lumbered to the water, I saw it had a long-pointed nose and a large hump; a grizzly. It still hadn't seen me, or if it had it wasn't paying any attention. Now at the water's edge, it was scooping up an already dead salmon and sniffing it. Slowly, quietly, I backed away. Glancing down before each step I took, to ensure I would not disturb any rocks. Very gradually, I moved backwards, with one eye on the bear. Then, I stumbled, slipping on the skin of a previously devoured salmon. The abrupt movement caused a rock to slip with a loud knocking sound that echoed against the opposite cliff.

The bear stopped working on the fish on which it had been snacking and reared up its head. It knew I was there now and it twitched and wiggled its nose, taking in great sniffs of the air around it. I could feel the breeze of the river gently blowing against the back of my wet hair and realised that the bear could easily detect my scent. Taking a nervous swallow, I hurriedly looked around, considering my options. Grizzly bears couldn't climb trees but anything that looked even vaguely scalable was deep into the woods, across ground a bear would easily cover far faster than I. Trapped, I looked back towards the animal I was starting to see as the vehicle of my death. As I did, I breathed a sigh of relief. The bear had clearly heard, seen and smelled me. Subsequently it had determined that I was not of interest today. It had sat down on the rocks and was settling in to work on the salmon, demolishing it with its teeth and claws. Again, I made my reversing movements until I made it to the tree line. Finally out of sight of the beast, I carefully made my way up-river. With a sinking feeling, I resignedly started making my way back to the city. The bear had sent me back. It would be my responsibility to face the demon after all.

After ten minutes of walking, I felt out of range of my encounter and started to calm down. Wanting to avoid any further encounters with bears, I started talking noisily to any that might be lurking in the woods, periodically clapping my hands. It took many hours but I finally started to recognise the landscape. As I found the outskirts of the city, I thanked my luck that I had enough money in my pocket for the bus. Catching the Number 3 back downtown to my apartment, I finally squelched my way across the floor of the lobby and let myself back into my home. It couldn't have been midday even, but I stripped off and collapsed into bed. Immediately, thankfully, I fell into a deep dreamless sleep.

*

I was rudely woken by a pounding on the door. Momentarily confused, I climbed out of bed, unsure what to do. Shaking the sleep from my mind, I remembered that security in the lobby was not supposed to let any unannounced visitors into the building. Worried now, I pulled on a robe and looked around the small apartment for some kind of weapon.

"Open up, Mr Gooch," the pounding visitor called out from the other side of the door. The voice sounded vaguely familiar which comforted me. "Come on, Mr Gooch. It's Detective Beech, Police." Breathing a sigh of relief, I opened the door, cinching my robe around me tighter. "Finally. What were you…" Detective Beech stepped through the door, gently pushing me aside, investigating my home. "Oh, you were asleep? I'm sorry… Maybe you would like to take a second to put some pants on?" He suggested as he walked past me.

I looked down at myself; my robe was open at the bottom and I saw my legs were covered in dirty river detritus. I gathered up the pile of stinking clothes previously discarded on the floor and scuttled to the bathroom. As I looked at myself in the mirror I heard the Detective make himself comfortable on the sofa, the leather creaking under his weight. I pushed the clothes into the washer and closed the door against the smell. Wetting a towel, I wiped the worst of the dirt from me and made a quick dash to the bedroom. Not making eye contact as I passed the lounge, I made it to my wardrobe and pulled on the first clothes I could find. Composing myself, I moved into the lounge and sat down in the chair opposite the Detective.

Chapter Eleven

It was easy to track down Edward Gooch. My thorough investigations into him had yielded a legitimate address and still no link to the victim or any suggestion of criminal activity. However, I informed the Captain that I wanted to chase up the witness with a follow-up interview and received a non-committal grunt that I took for permission. I immediately jumped into my car to drive to his residence. The building guard informed me that Mr Gooch was indeed in, having entered a few hours earlier leaving water stains all across the lobby floor. I decided that my day was already getting more interesting as Mr Gooch finally answered my pounding on the door and let me in. I let him dress and he sat himself down opposite me, ready for the questions to come.

When I had first interviewed him at the station, I had noted his physical attributes and demeanour as I had been trained to do. However, now, here in his home I started to notice him for the first time as a person. He was forty, I knew that from his records but looking at him, I could see it. He had wrinkles at his eyes and his dark-blonde hair had the beginnings of grey appearing here and there. As he studied me with his light blue eyes, I continued to assess him. He looked strong and was taller than me at over six feet. I would say he didn't look like a software engineer but in my experience, few did. The high wages and free time tended to make more than a few of them outdoors enthusiasts. I looked up to find his eyes drilling into me. Intelligent too, I decided. I knew from my research that he was extremely law-abiding, there wasn't a blemish anywhere to be found. His social media presence was conservative and inoffensive. But looking at him now I could see it was more than that; his demeanour was honest and open. He was also well off, which was obvious as I casually inspected his modern apartment, purchased outright. He already had a large house in the suburbs where his ex-wife lived, and now he was living in this prodigious new high-rise. There was just no reason for him to be involved in this crime.

Today, sat before me now, he also looked a bit of a state. He had a layer of grime all over his body and in his hair, despite his attempts to clean himself prior to sitting down. He smelled too, a little like dead fish, a lot like the outdoors. I smiled, pleased at how I had pegged him as an outdoorsman as he pulled some pine needles out of his matted mop of hair.

"Mr Gooch, you've been busy since we spoke last." I gestured to the grime and he swallowed and wrung his hands nervously.

"Yes, I visited the woods," He said, hanging his head slightly.

"Hunting?" I asked, thinking of the knife.

"Oh no, I find hunting despicable," he insisted with conviction. "Detective... Can I call you something else, something a little less formal maybe?" He replied.

"Why not? Call me Minty," I replied, wanting to put him at ease. 'A relaxed witness often let slip unwanted truths', I remembered from police college. However, looking at him nervously fidgeting opposite me, I could tell there was no truth to be extracted from him. I sagged in the sofa where I was sat. My case was still going nowhere.

"Minty?"

"Yeah, short for Montgomery. A nickname I'm trying to embrace."

"Okay. Call me Edward then." He said, leaning forward and shaking my hand. I shook his back and relaxed. My case might be over but there would be another one. In the meantime, I thought I could enjoy a chat, and chase the case to its conclusion by interviewing Edward. "You want a coffee?" He asked, standing before I could answer.

"Sure. Black, no sugar." He got up to make us a coffee in a fancy machine. Inserting a plastic pod and pressing a button was all that was required. I took the mug as he returned to his chair opposite. I pulled out my notebook and considered my strategy for the interview. In the end, I simply decided to be direct. "I'm here because of your dream, Edward."

"My dream? I thought that was all done and dusted," he was shaking a little now, remembering the dream no doubt, "There being no murder."

"It was... That was until we found a body."

Edward's body sank deeper into his chair and he squeezed his coffee cup, his knuckles turning white as he did.

"Like I dreamt?" He asked, warily.

"Well, I can't discuss an open case. But pretty close, yeah." I felt bad making it seem more serious than it was, but still; I was a detective on a murder inquiry and I wanted the interview to be legitimate.

"I knew it. It felt so real."

I nodded in agreement, "the thing is, Edward, your description, although vivid, could describe a number of crime scenes, or just stuff from the television. Do you remember anything specific, anything that would distinguish this crime from any other?"

"I thought I was specific... I was very descriptive."

"True, true..." I conceded, "but there were no witnesses to the crime I'm investigating. All I have is a body; your description could apply to any number of situations."

"Ah, yes. I see... You need something specific, something definitive... So, we can prove it was just a dream, a coincidence that there was a murder the same night."

"That's right," I noted in my book that he wanted it to be a dream. He didn't want it to be real; he wasn't claiming to be a psychic. I felt sorry for the guy as he twitched and wriggled in his chair, trying to remember something that would prove to himself that it hadn't been real. I almost mentioned the disparity in eye colour, but I wanted more. I needed some more information and just hoped that he could provide something. There certainly wasn't anything else I could do.

"Must be murders every night," he said to the room in general.

"Well, this is Canada not America, so not every night. But often enough it wouldn't be too much of a coincidence. You might have even seen reports on the news about recent stabbings."

"I don't remember, but yeah, maybe. Let me think... Something definitive..." he sipped his coffee, stilling his movements and concentrating. I sipped mine, waiting. "He was right-handed... He slashed the man's leather coat from left to right, then his stomach right to left... He didn't turn his wrist, so the knife must have been sharp on both sides..."

"Okay, that's good," I said, writing down that he had described the double-sided blade that had been used, "can you think of anything else?" I asked, knowing how common this feature was.

"No, I'm just not sure I can remember anything else. It felt astounding, the attack. Superhuman almost, but I guess pretty standard for you..."

"Yes, fairly standard I'm afraid. You don't remember anything after he cut the victim?"

"No, sorry... I blacked out, well, woke up I suppose... No wait a second, just before I woke up, I remember he reached into the man, with his right hand... He reached in and pulled his intestines out. I remember the noise sending me over the edge, I wanted to stop seeing. I woke up straight after that."

"Nothing more than that?" I tried to ask calmly, willing my heart to stop pounding as I noted that he did know about the killer removing the intestines after all. Then, just as quickly as my excitement built, I felt it fall away. Of course, the mutilation had been mentioned in the news just that morning. Some sloppy uniform had leaked it to the press, no doubt for a free drink. Edward was obviously going through a mid-life crisis, on the verge of a breakdown. He was fixating on a crime he had heard about on the news to distract himself from it. He was about to totally crack and I didn't want to be the one responsible for that.

He was talking loudly now, desperate for reassurance, "No, sorry, I don't know anything more. But is that what happened? Did I witness a murder?"

"I don't think so, no, Edward." I said formally, providing the reassurance he so desperately needed. I smiled, watching him step back from the brink. He looked up to me, moisture in his colourful blue eyes. I wanted to help this kind man, so I decided to confide in him, "look, in all honesty this case is going nowhere and I'm only here because I've got nothing else to investigate." He smiled weakly at that, uncertainty in his expression. "I'm sure that you just had a dream and it just happened to be on a night there was a stabbing in the city. If you had really witnessed it he would have stabbed you too, right?" I added with more enthusiasm than the comment really allowed and winced with disappointment at my lack of professionalism. "Can you keep all this to yourself though? It's an ongoing investigation and I don't want any details getting out." I added in a more professional tone of voice, trying to assert my authority as Detective.

"Yes of course. Please, this dream is really torturing me. That and what I did yesterday..."

"I understand. But like I said, your dream isn't definitive in any way and there are some discrepancies in your description, this sort of thing is very common on TV. Not in real-life so much but maybe you're just remembering a film or the news you overheard in a bar. Or more likely an amalgamation of a bunch of things you watched and read."

"But could it be something else? Could it be a vision, could I be channelling him?" His nerves were coming back and the look of desperation on his face was heartbreaking.

"Let's not get carried away at this stage, Edward..."

"But the bear, the bear made me..."

"The bear?" The mention of a bear from nowhere was worrying and I was thinking again that he was going to lose it. I was starting to regret coming to talk to him, all I had was a mention of mutilation that was in the public domain already and a witness about to have a break-down. This was getting me nowhere and it was really upsetting him now.

"Sorry, just something else... It isn't important, so the victim--"

"Sorry, Edward," I interrupted him. I wanted to end the interview before he broke down in front of me. "Open case and all that. I only came to see if you remembered anything else, something that could point to the killer. You know, just to dot the i's and cross the t's, so to speak. I don't believe for a second that your dream was real..."

"No, sorry, I don't remember anything else. Nothing at all..."

He sipped the last of his coffee at that point and that seemed to signal the end of our conversation. He was looking down into his mug, looking for inspiration, looking for escape. I finished mine and placed the empty mug on the coffee table. "Well, Edward. Try not to worry. Like I said; I'm sure it's all coincidence and just a weird dream. If you do remember something though..."

I handed him my card. Standing from the sofa, I walked to the door. Opening it, I turned and added again that he should keep all details of the case confidential. Leaving his apartment, leaving the building, climbing into my car, I considered the situation. I had a man with a dream of a stabbing and I had a stabbing victim. There was not enough detail in the statement that could prove a connection and one serious discrepancy, but I felt like he was describing the crime as if he had seen it first-hand. Believing something so impossible made no sense to me so I shook it from my head. "It's just because you like him," I told myself, "he's a nice guy, but totally losing it over a dream doesn't make him helpful." Finally finished, deciding to write up the interview and hand the case to the Captain, I started the car and pulled away to drive back to the precinct.

Chapter Twelve

I am outside, walking; once more I am in control of Edward's body and can revel in the sensations it provides. The heat of the sun is warming me even as the chilly air washes around me. I smile, revelling in the feelings I am experiencing. There is something so primal, so pure, about weather. I breathe in the scent of pine on the cool breeze and look all around. The aroma has awoken a need. I feel the need to run, to chase. I need to experience this now. I am on a pedestrian bridge that spans a park below. I walk to the edge and lean far over; the height starts my heart racing, adrenaline building with the danger. As quickly as the feeling builds, I acclimatise to the sensation and it fades once more. Below me there is a group of men, they have finished their game of basketball and are now chatting in the corner of the court. They look fit, strong and powerful. A slew of racial and personal slurs come to mind as ways to antagonise them but a new physical sensation that stirs inside me brings forth a better idea.

I shift position to my left, placing myself directly above them. I unbutton my jeans and pull open the fly. I pull out my penis. It is hardening with the anticipation of my action but a waft of chilly air softens it just enough for me to act. I step to the edge and let urine flow, laughing gleefully as I watch the powerful and constant stream flow from the bridge. I step to the edge, continuing to pee. Looking down I can see the confusion on the faces of the men below. To my delight they are looking up, trying to determine the source of the fluid. As they see me looking down, spraying penis in my left hand, my right waving at them. They realise the nature of the liquid and scatter. Their hands are on their heads, shaking the urine from them, they are shouting, swearing, gesticulating. I wave my dripping penis at them, smiling wide, grinning like an idiot.

My impromptu rain shower seems to have elicited the required reaction from the men. They abandon their belongings on the basketball court and race to meet me. They are rapidly climbing the steps to the bridge as I put myself away and wipe my hands on my jeans. I let them close, they are approximately ten seconds from me as I start to run. I flee the men. Despite my mastery of animal combat, I cannot defeat five prepared men easily; they are fit and strong, they are motivated, they are worthy hunters. Looking down at my feet, pleased I am wearing trainers, I pound the concrete of the bridge. As I run, I relax my knees and drop lower to the ground. I lean forward and allow gravity to drag my torso down, my legs converting gravity to forward momentum. I sense myself pull ahead as I grab for the handrail near the end of the bridge. I haul my body over the railing and drop to the riverbank below. As I hit the rocky surface, I allow my legs to collapse and I roll to the ground on my shoulder. Back on my feet now, I continue to run, heading for the grassy park alongside the river. Slowing to turn and look back, I am delighted to see that three of the men have followed suit and are leaping from the bridge. They do not land as elegantly as I, but they still chase me.

Three pursuers are now behind me as I reach the soft ground of the park. My heart is pounding in my chest, adrenalin is flowing. I am grinning like a maniac while struggling to pull enough air into my lungs. The cold air feels painful in my chest and my legs are throbbing. I feel alive, I feel powerful, I feel as an animal fleeing into the forest. Weaving and dancing around the people in the park, I leap over benches and rocks. I blast through planted bushes and let trees whip at my face. All hairs on my body are standing tall, tingling as the cold air flows over me. I am pure once more, I am the primal inside. I move as a liquid across the ground, nothing is an obstacle to me.

Hearing a cry from behind, I turn my head to check on my chasers and see that one has fallen. Having caught himself on a bench that I had leapt over, he has damaged his ankle and is lying on the ground, clutching it. Two now, two pursuers. I keep running, fleeing, enjoying the sensations coursing through me. As I run, however, the feeling fades. Two chasers are far less of a risk, less of a match for me. The park is ending as I climb a grassy hill. From memory, I know that it ends in a very steep downward slope of loose gravel. The sensations return as a new surge of adrenalin courses through me. Increasing my pace, I crest the hill. I leap over the edge, head-first, arms outstretched. As I hit the loose gravel with my hands, I tuck into a roll. Letting my legs slam into the hill, my feet dig into the ground. I feel the resistance slow me as I send dust and grit flying into the air from my heels. My fall feels vertical but it is at least fifteen degrees off as I am almost, but not quite, standing on the slope. I spread my arms and dig my elbows into the banks of the hill to arrest my fall even more. Despite my efforts I am flying down the cliff, grit hitting me in the face. Dust is everywhere and I cannot see the end. The feeling is sensational, my mind is totally engaged in the physical actions and consequences of my movements.

The slope of the cliff levels out a little and the loss of momentum means less grit in my face so I can now see its conclusion. I twist my hips and adjust my fall, aiming for one of the larger rocks at the base. Hitting the smooth granite, I allow my legs to fold, and I tuck into another roll. Finally, my movement ceased, I stand. Looking up, I find my pursuers halted at the top, contemplating following me. I throw them a wave and a smile. Seeing the path of dust tracing my descent, I grin harder and encourage them to follow. Knowing they will not, only a crazy man would do what I just did. Only I with my knowledge of the primal, would manage such a slide and they know it. They gesticulate and shout at me, satisfying their need for revenge somewhat with a verbal attack. Snorting derisively, I turn and walk away. I close my eyes as I walk and revel in the tingling throughout my body. As the adrenalin leaves me, my skin starts to sting and muscles burn. I concentrate on the sensations, walking back to the city, revelling in the exquisite pain.

Chapter Thirteen

Back at the precinct I sat at my desk, writing up the interview with Edward. The more I documented the conversation and my thoughts, the more confused I became. His strange half-mention of a bear was worrying. His horror at the dream was clear enough but his need for me to prove it was not real didn't sound like any other 'psychic' evidence I had read about. Most psychics I had researched craved the attention and insisted on the truth of their visions. It also bothered me that he didn't seem crazy. Most of the 'moles' I had interviewed were so obviously mentally ill. Edward seemed like a clever, switched-on guy. I liked him. He put himself forward as an honest and genuine man in a confusing and frightening situation.

Finishing my notes and placing them in the file I walked into the Captain's office and laid the folder down on his desk.

"One perfect, dead-end investigation of a stabbing. As requested, sir."

Motioning me to sit he collected up the file and started to read. To my surprise, he slowly and methodically read the whole document, cover to cover. Finally placing it down on his desk, he raised his head to face me.

"Nice work, Detective."

I smiled. "Thank you, sir."

"Any thoughts on progressing the case?"

"Progressing, sir? I haven't found any evidence, as you can see--"

"What about this Mr Gooch? He seems to know rather a lot."

"As yes, the dream. But he could be describing any crime, and what with the discrepancy of eye colour, just a disturbed man I think."

"I see that's the conclusion in your notes, but I disagree..."

"Sir?" I was confused. I had thought it was very clear and had said so in my conclusion. Just before my recommendation of, 'no further action at this time.'

"Look, Minty. You're a good detective. This is good work. But this is what I meant when I said you weren't ready. Any other cop would be all over this guy. The description isn't spot on but it's very close. Too close to be a coincidence, especially his mention of the slice from a two-sided knife. He doesn't say 'cut' or 'stabbing', he says 'slice'. From what I understand from the coroner, this is a good description of the wound. Before you say 'psychic vision' or 'dream', maybe you should be considering that he did it."

"But, he was appalled by the murder," I said rather louder than required. I was shocked, and a little annoyed at the rebuke. I added, "the very memory of the dream was sickening him."

"The number of murderers I've seen sickened by their actions would surprise you, Minty. They love it at the time. But after?" He held his hands out in an expansive shrug, "when reality sets in, they don't want to confront what they're capable of. Denial sets in, their conscience returns. Seems to me that this Gooch guy could have done it and be repressing the memory. Did you consider that?"

"Well, I," I stammered searching my mind for a counter-argument. I felt foolish, being reprimanded so quickly on what I had thought was a perfect investigation. "The eye colour," I blurted out finally. "He said the victim had blue eyes, the same as his. I checked, I was quite thorough. The victim's eyes were brown, nothing like Mr Gooch's." I sat back, relieved at my recovery.

"Do you remember your training on eye-witness testimony, Detective Beech?"

It was a loaded question, "of course, sir."

"How details of an account get swapped around, switched out through prejudice or just plain confusion? Did you consider that?"

"No sir... I didn't," I admitted, hanging my head. "He was so accurate, so descriptive. It didn't seem likely that he would get something so intimate, so wrong."

"Not even on purpose?"

I went again to protest but he held up a hand, stopping me.

"Look, I concede that you've done the background very well;

with no previous record, no connection to the victim, no motive, it's unlikely. He's a bit late in life to be a serial killer and doesn't seem to have any inclination to violence at all. So, it's probably not him, I admit. But we don't deal in probabilities, not where murder is concerned." He paused to look at me, steepling his fingers in front of me. "I'll ask you again detective, are you finished? Really? Have you done everything you can?"

My enthusiasm jumped back to me straight away. He wasn't taking the case from me, he was extending it. I thought quickly, "I would like to immediately put a tail on Mr Gooch and apply for a warrant to search his apartment for any physical evidence pertaining to the crime."

"On what grounds?" He asked with a raised eyebrow, testing me.

"That the suspect is aware of details pertinent to the case," I quickly replied. A textbook answer.

"Better. Now go and do that please," he said, handing me back the file.

"You're not bouncing this to Organised Crime?" I tentatively asked.

"Why would I? Does it seem like Mr Gooch is a member of a crime syndicate of which we know nothing?"

"No sir, definitely not," I quickly answered, almost saluting.

"Exactly. Last time I checked, this was your case and Mr Gooch is your suspect. Off you go now, Minty."

Grasping the file, I left the office with a grin on my face. True, I had missed an obvious lead, but I still had a case; a murder case. Now I also had a suspect. This was my dream come true, the culmination of all my efforts. I was the happiest detective filling out a warrant request form in the history of the Precinct.

Chapter Fourteen

The sun is going down. I am walking in the city still, feeling the sting of scraped flesh under my ripped and bloodied clothes. I smile, loving the sensations of pain. It makes me feel alive and raw. I see a woman walking toward me, causing a rhythmic clicking on the concrete. Her high-heels are making her hips sway provocatively as I allow her to pass me. Waiting for five steps of her loud gait, I turn and follow her. My animal is strong following the chase and her walk is making the feeling stronger. I feel myself press against the fly of my jeans and leave it unadjusted, allowing the pressure to build.

I hang back further in order to study her body, the distance allows me to see her alabaster legs through the complicated pattern of her black hosiery. Her wide hips and ass are contained in a short grey woollen skirt. The wiggle in her hips, caused by the high-heels, is swaying the flesh of her bottom in a most pleasing fashion. She is sporting a flowing cotton blouse that is billowing with her movements and the wind. Her long blond hair, constrained in a loose ponytail, is twitching back and forth. Like a ticking clock, her hair is counting down the time until I will act. Her body is calling to me, taking me to a place I so deeply desire. The pressure in my jeans is teasing me, building my arousal toward what will be a delightful climax.

To my dismay, three men step from a doorway and insert themselves between me and the object of my interest. I frown and calculate how best to be rid of them. They speed up, and, thinking they will overtake and be out of my way naturally, I steel myself and wait. Patience is not natural to me but I can wait the few seconds it will take for them to be gone. Then, as they pass an alley, they deviate into it. To my surprise, she too is gone. Intrigued, as I reach the entrance, I pause and look within. Seeing nothing, I enter the dark place, stealthily creeping deeper into the urban tunnel. Eventually, rounding an industrial air-conditioner, I see them. The largest of them, a bearded monster of a man, has the woman by the arm and is jerking her around. She is struggling to remain upright on her heels as he brutally manoeuvres her against the rough brick wall. His two compatriots are looking all around, checking for onlookers. Pointlessly they search for me; I cannot be seen by such amateurs. I press myself against the metal of the machine. My silhouette is merged with the angular outline of the equipment and the light is nearer them. They cannot detect me, yet still they look. I smile.

The bearded man releases the woman from his grip and slaps her across the face with the back of his hairy knuckled hand. She falls to the ground with a soft thud and the other two men turn to look. All three men are white, all are tall, all are overweight. They look threatening, but to me they are nothing. They are strong enough, however, to each be able to defeat the thin woman. The smallest of the men steps to her and grabs her ankles. He pulls her from her seated position against the wall, scraping her ass on the rough ground. The clean-shaven member of the group steps to her and grabs her wrists, forcing her down. She is pinned to the ground now, one man either end of her as the bearded monster stretches to his full height over her. In dragging her across the ground the men have caused her skirt to be bunched up around her waist, exposing her to them. The bearded man straddles her and lowers himself to his knees. They say something to her and her loud cries change to a gentle whimpering that barely carries down the narrow alley.

The largest man, the leader, the bearded monster, is pulling her pantyhose from her. Tearing them in the process, her underwear soon follows. They are casually discarded, and her legs are spread even wider by the one at her ankles. They are laughing loudly as the bearded one unzips his jeans and releases himself. She stops her whimpering now as he lowers himself between her legs. She is helpless, one man at her wrists, one at her ankles, a large fat man pressing himself to her. I remain hidden against the machine, unseen in the dark of the alleyway. My hand is down the front of my jeans, holding myself, feeling my pressure building. The bearded man begins his attack on her, thrusting forward to penetrate her. The woman bucks and writhes and manages to free her wrists. She whips her hands to the beard and scratches at his face. She is screaming into the alley, her cries cause the metal against which I lean to vibrate. The men are caught unawares and struggle to regain control of her.

I sigh as the pressure I was feeling in my hand drops. This is a pathetic display; it is no longer pleasing me. They seek to take this body. I understand that urge. Just one minute ago I too revelled in the feeling of it. Yet they are taking this beautiful need and corrupting it. They see the taking of a woman as a stab of the penis. They fail to realise that sex is not an act of violence; it is the taking of pleasure. Sex is the release of a tension felt, a sensation that needs to be built over time. Violence on the other hand is the culmination of anger, fear and hatred; released in an explosion of rage. This is what these pretend monsters of men do not understand. Receptive women are sources of delight providing an exquisite release. An unwilling receptacle can be a target for power, but it is a poor substitute for true violence. I look upon them and see that they will never understand. They think they can hear the animal within, but they are not listening. Mine is the roar of the lion, theirs is the squeak of a shrew.

I step from my hiding place as they regain control of her, the bearded one is trying to push himself inside of her again. They hear my movements and he stands. I look down upon his penis, his weapon, and sneer.

"You are trying to push that inside her?" I demand of him as his flaccid penis droops even lower. "Any weapon used for penetration should be hard, strong and sharp."

They look confused. They look to each other as the bearded man awkwardly pulls up his jeans and covers himself. "This is nothing to do with you, asshole. Just walk away," he pathetically calls to me.

One man, the smallest one, shifts to pull the woman to her feet and holds her tightly from behind, pinning her arms to her sides. The other two move towards me, threatening me with their wide stances and clenched fists.

"I'm afraid I cannot do that," I calmly inform them. "This is a pathetic display I cannot see come to pass. Also, I saw her first, and I desire her still." With this, her eyes widen even further. She had taken my arrival as a potential rescue, now she sees me as yet another attacker.

"You can have her after us," the leader informs me in a placatory move that contains not a word of sincerity.

"You misunderstand me," I smile, my tone as a parent might talk to a child, "I mean to take her properly, willingly. I am a man you understand. I am connected with my animal, I am it personified. You just pretend; I am pure."

"You're nuts. Get out of here!" The lesser of the two before me yells, supporting his leader.

"Again, I decline. I am instead inclined to show you the true power within." She is looking at me imploringly. Now, once more, she sees me as her saviour. It was not my intention but maybe I am. I am committed now.

Once more aroused, this time with the delightful inclusion of the prospect of violence. I step forward and point, "you, bearded thing. You are first. Come. Feel the power and purity of Id."

The leader steps toward me in one long stride. At the same time, he commences a wide-arching punch to my head. I drop to the floor and roll to one side, simultaneously gathering up a glass bottle I knew was there. As I rise, I smash the bottle against his temple and he collapses to the ground in a heap of fat flesh. I am still holding the remains of the bottle as his colleague steps to me, hands raised. Without pause I thrust the jagged remains in to his face and twist my wrist. The glass grinds into his features and slices his cheeks and forehead with ease. He falls to the ground, clutching his face and crying.

The last man standing is holding the woman from behind. Her skirt is still around her waist, showing me her pubic hair in the dim light of the alley. I step to them as he shuffles against the brick wall. I reach forward and grab the pinned woman by the material of her blouse. Pulling her towards me, I hear the material rip. However, the majority of her top holds and I use it to yank her past me. I hear her crash to the floor and the pop of her knees on the ground momentarily masks the sound of a man crying behind us. I lean back and lift my leg, lunging forward at the man against the wall. My foot strikes him in the chest, crushing his ribs against the brick. He is still standing, just about, so I bring my other leg up and knee him in the crotch. This action finally results in him sliding down the wall and into a curled-up ball on the floor.

Chapter Fifteen

Sitting outside the judicial offices in the courthouse, I was still sporting my stupid grin. I had ordered an undercover unit to position itself outside Edward Gooch's apartment building and shadow the suspect should he show himself. I couldn't keep still so I was jiggling my legs about, watching the movement of my feet. That's why I didn't see or hear Grace approach. She had been giving evidence in a courtroom downstairs and had heard I was there.

"Minty, I heard you had a breakthrough," she called to me, making me look up quickly with a start.

"Yeah, a genuine suspect. Just getting the warrant now, shouldn't be a problem."

"That's great, Minty."

She sat down beside me on the hard wooden bench, her hips touching mine. I stopped moving my legs and stared straight ahead instead. I could feel the warmth of her touch against me. Her breath was the only sound I could hear. I wasn't sure if this was heaven or hell at that moment in time. I wanted, with every fibre of my being, to turn my head, to face her, to press my lips to hers. Instead I just continued staring ahead.

"Yeah... Any moment now... The warrant..." I tried to talk but found myself failing in such close proximity to her.

"Exciting." She breathed the word in the most sensual way. I could feel she was facing me now; the exclamation of the word had tickled my ear with a warm wind. I looked down and saw the hemline of her skirt, high on her legs. Revealed to me were her perfectly formed thighs in dark pantyhose. Her perfect knees touched each other. She shifted her feet under the bench and they parted a tiny amount. My mind raced, picturing stockings, naked flesh beneath the skirt, tiny black underwear. My heart pumped audibly in my ears and I closed my eyes and swallowed.

"Yeah, exciting," I agreed wholeheartedly.

I was sweating now; my hands were slick and I could feel moisture on my forehead. I needed to get away from here. Or did she want this? Was she so close to try to get a reaction from me? Again, I fought the urge to turn and kiss her. I placed my sweaty palms under my thighs and rocked back and forth on them. She moved away from me, just an inch but it felt like a mile. My heart calmed back down and I dried my hands on the creaking vinyl seat. I swallowed and finally turned to face her. She looked amazing and it wasn't helping. She was wearing a formal jacket that matched her skirt and a cream silk blouse. Her hair was done up in a knot, held with a colourful clip. She looked devastatingly beautiful and it made my heart ache. Silently I said the words to myself that I had never before admitted, "I am in love with this woman."

It made my heart leap and then instantly plummet. I was in love with my best friend; my only friend. Not only that, I was in love with someone who did not love me back. As she sat beside me, no longer touching, I felt our friendship and nothing more. She was out of my league. Everything about her was better than me. I was this inept, untested detective. I had no experience with women. I had always been, and still was, the class nerd. I was sweating and having palpitations just because we brushed hips for a second; I was pathetic. Trying to calm myself again, I didn't notice the judge's clerk standing in front of me. He coughed politely and held out the completed warrant.

"Here you go, Detective."

Grabbing the document, I barely managed to shout my thanks to the clerk and farewell to Grace as I fled the building, paperwork flapping in my hand.

Chapter Sixteen

I stretch tall, enjoying the sensations that flood through me following my attacks. There is a woman on the floor behind me, crying. She wears a woollen skirt and a torn blouse through which her breasts are exposed. She has pulled her skirt down to hide her absence of underwear but, in my memory, she is exposed. I am throbbing with excitement having aggressively disabled her attackers. I am aroused at her nudity and coursing with adrenalin. Previous injuries from a chase are stinging my bloodied skin under my own damaged clothing. I am alive, the power of my animal is proven. Three men lie on the floor in various states of damage. Two are crying and one is unconscious. I step to the unconscious one. He is the bearded leader who sought to rape the woman just seconds ago. I collect a shard of glass from the bottle I used to defeat him. I cut and slice at his back. Without pause, I cut him deep in a frenzy of movement. Left and right, up and down; his copious flesh pierced and diced. Eventually the pain wakes him as blood soaks the tattered remains of his flannel shirt.

Noting his return to consciousness, I place my hands in the belt of his jeans. His fly remains open from his attempted rape so, with a yank, I easily pull them from him. I stand on his ankles and force his legs open; his hairy white ass exposed to the light looks ridiculous.

"You!" I point to the woman cuddling herself on the floor, trying to wrap the tattered remains of her clothing around her. "Stop trying to cover yourself and come here!"

She complies mutely. She drops her hands to her sides, causing her tattered blouse to fall to her waist, barely clinging on to her slight frame. She moves like a zombie towards me in her bare feet.

"Take up that bottle." I command her a little more gently. She collects a beer bottle from the ground and walks over to me quaking. No longer do I want to take her now that she is broken and vulnerable. Disappointed that my sexual urges have been dashed I decide to make up for it with viscera. "Cut him, slice him up. Taste the flavour of his blood..."

She does not move, I try to coax her. I guide her hand to his blood-soaked body but she jerks away. Standing stiff, bolt upright, all I see in her eyes is terror. Sighing with a frown, I take the bottle from her and gently guide her to the opposite wall of the alley, away from the scene. Setting her down on the ground I try to soothe her by making soft noises, I stroke her hair like I might a kitten. Finally, with her out of the way and soothed into stillness, I return to the men. The fat one is writhing around on the ground as blood oozes from the wounds on his back. Knowing he will slowly die from the loss of blood, I step over him to the other two. They are sitting now, facing me. Fear lights their eyes as I gesture that they should stand. As they do, I reach into my pocket and retrieve my knife. Extending the blade behind my back, I step to them.

With a frenzy of movement, I slice them open, diagonal lines of blood form on each of them from waist to shoulder. I come at them from the opposite direction as they react from the pain. They twitch backwards, attempting to retreat; their minds unable to process the solid wall behind them in their fear and confusion. The knife is flashing as I violently lacerate them, sending blood flying. I am unstoppable. Their insides spill from them and I rip spongey organs from their bodies, scattering them around their bloodied bodies.

They lie tangled on the floor. Clear and coloured liquids in equal measure ooze from them. Strange shapes and textures punctuate the scene. Looking back to the woman, I see she has covered herself and retrieved her shoes. She is hugging them like they might save her from this mayhem. Shrugging, I give her a wink, and leave the alleyway. My job here is done, I am sated.

Chapter Seventeen

Searching the apartment of Edward Gooch was a huge waste of time. Not only was there no blood-soaked weapon or anything relevant to the case, there was nothing of interest, period. He had all the modern necessities of living; kettle, toaster, cutlery, and so on. And that is all. There were no photos in drawers, no boxes of memorabilia, no ornaments. It was like he bought the apartment with fittings and furnishings and just walked in. There were clothes in the wardrobe, but not many. He had only two pairs of shoes; one formal, one sporty. I suppose he had a pair he was wearing as we had yet to find the man himself, but it was like he wasn't a real person at all. I toyed with the idea that he was a spy or some kind of foreign agent. I even searched on our databases for other rented properties, thinking that the apartment was merely a front for his murder organisation, but nothing checked out. I wanted to believe he was the murderer, just to be able to solve the case, but there was no evidence. There wasn't even a motive, just the dream. *Curse that dream*, I thought as I finished reading the catalogue of Edward's belongings yet again.

Slapping the file back down on my desk, now thicker with notes about the most boring suspect in the world, I leaned back in my chair. My thoughts, annoyingly, turned to Grace. I needed to get her out of my head. I didn't want to be infatuated with my friend. I was trying hard to replace the word 'love' with something else but I kept coming back to that simple, painful realisation. I was in love with Grace and I needed not to be. Opening up Facebook, I browsed to her profile. Seeking inspiration; I was hoping to find something to grab onto to diminish my feelings for her. Perhaps she had a liking for something I hated, I hoped. Quickly finding her page, I was immediately disappointed. Her interests, yoga, cycling and films, were lovely. Her friends were interesting. Her pictures. I got distracted, I must admit, by her pictures. There was an entire album of holiday photos of coy poses in a bikini that sucked me in completely.

My mental image of her had not done her credit, she was thirty years old and her body was toned and as hard as marble. Much better than me at my child-like twenty-four. My gut was starting to show and I had some unpleasant love-handles that I had been meaning to deal with for months now. Whilst being replete with muscles, she still looked soft and womanly. Even the colour of her endeared her to me, the slight brown tan of her smooth white skin caught the sun in the pictures. So much nicer than the pasty-white colour I permanently sported. Sighing, I closed the page, telling myself that she had no time for me. I was just a pale nerd who was six years her junior. She was a goddess, superior to me in every way.

A shout rang out from the Captain's office, calling me. I shook the distractions from my head and hurried over, closing the door behind me. On his desk was a crime-scene report.

"A new case, sir?"

"New, Minty? What happened to your suspect?"

"Nothing sir, I'm still waiting on the undercover unit to pick him up for questioning but there was nothing in the apartment and nothing in his background. He still looks clean, even cleaner if that's possible."

"That's disappointing... But no, not a new case. A possible connection to another one."

"Another stabbing sir?"

"Yeah, different M.O. but maybe the same weapon. Quite distinctive apparently, in the mugging scene. You'd better get over there."

He slapped the report down in front of me and I gathered it up in my arms. This was indeed a real case, not one but two attacks. If my luck held he might even go serial. Shaking the thought from my head, I chastised myself. I was forgetting the victims. People were dead. It was true that I was excited, but I should never forget the victims. I needed to catch this man, or woman, before they killed again. I quietly thanked the Captain and quickly marched to my car, leafing through the new file as I walked. I was fishing around in my pocket for my keys and pressing the remote unlock, as I looked up to see Grace. She was smiling at me as she leaned against the passenger door.

"Sorry, Grace. No time. Have to go..."

"I know, Minty. I'm coming with you."

"Sorry but this is getting high-profile, official. I can't afford to let you tag along. People will be looking at this one; there are two deaths now." I was talking quickly, babbling almost because she was making

75

me nervous and I had to concentrate on work. This was my chance and I couldn't afford to blow it.

"I know, Minty. Stop talking. The Captain needs two people on a multiple, so he assigned me to you."

"But you're not a detective, you aren't even police," I blurted out without thinking how insulting it would sound.

"I know that," she frowned, "but I am permitted to work cases you know, and he doesn't have another free detective."

"Sorry, Grace, I didn't mean it like that, I wasn't thinking is all..." I spluttered, quickly trying to take it back.

"Well don't forget again, okay? Now you're a proper detective, don't forget your friends." Smiling again, she climbed into the car.

As if I could ever forget Grace, I thought, as I climbed into the driver's side. Starting the car and pulling out of the garage, I looked across at her. She looked more serious now. Her hair was pulled back in a ponytail and she was dressed in dark jeans and a shirt. She was even wearing her hip holster with an automatic pistol strapped inside. Noticing my glance towards her side-arm, she nodded.

"I've got your back, Minty. I'm certified but would rather not kill anyone today, if that's okay with you."

"No. Me neither. You ever fired it?" I asked her as I started up my beaten-up Toyota.

"Nope, not in anger. Never even taken it out the holster."

"No, nor me. Let's hope we can catch the guy and he surrenders," I smiled as I pulled from the precinct parking lot.

"Yeah. I'm sure he'll come peacefully," I saw her smiling wryly as I checked for traffic and smiled back, previous friction already forgotten.

"D'you have the file for the new scene?" She asked, business-like.

Inwardly, I sighed. She was magnificent. *Indomitable*, I thought. "In the back. Summarise it for me?" I asked her. She pulled her seatbelt loose and turned to reach back to retrieve it. I was glad I was driving, it prevented me from looking at her again. My mind filled in the details, however. She was the kind of woman that an artist would sculpt, a muse for a work of art, I thought. Boudicca or Joan of Arc, I decided; a warrior. A woman of curves, beauty, power and intelligence.

She retrieved the folder and whipped it past me as she spun back into her seat. Reading the document, she gave me the salient details as I concentrated on driving. I sped up as she read. "Okay, let's see... another alley, the weapon is a knife... Minty, did you read this?"

"No time. Why, what is it?"

"It isn't just another victim... There are three new victims..."

Stunned by the news, I just grit my teeth and drove. He had killed four people now. This was serious, "how is it connected to our victim?" I asked as I considered turning on the lights and siren.

I heard her turn to a new page, "it's the knife apparently... just reading here. It's a very unique weapon for murder." Her voice changed as I heard her start to quote from the report, "'a thin short blade that retracts into a glass-reinforced plastic holder. It is a pressure-moulded ceramic blade that slices skin in a particular fashion. It is therefore distinctive and rare due to the cost over that of a regular retractable blade. Also, the short blade is not ideal for defence as would not appear threatening to a casual onlooker. Such weapons are not currently fashionable amongst the criminal element in Canada.' I am quoting here obviously, there's even a picture they downloaded from a catalogue. Says on the advert that it's for 'filleting sharks and other game fish while also being suitable for skinning', explains why it's so short I suppose."

"Nasty..." I commented, picturing being cut by such a knife.

"Definitely. I would say that our guy likes people to hurt, he likes the sight of blood."

"Our guy?"

"Yeah, only a man would do this sort of thing. Don't you think? Too dangerous for a woman to use such a small weapon against a man. Knives are a man's weapon, probably as a penis replacement."

"I agree, but let's keep our minds open..." I advised, trying to remember my Police College training. She was right of course, and I too was already referring to the killer as male, but I was determined to do this right.

"Nope, let's not…", she contradicted, "Minty… there's a witness…" almost stamping on the brakes, I looked across at her. She was smiling a grin of satisfaction. "She saw him, she might be able to give us a description. She's in the hospital, should we go there?" She asked excitedly.

"No, let's check the scene first," I quickly decided, "give her time to calm down and get the treatment she needs. We need to take over the case officially and you do that at the scene."

I fired up the lights and siren and sped up even more, wanting to get the job done. This was going to make me, and I didn't want to put a foot wrong. Grace gripped the door handle as I wove in and out of the rush-hour traffic. I was enjoying the movement; the control and the power of the speeding car. I hadn't used the blues and twos since I was a lowly beat cop. Screeching to a stop at a street-blocking angle at the crime scene tape, I turned and grinned at a very still Grace.

"Child," she tutted through a tight smile. Finally releasing her grip on the door handle.

"If you can't take the heat," I replied with a grin, adrenaline still pumping from the drive.

We stepped from the car as a pair and moved to the uniformed officer guarding the scene.

"Detective Beech?" He inquired as I approached.

"That's me," I stated confidently, showing my badge. "This is CSI Bouchard," I gestured at Grace as she presented her credentials.

"I've been informed you were taking over, sirs," he said, nodding to us, "the detective from our Precinct left already, he said that you can just start again as he hadn't done much anyways when he got the call."

He raised the tape to allow us through, but we ducked anyway. I was sure the attending detective had done a great deal already. His abrupt departure was a protest against us taking the case. Just a little inter-precinct rivalry and not a real problem, I told myself. The bodies had been examined and taken away already. Any trace evidence had been gathered and the photographs completed. With most of the crime already processed there was little to do at the scene. We stood by the tape outline of the bodies, trying to take in the larger picture.

"Looks pretty much the same as before," I ventured to a quiet Grace.

"Yeah, secluded alleyway. Hidden from the main street by that air-conditioner. Perfect location for a stabbing," she replied, clearly having being analysing the scene as I had been.

"Three victims though, and a witness. It seems to be quite an escalation. I wonder why he didn't kill the witness too?" I wondered aloud.

"Maybe he doesn't do women?" Was her reasonable response.

"Let's go and find out, shall we?" Without waiting for an answer, I turned and strode back to the officer guarding the scene. I signed his release so he could close down the scene and let the cleaners get to work on the blood. There was nothing more that could be done forensically and City Hall liked us to open up the streets as quickly as possible. Nothing scares the voters more than police tape, they liked to tell us in the monthly PR meetings. We climbed into the car and I backed out into the main street.

"Minty, please, no lights this time," Grace asked; placing her delicate hand on mine as I gripped the wheel.

I obliged, and we drove in silence. Still feeling the touch of her hand on mine, I focussed hard on the case as I drove on automatic to the hospital. A witness; it was unbelievable luck and I knew that she could give us something. In the space of less than a week I was going to eradicate my 'fresh' nickname as I brought in a multiple-murderer in record time. *This was going to be the case that made me, I could feel it.*

We arrived at the hospital and, after some wandering, found our witness. The attending doctor quickly briefed us on her status and we stepped into the private room. Even with the cuts on her face and bruises already starting to darken, she was stunning. She was as white as a porcelain doll and looked about as fragile. Her long blond hair cascaded down the white hospital pillow she lay on. I cleared my throat and stepped forward, a little tongue-tied in the presence of her beauty.

"Miss Wilmon, my name is Detective Beech, and this is CSI Grace Bouchard. I wonder if you are up to answering a few questions?" I asked her as professionally as I could.

"Of course, Detective," she answered in a soft trembling voice.

"I understand that our perpetrator may have initiated a sexual assault. Did the three victims come to your aid?" I asked, pulling out my notebook.

"No, Detective. It was the other way around," she replied calmly considering her ordeal.

"I'm sorry, the doctor said--"

"The doctor is wrong," she said with more passion and strength than I would have expected, "no-one has been listening to me since I got here. They keep saying that I'll remember when I'm better. I'm better now, I remember it all." With each sentence her confidence rose, her commitment clear in her intonation. Grace stepped forward, supplanting me as the leader.

"Miss Wilmon. Please, can you tell us in your own words what happened," she asked calmly and with a tone of respect.

"Of course, thank you," she said more calmly now, "those three men, those monsters, the fat bearded one mostly. They grabbed me and shoved me into this alleyway. They came from nowhere, I was just walking home and the fat one grabbed my arm and shoved me in, the other two followed. They said they just wanted my money and to be quiet or they would hurt me..."

"Please, take your time. They can't hurt you now, you're safe." Grace was reassuring and helpful, but at the same time getting all the information we needed. I backed away and continued taking notes. Grace had already placed her phone on the side of the bed and was recording everything, but I wanted to write down the salient points too.

"I know I'm safe, because my rescuer came."

"This was the man that killed the three attackers," Grace clarified.

"Yes. Although I don't think his motives were much better. He took his time..."

"He was with them?"

"No, he was alone. The fat one was on me, the other two holding me down. He almost managed to start it... the, the..." she started to cry but swallowed it back.

Grace finished the phrase for her, "the sexual assault."

"Yes, that...", the victim agreed, "but finally, he, my rescuer, stepped from behind the big metal box thingy."

"The air-conditioner," Grace clarified again.

"Is that what it was? I don't know, just the big silver thing closer to the street."

"Yes, it's an A.C. unit," Grace answered, nodding.

"Okay, well he stepped from there. He'd clearly been hiding, watching. His hand was down his pants and he said something about wanting me for himself. I almost died there and then. I thought I was saved, then I thought my ordeal was going to be with four of them instead of three. I wanted to die."

"That must have been very difficult..." I added, not wanting to be forgotten from the interview. Grace turned and faced me, the expression on her face clear. I was to stay out of it. I gave a sheepish smile and nodded gently, agreeing to be quiet.

"Yes, well..." the witness continued, "the fat one got off me and they had some conversation. The skinnier one held me, pretty tight. I couldn't get away. I thought they were going to have a fight over who was first or something..."

"Then what happened, Miss Wilmon?" Grace coaxed.

"Please, call me Joy," the woman in bed asked with a genuine smile aimed clearly at Grace alone.

"Okay... What happened, Joy?" Grace said, smiling back and touching her hand as she had mine just minutes ago in the car.

"I don't know really..." Joy carried on, reassured and

strengthened by Grace's touch, "all of a sudden the fat one was on the floor, knocked out. His friend was rolling around by him... Then the rescuer just pulls me away from the guy holding on to me and throws me on the floor. I just crawled away as far as I could. When I finally looked up, I saw him cutting and slicing the fat one up real good. He wanted me to cut him too, he made me get a bottle from the ground."

She faltered at the memory and Grace pressed her to continue, "he wanted you to join in?"

"Yes, I didn't though. I couldn't," Joy stammered, again swallowing the memory, "so he just pushed me to the ground again."

"So, you were safe?" Grace asked.

"Yeah, well, I didn't think I was. The guy, the one still standing, had just cut the other three to pieces. I never saw anything like it. I think I fainted, sorry. I thought I was next, you understand? The next thing I remember is some guy asking if I was okay. Then the ambulance, then here. I'm sorry but I couldn't take the blood. The smell..." She started to cry, unable to hold it back this time, the memory of her trauma overwhelming her.

"That's okay, Joy," Grace slipped her hand into hers and gently squeezed. "Don't go there right now, push it away. It will get better, but for now don't make yourself think of that..." Grace turned to me, sensing the end of the interview. "Minty, maybe we should go..."

"Wait." Joy called, raising her head and wiping the tears from her eyes with the palm of her hand. "I know this guy saved me but he's crazy. He didn't care about me, he just liked hurting those men. I saw it, I saw him. It was like he was an animal. You have to catch him. Please, catch him."

"We will do our best, Joy. Don't you worry, we'll find him," Grace assured her confidently.

"But don't you want a description?" Joy asked, confused.

"You seem tired, Joy," Grace said, "these things are best done when you are feeling better. The doctors are right, the memories will return, the image will clear. So close to the assault, your recollection will be fuzzy. We have to think of you, being made to remember in such detail isn't good for you right now."

"No, you have to know now, he might attack someone while we wait," she insisted, reaching towards us as we were moving away.

"That's unlikely," Grace replied, "just wait a couple of hours."

"No, we have to do it now, I remember every detail. He would kill again in an instant; we have to stop him now." Grace looked at her with concern, but she continued, "it's not fuzzy either. He looked right at me, I looked right at him. I thought this was the last face I was ever going to see. It's etched into my mind," Joy asserted.

"Ok, I'll get a sketch artist here as soon as possible," I said quickly, stepping forward eagerly.

"Please, quickly. I want you to get this guy, he's not okay. He's going to hurt someone else," Joy predicted ominously.

Chapter Eighteen

I emerged from the tunnel in which I had been trapped; returning to conscious thought, sitting in a coffee shop. This was not good, I thought to myself, looking down at the hot coffee in front of me; not only was I experiencing visions of a crazed killer, now I was blacking out. With a wince, I carefully placed my hand on my arm. My bruised and battered torso had suffered badly from its comatose trip down the river, but it felt much worse now. I raised the coffee to my lips and took a sip. Its warmth soothed me as I tried to take stock. Firstly, I'd had a dream about a killer mutilating a man in an alley. This was pretty disturbing but nothing that watching too much television couldn't explain. The second incident was more problematic because something had taken control of me. Something foreign had made me push excrement into the mouth of my subordinate, Johnny. I wasn't sure if it was the thing inside me, or me trying to escape it, who had jumped into the river. However, that detail seemed unimportant somehow. Now I was in a coffee shop, somewhere in the city with no memory of how I got there.

I ordered a muffin to go with my coffee and considered the evidence. I wondered, hoped really, that is was all in my mind; a complete fantasy. I cast my mind back to university; my abnormal psychology class contained many instances in which people had created elaborate mental fantasies from nothing. This quickly fell down, however, because the police had visited, and I was in pain, so something had happened, that was for certain. It was not just a vision either, as visions don't take control of you. This wasn't a psychotic break because, again, it had actually happened. Detective Beech had told me that the murder was real, or might be real. Okay, so I was not crazy, that was something. Looking around the quiet café, I realised that I needed some space and privacy to work it all out. I didn't want the police to bring me in for any more questions, or worse, the excrement assault. Looking around me, I concluded that, for now, I was safe; they wouldn't find me here in this random coffee shop. I sighed, pondering my situation. The explanations that remained were things I didn't believe in. What remained was either psychic vision or demonic possession.

The latter made some logical sense. I'd had a vision, not of a person, but of someone possessed. This man, overcome by evil, killed another. My witnessing of it had opened the door for this demon to take control of me. Thinking on it, I decided that it was a poor hypothesis. Even with my rudimentary knowledge, from watching *The Exorcist* more than a decade ago, the explanation seemed too outlandish. Still ridiculous, but more likely, was that it had been a vision of a man killing another man. People talk about it all the time and just because I don't believe it, doesn't mean it isn't true. Murder cases are solved by psychics, I had heard, so maybe there was something to it.

Letting that settle in, I decided that the vision could have connected me to the killer in a way in which his rage had infected me. Diving back into my muffin, I decided that I liked this explanation more. I had been overcome by the emotion of the killer. He had made me do something I actually really wanted to do anyway but was too afraid. I had felt detached, but it was still me shoving shit down Johnny's mouth. This explanation still left many questions unanswered, questions that I consciously forced out of my mind, trying to let my theory, however tenuous, settle me.

I looked down at the Formica surface of the table before me. Sterile, that is the word that came to my mind, with smears of disinfectant spreading patterns across it. The marks of the remaining fluid reflected in the sunlight that was making it through the high glass front of the café. The dirt and germs of the person before me had been wiped away, just as my thoughts and actions were being eradicated by the separation of time. I looked up; the café was a soulless place. Devoid of personality, created only to sell and serve coffee. The people around me might have been dummies for all the connection I had to them. Even the man at the counter, he who had so happily handed me a little plate with my muffin on. He had not touched anything that I might too be touching, such was our disconnection. He might as well be a robot. Me too; of course I was worried, concerned about my situation, but I should have been screaming. I should have been running to doctors, the police, someone. Instead I was sat in a café, calmly eating, warming the soft material of the food with sips of warm coffee after each bite.

Even my apparent detachment from the situation didn't really concern me. I felt almost at peace; the idea that I was somehow infected with the emotions of another person alleviated me of any responsibility for my actions. It occurred to me that I could use my gift to help the police. The other thing, the incident at work, just showed me that I had to be stronger and fight the contamination that I might get from the visions. However, there remained the disconcerting variable that was the blackout. The fact remained that I still had no idea how I had arrived at this place, or what I had done in the meantime. Had I experienced another vision? Why had I forgotten it all this time? I stood and resolved to head home, to face the situation from more comfortable, familiar surroundings.

Chapter Nineteen

The wait outside the hospital room, first for the artist to arrive, then for him to finish, seemed interminable. It didn't help that Grace didn't seem to want to talk either. I sat on the thinly padded bench outside Joy's room and fidgeted. Finally, the silence was broken with some softly spoken words from Grace's barely parted lips, "you find her attractive."

"Sorry?" I asked, confused at the abbreviated sentence.

"Joy, Minty. You find her attractive," Grace elaborated.

"I hadn't really noticed…"

"Minty, your jaw practically dropped when we went in," Grace retorted with a change in her tone of voice that edged it towards annoyance.

"I wasn't that bad, I just thought she looked vulnerable. I felt bad," I innocently replied with what I thought was the truth.

"So, it was a 'saving a girl' thing then?" She asked.

"Maybe… it's my job to catch this guy you know," I answered, defensive now I realised she was criticising my behaviour.

"Our job, Minty," Grace asserted herself.

"Well yes, now it's our job, but it was my job when she was attacked," I replied, even more defensively.

"I suppose," was Grace's grudging reply.

"Suppose nothing, it's my fault she's there, in that hospital bed," I said with a raised voice now I was annoyed.

"Although if you had caught him, she would have been raped too," Grace said, calmer now and more like the Grace I knew.

"There is that…" I conceded, quieter as I realised I had been over-reacting. I smiled, trying to diffuse the situation. Looking at Grace I could see that she too was trying to calm down our small argument.

"But you didn't answer me. Do you find her attractive?" She asked again with a tilt of her head.

"Yes, I suppose," I finally conceded. I wasn't sure where this was headed. Intellectually it sounded like she was jealous, but I knew that couldn't be the case. However, I rolled this idea around in my mind, finding that I liked the sound of it. Grace was jealous, I liked that. Then reality hit me, the real reason. "Grace, I'm not going to ask out the only witness in my most important case ever."

"You're about the same age, she's pretty, you're a good-looking guy..." she pointed out.

She thinks I'm good looking, the words bounced around inside my head. I almost hit the ceiling. Grace thinks I'm good looking. All other facts left my brain. "You think I'm good looking?"

"Shut up, Minty," Grace said, turning away now.

"No, you said something interesting there..." I pressed.

"Minty..." she warned me.

I wasn't listening, I was enjoying myself now, "ooh come on, you can't take it back..."

"No. The artist is done, look."

She was right, the sketch artist had come out of Joy's room and was showing me his clipboard, which contained the sketch of our perpetrator. One look and I knew. I knew that face. It was Mr Edward Gooch; the man with the dream.

Chapter Twenty

I awoke, but I was not awake. I remembered coming home from the coffee shop and going to bed. I was still there, lying under the covers. But my eyes would not open and I could not move. I considered this and arrived at the conclusion that I should be concerned. I was not. I was calm. It was just that I could not move or open my eyes. It occurred to me that I was still asleep even though my mind was awake. This must be another vision, I thought, but it did not feel like one. I was myself, I was Edward, but I did not feel entirely like him; detached as before, but far more so. Suddenly I perceived a flood of light and a vision of my bedroom ceiling. My eyes were open. In a flash, I was up and moving to the bathroom. This was odd, but I was not worried as I urinated into the toilet. I had no control, but unlike before, I didn't mind.

The time before, when my body was not mine to control, I could still feel myself. This time I could feel nothing. I could see through my eyes but had no sense of the rest of my body. I was a floating thought; a consciousness inside the mind of another's physical being. The body in which I was contained moved to the bathroom mirror. I looked into the eyes of what I thought would be Edward. This was not who I saw. I saw the eyes, the face and the expression of someone I knew very well. I saw the eyes of an animal. I recognised him immediately; the instinctive impulses and primary processes of Edward separate and looking back at me. The words of Freud echoed in my mind; his name was Id.

Id stared back at me through the mirror. The face was that of Edward Gooch, but the eyes were changed, the person behind them was something else now. Just a portion of the man he had been. I too used to be a part of Edward; that, I recalled, but Id had taken him. It was Id's body now. Considering the issue, coldly and calmly, I determined that I must be Ego. That is why I wasn't panicking, I realised. Such emotion was Id's to control whereas I was the self; the higher being. I considered for a moment if I cared, discovering that I did not. Searching my mind, I discovered that I could access all of Edward's memories. I could recollect Id's work last night too. Each cut and slice was as clear as day, the edges of the memories as hard as diamond. I vividly recalled his desire to take the woman and his disdain of her attackers. The memories made me sick. It was a strange sensation for a mind without a body to experience and I did not care for it. The realisation that I contained a conscience suggested that I was both Ego and Superego. This filled me with dread as it suggested that Id was in complete control. With all morality residing in me, his self was totally detached; leaving only the animal within to run rampant.

I tried to take control by pushing myself back into Edward's mind. But how do you take control of something you always had control of? It was not a problem I had ever considered and had no idea how to achieve such a thing. In the mirror, Id smiled back at me. He knew. He knew I was watching and had no influence. He had won and all I could do was to float around in his mind and watch. I would have wept, had I eyes. I would have screamed, had I lungs. If I had hands, I would have taken my life. Yet I had nothing. So I sat, cursed to inaction, locked within the mind of a free man; an evil man. Edward's Id was loose. I, Ego, was caged.

Chapter Twenty-one

"We breach in five...

Four...

Three...

Two...

One..."

The steel battering ram slamming against the door was like an explosion in the tight confines of the corridor. Waves of blue fabric burst through the now open entranceway. Flashes of white filled my vision as the words 'police' strobed past.

"Get down!"

"Police!"

"Clear... Clear... Clear..."

The cries were loud, confident, final.

"This is it," I thought as I stepped over the door that lay shattered and hanging from a single hinge. The members of SWAT who had burst through were now hanging around relaxing. They just loved to show everyone else that they do this kind of thing every day. Their whole demeanour screamed out casual professionalism. Guns were held by a few fingers, clipped to their body armour. Faces remained hidden under balaclavas with dark eyes inspecting me from behind thick goggles. I tried to remain casual too, as I calmly entered the flat of Edward Gooch. A flat I myself was in just a day before. It was my scene after all; it being my case and my perpetrator.

"Report," I barked at the leader of the breaching team.

"Sorry, sir. No-one home."

"What! We have positive identification of the suspect being in this flat," I cried at the impassive face before me.

"What can I say, sir? He ain't here, look for yourself," he gestured with the butt of his compact machine gun.

I did, foolishly looking around the empty flat as he and his team left in the elevator. He was indeed gone, but the man on Reception had been sure. Edward Gooch had definitely been in.

Chapter Twenty-two

The police are so stupid. I sensed their approach a mile away. I heard their over-sized vehicles shuffling around, closing the street. They entered the building and deactivated the elevators, causing distinctive noises that were clear to my senses. They think their procedures and experience make them formidable but they are wrong. Even as they were closing the street, I was walking down the stairs. As they were packing themselves into the elevator, I simply walked past their guards. They stood in the entrance, machine guns in their arms, body armour on, goggles and helmets like they were about to fight a war. They were not expecting their suspect to calmly walk by. They believe themselves to be frightening and threatening to the people they want to contain. But I am in control. I have no fear. I am instinct. Excepting the simple addition of a hat, I disguised myself with confidence. They expected me to run, to look furtive. A man striding across the lobby did not figure in their psyches, I even smiled as I passed by, exiting the building and hailing a cab.

I am thrilled to finally be rid of the worm of a man that was Edward Gooch. I am excited for the future, for what I might do, for what I might be. I am Id, and I am free.

Chapter Twenty-three

They took my case from me. It was understandable really, given the circumstances. No-one blamed me for the disappearance of Edward, the Captain had been clear on that, but I did. I had him, I was sat opposite him drinking coffee. We were calmly discussing his dream and what it could mean, if it could be real or imagined, and I let him go.

*

"Oh, Grace. Why am I so stupid?"

"Come on, Minty. This wasn't your fault, you found the guy," she was tiring of the conversation, but I remained stuck on topic, obsessing.

"But then I let him go," I complained.

"No, you discovered that he's the guy. We're hunting him now because you solved the case. Now all we have to do is find him," she repeated with more force as her patience wore thin.

"I suppose…" I conceded, trying to see her point of view, "The case kind of solved itself really, once there was a witness…"

"But that's ninety percent of police cases, Minty. We gather facts, follow procedure, which inevitably leads to us finding the suspect. Boring really. The other ten percent of course, remaining unsolved."

"It was his eyes," I was whining now, "the eyes being blue. That was what stuck with me. Why did he say that the man he killed had blue eyes?"

She looked down, thinking, "he said they were like his own, didn't he?"

"Yeah, he said they were identical," I remembered.

"So maybe that's it," she said, "he transposed himself into the victim as he remembered it. Placing his own eyes in him, looking back at himself."

"Why would he do that?"

"Well, what's his motive?" She asked, "we still don't know why he's suddenly killing people. I bet when we catch him, we'll find out why, it'll become clear."

"I suppose…" I conceded.

"Suppose nothing, let's go get a beer." She suddenly declared, "we'll find him, his picture is with every cop in the country now, someone will see him, and it'll be case-closed." She didn't wait for acceptance, instead she grabbed me by the arm and dragged me to my car. I didn't complain as I drove us to the bar. Soon we were sat at our usual table with bottles in hand and I was already feeling better.

"I don't know if I feel better or drunker…" I said, slurring slightly.

"What?"

The music was pounding tonight, the crowd stomping harder than usual. At least that's how it felt as my beer vibrated on the table.

"I don't know if I feel…"

"What?"

"Forget it… LET'S DANCE!" I screamed at her. She heard that, and nodded as she walked to the dance floor. This was not usual, but I was drunk and wanted to move. Really, I wanted to find Edward, but that was out of my hands now, so instead I thought I could dance. Pretty soon I was stamping my trainers on the floor as loud as I could, trying to turn when everyone else did. My hands were on my hips and I was trying to blend in but failing. Grace was already laughing. I was rubbish and didn't care, drink was definitely overriding my usual embarrassment. Her laugh was intoxicating. I looked stupid but the effect on her was worth it. Ignoring the fact that I was repeatedly knocking into the man beside me, I turned in the wrong direction yet again. I was busy trying to copy the moves he was performing and that was the cause of my failure. In trying to mimic the man, I was always one move behind.

"Why do we have to dance like this?" I shouted to Grace over the music. "Why all line up like robots, why can't we just let loose?"

I punctuated my point by going free-form. In what I thought was an expression of pure movement, I waved my arms in the air and wiggled my ass at Grace. She laughed even harder but the reaction around us was not favourable. After a very short display of my dancing prowess I found myself being pulled from the floor by a very insistent, still laughing, Grace.

"Minty, do you have a death-wish? You can't break the square like that," she told me in a loud voice as she pulled me back to our table.

"Ahh come on... Where's your *senshe* of adventure?" I asked in a drunken slur.

"I'm still two beers short of mine, I'm afraid," she replied with a smile as she slid into place on the smooth vinyl of the bench her side of the table.

"Then let's get two more..." gesturing with two fingers at our waitress I sat back down with a thump in our booth.

"Minty, what's got into you tonight? You don't dance," Grace pointed out.

"We both know that was hardly dancing..."

"That's for sure, you are a funny one..." she smiled her warmest smile of the night.

"And you are a beautiful one," I blurted out.

"What?" She quickly asked, the look of surprise on her face complete.

"You heard me. You are the most stunning, most amazing woman I know, have ever known," I forged on.

"Minty..." she started to say.

"Yeah?" I asked reluctantly, sensing her imminent rejection.

"I don't know--"

"I know. And that's fine," I admitted. I was just so relieved to have finally said something. Having committed myself to the embarrassing truth, I forged on. "It's just that it's been driving me crazy, not saying. I have to say it, then you can reject me, then I can get over it. What d'you think?"

"Think about what?" She asked me, still having to shout to be heard.

"Telling me that I'm not your type; too young, too pale, too flabby, too boring," I said for her.

"That isn't true. I think you are very handsome. Nice, too."

"But?" I needed the truth, I wanted to move on. I felt an urgent need to move away from my obsession back to a normal existence. I was being eaten alive by my feelings; I needed some peace, some rest from the endless torment.

"Let's not do this. You've had too many beers and I'm on my way to doing the same. Let's just go..." she decided as she slid out from the table just as two new beers arrived.

I threw a note on the waitress' tray. But she was already standing from the booth, heading out of the door. By the time I had extracted my uncertain legs from under the table and followed her out, she was gone.

"Well that solves that, then..." I muttered into the night. Certainly telling her how I felt whilst drunk in a night-club was one way to ensure we never spoke to each other again. "I suppose now I can move on," I told myself, as I trudged home. I collapsed into bed face down on my pillow and fell asleep with a long throaty groan.

*

The next morning as I walked in to the Precinct I wasn't surprised to find there was no sign of Grace. My day had started off badly. Hungover and embarrassed about my display, I was devastated at the probable loss of my best friend and love of my life. To top it off I found Detective Booth sat on my desk, grinning.

"Booth, I'm not really in the mood today," I grumbled at him as I sat down.

"Well, I just wanted to say, well done..." he surprised me by saying, not moving from his perch on my desk.

Well done? This was Detective Booth, my tormentor. Where were the jibes, where was the 'Minty-fresh' mocking nickname? Could I have done something right? "Well, thanks." I managed to splutter as he held his hand out. I shook it as he looked me in the eyes.

"Difficult to spot a killer," he told me with sincerity, "well done for finding the guy, I just hope we find him before he kills again."

"You and me both," I replied, as he hopped from my desk and returned to his. Despite my depression, I smiled. Maybe things were looking up. Perhaps I was finally no longer the new guy. I powered up my computer, thinking how surprising life can be, and checked my email. There had been no sightings reported yet. Looking up in response to a polite cough, I saw a tall woman in a black cowboy hat standing in front of me.

"Detective Beech? I'm Officer Cote, from the Force," she said.

The Force was what the Mounties called themselves. The Royal Canadian Mounted Police are the Canadian equivalent of the FBI in the USA. Clearly this was the person who was going to take my case from me.

"Please call me Minty," I replied, still determined to take the nickname on as my own, without the 'fresh' of course. I smiled as I stood to shake her hand.

"I'm Elisha."

She removed her hat and let a bun of long blond hair loose. It cascaded down over her shoulders as she pulled up a chair from another desk and sat beside me. Her tall frame struggled to fit in the small chair and her long legs reached towards me from beneath her fitted black skirt. Not wanting to go down that road, I determinedly maintained polite eye-contact, "Elisha," I nodded to her, "I presume you're here for the Edward Gooch files."

"Yes, please. But more importantly, your impressions of him. You met him, what can you tell me about him," she asked, looking at me intently.

"Sure, yeah, I let him go..." I responded, a bit petulantly.

"Detective, this is no reflection on you, you understand? This is RCMP business now because he's fled the City, probably the Province. Your jurisdiction runs out so we take over. You work out who, we find out where. It's that simple."

She said it with such a genuine expression on her face I had to believe it. "Thank you, Officer," I replied as another part of my depression lifted from me.

"Like I said, Elisha," she said with a warm smile. "You're going to beat yourself up for a while over not spotting him right away, but I've worked these before. He's a psychopath. They feel nothing so there's nothing to see in them. You followed the evidence, there was nothing else to do."

"Thank you, I appreciate that..." I liked her; her easy manner and friendly smile. Suddenly I felt better about handing the file to her as I did so. She was right, this was just a change in the case. I had identified him, now she would actually catch him. As she flipped through the paperwork, I patiently waited.

"So, anything you can add, any impressions?" She asked again.

"Not really, it's all in the report. He's no family, no friends outside the city, he's nowhere else to go. What still bothers me is the lack of motive, of any reason at all really. I'm sorry there isn't more, but he seemed so normal. So innocent," I concluded.

"I know, motiveless killers often do. Well if you think of anything, give me a call." She handed me her card and left me thinking. What was it about him, why did he kill when he seemed so nice, so straightforward?

Chapter Twenty-four

I am on the move. I am not running but I am evading. I must leave Calgary, I know that, but how? I have no money, and if I did, I couldn't rent or buy a car, for surely the police would detect that. The same is true for train and airplane tickets. I cannot walk, Canada is too large a country for that. I could hitch-hike but that would constrain my movements. I ponder the situation and stick out my thumb as I walk down the road.

No-one offers me a ride and soon I find myself sitting on a bench in a rest area. I know that some opportunity will arise, when it does I will take it. Until then, I am satisfied to be at rest. There is an old man here too, waiting for his friend to come and collect him. He is going to the airport, on holiday, I am not interested but am content to let him talk. He tells me of a cabin in the woods, of the solitude of the place; it sounds attractive. Eventually his friend comes and he offers me a ride to the city. I do not want to go backwards, so I refuse. I debate for a second taking the car, taking it from them, but decide against it. It is not to my liking.

Chapter Twenty-five

I spent the entire day thinking while I paced around my apartment. I doodled and made notes, sticking them to the walls, anything I could think of to get to the root of the problem. I had written, one letter at a time, on notes stuck to my window; 'what had driven Edward Timothy Gooch to kill?' I wanted to know why, at forty years of age, did a respectable man become a blood-thirsty murderer? There had to be a reason, an explanation. Maybe the explanation could provide some insight into his next move. It also helped distract me from the apparent disappearance of Grace. She was no doubt avoiding me. I was embarrassed about my outburst and happy to give her space.

Wanting to move my mind away from my personal life, I picked up the notes from my coffee table and leafed through to the official statement from Joy Wilmon, the witness. Reading through the heavy document, I was amazed at how thoroughly she had remembered the event. Often victims of traumatic events block things out, but given a little time and space, Joy had remembered every little detail. It was interesting to me how Edward had hidden, biding his time, maybe enjoying the view. He had only revealed himself when he thought the efforts of the men were 'pathetic', Joy remembered. It seemed significant that he had described them as not being worthy. He was an animal, a thing, a force of nature. This was not the Edward I met in his apartment just a day before, this was someone very different. Reading on, I highlighted one particular entry. Joy described how he had called himself 'Id' not Edward, not Ed, but 'Id'. I wondered, was that a typo? Did she hear him correctly?

Looking up the word on Wikipedia, I thought that maybe Joy was right; '...the id is the animal-like desire for gratification.' If a person were pure id, then they would be nothing but instinct and desire. That made sense, a person with no morality could and would certainly kill and attack like Edward had. It seemed to me that this might be the key to Edward's behaviour. Could it be that Edward was in fact two people, a disassociated killer? While he was Id, he was dangerous. While he was Edward, he was once more normal and calm. That was a good explanation as to why I hadn't suspected him. The man I had interviewed was not the killer, he was somewhere else at the time, hiding inside Edward.

I called Grace. I didn't want to, but I needed to talk to someone, to explain my theory. To my surprise not only did she answer the phone, she said she would come straight over. I tidied up whilst waiting nervously for her arrival. Finally, she knocked on the door and I opened it to the vision of my dreams. I hadn't helped my situation in any way by getting it off my chest. I was so deeply in love with this woman it hurt. Casual reflections on the appearance of Joy, or the impressive nature of officer Cote hadn't dampened my longing for Grace. She marched in and positioned herself on the sofa. I sat in the opposite corner of the room. We were respectably apart, while close enough for my heart to be pounding in her presence. I waited for her to speak.

"So, what's your theory?" She surprised me by getting right down to work, ignoring the elephant in the room.

Pleased not to be addressing my embarrassing admission, I followed suit, "I think he has multiple personalities," I summarised.

"A bit obvious, don't you think?" She pointed out.

"Well, yes I suppose. But there is evidence. In Joy's witness statement--"

"Ooh, Joy, now is it?" She cooed playfully. I was glad to see we were back to being normal straight out of the gate, so I forged ahead, ignoring the comment.

"Yes, Joy," I said with more emphasis on her name, "says he referred to himself as an animal. He called himself Id. Like Freud--"

"Yes, Minty. I know what the id is," she quickly interrupted. "It means, 'that'. You might be interested to know that Groddeck used it first to mean a part of the psyche."

"Right, yeah. Okay then," I mumbled, remembering that Grace had studied psychology as part of her degree. "So, the killer is Id. He comes out, kills people and goes away again. Id goes to bed, Edward wakes up. What he did the night before, lingering as a memory, real but not real. Hence the dream."

She nodded as I spoke, carrying the theory on and padding it out herself, "okay then. So later at work, Edward is all annoyed at the coder guy for messing up and out pops Id again to shove shit down his throat."

"Yeah, I wish they'd reported that sooner, it might have given us a hint as to what Edward was really capable of." I lamented. The embarrassment of the victim and the company wanting to hush it up had hurt us. They only reported it when we had visited the office, enquiring about Edward's whereabouts. Still, we were rolling now, just like old times, "yeah, yeah. Then it happens again, Id is out, following Joy down the road. Wanting to get some, or whatever. But then the three guys attack her and he goes after them instead."

Grace took over again, asking the question; "okay, so why attack them if he just wants the girl?"

"Because they were doing it wrong," I realised, "it's in her statement. He says they were confusing sex for violence and that he'll show them the right way."

She was nodding more now, agreeing as each event backed up the theory, "right, okay so sex for him isn't violence. So, he wasn't going to rape her..."

I flipped through the notes, looking for the correct passage. "No, here. He says that he would have done it properly, 'willingly'. Joy took it to mean that he would have made her pretend to enjoy it, but I think he meant it literally. A person driven by the id would be pure desire. Desire for sex and desire for violence are two different things. I think an id would either have sex, or kill, not the two together."

We paused while Grace removed her coat and made coffee. While she operated the equipment in my kitchen to prepare the drinks, I watched her. I had vowed to myself to not do this, to not torture myself, but her presence and movements drove me crazy. Looking away, I tried to get a hold of myself, I needed to pull it together or my own id was going to take over. Returning, she handed me a mug and sat back down.

"I like it," she stated simply, "thinking it over, it seems to make sense." Pleased, I sipped the coffee and smiled. "Hmm," she added over the top of her own mug, "there is one problem though... if his personality really is split... then where's Edward?" She asked me.

"Well, that's what we're trying to find out," I pointed out the obvious.

"No, you don't get me," she said as she shook her head, "Id is the cunning killer, right? So, Edward is... well he's just Edward. He has no reason to hide, no reason to run. In fact, he would probably wake up somewhere with blood all over him and memories of what he's done. He would freak out even if he didn't remember. What would Edward do then, Minty?" She asked, seemingly knowing the answer.

I thought to myself, what would Edward do? He was a normal guy, a nice guy, "he would call the police. He would call me, in fact," I admitted.

"Exactly," Grace stated, glad that I had confirmed her hypothesis, "if he's Dr Jekyll and Mr Hyde, then where's Jekyll right now?"

I thought about it and slowly realised that she was right. We might not be able to find Id, but we should be able to find Edward. I thought that maybe he was scared and running now. Thinking back to our conversation, however, I remembered how scared he was at the thought that he had done something as wrong as murder. No, Edward was a good guy. Scared or not I thought he would be more scared of hurting people than the consequences of turning himself in.

"Minty?" Grace knocked me from my train of thought and I grunted an acknowledgment of her. "There is one thing you could consider."

"What's that?" I asked.

"This guy, Id. He's a pretty ruthless killer... maybe he killed Edward," she suggested.

"What? But he is Edward," I said, confused.

"I know that," she nodded lightly, "but maybe Id is stronger. Maybe Id has taken over totally now. It's been getting worse and worse. First; total control while Edward was sleeping. Second; he gains control while he is conscious at work. Third; a triple murder and potential rape. Then there's no sign of Edward. Maybe he's escalated to the point at which Edward has no control. Maybe he's just Id now."

"That sounds bad," I said.

"Yeah, that's bad," she agreed, clearly thinking what I was. "An

Id loose is a danger to everyone. But maybe also good? If Id is just instinct, satisfying his needs when and where he wants, then he'll be rubbish at covering his tracks. He'll just kill and take what he wants indiscriminately. That guy will leave tracks a mile wide. That guy is easy to catch."

I thought it over and decided she was right, as usual. But he had evaded us in his building. He had moved so easily and confidently in the security footage we later watched of him walking past the guards. "He would be easy to catch," I agreed, "but we're wrong..." I said, forming the thoughts as I spoke, "he can't be just an id. There's still a full personality inside, otherwise he wouldn't operate at all, he would be helpless..."

"Yeah," Grace agreed, "he would steal whatever he wanted, fight whoever he saw. He'd get caught in an instant. We would have caught him at his apartment, he's got to be smarter than just an id."

"He's got rid of Edward," I added, "but not totally, 'cause he needs him to function. Id's in charge, but the rest of Edward must still be in there somewhere."

"Well I hope so, for Edward's sake," Grace said, "but for our sake I hope not."

"Why not?" I asked, finishing off my coffee.

"Well a person of Edward's intellect with Id in charge is a far more dangerous fugitive. He would be both impossible to catch and insanely violent," she pointed out.

If we were right, then Edward was going to be difficult to find and even harder to catch. Grace shifted on the sofa, distracting me once again. "I wish I could let my personality split," I muttered to myself as she rose to leave.

Chapter Twenty-six

Eventually, what I want comes to me; I knew it would. A truck pulls into the rest-stop and I see it is sufficient for my needs. A young man descends from the cab and hurries from the idling truck, he is heading for the restroom behind me. He smiles at me.

I rise from the bench on which I am sitting and, as he passes, I strike. There is a rock in my hand and I smash it to his temple. He crumbles to the ground with a gentle hush of material and flesh as I step over him. Briskly, I stride to the truck. It is still running. The door is open, so I simply slide in and close it. Pressing the accelerator, I pull on to the highway. I had paid attention to the old man as he told me of his property. I know where his cabin waits for me.

I smile, pleased with my progress. Suddenly, I hear movement to my right. There is someone beneath the coat that lies there. I hear a soft sigh, the noise of a woman at rest. My smile grows; I will have company, it seems.

Chapter Twenty-seven

"Minty!" The banging on my door was incessant. "Minty, get your ass out of bed now!"

The sound of the voice was familiar, but my sleep-addled mind couldn't place it.

"Minty-fresh," it called in a sing-song voice.

It was Booth. I groaned; the nickname was back, obviously my reprieve had only been temporary. I climbed from bed and opened the door. Without acknowledging his presence, I turned back to my bedroom to get dressed. He entered the apartment behind me, closing the door.

"Damn, this is a nice place," he shouted to me, punctuating the comment with a whistle.

"Thanks," I murmured as I started to dress, "what's happened?"

"Someone just got beaten up by your guy. RCMP wants you out there," he informed me casually. I looked out from the bedroom to see him inspecting an ornament of a duck my mum had bought for me when I had moved in.

"And you are here because?" I asked, wishing he would put the duck back.

"I'm yours, Minty my man. Assigned to you for the duration," the duck went down with a bang. I winced, but at least he hadn't broken it.

I poked my head out from the bedroom and looked him over. He was both serious and smiling which was unexpected. "And you're okay with that?"

"Sure. Look, I know I've been riding you, but that's just part of the job. Pick on the new guy, ya know?"

"Yeah, I get it," I said with some venom in my voice.

"No, you don't. You will when there's another new guy and it's your job to ride him--", he started.

"I wouldn't do that," I insisted, but he interrupted me by

holding up his hand.

"Look, Minty. If we're going to work together, you have to get this... The new guy comes in, we pick on him. It's partly to make us oldies feel better but also to put you in your place. When you started, you thought you were going to walk in and solve all the big cases, right?"

"No, I didn't think..."

"Really?" He pressed.

"Yeah, okay, that's what I thought," I reluctantly conceded.

"Right, then we all started picking on you, calling you Minty-fresh. The Captain gave you rubbish cases and you settled in, right?"

"Right..." I couldn't believe that I was agreeing with Booth. But what he was saying was starting to make sense. I carried on dressing as he talked to me from the other room.

"So, you were put in your place. And when you got a real big case?"

"I messed it up..." I answered, depressed instantly at the reminder.

"No," he pressed, "you were ready. I read the notes, you did it all properly, by the book. Why?" He asked.

"Because it was a big deal, I didn't want to prove you right. I wanted to show you I wasn't fresh and wet behind the ears," I admitted.

"Exactly. You might not have liked it, but you were properly ready. Not just thinking you were. Because you were humbled," he crossed his arms over his expansive chest and looked at me, appraising me, daring me to say different.

"Maybe..." I conceded, as I stepped from the bedroom, gathering my badge and gun, and ushering him from the apartment.

"So, no hard feelings?" He asked as we waited for the elevator. He held out his hand, which I accepted, and we shook. As expected, he squeezed hard, trying to get a reaction. I grasped back and resisted the urge to wince. Finally, he released me and stepped back.

"Not exactly, but we're good I s'pose..." I said, deciding to be the bigger man.

"Right then, let's get going, sir. I brought my car, so we can go in comfort rather than your box of rust and rubbish," He jabbed at the elevator button again, impatiently trying to hurry it along.

I was going to complain about his description of my car. I was getting ready to explain the virtues of my cheap old rust-bucket, but then remembered that Booth drove a gorgeous new Mustang. Since first setting eyes on it in the Station parking lot, I had secretly admired the machine. As the elevator deposited us in the underground parking lot, we strode to the magnificent machine and I happily slid into the passenger seat. As I clicked my seat-belt into position, he fired up the big muscle car. The rumbling engine shook the entire vehicle from side-to-side and he powered out from the front of my building toward the Trans-Canada Highway, lights flashing and siren blaring.

The journey was noisy, but fast and smooth. The Highway was quiet, and people pulled over for the dark-blue Mustang with its bright strobes flashing behind the grill. We pulled into the crime scene just over an hour after leaving the city and Booth let the engine run while it cooled gently in the morning light.

"Nice car." I commented, speaking for the first time on our drive.

"Yeah, I saved up a long time for this beauty. I'm just letting the oil settle," he explained as he blipped the accelerator a little to juice the engine. The throbbing from all eight-cylinders coursed through the seats and up my spine. I caught Grace's eye as she was standing, waiting for us, and she rolled her eyes.

"Women. Just don't get the muscle-car thing, do they?" Booth said as he gestured to Grace.

"Yeah," I agreed. I was agreeing with Booth. This was a strange day indeed. Finally, the oil pressure having apparently dropped to a satisfactory level, he shut down the car and we both climbed out. Stretching my back, I lightly cursed the hard racing-seats and walked over to Officer Cote. She was standing at the back of an ambulance, talking to a young man cradling his head.

"We know who we're after, but we'll need the physical evidence to secure a proper conviction," she firmly informed a waiting officer. "Collect everything on and around that bench," she commanded, sending him over to an area segregated by crime-scene tape. "Minty, I got your email and I must admit I'm intrigued. Does this fit your theory?"

"You're asking me?" I was stunned.

"Yes. I have an opinion of course, but I want yours," she pressed.

"What can you tell me?" I asked in a flat tone, switching to professional police mode in a second.

She nodded, starting her summary of what she knew so far, "well, it's not good. David here walked by a man on a bench, on his way to take a leak, next thing he knows he's on the ground unconscious. Another couple found him here sometime later and called the police. The arriving cruiser had a picture of Edward, David identified him as his attacker as soon as he regained consciousness. He was going hiking for two weeks and had a truck full of camping and hunting gear, which is missing. Worst of all, his girlfriend was with him, there's no sign of her either. We're searching the woods now." She finished, gesturing to the trees that stretched away from the rest area.

I didn't say anything for a while, considering the problem, weighing the consequences of what she had told me. Elisha stayed quiet, letting me think.

"You won't find her." I stated, "He wouldn't move the body; he's made no attempt to hide any evidence before, he's unlikely to start now. It's interesting that he didn't kill David," I said, trying to expand on my thoughts as I stood talking. Everyone was listening, and I wanted to get it right. "It's not good," was my summation, "the last few attacks, he didn't take anything. If he's taken the girlfriend then it's because he wants her. Probably the car too. He took the hunting gear because he wants to hunt. I'd say that Id's in command now. He'll take what he wants..." I tailed off, imagining the worst. I looked at Elisha and Grace who, from their sombre expressions, were doing the same.

As Booth rejoined our little group, we all looked out over the massive expanse of green before us. Over ten-thousand square kilometres of trees, mountains, lakes and glaciers. I knew that they stretched out far beyond what we could see. Finally, Elisha broke the silence.

"If he's out there, hunting... we're never going to find him."

Chapter Twenty-eight

I slide from the driver's seat of the truck to the ground in a fluid movement. Admiring the cabin I have pulled up to, I am happy with my situation. I breathe in the distinctive smell of the Canadian wilderness and smile. I am home. There is a whimper from the truck and I smile more. Delighted at how my latest acquisitions have come so easily.

She woke as I drove, screaming and attacking me as she realised her predicament. A firm slap to the face had subdued her and a report about me on the radio subsequently ensured her silence. Her fear delighted me during the journey, glances at her wide eyes in the rear-view mirror frequently distracting me. I had also been admiring her clothes. It struck me how little noise they made as she moved about the cab. I enquired about the camouflaged items; she nervously explained their purpose and construction with a quaking voice. Made for hunting, they were strong, rip-resistant, and blocked escaping scent. More importantly, they were made of a special fabric that did not rustle or squeak as it moved. I was delighted when she added that there were more in the bed of the truck, "his clothes", she said. "Mine," I corrected her.

She talked no more after that, I required no more information of her and she didn't make a sound as I completed my journey to this place, this cabin of solitude.

*

I gather my two rucksacks from the bed and throw them to the ground. I open the passenger door and hold out my hand to her. Tentatively she takes it and I help her from the truck.

"Come, let us go and investigate our cabin."

I take her by the hand and she compliantly follows me inside. It is a roughly constructed wooden cabin in the woods, set back from a large lake. There are many windows revealing the wilderness without. A sofa, armchair, bed and kitchen area, make up the meagre interior. There are no curtains, but I see that privacy is ensured by the absence of people or buildings anywhere in sight. However, we arrived here on a rough, but well-used road. There will be people nearby and although my woman is compliant now, she might well rebel if rescue seems possible. I look around and see that part of the floor is hinged, a metal ring is recessed into the wood.

"Open that," I command, releasing her and pointing to the hatch in the ground. She pulls it open to reveal a small cellar. Filled with shelves, I can see cans of food, a propane tank and various tools and other equipment. I direct her to descend the short wooden ladder and follow her down. The ceiling of the small room is not high enough for me to stand so I stoop and shuffle forwards, deeper into the cellar. She can just about walk upright and walks ahead of me easily. I see a plastic tub of cable ties on a shelf and pull it down as we pass.

"Sit."

I am gratified to note that she immediately falls to the floor on her knees.

"Turn."

Again, she immediately complies, rotating to face me.

"What is your name?"

"Jessica..."

Her voice is high and trembles, she is looking down at my feet. She is still on her knees, sitting down on the backs of her legs. Her hands are still in her lap as I place a finger under her chin and raise her head to face me.

"Look at me Jessica... Jessica Rabbit... Rabbit..."

She looks me in the eye and I am pleased with my acquisition. She is young, her features soft and curved. Her skin is a light brown colour, from birth rather than a tan. As I assess her appearance, I wonder at her parentage. She is beautiful, her frailty and vulnerability enhancing her appearance. I stroke her long dark hair, currently constrained in a ponytail.

"You are my Rabbit, you understand? Behave and no harm will befall you. I mean to cause you no harm but for now you must be restrained, little Rabbit."

Pleasingly she responds by holding her arms out to me; they shake as her whole body is quaking with fear. Tears fall from her eyes as I produce the tub of ties. I wrap a cable-tie around her wrists and pull tightly. Slipping another through this loop I bind her to the gas pipe that extends from the large tank and through the ceiling above her head. I pull her feet from under her and extend her legs, sitting her down on her buttocks. Another cable-tie secures her ankles. Looking around I see a pile of rags on a nearby shelf. Pulling one down and folding it into a square, I place it inside her mouth. She starts to cry, the noise muffled by the dry rag. Two connected cable-ties go around the gag, securing it in her open mouth. Standing back, I check that my efforts will hold her here. Satisfied that they will, I climb back out of the cellar and into the light of the cabin. I slam down the hatch, shutting my prize within.

Stripping myself, I walk back outside and stand in the centre of my domain, bathing naked in the sun. I have taken a truck, I have taken a cabin. I have taken a woman. I have a little Rabbit of my own. I am a wolf in the woods, a hunter supreme. Arching my back, facing the sky, I let out a howl. I scream into the woods that I am here, I am Id, and I am hunter once more.

Chapter Twenty-nine

"What do you mean we aren't going to search the parks?" I was shouting at Elisha as she explained the strategy the manhunt was taking. She was talking calmly, with authority

"The Force's shrink doesn't agree with you. She thinks that it's much more likely that Edward has had a psychotic break following his divorce. That's why he took the girl, she's a replacement for his wife."

"That's rubbish…" I implored, a little more calmly now as Grace and Booth looked at me, willing me to act more professionally.

"I know, and actually I agree. But it does make some sense. Doctor Crown says that if she is a wife replacement then he will be seeking to re-establish his life somewhere. A town like where they lived before. Probably across the border to evade us. So our efforts are needed there, filling the gaps in the border."

"I still think he'll go north, into the woods. He's a hunter now, with the equipment to survive in the wild. South is civilisation, south is people. He won't go south."

"Look Minty…" Elisha placed a hand on my shoulder and looked me in the eye. "The Force is deploying south, across the border. Patrolling the woods where he could drive over. The Americans are on the official border crossings. That is happening."

"And that is wrong!" I shouted again, shrugging her hand from me, "he's going north, I tell you."

"Right, so where are you three going?" She asked, remaining calm in the face of my anger, "you aren't RCMP, so I have no direct authority over you."

"What? Wait… really?" I asked, gradually realising the implication of her words.

"Yes, really. You are assigned to my case, but you're in charge, Minty. Right?" She asked, practically winking at me.

"Hell, yeah!" Booth interrupted with gusto.

"Right!" Grace joined in.

"Okay then," I said, turning to my team, "we'll trawl the parks, asking people if they've seen him. We'll check the cabins and campsites. He has camping gear now, he'll probably isolate himself in the wilderness."

"It's a big wilderness," Grace pointed out.

"I know," I responded, looking to the woods, "but we have to try. We have to find him before he kills again. Before he kills Jessica." I wasn't really talking to them, but they nodded anyway. We all knew it was going to be hard, probably impossible, but that's why we had to try.

Grace had driven out to the scene in her CSI van, so she climbed into that while Booth and I got back into his Mustang. We drove to the park entrance in convoy and soon were sat with the Head Ranger for Banff National Park in his office. The Head Ranger for the adjacent Jasper National Park was on the phone as I explained the situation. I calmly informed them that we believed a dangerous fugitive was hiding somewhere in one of their parks with a female hostage. They agreed with each other that there was no way to search every wilderness retreat in the area. Fairly enough, they were unwilling to even have their rangers try. All were volunteers and experienced only in dealing with tourists and wildlife; they were not prepared to undertake a manhunt for a serial killer.

We finally agreed that a warning would be issued to all rangers to be on the lookout and to report anything unusual, but not to approach anyone matching Edward's description. They supplied us with detailed maps and apologised but were adamant that the search itself was up to us. We split the parks between the three of us, and swapping our cars for a park Jeep each, we set off on our search. We also agreed that we would investigate and search only; one-on-one against Id was not a good idea for any of us, particularly Grace. Not because she was a woman, I quickly pointed out, but because she was tiny compared to Edward. Besides that, she was not even a police officer. I must admit that I wasn't too keen on searching for Id on my own, and I doubt Booth was either. We had no choice; finding him was going to be a mammoth task. Splitting up increased our chances from non-existent to infinitesimally slim.

I watched as Grace pulled away with a grim smile in her borrowed Jeep. Miming that she should radio if she saw or learned anything, I climbed into my own.

"She'll be fine, Minty," Booth tried to reassure me as he climbed into his own Jeep.

"I know, she's capable," I admitted.

"She's as hard as nails, that one..." he called as he skidded the Jeep up the gravel hill and away from me. I sat there a while, contemplating our decision to separate. Not liking it, but realising it was our only choice, I started up my own Jeep and powered up the same gravel hill as Booth. I followed him for a while but soon had to turn off, to search for the most dangerous man any of us had ever hunted. I wondered who would be the victor. The hunter? Or the hunters of the hunter? Only the most proficient would win, I realised. I shuddered, a feeling of dread filling me as I admitted to myself that Id was the best there could be.

Chapter Thirty

I am in my home, my cabin, my wilderness. I am naked as I prepare my Rabbit a meal from the selection she and her previous boyfriend had carried in their rucksacks. I whistle with contentment as I heat the packaged meal on the propane stove in my kitchen. Carrying the stew down to the cellar where I am keeping her, I smile at my consideration of her wellbeing.

"I have prepared you a meal, little one." She still looks scared. I hope to remedy that as I cut the plastic strip securing her gag. "Eat."

I slowly approach her open mouth with a spoon of the food, but she refuses to partake. Sighing, I place the hot pan on the floor beside her. Using my knife, I go to cut her wrist restraints. Quickly she recoils from me.

"Please, I will not cut such a beauty."

I release her hands and feet and she rubs her wrists and ankles where the plastic has cut into her. Looking at the marks, I am displeased.

"I am sorry, I do not want to hurt you, but I fear you would have tried to run. A running Rabbit gets hunted down by the wolf I'm afraid."

Fear and confusion in her eyes, she takes the spoon and starts to eat. I sit back, giving her space, room to breathe and think.

"What do you want from me?" She asks, finally speaking.

"Why, sex of course, silly Rabbit," I inform her.

"Sex?"

"Yes, why else would I bring you here? Why else would I keep you?"

"You're going to rape me!" She cries.

"No, silly little Rabbit," I chuckle. She does not understand but that is understandable. She has only seen the hunter, the killer, she has yet to see the lover. "You misunderstand. I want to have sex with you yes, but you will enjoy the process, there will be no rape."

"But I don't want to. I want to go home. I want David," she

starts crying, blubbering pathetically into the pan of food.

"Do not do that," I command her, but she continues to cry. The intensity of her tears increases and she starts to shake. "I said stop crying!" But she does not, she cannot stop. I try to be patient, but patience is not within me. Patience is for the weak, patience is for people who do not know how to take what they require, when they require it. I lurch forward and strike her across the face with the back of my hand.

"I require sex from you, comply now!" She doesn't understand, she just looks at me, rubbing the red mark appearing on her cheek. "I don't want to explain myself, comply with my demand. I will not wait, Rabbit."

Slowly she unbuttons the top of her camouflage shirt, gently crying, "why, why are you doing this?" She looks up, into my eyes, defiance appearing. I like that look. It excites me. "And my name is Jessica."

"No. You are wrong. You are my Rabbit. Don't you forget it. I am the wolf, I am the hunter. I am Id!" I am shouting, I realise. I calm my voice before adding, "but now... let's be friends, look how your actions are pleasing me, affecting me, that should please you also."

She has undone her top but not removed it. I lurch forward and pull it roughly from her. The time she is taking is frustrating me; I want compliance, not teasing. I am ready, I demand it from her.

"Now the trousers! And be quicker about it."

The sight of her perfect breasts make me harder. I am pointing directly at her now, wetness glistening in the dim light that is reaching down through the floor of the cabin above us. The dark circles around her nipples become exquisite targets for my passion. Eventually she slides the trousers from her body. Finally, she is recognising my power as she lies down before me and opens her legs. She is trembling with the anticipation of my actions. I move over her.

"I am pleased to see you finally understand... Rabbit..." I reach down with my hand, to guide myself into her. "You are not prepared at all!" I shout as I recoil from her. I can feel without touching her that she is not ready. "Look at me!" I command, screaming at her. Why does she not understand, how could she not understand? "Look at it! Why are you not aroused? Why are you not ready?"

She looks, but she is still shivering. I realise that she is shaking from fear, not anticipation. I reach forward and grab her crotch. She recoils but cannot escape me in the tight corner of the basement. My suspicions confirmed, I rise as tall as I can in the low ceiling of the room and smash whatever sits on the shelves beside me. My rampage continues for minutes, destroying various cans and packets without mercy.

Finally, calm enough to talk again, I demand of her, "why are you afraid? Have I not explained?"

She cowers in the corner, against the propane tank, shivering.

"Whore! Slut! You have sex with the pathetic worm that I defeated so easily. You sell yourself to that non-man. You WILL give yourself to me!"

I resume my attack on the goods on the shelves. It does not help, I am furious. Grabbing at the tub of cable ties, I stomp towards her.

"Roll over, you will learn to respect me!"

Without giving her the option to comply, I roll her over in the loose dirt and drag her arms behind her. I place a plastic strip around each wrist, looping them through each other. Ensuring that each lies in the red groove previously made, I pull them tight. Smiling at the pain I am causing her, I click them even tighter, cutting into the tender flesh.

"Good, you are feeling what I feel. The pressure in my penis is not pleasure, this is how you are making me feel. Feel it. Learn from it, do not make me feel it again."

Satisfied, I perform the same action for her ankles. Gagging her as she was before, I throw a blanket over her naked body and stamp up the ladder, slamming the trap-door down behind me.

I am not satisfied. Not satisfied at all. She did not give me what I require, I failed to take what I desire and this new feeling is not satisfactory. The pain I caused her, the red skin, the damage, it has stirred another need within me. I need blood. Yes, blood will satisfy me now. I pull on the camouflage hunting suit I took from her boyfriend, David.

Treading lightly, I stalk the area around the cabin, practicing my movements. I am delighted to hear that I can pass silently through the undergrowth. I navigate the lakeside on which my home sits and realise that my previous assumption was correct. There are indeed people here; the buildings are sparse and potentially vacant, but I need to be circumspect. My movements remain unseen and unheard. I am the hunter, perfection moving without leaving any trace. I am a wolf in the woods, a tiger in the jungle. I halt, there is a sound in front of me, I detect a twig breaking and leaves being disturbed. There is another animal there, a hunter. Not the hunter, not Id, but a hunter nonetheless. I look up to the branches of a large fir tree. Softly, silently, I move to the far side of the wide trunk. Out of sight from the hunter I now hunt, I pull myself high into the branches.

Lying on a wide branch above the bed of the forest, I slide forward on my belly. My clothes make no noise, my breathing is light, I am a silent wraith. I am part of the tree, unseen and unseeable. I see the hunter below me, wearing similar clothes to mine but with orange patches on the shoulders. He carries a gun. It is a long rifle with a wooden stock and he grips it as if his life depends upon it. It does.

He raises the sight on the rifle to his eye and crouches down on one knee. I check the area, searching for any fellow hunters. There are no more than us two. One vastly superior. I slide forward to position myself above this lesser being. He is distracted, concentrating on a distant deer. I sense he is about to fire as his breathing calms and the tip of the gun settles. Just as the muscles tense in his trigger finger, I drop from the branch above him. My hands land on his shoulders and my feet on his chest as I bend him over backwards. The gun fires uselessly in the air and the deer leaps away in a single elegant bound.

I pull the rifle from him as he protests impotently to the forest, for I am certainly not listening. Quickly, I use the butt of the gun to smash his face into the ground, not stopping until his head is nothing but a pulp. Bone and grey brain-matter lay mashed into the soft dirt. I raise my head high and howl into the canopy. I am satisfied, the violence is catharsis for my unsated sexual need. I curl my nose up at the gun, inspecting its bloodied structure in my hands. It is a cold lifeless machine that serves only to separate the hunter from the kill. It's very nature offends me, so I hurl it into the lake. I take my knife now and complete my ritual, spilling his organs from him. I plunge my hands deep inside his warm body, washing myself in his fluids, revelling in the palpation.

I drag the remains of the deer-hunter into the undergrowth, smiling, knowing that the animals will feast tonight. Eventually coming down from the high of my actions, I wash myself in the lake. I dive in, plunging deep, fully clothed, into the icy waters. I am renewed. I know that what I desire will come to me, it always does.

Chapter Thirty-one

We had been searching the park for three days; three days and nothing had been discovered. The rangers were doing an excellent job and reporting activities and behaviours that they thought strange. Each were noted on a coloured piece of paper and pinned to a map on the wall of the ranger's hut we had appropriated between the two adjacent parks. Each morning we would take a collection of notes from the map and investigate individually. Meeting at lunch, noting how the number of pins on the map had increased, we would take another set. Endlessly we travelled from campsite to campsite, cabin to hotel, checking on missing hikers, empty lodges and bear sightings. Anything that might have been Edward and his hostage. Everything either had an innocent explanation or no explanation at all. Our problem was all the people. Even though there was a wilderness out there, most people walked the same trails and stayed in the same organised areas. He had all the advantage, a huge area in which to hide and a large group of people to blend in amongst.

We gathered for our morning meeting and Booth had brought coffee and doughnuts. Taking a sprinkled one from the box, I chomped on the sugary topping and took a collection of notes from the board.

"Don't worry, Minty. We'll get him." Booth reassured me, walking to the board himself.

"I'm starting to think he isn't even out there," I sighed, slumping my shoulders.

"He is, don't worry. Anyway, if he isn't, the Mounties will get him. At least this way, both ends are covered."

He was right of course, it was either this or just sit and wait somewhere for news. This way we at least got to do something to take our minds off it. Not that my mind was totally focussed on it anyway, I thought as Grace entered.

"Morning boys..." she called lightly, chipper as always. Fresh as a daisy it seemed, despite the limited sleep we'd all had.

"Later people, got me a killer to catch..." called Booth, making himself scarce as he always did when Grace and I were together. He made some gesture behind her back as he exited to signal that I should kiss her. I rolled my eyes and shooed him off. After a short pause, I heard his Jeep start up and pull away.

"Morning, Grace. You look lovely and fresh as usual. How do you manage it?" I said to her back as she was looking at the board.

"Just a morning person, I guess." She smiled and turned. After inspecting me for a second she reached forward and brushed doughnut sprinkles from the side of my mouth. Taking her coffee from the table, forgoing a treat, she returned to the map to inspect the latest reports. I took the opportunity, as I always did, to watch her. She had taken to wearing a pair of tan jodhpurs, borrowed from the ranger she was sharing a room with, and they were driving me crazy. They were tight, too tight really. However, no matter how hard I looked, and I looked hard, I could not detect the shape of her underwear beneath them. I was convinced she wasn't wearing any and it drove my senses to the brink. I was having very vivid dreams about Grace and those tan jodhpurs every night. Interspersed with visions of Id slicing me open, or her open. My mind was very confused in the mornings, to say the least.

"Oh…" she sounded disappointed.

"What's up?" I asked, jogged from my reverie.

"Oh, nothing. Joan said that she'd put a note on the board about a missing hunter. I was going to check it out."

"Around the Red Deer Lakes?"

"Yeah, sounds right. We were talking about it last night before we went to sleep. Isn't it fun here? Like camp with bunkbeds and everything," she chuckled girlishly.

I smiled. She thought it was at her comment but really it was at her. I loved how positive she always was; everything was fun, everything was an adventure. I marvelled at how she somehow managed a girlish enjoyment of our accommodation amidst our arduous searches. "Yeah, great. You forget I bunk with Booth. My room-mate snores and arrests people in his sleep."

"Well, we have lots of fun…" she said, somehow verbalising a dot-dot-dot.

Fighting visions of pillow-fights and lacy underwear, I swallowed my wandering thoughts, knowing they would reappear in my dreams tonight.

"Sorry, Booth drove off to Red Deer today, said he liked how a few reports were clustering out there."

While I was stuck marvelling at playful Grace, serious Grace had appeared for work, "you think there's anything to it?"

"Probably not, I asked Ranger Joe and he said that there's always something going on out there. It's far enough out for people to think they're out of civilisation, so things get a bit raucous, is what he said."

"Raucous?" She raised an eyebrow.

"Yeah, I wondered about that. Apparently though, just some unlicensed hunting, fires without permits, stuff like that. Park stuff..."

She turned back to the map, disappointed, "oh, okay then. I'll take this batch." She pulled a stack of notes from the map clustered to the north. "It's a long way north, on a tarmac road... in that rough riding Jeep... so I might just take--"

"No, you know how he is about that car," I interrupted her.

"What Booth doesn't know, Booth doesn't mind," she said. Besides, he's a big pussycat." She blew me a kiss and I followed her from the cabin to watch her slide into the Mustang. A loud gurgle shook the trees as she revved the engine. I walked to my Jeep with my own stack of notes, turning my head to one side as grit flew from under her spinning tyres. I sighed; between the unfindable fugitive and Grace ever present in my mind, I was weary. I slumped into the Jeep and started the engine. Trying to shake the fatigue from my head, I told myself it was time to get to work.

Chapter Thirty-two

I had lived in my cabin for three days, I was happy. It was a pleasant sensation and I was whistling to myself as I prepared my meal. I had travelled to the town that first day, frustrated despite my kill. I had wanted something, I wasn't sure what it was but I knew it would be there. The first shop I entered, that is where I saw her, the shop assistant, looking at me. She was placing items on the counter to sell to gullible tourists. It was a tray of bear claws, each turned into keyrings, a grisly item, I thought. She insisted on telling me how grizzly bears often lose their claws in trees and how I could purchase one as a souvenir. I quickly realised their potential, purchasing ten and securely wiring them to a pair of cycling gloves I took without paying for from another shop. Now when I killed, I would kill with the ferocity of ten knives.

I had thought of taking her there and then, but something prevented me; it was unsettling until I realised what it was. I was determined to save myself for the prize that lay in the cellar, my Jessica would be the trophy I would collect; a true reward for my hunts. I sat in the truck, inspecting my claws, I wanted to use them, they excited me. I wouldn't have to wait. The very next day I found another hunter in the woods. Without warning I sprang at him from a clutch of ferns. I slashed at him with my claws and ripped his jugular from his throat before he could even make a sound. As he collapsed to his knees, clutching his neck, I drank in the spray of his blood as it bathed me. The kill was ecstasy.

*

Stirring the pot of food I am heating, I look behind me. She is there, my Rabbit. Looking at me as always. I have improved her bindings to allow her to accompany me upstairs. I have determined that no-one can approach the cabin without my hearing. I have guaranteed her silence by showing her the results of each of my kills, negating the need for a gag. She still has dried blood on her hands from my last trophy as I made her dip her hands in him, feeling the warmth of fresh death. She still maintains an air of defiance about her that I hope will soon dissipate. I hear the rattle of the chain as she moves behind me.

"I could remove that if you would just participate," I inform her once again. I have ensured her continuing presence by locking a solid bicycle lock around her neck. It remains loose about her throat but small enough that it cannot pass over her head. Through this I have attached a long length of silver chain that is padlocked to the floor of the cabin. It makes an annoying noise as she moves but I know the sound reminds her of her bondage, underlining her subservience to me. Pouring the food onto plates, I motion that she should move to the table. She does so, and we eat as we do every day, in silence. She finishes her food and moves to the bed unbidden.

"Good, I am glad to see you are learning. You will relent. You will relent and enjoy."

Moving to the bed as she removes her loose clothing I have purchased for her, I remove mine. As I do each evening, as I plan to do each evening until she is ready, I touch her. She closes her eyes. I know she is concentrating on overcoming the feeling, but I know she eventually will succumb. Everyone succumbs to Id.

Taking some soft fabric cut from the clothes of my latest kill, I secure her hands gently. Not removing my hand that is gently stroking her, I spread her arms and legs open. Securing them to the bed, I also apply a strip to her eyes.

"That's it, now you have nothing to think of but the feelings I am gifting you."

She moves to speak.

"Shh, you know the rules, Rabbit. No words except to accept me."

That silences her, and she bites her lip.

"As certain as the sun rises, your id will rise. You will become sex, you cannot suppress what is a part of you forever."

An involuntary movement shifts her slightly as I find a new location for my attentions.

"Yes, well done, Rabbit. Let yourself feel it. Let your id come to the fore. You will feel better for it. You will like it."

I feel a small quake in her body, her stomach dips in and her pelvis shudders.

"Ah, Rabbit. I do believe you are learning. If you want, once it's over, if you truly desire so, I will let you leave."

A whimper escapes her lips. My passion starts to grow, this is to be the night, this is to be the evening I will take her. I will defeat her, nothing can defeat id.

"No!" She speaks. That is not the rule.

"Rabbit, you know..."

But she rips the soft bindings from her body, pulling her arms from the bed to strike me about the head. I lift my arms to protect me against the feeble blows. She releases her legs and the blindfold falls from her. I have my arms about my head so do not notice her knee rise and strike me in the groin. My genitals explode in pain as she accurately strikes me with her kneecap. A wave of sickness quickly flows through me.

"Get off me, you monster!" She shouts at me as I roll from the bed. She lunges at me but the chain comes up short. The bicycle lock chokes her and she abruptly sits down on the hard floor. She grabs at the lock, pulling it from her throat. I laugh, fighting the feeling of sickness she has caused me. Raising my head, I let out a loud guffaw. Now, instead of fighting the feelings of pain in my groin, I stretch to magnify them. I both scream and laugh simultaneously. Then, bending over, I throw up.

"Excellent, excellent, little one," I applaud her as I wipe the vomit from my mouth. Clutching at my testicles I squeeze them in front of her, causing more pain to emanate from their tenderness. Shuddering at the exquisite agony, I laugh again.

"Quite a treat. Quite an unexpected treat. Now clean up this mess."

I change my mind about her expected level of compliance now. I allow her to finish cleaning up and move her back into the cellar. Using a smaller length of chain and a rag to gag her once more, I slam the trap-door shut. Pulling on my bear-gloves, I leave her for the night.

"I will hunt again and bring you back a prize for your behaviour, little Rabbit," I shout to her as I leave.

*

I have moved to the lakes the other side of the hill, a favourite hunting zone as the docile deer seem to attract idiots with guns. I am nude. I feel the air around me. The sun is dipping below the surrounding mountains causing a premature darkness to fall over the area. Covered in dirt from the edge of the lake, I am nature personified. Unseen to all. I carry no weapon except for my bear-claws. I am the antithesis of man, I am the animal. The apex predator, hunter of hunters.

I hear movement, but not the usual movement. Normally, in these woods, I detect the men, for it is always men, trying to disguise their sounds. Not this man. I sense his weight blundering through the undergrowth, staying on the rough path between two of the lakes. Curious, I drop to the floor and slide into the tall ferns that grow on the side of the path. I wait as still as a rock, for I know he will pass me by. Sometime later, he does just that. I hear him, muttering to himself, and let him pass. Gently, I slide from the undergrowth and rise to my feet behind him. I just stand there, daring him to hear and turn around, but he does not. He is carrying a hand-gun on a holster. He is wearing boots, dark stiff trousers and a windbreaker; a police officer for certain. I could take him. I could charge forward or slip silently to him and rip his throat from behind. There is no challenge in that. Instead, I slip back into the ferns. I slink to the edge of the lake and move rapidly to intercept him once again.

I choose my place carefully, balancing the need for a challenge with the risk of his gun. I slide myself up a tree that overhangs the path closer to the lake. He will come by here soon and I hug the branch closely, disguising my silhouette against discovery. I see him now, he has his torch out and is lighting his way. This is a complication as it is an advantage in his favour, potentially blinding my attack. Still, I will not back down, Id will vanquish this man soon. Letting him approach to within five strides I drop from the tree directly before him.

"What the..." he exclaims, confronted by my naked body. He twitches for his gun but leaves it in place as his training dictates with an unarmed man. I allow him time, time to process my face, my form. "Edward Timothy Gooch, I am Detective Booth. You are under arrest." He parrots monotonously.

"Do not go for your weapon, Detective. To do so is to die. For I am the hunter of hunters."

I stretch my arms, showing him my claws.

"Oh my…" he reacts, as I knew he would. The sight of me has already put him on edge, the realisation that I too am armed causes him to reach for his gun. As he does so, I am in motion.

His hand touches the pistol butt, I am five steps away.

He releases the clip holding the gun, I am four steps away.

The gun comes out, I am three steps away.

The gun is raised level to the ground, I am two steps away.

He slips the safety off, one step.

The gun is against my chest, touching. He pulls the trigger.

There is the click of metal against metal. There is no bullet in the chamber. My claws come up, slicing through the air with a whistle. I go to cut his throat from him, to tear into him, to destroy him. He sees death approach, he sees me. I scream my name.

Chapter Thirty-three

Grace and I were sat in the ranger's cabin, waiting. We had put the latest notes on the map, sorted through the paperwork and planned the searches for tomorrow. We had drunk three cups of coffee and finished off the dry doughnuts Booth had brought that morning. We were killing time.

"Minty..." Grace said.

"I know, Booth should have been here hours ago," I agreed.

"Radio again?"

I nodded, picking up the radio, making sure it was tuned into Booth's channel, I keyed the microphone, "Booth... Minty to Booth... Come in Booth..." nothing. Grace tried calling his cell again, knowing that there would be no answer, no connection. He was out of cell range. "Booth, Grace has crashed your Mustang..."

"Not funny, Minty."

"I know... come on." I jumped up from the swivel chair, sending it skittering across the cabin and crashing into the wall. Grabbing Grace by the wrist, I practically dragged her to the Jeep. I floored the accelerator and sped out of the parking lot. Gravel flew in the air from all four wheels as I found the switch to activate the lights. Grimly, we sped down the road towards the distant lakes, towards where Booth had been heading just this morning.

Grace moved around the inside of the Jeep in the dark. She bumped into various parts of me as she searched the dashboard for something. I was so concerned about Booth, I barely noticed the touches that would have been so desired just a few hours ago. Finally, she found what she was looking for and the lights mounted on the roof-bars of the Jeep came to life. The road ahead was a sea of light now and I sped up with the improved vision. She also found the switch for the strobes and soon red and blue flashes were added to our mobile illuminations.

I was pushing the Jeep hard, managing to get the off-road vehicle up over a hundred and forty kilometres an hour. We passed equal numbers of tourists and animals on the road north, barely in control of the swaying vehicle. It wasn't set up for highway driving and it was taking all my concentration just to keep it on the tarmac. Grace read the map, occasionally calling out turns and junctions I should be wary of.

Finally, eventually, we found the rocky road that led to Red Deer Lakes. I had to slow down else the rocks would have thrown us from the road. As I concentrated on the rough terrain, the noise of the Jeep finally abated to a level at which we could hear each other.

"What are we going to do when we get there?" Grace asked me, fear in her voice.

"I don't know. Find him I suppose," was my unhelpful reply.

"Just the two of us?"

We had radioed the rangers on our outward journey, but they could not be there until dawn. I didn't know if there was a logistical problem or not, but I suspected that fear was keeping them from the scene. I didn't blame them.

"Yes, just the two of us. We can't leave him, Grace."

"I know that, and I agree, it's just that we should have a plan."

"Okay..."

I turned the wheel hard to avoid a large pothole and floored the accelerator to climb us over another boulder.

Grace, swaying in the seat beside me, looked up from the map she was studying, "the map shows that the trail is a loop, if I go clockwise, and you anti-clockwise..."

"No," I asserted, "if Booth is hurt, then it's because someone hurt him. If someone hurt him, then that someone is dangerous. It must have been Id. We can't split up."

"He could have just tripped, fallen, be hurt somehow... maybe a bear..." she said.

"Maybe, but we both know it was Id. And if Booth can't take him, what chance do we stand alone? We stick together."

"Okay, together then. But can we handle Id? I mean can we

handle him together?" She was worried, I was too.

"I don't know. I hope so..." was all I could say.

We drove on into the dark, our powerful spotlights harshly lighting the woods as we penetrated deeper into the wilderness. Finally we arrived; I stamped on the brakes and shut down the engine, dripping water from the trees overhead hissing on the hot vehicle. Grace shut down the lights and we sat in darkness.

"It's dark," I commented dryly.

"No kidding. There's no light at all. I can't see a single star."

She leaned out of the window and looked up to check. The canopy of trees was complete. Under the shadow of the mountains, beneath the cover of the trees, we were in a natural cave that was devoid of light. I felt her hand me the cold metal tube of a flashlight and I pressed the button. Again, we were awash in artificial light; it was a lot weaker than the spots of the Jeep, but it would have to do. I climbed down and swept the parking area. The beam of my light passed over Booth's Jeep in the corner. Pulling my gun and chambering a round, I approached the vehicle. It was empty, as I knew it would be. I turned to see Grace looking around inside the lock-box in the back. She rose up brandishing a shotgun, its black metal gleaming in the glow of my torch.

"Crikey, Grace," I exclaimed as she cocked her gun with a loud crunch. "Got one of those for me?"

"Sorry, this is mine." She clicked on the small torch that was slung under the barrel and swept it around the woods, "you're a better shot than me, but this increases the odds that I'll hit the bastard."

She was right, and this configuration increased our firepower and lighting. She had the big gun and I had the big torch. Because of this, I led the way as we started down the trail signposted to the lakes.

Every noise we heard was ld in the trees. With each crack of a twig and rustle of a leaf, we would spin to the source of the sound. My torch would flood the area with light to be joined by the narrow beam of Grace's shotgun light. We would stop and watch, waiting for a new sound, hoping to identify the source. Sometimes a squirrel would move, or a bird would take flight, moving us on. More often there would be nothing and we would slowly walk sideways, pointing our weapons at the imagined danger. After quite a few false alarms, we heard a new noise and spun to face it. A large ground bird took flight with a massive sound. Its rapidly beating wings thumping the air sounded like a helicopter taking off. The noise and movement scared the hell out of me and I leapt backwards with a yelp. In response, there was an almighty boom as Grace fired the shotgun into the dark.

"What the hell, Grace?" I cried out, my ears ringing from the blast.

"What was that? What the hell was that?" She was shouting.

"Calm down... wait... stop..." I shouted back, "it was a bird, it was just a bird... a massive, scary bird..." breathing hard, I started to chuckle. Grace joined in and soon we were loudly laughing in the dark. I finally let out a long breath of air and Grace did the same. "This is stupid."

"What?"

"We can't react like this to everything we hear, we'll be here all night."

"I know, but I'm scared," she admitted aloud for the first time.

"Me too..." I replied honestly.

"Look. Let's think this through," she stated, resting her shotgun on a log for a second. "If Edward, Id, whoever, was here, then he won't be now. He kills and moves on, he won't hang around," she reasoned.

"Kills?" I asked.

"Sorry, you know what I mean. I'm sure Booth is fine. Id left Joy alive, right?" She reassured me.

"You're right," I shook the bad thoughts away, "after that announcement I think he knows we're coming anyway."

She smiled in the light reflected from our torches and I felt warmed by her. She nodded and we carried on, still sweeping our lights towards the noises in the woods but no longer stopping each time. We started to call for Booth. We shouted his name and walked a few steps, then shouted again. Periodically we would stop to listen. It was slow moving, but we were finally making progress. We could see light ahead;

the lake clearing a gap in the trees meant that the light of the sky could finally penetrate to the ground. I was thankful for it, as instead of a tunnel of pitch dark, I could finally see some of the wider landscape around us.

"What the...!" I exclaimed, almost jumping out of my skin as my feet and shins encountered something soft on the trail ahead of me. I had found Booth, or Booth had found me, I'm not sure which. I had been looking into the trees, sweeping my light across the ground to my right when I had walked into him. As I did so he had caught and grabbed hold of my leg. Dropping to the ground, I quickly started to check him over; he looked in bad shape. In the harshness of the white torchlight a bloodied red face stared up at me.

"Minty, he's here, he got me," he croaked.

Grace stood tall and swept the woods for any sign, the narrow beam of the shotgun light turning like a lighthouse, seeking him out. Booth gestured at his chest and I rolled him over on his back. Grace paused her searching to drop her backpack beside me.

"First-aid kit inside," she said in clipped tones.

"Well done, keep checking the woods..." I commanded, forcing the fear from my own voice.

She resumed her vigil, stepping closer to us so her legs touched mine as I crouched next to Booth. Using the scissors from the kit, I cut the shirt from Booth. Easing it from him, I also pulled away the dried blood holding it there and he winced in pain.

"Hey, Booth. Stay with me, okay? If it hurts that's good, it means that you're not in shock. Pain is good, remember?" I said as I worked.

"Yeah. Pain is good, pain is good..."

He gritted his teeth and repeated the mantra as I peeled the shirt off his chest. I squeezed the contents of a bottle of water over his torso and wiped the blood away with a cotton pad. I applied temporary stitches to each cut, repeating the action for each of the multiple wounds; water, wipe, stick. Eventually they all had sticky strips of white tape holding them together. Finally, no more blood ran from him.

"Did he get you anywhere else? Booth, are you hurt anywhere else?"

"Yeah, Minty. I am," he croaked.

I was really concerned now; the cuts were bad, but it sounded like there was something much more serious. Frantically I started searching his body for blood or broken bones. I patted him down, running my hands up and down his legs.

"Where, Booth? Where?" I shouted at him.

"Minty... Minty..." he whispered.

"Booth, what is it? Where are you hurting?"

"Minty... If you're going to touch me like that, I think you should call me Mike."

I turned to look at him and he was smiling inanely back at me. I had my hand on his crotch, checking for any injuries there and quickly I pulled it away.

"You bastard. Are you even hurt?" I asked, shocked, annoyed and embarrassed.

"Yeah," he chuckled, "I landed on my coccyx, my ass is on fire. Kiss it better?" he joked with more strength in his voice now. Playfully I punched his arm.

"Yeah, later Booth, when we don't have an audience," I replied in good humour.

"What happened to 'Mike'?"

Ignoring him as he started to chuckle, I applied the remaining tape to the larger of his cuts, sealing them more securely. Patching each repair with sticky bandages from Grace's kit, I finally pulled his shirt together and zipped his coat closed.

"Do you think you can move, Mike?" I asked him, finally finishing the first aid.

"Yeah I think so... I couldn't on my own, I was worried about the blood and I feel a bit woozy. Not to mention it's as dark as the devil's ass-hole out here."

"Yeah, lovely place you found to have a lie down, buddy," I agreed, looking around.

Together, we back-tracked to the cars, Grace under one arm, me under the other. We each took a Jeep, Booth sprawled in the passenger seat of mine. We drove slowly, both to be safe and to prevent jarring his injuries. Finally, after a long and painstaking journey, we pulled into the Park Medical Centre, helped Booth to a gurney, and watched as they wheeled him inside.

"That was intense." Grace commented, searching for and finding my hand to hold. I squeezed her little hand in mine.

"Yeah, too intense," I agreed wholeheartedly. The ordeal finally over, I found my eyesight was blurring as my eyes filled with water. I swallowed back the tears I knew were coming. I was trying to breathe, to control the overwhelming feeling that was flooding through me. Quickly, I was interrupted as Grace squeezed my hand, causing me to look at her.

I looked into her eyes, just about visible in the dark. They were wet; she blinked rapidly, and tears fell to her cheeks. Her eyes spoke to me, they needed something. I needed the same thing and I turned to her. She wrapped her strong arms around me and I wrapped mine around her. I pressed her tightly to me and felt her body quake with silent tears. Mine came now too, I couldn't hold them back.

Chapter Thirty-four

Finally, I am back at my cabin.

"Rabbit..."

I call to my pet in the cellar. I hear movement through the floor. I feel her presence. I pull open the hatch and poke my head through. I see her, cowering in the corner. I throw the key to the lock at her, striking her in the head with it.

"Unlock yourself and get up here..."

Turning and moving to the sofa, I sit and wait for her. She emerges slowly; she has removed the lock from around her neck but still has the gag locked in her mouth.

"If I give you the key to remove that, you will be quiet," I inform her. She confirms it by nodding. "Okay, but first you have to give me something."

She swallows, anxiously.

"I want you to clean this cabin."

Suddenly she is relieved. Thankful for the straightforward request she walks to the kitchen area and starts to tidy up the dishes.

"Naked..."

She stops moving. She is facing the sink, the tap is running, filling it with hot water. I can hear the propane flame working beneath me. She is wearing simple sweat-pants and a tee-shirt. Hardly suitable for a strip-tease but the sight of her removing them stimulates my already agitated body. I watch her posterior move up and down as she continues to wash-up nude. I study her form. She has nice thin legs ending in a tight, small ass. Her hips are slim, and her waist is even thinner. Her skin is smooth and tight with the undamaged quality of youth. Her hair is falling down her back, ending at her shoulders in a neat straight line. I can see her thin arms moving back and forth, washing a plate.

I am still nude following my hunt. I look down at my body, realising that I am covered in blood and mud from head to toe. She finishes the dishes. Staying at the sink, she continues to tidy. She does not want to face me.

"Come here."

Again, immediately, she obeys. I am pleased. As a reward, I unlock her gag and throw it down the open cellar door.

"You may wash me now," I command, gesturing at the grime covering me. She turns and collects a pan from the sink; filling it with hot water and soap she comes to me with a cloth in her hand. She proceeds to wet the cloth and wipe down my chest.

"Harder, Rabbit. Work at it. The blood. Scrub it from me."

She starts working harder, scrubbing at my skin. The pain as the hardened dirt and blood is scoured from me is arousing me further. She pointedly avoids that area while she cleans the rest of me pleasingly thoroughly.

"Do you know whose blood this is?" She does not answer. "This is from the police officer who came here to save you."

She doesn't look at me, but I can see from the shaking of her shoulders that she has started crying again.

"You know the only way for you to leave this place is for you to free yourself." I wait, she is still crying, still washing me. "I am a man of my word, Rabbit. You only have to give me what I require, and you can leave. I would leave too. We would go our separate ways. You to your home and me into the wilderness. I have nothing to fear from you. Your escape would not lead to my capture."

Her crying slowly abates; she is thinking about it.

"They even know who I am. Who I was, that is. My name was Edward Gooch, they have photos, fingerprints, everything. You have no knowledge I fear, you just have something I require."

Still she does not look at me, but her hand moves to me. I am hard from the sight of her, the anticipation of taking her, her touch is exquisite.

"Yes, little Rabbit. Perform your duty and you can leave. If you want to."

She begins to massage me, to move me, to excite me.

"Careful, Rabbit. That is not what I require, and you know it. I require you, remember?"

"I remember," she says, finally speaking.

"Are you ready for me?" I ask of her, gently.

"No, no I'm not," she admits to me, demurely.

"But you could be, couldn't you?"

"Yes, yes, I think I could be," she says with a broken voice. I have broken her.

"Prepare yourself then, Rabbit. Prepare yourself for Id."

She places her other hand on herself.

"Yes, little Rabbit, touch yourself--" I softly tell her.

"Do not do that, Jessica!" I suddenly shouted.

"I'm sorry? What should I do?" She asks.

"Prepare yourself, of course," I tell her.

"But you said not to, you told me not to do that."

"I said no such thing, Rabbit. Now. Prepare yourself, get ready for the event of your short little life--"

"Do not have sex with Id, Jessica!" I sharply snapped.

"Please, sir, please explain. I don't know what you want," she asks, starting to cry again.

"I am getting tired of this game, Rabbit. You know what to do, now do it," I command her. I am shouting now; the girl is wearing my patience thin. Is she going to do this or not? I am in pain from the waiting. The anticipation hurts me, and she keeps asking stupid questions.

"Do not sleep with Id. Please, Jessica." I implored.

She stops; I cannot believe it. She has stopped, she is dressing herself.

"What are you doing, where are you going, Rabbit?" I scream.

"I'm not going to have sex with you, Id. You might as well get used to it," she barks at me.

"Yes, you are, you most certainly are," I scream back at her.

"Well done, Jessica. Be strong. You can beat him. You can beat Id." I calmly whispered to her.

I cannot believe my eyes as she dresses. She walks back down the cellar ladder and I follow her. Waiting at the trap-door, I watch incredulously as she replaces the bicycle lock around her neck. My eyes are bulging from my head as she even replaces the gag, locking the padlock with a click. I slam down the cellar door with a bang. I am as mad as I have ever been as I start to smash everything in sight. I use the pan to demolish the sink. The glasses and crockery I hurl to the ground. Using my bare hands, I tear the bedding to shreds. Methodically, with great rage, I tear and smash the contents of the cabin to pieces as I scream inside the walls of my cage of indignation.

Chapter Thirty-five

I waited in the small reception of the Park Medical Centre. Booth had found Edward. Or more accurately, Edward had found Booth and he had almost killed him. How were we going to manage this? He was too formidable. How was I going to solve this? Booth almost died because of me and I dared not think of what was happening to Jessica. That innocent young girl was being held by a monster and there was nothing I could do about it. Finally, I saw Grace come in, holding two coffees in polystyrene cups. I took one from her and she sat next to me.

"How are you doing,?" She asked, gently.

"Oh Grace, this is all my fault. What was I thinking, us splitting up like that? What if Mike had been killed, what if you'd been killed? I never could have forgiven myself," I said, starting to cry.

"We all chose to do it, Minty. Besides, Booth is fine, just a few stitches and he'll be as right as rain," she reassured me.

"But it could have been far worse," I said, sniffing away the tears, trying to compose myself.

"It could have been, but it wasn't," she said more firmly now, "come on, Minty. We did it. We found Booth, he's okay. Pretty soon we'll find Edward too."

I broke down; tears were building in my eyes and as they broke free and rolled down my cheeks, I started to sob. My shoulders started pulsing up and down and I spilled my coffee. Grace took the cup from me and placed it on the floor. Rising from her chair she knelt between my legs and I let the tears flow. I was crying now, unstoppable, unmanly, wet and pathetic. I wiped my nose with the back of my hand and sniffed. Grace placed her hands on my shoulders and pulled me to her.

I rested my forehead on her shoulder and let her comfort me. I was crying hard and breathing deeply, weeping into the softness of her sweater. Grace stroked the back of my head, making calming noises. I was ashamed. Gradually pulling myself together, I straightened slightly to look at her. Grace's eyes too were moist, and she looked at me with sympathy. We paused there for a heartbeat, then she rose toward me and I moved to her. Our lips met, and we kissed lightly. We paused another heartbeat then kissed again, longer and deeper. Breaking apart,

I moved back. Looking at her looking at me, I moved fast towards her and our lips struck. Our kiss now had no pretence of friendship or comfort. We were locked in a passionate embrace.

Eventually she rose from her position on the floor and sat beside me. We stayed there, not speaking but waiting and holding hands. After a long time, we heard the door open and turned toward it as one. Officer Cote from the RCMP entered with a colleague I had not met before and Grace discreetly released my hand from hers.

"Elisha, I'm glad you came," I said to the Mounties.

"Minty, Grace. Of course we came, how is Booth?" she quickly asked us.

"He'll be fine, Edward let him live apparently," Grace said.

"Edward? I think we're hunting 'Id' now, don't you?" She replied.

"You believe my theory then?" I asked her.

"The fact that he's here in the park and not across the border proves it. That, and Booth says he screamed it following the attack, which is a good indicator."

"You spoke to Booth?" I asked on hearing his name.

"A little, I thought we could do the proper debrief together," she said, tilting her head toward me and Grace.

"Thank you. Don't you think you need to take me off the case though?" I said.

"Why on earth would I do that?" She asked, genuinely surprised.

"Because of Mike... Booth. He was hurt because of me."

"You found Id. Booth found Id. That's nothing short of miraculous. Yes, he got hurt, but that's the job. Now pull yourself together, we've got a monster to catch," she commanded me.

"And hopefully a girl to save." Grace added, rising from her chair.

"Yes, the fact that he let Booth live does bode well for Jessica,"

Elisha commented.

"Hmm, just why did he let Booth live though? That's the question." I asked her.

"Well, let's ask him..." Elisha said and turned from our little waiting room. We walked in together, the other Officer waited outside, guarding the door. Booth greeted us with a smile and a wave.

"How ya doing, Mike?" I asked sympathetically.

"Great. Apparently, you did some good first aid and the cuts weren't too deep, so no surgery required. They should leave some neat scars though," he explained with a smile.

"I'm so sorry you got hurt," I said, my voice catching in my throat.

"Not your fault, buddy," he said grimly, "if I had loaded a round into my gun you would have one Edward with a hole in his chest to look at instead of my beautiful body. So, this feels very much like my fault."

"Still--" I said.

"Still nothing. Besides, I survived, so no harm, no foul," he said, smiling again.

"Detective Beech, can you describe for us what happened?" Elisha asked as she started her recorder, placing it on the side of his bed.

"Okay..." he arranged himself in the bed and prepared to give his statement. "Edward dropped in front of me from a tree, freaked me out, I can tell you. The guy was totally naked and very pleased to see me if you get my drift... so I go for my gun and he just sprints at me. I manage to get it out, the gun that is. I manage to get it out and to his chest as he gets to me. Then, click, nothing, I hadn't chambered a round. Stupid. Then the naked nutcase, he's made bear claws out of gloves, he goes to cut my throat out and I think, 'this is it, time to die buddy'. But nope, he stops, instead he just slashes a load at my chest. Hurt like hell I can tell you. I'm ashamed to say I fell backwards. As I fell, he screams 'Id', stretched out real long, like a wolf howling. I think I hit my head as I landed, 'cause the next thing I can remember is that I'm lying on the floor, bleeding, in the pitch black. I think I went in and out of consciousness until you woke me up by walking into me. Thanks for that, by the way."

We all politely smiled at the humour in his story but the attack sounded terrifying. The memory of how he had looked at me came flooding back. His relief that I had found him, his terror after having lay there for hours, wondering if he was going to live or die. I looked at him and he looked back. He nodded, a tiny subtle movement that no-one else would see. I saw him swallow back the emotions raised by remembering the attack and I nodded back with a thin-lipped smile.

"I wonder why he let you live?" Grace mused out loud.

"No idea," responded Mike, coughing first to clear his throat, "glad he did though... have you seen my nurse? The good-looking one."

We all nervously laughed again as she came in; she was indeed pretty, and Booth wiggled his eyebrows at us as she approached. We left him to recuperate and went outside with Elisha who walked purposely to her car.

"You two can go home, try to get some sleep. The Force is here now and we're closing down the Red Deer Lakes. We have some trackers coming in from Toronto, we should have him by the end of the day."

Looking out over the parking lot, I saw that the sun was finally rising after a long and emotional night's work. Grace gently took hold of my arm and walked us to our Jeep. I didn't even think of complaining.

As we arrived at the ranger's station where we were bunked, Grace's room-mate was waiting at their door having heard us arrive. Disappointed, I watched Grace exit the Jeep and walk to her cabin. She didn't turn back once and Joan closed the door to the cabin and my hopes. Sighing, I climbed down from the Jeep and walked to my private hut now my room-mate was in hospital. I lay on the bed and pondered the night's events. Unsurprisingly, thoughts of Grace and the kiss dominated my mind.

"I'm not going to get any sleep." I said to no-one in particular. As I rolled over though, the evening's exertions immediately pulled me into a deep, dreamless stupor.

Chapter Thirty-six

I'd had a breakthrough; it was an interesting experience. Still I remained without body, without form. I existed only as a floating mind in a sea of black molasses. My only sensory input was through the eyes of the skull in which I resided. All I could do was think, so I considered my world in depth and breadth. My thinking had been productive, and I had arrived at a number of conclusions. For a time, I thought I was Edward Gooch, software engineer, male, forty. But then I considered that when I look in a mirror, correction, when the body in which I reside looks in a mirror, I see Edward. If I can see him, but not feel him, then I am not him. I am not Edward. Therefore, if not Edward, then who am I? This I rolled around my mind for quite some time. Finally, I came to the straightforward conclusion that I was Ego. I think perhaps that I am also Superego, but for simplicity's sake I have chosen to call myself just Ego. It seems an elegant solution as my physical body appears to be calling himself Id.

It is as this new person that I began to experience the world in which I now exist. I am in a body, the body of Edward Gooch. This is completely and totally controlled by a new personality calling himself Id. I have tried to take control and influence the actions of Id. At every attempt, I have failed. What I have seen through his eyes, felt through his skin, has horrified me. He has killed in the most disgusting and evil ways while I have been forced to observe and bear mute witness.

Interestingly I see what he sees and feel what he feels, but there is something missing. The emotional component, the drive, the instinct. These are all his and I am missing them. I am logic, I am thought, I am perhaps personality, as I feel more like Edward than Id does. Also, I am moral. I see these acts as wrong, evil and deviant. This is why I have decided that I too am superego, as I am the morality of Edward. Therefore, I have determined, that Edward has fractured. His being has split. Rather than multiple personalities, he has separated out the id of his psyche and placed it in charge of his body. I, on the other hand, remain trapped in some dark corner of his mind.

I would like, as much as I can like, to regain control of my body and stop Id acting as he does. I have tried. I have tried yelling, whispering, moving and controlling, using everything at my disposal. I have tried while he sleeps. I have tried while he is murdering. Nothing has worked. That was, until last night. He was attacking a police officer in the woods, he was nude and rampant. As he was about to cut the throat of the man using his vile bear-claw contraptions, I decided that I did not want to watch. Unable to close my eyes and knowing that I was unable to prevent it, I attempted to distract myself. I thought of memories of my life as Edward, of pleasant times past.

My thoughts, conjuring memories of Edward, had a wholly unexpected effect. I suddenly felt connected to Id. I felt as if I were Edward again. Not completely, just a little. I felt some of Id's emotion seep into me and, together again, some of my influence returned. I couldn't halt the attack completely, but I managed to re-direct his rage from the throat to the man's torso. Hopefully I saved his life. The effect was temporary, but it worked. Soon Id was running back through the woods, back to his cabin. From within his mind, safe and separated, I started plotting. I knew he would try to hurt Jessica on our return and I could not allow that.

My theory was that I couldn't overpower Id because the id is stronger than the ego. The id is primordial, the biological drive that keeps Edward alive. The ego is just an arbitrator between the id and the superego. Therefore, the ego cannot override the id. I cannot be stronger than Edward's instinctual drives. This is what I had been trying and this is why I had failed. But Id is not separate from Edward, he is a part of him. So am I. Instead of trying to overwhelm Id, perhaps the key to control is to resurrect Edward by combining myself with Id. Once Edward's personality is reconstructed, then the ego can dictate his actions once more.

This was my plan as I watched him prepare and manipulate Jessica. I could see from her actions that he had indeed finally broken her. She was going to give herself to him and I could not permit that. I bided my time, building my strength. I let Id become distracted by her. When the time was right I let myself feel him, feel his desire and his passion for her. In doing so I managed to become a part of him. For a second, we became Edward. As Edward, I spoke to Jessica, warning her. It confused her greatly and I had to repeat the warning a number of times. However, it worked. She found her strength once more and refused Id his passion. The activities exhausted me, depleted my strength and once more I had to sit back while he vented his rage. Once he had destroyed the interior of the cabin, he slept, and I tried again.

Unfortunately, I failed.

To my great disappointment, I discovered that when Id sleeps I am unable to merge our disparate selves into Edward. It seems he remains in charge. However, I take encouragement from today's victory; that I can influence Id, take control, even for a second. Despite this, I have no idea how I am going to defeat him. When we are together, the strength of Id overwhelms me quickly and decisively. However, I will not stop, I will not rest because I cannot. I am Ego and I intend to return.

Chapter Thirty-seven

Three more days... three more days without any leads. Grace and I were seated on small plastic chairs in the auditorium of a tiny school just outside Banff. The RCMP were now in the parks in force and had appropriated the hall for their Operations Centre. Their methods were not too different from ours; reports and sightings came in from the rangers and public, they were collated and filed and then assigned to officers to investigate. We were still there as a courtesy and patiently waited as assignments were handed out again. Elisha, learning from our failure, kept investigators in teams of two now and, as she read out their names, they rose and walked to her. Collecting their cards, they departed just as Booth had done that fateful morning. He should be at home recovering, but instead he was seated against the opposite wall, working hard. He had refused to leave, instead installing himself behind a large desk, arranging reports as they came in on the radio.

Twenty Officers from the RCMP and us. Eleven teams were searching all day and sorting reports all night. We had missing hikers, absent locals, sightings of strangers, Bigfoot and bears. Slowly, inexorably, we investigated, with the same results as before. Nothing to follow, nothing to chase, nowhere to search. It was infuriating. The last of the Force finally left, driving from the parking lot. Looking around, I saw that Grace and I were the only ones remaining as Elisha came over to us.

"Guys, why don't you take the day off? We don't have anything significant, so we could spare you for a day," she informed us.

"There must be something, we're good to go," I insisted.

"No, you're both tired; you look like you're about to keel over."

Quickly, Grace interjected, interrupting my building response to Elisha's observations, "Minty, perhaps Elisha's right. I know I could do with a day off. We could go to a spa?" She suggested.

"That's a great idea, Grace. There's one close to here that's fed by natural springs. It might rejuvenate you." Elisha responded with barely a pause.

"I'm being ganged up on by women here..." I called out to Booth. He hung up his phone and answered back with a grin.

"Sounds like this dream I had..."

"That's enough from you, Booth. You shouldn't be here at all." Elisha was mockingly firm, and he picked up a ringing phone. "Look, I'm not sure that if you found him, you'd be capable enough to apprehend him anyway in your current state," she added, gesturing to us.

"But..." I complained.

She ignored me, "the other thing you can do for me, and everyone else, is to buy some new clothes. Sorry to be personal, but you smell pretty bad."

I sniffed under my arm, detecting nothing. But I had worn the same set of clothes for a week now, not having any more with me, so I probably did smell.

"Fine, let's go to a spa then," I surrendered.

"Take my car..." called out Booth, obviously still listening.

"Okay, what's going on. Who replaced Booth at the hospital?" I asked loudly across to him.

He simply grinned and threw the keys to Grace. She caught them with one hand and shoved me toward the car with the other.

Two hours later, having bought some new clothes, we were at the spa. I was first to change, and wearing a new pair of trunks, I padded over to a hot, swirling pool of water. As I lowered myself into the soothing waters, I realised that Elisha and Grace had a point. I was exhausted and suddenly feeling my aching body, I decided I did need a day off. I relaxed and closed my eyes, letting the water do its work. Sensing a disturbance in the surface around me, I opened my eyes to find Grace smiling back at me. "How is it?" She enquired.

I just made a long groan of satisfaction in response, as she removed a robe rented from reception. Finally, here was something to take my mind of the case. As she rose on tip-toe to reach the hook for the robe, her tiny feet stretched and elongated her calf muscles. I watched as her tendons straightened under her smooth skin. I breathed in deeply, admiring the view. She turned and I lifted my gaze to her eyes, "come on in, it's really nice."

She dipped a toe, testing the water. Gradually she lowered

herself into the water and I moved around so she could sit next to me. She exhaled noisily as she immersed herself and I looked away, trying to relax. However, I was singularly failing now she had joined me. Wearing hardly anything, with warm water wafting over our bodies, all I could do was sit there, frustrated and frozen in action. I had tried a number of moves since our kiss in the hospital. I had brushed close to her, opened doors for her, accidentally stroked her leg while changing gear. Nothing had elicited any kind of response, except that the time I touched her leg she had moved away. She must have thought the kiss was a mistake and, again, did not want to talk about it. It was killing me though. When I wasn't hunting Id, I was thinking of that kiss.

"Grace?" She didn't answer, probably due to the noise of the spa, so I spoke up. "Grace?"

"Hmm."

"I've been thinking."

But my enquiries were cut short as a group of three entered the water. We exchanged greetings and they settled themselves in. I closed my eyes and tried to relax, to forget Grace's proximity. In an attempt to distract myself, I ended up listening to the new arrival's conversation.

Suddenly, I sat bolt upright in the water, causing a wave to slosh towards the three people opposite. The content of their conversation had only just penetrated the shell of my relaxing mind. They looked at me with concern as I blurted a question at them.

"Where is this, where's this cabin?"

Grace was sat up now too, "Minty, what are you doing? I'm sorry, it's okay though, we're police officers. We're here investigating a case in the area." She calmed the strangers who were understandably looking alarmed.

"Grace," I practically shouted at her, "they were talking about their neighbour, who's not their neighbour."

"That's right," the woman among them nervously said. "Jerry, our neighbour isn't in his cabin. Some other guy is."

"What does he look like?" I barked at them.

Stunned, the woman had little choice except to reply, "sorry, we're not sure really, he keeps himself to himself and Jerry always wanted privacy so we tend to leave the cabin alone."

"How d'you know it's not Jerry, then?" I was interrogating them I knew, but I didn't care. I wanted answers.

The woman looked at the man to her left, who seemed more relaxed about my excitement. He replied for her, "oh, you can tell. Jerry's old, he moves slow, with a stoop. The guy there at the moment, he's young and athletic. I'm a hunter, you learn to see how people move, watching animals all day." His comment seemed to stir something in Grace's mind.

"Would you say he moved with grace? Like a hunter himself, like an animal?" She asked, far more calmly than me.

"For sure. He moves smooth and balletic-like. I saw him go out hunting one evening and I didn't hear him shift a single plant. The guy's good, great even." This was the second man. I looked at all three of them.

"We need the location. And you're not to go back there today. Understand?" I brusquely informed them.

"Okay... can I see some credentials though? Like I say, Jerry likes his privacy." The woman was still talking as I was climbing from the pool to fetch a map and my wallet.

After drying and changing, Grace made me shove my old clothes into a donation bin nearby. Finally, we had a lead. A point on a map where a strange man with outstanding athletic ability was living. We called Elisha and, despite her misgivings about us going to investigate, she authorised us to proceed. Swapping Booth's car for a park Jeep, we were soon bouncing up the gravel road to the cabin marked on the map.

"This lake is just a short distance over the hill to the Red Deer Lakes." Grace said, studying the map.

"Yeah, he must hunt over there where he caught Booth, and live this side."

"Clever, very clever," she commented, sounding genuinely impressed.

"Yeah, he's definitely dangerous... how d'you think we should play this?" I asked her, as I tried to concentrate on driving.

"I think stick together, go in hard. Our priority here is Jessica. Also, he's a hunter, far better than us. I think sneaking up on him is a non-starter," Grace said, obviously having thought about her strategy during the drive.

"I agree, he'll hear us coming regardless of how we approach. Let's drive right up to the cabin, fast. You take the shotgun and I'll have my hand-gun out ready. You go to the right of the door, I'll stay on the left." She nodded, confirming our tactics. I was trying to plan for every eventuality. "His instinct will be to attack. But he's all about knives and cutting. Let's stay apart, at least three metres. That way one of us can always cover the other. If he goes for one, the other shoots. Understood?" She looked uncertain as I glanced across at her. "Grace, you have to be clear on this. We cannot give him even a second. You have to shoot."

"What if you're in the way?" She asked, worriedly.

"Just shoot him, Grace. Even if it means hitting me. If you give him an inch he'll kill us both. Promise me."

"Okay." She said it quietly, but I believed her. She was tough. She would do it.

"Besides, shotgun pellets shouldn't penetrate him. If we're fighting, just shoot him in the back, I'll be fine."

She nodded, and I turned back to the rough road, increasing our speed.

We pulled up to the cabin fast as planned. Slamming on the brakes I lurched the Jeep to a stop behind an old pick-up. We dove out of the doors, weapons out, pointing at the cabin door. We paused there, looking at each other. It took a mammoth amount of effort to move from the protection of our Jeep but with an unspoken agreement we stepped away. Walking slowly, either side of the truck, we moved to the cabin, guns raised.

Chapter Thirty-eight

I hear them coming, a vehicle in the woods is a distinctive sound and I focus my mind and ears. It is not a beaten-up old truck, therefore it is not a local, it is not my neighbours. I move quickly. Rabbit is on the sofa, compliant, the chain limiting her movements. Quickly, I retrieve her gag and have her lock it to her mouth with the chain and padlock. I stroke the smooth skin of her cheek with the backs of my fingers, revelling in the touch. I dart from the cabin. They will regret coming to my place, my home. Finally, Rabbit will get to witness my prowess as a hunter. Maybe then she will succumb to me, to my superiority.

I am Id, I am perfection. I am, once more, hunter.

Chapter Thirty-nine

Grace was moving on the right of the pick-up and I was on the left. We stepped forward in unison, maintaining an invisible connection with each other across the wide expanse of the vehicle. We were watching the door to the cabin but nothing had moved. She paused and looked at me; I signalled for her to wait a second whilst I scanned the surroundings. Luckily for us the clearing for the cabin was a good ten metres in all directions. There was no Id, and no-one was attacking. Yet. I nodded to Grace and we stepped closer to the cabin. She moved her hand from the pistol grip on the shotgun and wiped it on her leg. Replacing it, she nodded again and we moved forward.

There was no sound. No birds sang and the cabin was silent. It felt empty, dead. But the emptiness itself had a message. I knew all too well that an absence of noise, especially in the wilderness, can signal danger far more. It was as if the local animals could feel the presence of a predator in their midst. I looked down at the tyres of the truck. They were soft and had sunk into the dirt of the clearing. I whispered to Grace.

"This truck hasn't moved in days, look at the wheels."

"Yeah, and why no noise? Why hasn't someone come out to investigate? Should we announce ourselves?" She asked in a hushed tone.

"Procedure says yes. But I don't know..." I whispered back. I hadn't thought about that; we knew that we should always follow the rules, but Id transcended them. Should we fight him with different rules, with more brutality, or less? I was uncertain, and my fear silenced me.

That was it, that was why I was moving so slowly, so cautiously. I was afraid. I took another step forward; the barrel of my gun was shaking. "When we get to the door, I'll go in first and clear the room. You stay outside to cover and protect me," I commanded Grace, taking charge as the police officer. Looking at her, I remembered she was used to scenes after the crime, not hunting down dangerous criminals. She looked scared, as scared as I was. "Are you okay?" I asked. She nodded. Her gun was steadier than mine, I noticed. I inched another step forward.

Suddenly, without warning, I felt something on my leg. A hand wrapped itself around my ankle. I looked down to see an arm extended from underneath the truck. I hadn't checked under the truck.

"Grace...!" I cried out as the hand, with super-human strength, pulled at my ankle. One side of my body slammed against the cab of the truck as he dragged me into it. As I hit the door, my back crashed against it, making me drop my gun. My head hit the glass hard. I resisted his strength as he grabbed my other leg. But I couldn't stop myself from falling forward as my legs disappeared under the truck. Falling with such force and speed, I failed to put my hands out and my face hit the ground even harder.

Chapter Forty

It is so easy, so simple to defeat these lesser men. Running from the cabin I saw them speeding up the road. Clever, arriving before I had time to position myself, but they are not fast enough, not clever enough. I slide under my truck.

Their vehicle rocks to a stop and they jump out. They are tentative, cautious. Clearly, they have come for me, they know of my strength and my prowess. I smile as they creep from their vehicle towards mine. I roll over onto my back and lift myself from the ground into the belly of the truck, out of their sight. I needn't have bothered, as they fail to even cursorily check the underside. I have to suppress a chuckle at their ineptitude as they move closer, discussing the state of my wheels. Their trivial conversation continues as I lower myself to the ground, shifting closer to the leader. He is commanding her movements, I will take him first.

Striking snake-like, I pull his legs from him. Satisfyingly, it causes him to twist to face away from me. I pull harder and cause him to slam face-first into the ground. I smile as I hear the sound of his skull popping against a tree-root. The muscles in his legs go slack as he loses consciousness. Instantly I turn my attention to her. I see that she has a shotgun, its barrel probing the underside of the truck. Before she can lower herself to look under and shoot me, I shuffle in the opposite direction. I climb over the prone form of the unconscious man as she drops to her knees and sweeps her gun at my departing figure.

Without pause, I use the body of my victim as a springboard. I leap over the cab of the truck, across the roof and drop down on her. She cries out but cannot do anything to prevent me landing on her. My hands grab her wrists and my momentum throws her to the ground. I am on her as she lies spread-eagled on the ground. The gun has flown from her grasp and she is at my mercy. I see her terror as her mouth opens in a silent scream. I stare deep into her green eyes and smile. I release one of her hands to show her my claws. She cannot take her gaze from them. They are items of elegance, tools of death. They transfix her as I use one to point to the cabin door.

I climb from her, placing myself between her and her gun but she doesn't even look at it. Instead she does as commanded. She walks slowly to the door, looking back only once to the unconscious form of her partner. I follow her. She opens the door and enters the cabin. She gasps, no doubt at the sight of my Rabbit. I shove her deeper inside, closing the door behind us.

I am wearing my hunting suit, stained by the blood of my victims. I stand before the women, crouched and panting from my exertions. I appear as I am, for I am animal and they are at my mercy. Accordingly, they shake with fear and expectation. I have defeated the only real threat, the man, with ease. The action did not sate my need to hurt. I step forward and strike the policewoman. I roll in my claws, so as not to cut her, and punch her in the stomach. She folds over with a groan and slumps to the ground. I scrape my claws down her back. Ten red lines rip her shirt to shreds. I wrap my fingers in the remains of the cloth and tear the garment from her. Arching my back, I howl at the ceiling above me.

I slice at my own chest, feeling all ten points pierce my skin from arm to arm. Bending down, I cut myself from ankles to waist. I throw the gloves to the floor. Using bare hands, I rip the hunting suit from my body. I feel everything, and everything is rapturous. I start laughing, I cannot help it. The pain, the excitement, the emotions; they cannot be contained.

"Rabbit, where are you?" I ask of my pet. I know she is behind me, I want her now. "Rabbit…"

My command is interrupted by a new feeling. There is something cold around my neck, something hard.

"No, Rabbit…"

But something is happening, it is becoming difficult to breathe and I cannot speak. She is tightening her chain around my neck. I cannot believe it, she is trying to strangle me. I laugh at the pathetic attempt, twisting to face her, to punish her. But she has positioned herself behind me. I realise suddenly that she is standing on the bed. I awkwardly arch backwards as she presses her knee into my back. I cannot breathe now; soon I will lose consciousness. I am grasping at the chain, trying to pull it from my throat. I cannot. How can this frail female be overpowering me? I relax my arms and let my body slump.

Here is her mistake. She is releasing the pressure on the chain. She cannot kill, she does not understand her id. I whip my hands up and squeeze them between my throat and the chain. Shocked, she renews her efforts, but they have little effect now that I am holding the chain. I gasp in the air I was lacking, reenergising myself. I twist to face her. I laugh at her failure as she releases the chain. I slap her, hard in the face. She falls down onto the bed. I loom over her, I will take her now. Ready or not, wanting it or not, she will be mine now as I step to her.

Suddenly, a new sensation; a sharp pain to my right temple. Overwhelming agony forces me to the ground. The policewoman has struck me with something hard. I see her standing over me wielding a frying pan. Jessica joins her. She is no longer my Rabbit, no more my pet, she is a threat. As the policewoman attacks again, I roll under the bed. She appears momentarily confused and I take the opportunity to rise on the other side. They stand against me.

Stalemate. They are armed, I am not. They are prepared, but I am also. I am Id. I look to them, they are both shaking. They are frail, they are pathetic. They only managed to hurt me because I was overwhelmed by my emotions. I only have one emotion now: anger. I smile, baring my teeth. They have aroused the hunter; the killer will act. They will die.

"Ladies, congratulations. You hurt Id. But Id has truly awoken now, prepare yourselves for death."

"Back off, Edward!" The policewoman yells at me.

"You misunderstand woman. Edward is not here, Id is here, and Id is death. Id is the hunter of hunters, unstoppable."

"Stop!" The voice came from my mouth, from my mind. I was about to lunge at them, to end them, but my body betrayed me.

"What?" I yell out, "I will not stop, I will end them."

"You will not, they are not a threat, they are not your enemies."

"But they hurt me. They hurt Id," I scream.

"You hurt them first."

"I don't care," I cry out so loudly I feel the damage in my throat.

Finally, I have control of my frozen body. I launch myself at the policewoman because she has the weapon. She pulls back the pan, ready to strike me with it. I simply grab it and take it from her. I throw it to the ground and punch her in the face. She collapses to the floor and I move to finish her.

"Jessica, kick him!" My voice yells out. I am paralysed. She does as I command and kicks me in the back. I fall on top of the other. She raises her knee and strikes me in the genitals. The pain is crippling, it has no edge of pleasure, no exquisite tingle.

"Id, you are no more, I am Edward now," I scream, triumphantly.

This is confusing, this is not pleasurable. I keep losing control of myself. These women are taking advantage of whatever is happening to me. I steel myself and concentrate on the pain, focussing on my hatred of them as I stand in the doorway. They seem more confident now, prepared for me. I realise that, once more, I am unable to move. However, just as quickly as I had lost control, I regain it.

I take my opportunity. I turn and run from the cabin. I run past the policeman on the ground. I sprint to the lake and dive into the woods beyond. I don't stop. On all fours, I run. Run from these women. Run from whatever was taking control of me. Suddenly I am the deer, bounding through the wilderness, escaping the wolves that want to devour me.

Chapter Forty-one

I stopped him. That was my thought as I allowed him to run from the scene. I was tired, my interventions had drained everything from me. My hypothesis had been correct. It took a great deal of concentration and effort, but I had managed to combine myself with Id. I achieved success at critical points during his attack. Each time, we had become Edward. And each time Edward was revived, I, Ego, was in charge. It was simple at first to override his actions. However, Id was strong. Much stronger than I or Edward, it seemed. Each time I took control, each time Edward resurfaced, Id pushed him back. I found myself separated once again, impotent.

It was promising, my progress, but also infuriating. He was in charge; I was simply a pause button on the runaway train that was the power of his personality. I cursed him as he ran through the woods, running from capture. I was resolved; I will combine with him. Edward shall return. I, Ego, will ensure it.

Chapter Forty-two

I woke up, or was I dead? The view to my opening eyes was confusing. It appeared to be a bra. A barely covered breast touched my nose and I realised that was indeed what it was.

"Huh?" The breasts disappeared.

"Minty, are you okay?"

Fine, that was a good noise. That was Grace, I must be alive. Unless she too was dead.

"I don't know, are we alive?" I asked the voice.

"Yes, Minty. We're alive." She laughed, I took that as a good sign and sat up. She was sat beside me, just wearing jodhpurs and a bra. There was blood on her and her face was swollen. I remembered Id.

"Where is he? Where's my gun?" I asked, panicking.

"Here it is. It's okay, he ran off into the woods. Jessica and I chased him off." She calmly informed me.

"You did? Jessica, she's here? She's okay?"

"Yes, we're both fine, you don't seem to be alright though. Can you see okay?"

"Yes, yes I'm fine. It's just a bit confusing..." I admitted.

"Yes, I know, do you want to try and stand up?"

She helped me up and I stood, wobbling from side to side. She was holding her shotgun in one hand and I could see my gun on the floor. I bent to retrieve it and she steadied me as I stood again. My vision swam in and out of focus but finally settled down. A massive headache was pounding between my temples, but nothing else seemed to be seriously wrong so I stepped towards the cabin, finally able to stand on my own.

"Grace? Why aren't you wearing a shirt?"

"Come on, Minty. Come and meet Jessica."

Everything in sight was smashed to pieces, the inside of the cabin was devastated. Jessica was attached to a pipe via a long length of chain that was secured around her neck with a bicycle lock. The weirdest sight, however, was that she was whistling and making three cups of tea.

"Okay..." I sat down on the bed and she passed me a mug. "Are you sure I'm not concussed, this is kind of weird."

They both laughed, which I took as another good sign. Everything looked disastrous, frightening and dangerous. Two women standing, mugs of tea in hand and laughing, seemed very out of place. The sight comforted me, however, so I just sat there, sipping the tea that Jessica handed me.

"Grace, don't you want to put something on?" I asked her after a delay. I didn't mind, the view was very nice, but in my confused state it was very disconcerting.

"My shirt is torn to pieces and there isn't anything here, Minty," she informed me, logically.

I removed my shirt and, a little reluctantly, threw it to her. Surprisingly she didn't even try to catch it, she just let it hit her and fall to the floor. Her laughing stopped as she started to cry. As she started to weep, so did Jessica. They dropped their mugs of tea as I stood and moved to them both. I wrapped my arms around the two of them and drew them into me. I felt a wetness against Grace's back and she winced at my touch. I reduced the pressure of the embrace, but she pressed herself to me and I resumed my tight hug of them.

We stood there, the three of us, for many minutes. They were weeping into my naked chest as I held them close. I consoled them, telling them everything was going to be alright. It felt hollow and empty, but it seemed to work. I was comforting the women who had rescued me, saved my life. I didn't know how, but looking around the inside of the cabin, I knew it hadn't been easy.

Id was gone, there was no point in trying to chase him into the woods; our priority had to be Jessica's safety. And ours. We found the keys to the bicycle lock and freed Jessica from her chains. We secured the crime scene as best we could by wrapping police tape between two trees leading to the clearing. Eventually we found some phone reception after driving back to the road; by the time we had informed Elisha of our discovery two hours had passed. She set up roadblocks and redirected all her officers to the area but we held out little hope for catching Id.

*

The news of Jessica's discovery was met with cheers and whoops in the situation room upon our return. Following her debrief, we placed Jessica in a car to be driven home to her parents in Calgary. She kissed and hugged us both, thanking us for her rescue. We waved her off as she sat looking forlornly from the back window of the departing police car.

"It will be difficult for her to recover from that." Grace commented, waving goodbye.

"What about you, Grace? Will you be okay?" I asked her.

She was wearing a ranger's shirt now, matching her tan jodhpurs, and she really looked the part. A ranger through and through, tough and hardy, outdoorsy and strong.

"Me? Oh, I'll be fine."

"But he attacked you, tore your…"

"It was just a fight. Sure, it was tough, it was scary, but I was never at his mercy. I was never his prisoner. Hell, he only cut me a bit, hardly even very deep. The tetanus shot was worse than what he managed."

She smiled and I think I saw the truth; that she was going to be fine.

"You are one strong woman," I observed.

"Sure. But you knew that already didn't you, Minty?"

She turned from me and walked back to the situation room. There seemed to be an extra wiggle there as she moved away from me, looking back at me over her shoulder.

"She knows I've been staring at her ass, then," I admitted to no-one but the birds as I followed her in, taking another long look.

Everyone in the situation room was jubilant and the space echoed with loud conversations. As Grace and I walked in to find our seats, the officers of the RCMP rose and applauded, and a few slapped us on our backs as we passed. Grace winced at each touch but didn't shun the attention. I gestured that the applause was for Grace alone as we sat. Elisha was standing at the front, behind a lectern. The map of pins behind her had been cleared. One red pin remained, centred on the cabin where we had found Jessica.

"Okay people, today was a good day. We saved a life, rescued a girl," she nodded in our direction, "thank you Detective Beech and CSI Bouchard."

Another round of applause thundered around the room which Elisha quickly quietened with an expansive wave of her arm.

"But Id is gone. We have officially started calling him Id, so we can all remember the danger he poses to us and the public. He used to be Edward Timothy Gooch but he is far more deadly now. He is an animal. An expert hunter. He has no morals and no qualms about killing and torturing anyone who stands in his way."

She paused, letting the room become still as the facts settled in. We all knew that Grace and I had been lucky, Jessica too. Now he was free again and running wild. The body count could only get higher.

"We have no idea what he will do next. Our psychiatrist agrees that he is working on instinct alone, so our predictive patterns will not hold. The only thing we can do, I'm afraid, is to wait. Wait for him to act so we can react."

We slowly dispersed from the situation room. We had all been assigned points on a map to try and catch him fleeing the park. The rangers had warned us that the chances of finding or intercepting him were minimal, but we had to try. Grace and I drove out to our location in silence, listening to the radio in the Jeep. News of Id had gone national now and the report of his presence in the park was playing after every song. People were scared; we saw a long line of vehicles leaving ahead of us. We pulled off the main highway to the service road assigned to us and stopped. Looking out over the road below that twisted through a valley, we settled in with our binoculars.

"This is pointless," I complained.

"Agree to disagree," Grace responded. "You never know, he

might come this way. We have to try."

"Yeah, I s'ppose. And what else are we going to do?"

We sat for a few seconds, scanning the road.

"Yes, what indeed?" She answered, after a delay. I glanced across at her, thinking she'd said that in a suggestive manner. I watched her for a few seconds as she continued to scan with her binoculars. Then I joined her, searching for our fugitive.

"Where are you Id?" I asked the wilderness.

Chapter Forty-three

I am wraith, hiding from hunters. They are a pack, dangerous and to be avoided. But I am the apex predator. More dangerous than any of them, yet still I must fear the pack. For that reason, I re-clothe myself from a cabin I come across on the edge of a lake. The occupants are no match for me. An older couple sit on lawn chairs on their porch. The arrival of a naked man shocks them. He goes down with the first blow to his head, his silver hair hitting the dark stained decking most satisfactorily. She darts to his side immediately to hold him. I could easily end them now to prove myself worthy, but it seems hollow somehow. I just leave them there. I take his clothes, boots, food and water in a rucksack and depart. I head south, away from the park, away from the pack.

Chapter Forty-four

I was resting my eyes as I slouched in the driver's seat of the Jeep. Grace was searching the road below us through her binoculars. The engine was running to keep us warm when she shouted out.

"Minty!"

I sat bolt upright, grabbing at my binoculars, "what?"

"There, a man, crossing the road, just past that large maple."

I found the area and turned my focus wheel to see the man, who was tentatively crossing the road. "D'you think? Could it be him?" I asked her.

"It could be, it does look like him."

It did. A tall figure was moving softly and elegantly across the road. He was wearing dark trousers and a green coat; it could be Edward, I thought. *Id*, I quickly corrected myself. Putting the Jeep into gear, I started down the rough road towards the figure.

As we bounced down the road, I debated how close we would get before he saw us when Grace answered my internal question.

"He's seen us!" She called, still looking through binoculars. I sped up; flooring the accelerator, sending gravel in all directions and sliding awkwardly down the road. Grace put the binoculars down as they hit her in the eyes for the third time with a thud. She held on tight as we bounded down the road, struggling to reach the radio on the dashboard. Finally she grabbed the microphone as we transitioned up a short rise.

"Jeep four to base, four to base…"

"Base here." It was Booth, manning the radio back in the Operations Centre.

"Mike, Grace here. We think we have a positive sighting, crossing our road north to south, about halfway down. We are in pursuit."

"Copy that, Grace. How certain are you, over?"

"Not very, Mike. The suspect is in a long green coat, seen only at a distance."

"Okay. I'll transition one unit to the south of you. If he runs, try to move him to the Collins River crossing, over."

"Roger that. Grace out." She threw the microphone to the floor as I slammed on the brakes. It swung around the inside of the cab on the end of its cord. Grabbing her shotgun from the rack, she leapt from the Jeep, shouting. "This is the police! Come back! We just want to see if you're a fugitive we're searching for."

"Grace, you're not the police."

"Shut up, Minty," she said to me. Into the woods she yelled, "we just want to find our fugitive; if you do not return here we will have to assume you are him!"

"He must have heard you," I pointed out.

I joined her, gun in hand. She turned back to the Jeep and reached for the radio through the window. She informed Mike that we had more evidence that the man was Id and he sent another two units to the river crossing as we entered the woods.

Suddenly we were blasting through a solid mass of vegetation. I led with my arms in front of me, pushing branches aside as I squeezed through the trees. They snapped back behind me, striking Grace in the face to yelps of protest. Looking back, I could see that the bruise where Id had struck her was darkening, it was now joined by various lines of blood from the whipping trees.

"D'you want to go ahead of me?" I asked.

"No." She replied with certainty. Instead, she lifted her shotgun vertically in front of her, shielding her from the worst of the damage. We forged ahead, I breaking branches and bending foliage as we went.

"This is no good, Id will hear us from miles away," I pointed out.

"But he might just come and get us then." Grace said, her jaw set determinedly. She crunched a shell into her shotgun and motioned that I should proceed.

I gripped my hand-gun hard; I would not drop it this time. This time I would get him. "Yeah, he's going down this time," I agreed with her.

We crested a low ridge and the trees thickened, darkening the woods as foliage spread out above us. However, the lower branches thinned and there were fewer bushes and ferns. Our progress quickly improved and our movements became quieter. We spread out and walked on side-by-side, scanning for any sign of Id. After about half an hour of this I suddenly stopped; I could hear something.

"Grace, do you hear that?"

"Yes, water?"

"It must be the river."

Quickening our pace, we arrived at a wide gorge. A five-metre cut in the ground, its sides were solid granite; a grey scar across the forest.

"There's no way Id could climb down there," I declared.

Grace nodded, "yeah, I'll go upstream, you go down."

"No. We have to stay together."

"Which way, then?" she asked me urgently.

I was glad she wasn't going to argue. Not only did I want to keep her safe, I needed her to keep me safe too. She swept the area with her shotgun, a determined look on her face.

"Let's go down-river," I decided. "He wants to leave the park. Downstream is more south than up so he would go that way."

"Unless he wants to throw us off by heading up?" she said.

"I know, let's just take the odds though, we have to pick something. Besides, down is towards the crossing where backup is. We might just drive him to them."

We spread out again; Grace took the riverbank and I stayed beside her, a few metres deeper into the woods. The shotgun made her movement through the trees more difficult than my pistol so this way we could move at the same speed, covering each other.

We walked for another hour in silence. We listened and

searched for Id, but there was no sign. No sounds penetrated the trees except for the roar of the river. Grace stopped. Sensing her sudden tension, I turned to look at her. One eye on her, the other on the river in front, I scanned the woods. Seeing nothing, I slowly moved to her. She stood stock-still, shotgun raised out in front of her.

"Grace?" I whispered. She motioned ahead and I looked to where she was pointing. I could see nothing but I raised my gun anyway. "What is it?"

"Just to the left of that fallen tree, behind that mossy rock," she whispered, pointing again with her shotgun. I stared into the woods, trying to see what she saw. Then it moved. There was a dark hairy shape behind the rock, black and ominous. A bear, there was a bear in our path.

"What do we do?" I asked her.

"We could go around?"

"We need to follow the river though, we need to chase Id down to the backup," I said.

"But he can't have come through here, the bear wouldn't be here if he had."

She had a point, if someone had passed by, the bear would have run away. Being notoriously wary of people, even the scent of a person long-gone would keep them away from an area. The bear was sniffing around the side of the river, no doubt looking for a way down or across. Perhaps even for some early-season salmon.

"We could scare it off," Grace suggested, raising her gun to the air.

As she did so, the trees above us exploded.

Chapter Forty-five

I am slicing through the trees with ease. My new clothes make noises that I am not accustomed to, but I am still as quiet as a wraith. I am pleased that Edward had met my pursuers previously. Through his interactions with the leader and mine with the woman, I know their tracking abilities will be non-existent. I make good progress as I don't have to worry about leaving a trail. They are not hunters at all, they are city police. In the wilderness, I will evade them with ease.

I am making my way down the river, looking for a place to cross, when I detect a problem. Before me, eating berries from a bush is a large grizzly bear. She cannot see or hear me, but if I approach she will smell me. Luckily, I am upwind of her, so as long as I keep my distance I can avoid detection. I am about to make my way around when I hear the two police behind me. They are attempting to move silently, I can tell, but are failing miserably. I sigh at their ineptitude and change my mind about circumventing the bear. It will be a good choke point, I realise, as I study the terrain around me. Climbing a suitable tree, I lie on a wide branch, waiting for their arrival. I don't have to wait long. They were closer than I had thought. They might not be silent, but they have some proficiency in movement.

I lie still on the tree, letting the breeze soothe me. The sound of the river masks the noises my clothes are making in the wind and I take a deep breath. They are armed and prepared, ready for my attack. Standing tall on the wide branch, I disturb some pine needles. Watching as they gently fall to the ground I judge their distance from my prey. Just as they are about to strike the head of the man, I drop from the trees. My descent is not elegant or silent. There are many thin branches beneath me and I smash through them on the way to my target. There is a long rustling crash, snapping branches and falling pine cones herald my approach. Not with enough warning, however, as I strike the woman with my feet. Using her to cushion my fall, I plant a shoulder on the ground and roll to complete my attack. Coming back up to my feet, I stand before the man; his gun is out, pointing at my chest. He thinks it over.

"Don't you move!" He commands, the waiver in his voice betraying his lack of confidence despite the firearm in his hands. I raise my own hands in compliance and bend my knees in preparation for movement. He bends to check on his fallen comrade, placing his fingers on her throat to check for a pulse. I realise I can use this compassion against him. Feeling the nagging presence in my mind, reaching out as it always does, I close my eyes and let it come; I let Ego blend with me.

"Detective Beech, Minty?" I implore the crouching man, who rises quickly to his feet in response to my speaking. "Is she okay?" I ask him, reaching my hands out in a placatory gesture.

"*She*? She is called Grace!" He shouts in an angry voice, jabbing his gun forward in my direction.

"*Good*," I think, Ego's compassion has given him pause, calmed the situation. Retaking control, I realise he is emotionally involved with the woman, he is angry, he is failing to remember his training. The volume of his voice is having another interesting side-effect. As I look over his shoulder, I see we have attracted the attentions of the bear. She might have run away earlier but now we are too close; we are in her territory and the shouting policeman is agitating her.

"Is she dead?" I let the scratch in my mind return to ask him.

"No, lucky for you, or you would be too right now."

I retake my mind, forcing Ego away again with ease, "I won't kill her, Minty. I will take her, however. Take her like she wants to be taken. She is ready, she is willing. I will bring her to the pinnacle of ecstasy and tip her over the edge. She will beg me to take her there. She will scream my name." I taunt him with one eye on the bear; she has risen on her hind legs now, sniffing at the air.

"In your dreams, you bastard! You're forgetting I've got the gun."

The bear hears him and takes a large pull at his scent, trying to determine the source of the noise.

"I will take it from you, you are nothing in comparison to me," I calmly inform him, "but you will not die so quickly. No, Minty. You will get to watch me give her this gift. You will hear her screams. You will hear them change as, at the moment of her greatest pleasure, I slice her open. I will cut her from pelvis to throat and have her watch with her dying breath as I eat her intestines."

"You will never touch her, you evil monster!" He screams at me, his gun shaking with rage.

The bear's ears twitch. She does not like his noise and drops to all fours to start her charge. I smile. The policeman looks confused. I gesture with my chin that he should look behind him as I raise my eyebrows in a knowing look of superiority.

Chapter Forty-six

He gestured that I should turn around, but I wasn't going to fall for that. My rage had almost overwhelmed my senses but not completely. Grace was badly hurt and she needed help but this monster was standing in my way. I almost shot him dead as he taunted me. Had he not temporarily concerned himself with her well-being, I think I would have. It had made me think that Edward was still in there. At that moment, I had seen him change; his eyes had softened and his demeanour had calmed. Then, in an instant, I watched him switch back. His stance had adjusted, somehow making him more animal-like; his eyes had hardened once more and his smile had re-emerged. It was Id that wanted me to turn around, not Edward. I was not going to do anything Id wanted. But then I heard it, a huge sound, a beastly presence behind me. A snort of air penetrated the noise of the river. It was then that I remembered; there was a large grizzly bear behind me. I turned too late. A mass of hairy flesh smashed into me.

As I hit the ground, I saw Id's feet departing in a flurry of movement and I tried to point my gun. The mass of the bear stopped me, and my attention was instead drawn to its weight pressing down on me. It was on my legs, crushing me into the soft dirt. I turned my head and was confronted by teeth. The bear roared and a line of spit fell in my eye. The warm breath of the beast blew across me as I tried to bring my arms up to protect my face. It reared up, snorting. Collapsing back down it swiped at me with its paws. I felt an intense pain explode from my chest as the strikes hit home. I tried to roll away but was met with another blow. Its paw felt like an iron bar against my arm as it knocked me back beneath it.

It roared and barked at me. Since the first swipe with its claws, however, it had declined to use them again. Nor did it bite me. I had no idea where my gun was. At one point I tried to reach out with a hand to feel for it but another blow struck me and I returned to my curled-up defensive ball. Gradually its blows slowed and had less strength behind them. I remained still; eventually the bear backed away a step and rose on its hind legs. It barked into the air once more, a disturbing sharp sound that seemed to shake the trees around me. It collapsed again to all fours and, with a derisive crinkle of its nose, it turned and walked slowly away. I poked my head out from under my arms to watch its wiggling posterior departing. I saw my gun, only thirty centimetres from my hand, and snatched it up. Checking its operation by pulling back the slide, I saw the deadly copper tip of a round in the chamber. Allowing the slide to click back into place I pointed the steel at the departing beast. It turned over its shoulder to look at me, seemingly hearing the dangerous sounds and movements. Seeing her face, her expression suddenly now one of pure peace and gentility, I had no option but to lower my weapon.

I rose to my feet as it continued to quietly depart into the woods. Pain emanated from every part of me but the cuts on my chest were not deep and the flow of blood was already slowing. I was bruised and bloodied from the attack, but it could have been far worse. Thanking the bear for my life, realising that it could have taken it whenever it wanted, I crawled over to Grace.

I sat on the ground beside her, watching her chest rise and fall with a steady rhythm. I ran my hands over every inch of her still body, checking for broken bones or blood. I didn't want to move her. Id had landed on her hard and she might have broken her back for all I knew. I pondered the problem; I couldn't move her, I couldn't leave her. With each passing second Id was escaping further into the woods. I tried to rouse her, tapping her face gently but there was no reaction. Taking out my hand-gun, I fired three quick shots into the air. This, I knew, would attract the attentions of the units at the river crossing. My nine-millimetre automatic sounded nothing like any gun a hunter would use. The sound of it firing so rapidly would only mean one thing to an officer of the RCMP.

That done, I turned my attentions back to Grace. I was worried, but also intrigued. Id's words rolled around in my mind. How he was going to have her, to bring her to the point of ecstasy. I had been beyond furious at him. Not because I believed he could, I would have prevented it, but because it was what I wanted too. Looking down at her small body, I wanted to do everything he had described to me. It was my name that I wanted her to scream into the woods.

Remembering my first-aid training, I carefully removed her walking boots. Scraping the soles of her feet with a twig, I watched as her toes curled. Satisfied at the correct instinctual response, a sign that there was no spinal damage, I returned to my non-medical intentions. My eyes traced a path from her dainty feet, up her sleeping form. I wanted to take stock, to memorise the shape of her. Her feet were tiny, perfectly formed at the bottom of thin, delicate ankles. Her legs, revealed so clearly to me under her tight jodhpurs, were perfection to my eyes. I moved my attention to her flat stomach, flesh peeking out from her dishevelled shirt, and paused at her belly-button. I wanted to bend over, to kiss it, to flick my tongue in and out of the depression. I resisted, instead letting my eyes fall to her waist.

I stared at her exposed stomach for a prolonged time, taking in the colour and texture of her fair, tanned skin. Then, steeling my resolve, I lifted my gaze to her breasts. Contained by the thick coarse material of the ranger's shirt, shackled by a patterned bra, they still managed to excite me. I couldn't resist; shifting my seated position, I moved down to look though a gap between the buttons of the shirt. The bra beneath was black; pink floral patterns disappeared into the dark. A delightful glimpse of what might never be. I allowed my eyes to move from this view to inspect the taut skin of her neck. The tendons and muscles were pulled tight by the position of her head, the skin there was perfect, without a single blemish.

I took in her face, a face with which I was so familiar. This was the face of the woman I loved, the target of my infatuation for two years. Her petite features carved from soft pink marble. The small nose, the tiny ears, wrapped in the gentle curls of her dark brown hair. I knew that if she were just to open her eyes I would be greeted by two circles of complex colour. Green, brown, blue and grey, they sparkled and danced in the light, defying classification as one thing or another. My attentions were drawn to her slight, soft, lips as they parted. They opened, dryly, painfully.

"Minty?" She spoke with a croak.

"I'm here, Grace. Try to lie still, help is on the way," I softly informed her.

"Id?" She asked.

"He's gone again, I'm so sorry. I let him escape."

"Are you okay?" She spoke with more strength now. Her eyes fluttered open and eventually focussed on mine. She glanced down and her gaze settled on my chest. "Minty, he hurt you..." she said, startled. Sitting up, she grabbed at her head, the other hand reaching out to me, steadying herself.

"You should lie still. I'm fine. It wasn't Id."

"What? No, I'm fine, just woozy, I think. It wasn't Id?"

"Believe it or not, it was the bear."

"What?"

I laughed, releasing the tension I was feeling now it seemed that Grace was, in fact, definitely unhurt. "Here we are, chasing down the country's most dangerous fugitive. We catch him. I have my gun on him even. Game over. When the bear I had totally forgotten about attacks me from behind."

"A bear saved Id?"

"Well, I think I accidentally provoked it into attacking me. That's probably more accurate."

"What?"

"Id provoked me, made me angry. I think my noise provoked the bear. I totally forgot about it when Id turned up."

"Understandable, I suppose."

She lay back down, satisfied that I was okay, and closed her eyes. I was so immensely relieved that she wasn't hurt I almost wept. She was alive, and I was alive. Those simple facts were amazing revelations to me as I sat in the dark woods listening to the pounding river thundering through the trees.

The noise of the water seemed to mirror the flow of blood in my veins. My heart was pounding, I could feel the pressure building in my ears. I was sitting beside Grace, looking over her. Her eyes were closed and she had a hand on her head. Her position had further opened the gap in the shirt at her cleavage and this is where my eyes lingered. Id's words rolled around in my mind again and I stirred in my underwear.

I looked up to her and saw that she had her eyes open. She was looking at me, looking at her. I could no longer resist. I bent over and kissed her. I pressed my mouth to hers. Her lips parted, and her tongue met mine. We slowly explored each other's mouths. I stretched an aching leg over her and straddled her hips, quietly groaning through the kiss.

"You're in pain," she quietly whispered to me, mouth against my ear. Her hot breath soothed me, its tickle sending a shiver down my spine. I closed my eyes and breathed in the scent of her. Her hair was spread out on the ground and the fragrance of the forest mingled with her own to produce an intoxicating mixture. Her hips rose, pressing against me. I reached down and placed my palm against her breast, gently squeezing it, feeling the hard material of her bra.

She said nothing, just closed her eyes. I rose up, and using both hands, undid the buttons of her shirt one-by-one. She sat up and pulled it from her. Reaching behind, unclasping her bra, she slid it down her thin arms before flicking it away. I gingerly removed my own shirt and threw it to hers. I cupped her breasts in my hands and explored their shape. Bending down I flicked my tongue across her nipples. She lay back down as I proceeded to tenderly kiss her body.

The experience passed in a fog of pleasurable exploration. We touched, kissed and probed each other's bodies from head to toe. Eventually she guided me to her. Without a word spoken, our breathing and exclamations took each other to where we wanted to be. We became one. It was as if we belonged together as we tenderly made love on the soft forest bed. Afterwards, I rolled onto my back and we both looked to the sky through the thick canopy of pine trees. From the corner of my eye I could make out her bare chest slowly rising and falling. A bird started its song, playing us a lullaby, as we held hands in this place of perfect peace.

Chapter Forty-seven

Id had made a mistake. He had let me in, let me combine myself with him. It was for his own purposes, he had thought; to prevent Detective Beech from killing us. What he didn't know is that it was more useful to me. For I, Ego, now knew better how to combine with him. My previous attempts had been akin to merging myself with a beanbag. I could try to mould myself to its form. I would push here and press there, to fit our shapes together. It was difficult and cumbersome and formed only a trivial combination. We combined as strangers, temporary and without meaning or depth.

As he had let me into his mind, however, we connected at a richer, deeper level. I could feel him, I was him, and he was I. I felt I could have retained control, but he was still strong and I feared permanent exclusion. I approved of his actions at the time, letting the police escape, so I let him eject me. I actually left of my own volition, testing the perimeter between our minds in both directions.

I will bide my time, I will wait and practice. I will let him let me in, permit his use of me. When the time is right, when we are together, I will strike. Edward shall return.

Chapter Forty-eight

Four officers from the RCMP found us not long after we had re-dressed and started making our way back down the river. We had walked hand-in-hand for a time. We hadn't spoken but our stolen glances at each other, as we struggled through the undergrowth, said it all. She'd wanted it as much as I had. I dared not say it out loud, I barely dared say it in my mind, but I felt like we were boyfriend and girlfriend. It made me feel like an awkward teenager again. The officers approached us with their guns drawn. We waved them down and they holstered their firearms, approaching us with less caution now they knew they were safe.

"I take it you didn't come across Id on your way here, then?" I asked the first to arrive.

"No, nothing. He must have looped around us, probably heard us coming. I'm afraid we abandoned stealth for speed once we heard your shots. I assume that was you?"

"Yeah, we're okay, but Grace got hit pretty hard." I motioned to where she was taking a moment to sit on a rock. "I almost had him, I had him under the gun, literally."

"What happened?" The officer asked.

"Believe it or not, a bear attacked me," I motioned to the cuts on my chest and he whistled while the others gathered round. "What's the play here, then?" I asked as they inspected our wounds.

"We head back the way we came, spreading out and looking for any sign. There should be half the Force deployed across the river by now so maybe we can drive him into them."

"Or he's already crossed the river and is away by now." I grimly forecast. The officers nodded in agreement. None of us had much confidence as we spread out and set off in a line downriver. Grace was alongside me, by the water's edge. As we searched hopelessly for any sign of Id, I couldn't help stealing a glance from time to time. I was pleased to notice that she was doing the same.

We arrived at the river crossing to shouts and challenges from five more Mounties. Confirming our identities, we emerged from the woods. Our clothes were cut and scraped from our travels and we looked like a dishevelled, defeated group as we climbed into the vehicles. Radioing in, we checked with Elisha for our assignments.

"Minty and Grace, get someone to take you back to your Jeep and then report to the Medical Centre."

These were our orders, which we gladly obeyed. Id was gone, had vanished ghost-like back into the woods. Looking to the south, beyond the river, I could see the Trans-Canada Highway. Beyond that, the Park became private land, filled with people, vehicles, and roads. If he was past the river, which he certainly was in my mind, he was gone. Gone until he killed again, that was.

*

The nurses at the Medical Centre were concerned about Grace, as she had lost consciousness for a prolonged period. As I had also previously been knocked out at the cabin, they finally insisted that we both be sent to the hospital in Calgary for proper attention and monitoring. As there was nothing more we could do for the case, we let them call an ambulance. We slept in the back, happily allowing fatigue to overwhelm our minds. I dreamt of Grace, our time together. Together we slept in perfect harmony.

Chapter Forty-nine

I was away, I was safe. I had allowed Id to take me across the river and through the woods to the highway. From there he walked to a small town where I allowed him to take a vehicle; there was no violence. The keys were in the entranceway of a small house and we simply took them and drove away. He stopped in a rest area and I coaxed him to swap number plates with another vehicle parked beside us. Carefully and precisely he replaced the other vehicle's plates with ours. The driver was unlikely to notice this change, so finally I felt anonymous and protected. We drove west, across the highway at the speed limit. Again we stopped, this time to take money. I persuaded Id to break the glass of a parked car that contained a large purse. As expected, inside we found a pocketbook filled with credit cards and a sufficient amount of cash. Using the cash we filled up our stolen truck and ate at a fast-food establishment. Together we seemed to make an effective criminal; I provided the brains, he the action.

As Id drove, I rested. He seemed to have a boundless energy that I lacked. I remember being aware of filling the tank of the large pickup truck twice more before the lights of a city appeared. I did not want Id rampaging around a large populous without my supervision, so again I lightly joined with him. It was fairly easy, I was discovering, to join with him in a superficial way now. Slowly, gently, I would consider him and his thoughts. Pondering on his emotions, letting them penetrate my mind, I softly became him, and he I. Stopping short of merging completely and becoming Edward, lest he detect the change, I communicated affective thoughts to him. These he seemed to hear as an urge, an instinct. My previous mistake had been to talk to him, but as Ego, I thought logically and verbally. Id, therefore, heard me as a voice, an intruder. This he fought, this he resisted. Instead, now I conveyed a desire; a need to sleep and to rest. This he heard but did not resist. Pulling over, he parked the truck, reclined the seat, and fell asleep. Satisfied with my progress, my influence over him, I too slept. Together we slept in perfect harmony.

Chapter Fifty

I sat back, pushing myself into the soft sofa cushions. Stretching my arms above me I clicked my neck with satisfaction. This was Grace's apartment and she was in the bathroom, taking a shower after an amazing night together. I was wearing my pyjamas, having brought some things over to hers a few days ago.

"This is the life..." I quietly informed the City through her picture windows. We had both been given two weeks leave to recover from our injuries. This was partially as a reward for our endeavours despite our failure to apprehend Id and partially because we had accrued far too much overtime during the manhunt. A wet, steaming Grace stepped from the shower, wrapped in a large green towel. A matching one was wrapped around her head. "What a sight..." I informed her.

"You. D'you ever stop being horny?" She asked, bending her knee and dropping her hip to one side.

"Please, I couldn't if I wanted to. Last night practically killed me."

She chuckled and went into her bedroom to change. We had slept in, because of the aforementioned night of activities, and had no plans for the day. It was exactly the kind of day I was enjoying on our enforced sabbatical.

"D'you want to do anything today?" She called in a sing-song voice from the bedroom.

"Not sure, not really. I s'pose we should get out, though."

"Yeah, I'm feeling a little cooped up in here. We could just wander into downtown?" She suggested.

"Sounds nice, I'll get dressed then." I dragged myself from the sofa and trudged reluctantly into the bedroom. There I found Grace. She was spread out completely naked on the bed, towels thrown to the floor.

"Are you sure you couldn't manage just a little?" She teased.

Casting off my own clothes, I climbed onto the bed. "I guess we'll find out." I replied as I climbed on top of her.

*

We did finally manage to leave the apartment. We went for a stroll around a city park and visited some shops. We didn't buy anything, just browsed. We tried on clothes and joked around. It was magical, wasting time with Grace was a pastime I could never grow tired of. Deciding that we were both hungry, we were soon relaxing in a bar waiting for food to arrive when she suddenly stopped talking and stared at a television instead.

"Hey, pay attention to your man, please." I joked with her, finally getting revenge for all the times I had been distracted by televisions in the past.

"What?" She replied, confused.

"Didn't you even hear me? What's so interesting?" I asked, turning to look. As I did, I saw what had grabbed her attention. There was a news report about a gruesome murder in Vancouver. The sound was down but the subtitles spelt out a sorry tale. What was disturbing to us both was the headline above the reporter's head.

'The Id Killer hits Gastown.'

Our food arrived. Neither of us acknowledged the waitress as she put the plates down and arranged our cutlery. Our failure to answer any of her questions delayed her leaving but eventually she wandered off. Grace said nothing, I said nothing. We both ate our food in silence, staring at our plates. Finally, as we finished the last of our food, the same waitress came and took the plates away without saying a word. She returned and replaced our used cutlery with a bill. Grace put down some notes on the little plate and we both stood to leave. We left the bar in silence, both knowing where we were headed as we walked slowly to the Precinct.

*

It was no surprise to either of us to find Booth also there as we walked into the detectives' office from the elevator. He was waiting for us and stood as we arrived. Nodding hello, he turned and we followed him into the Captain's office.

185

"The answer is no," said the Captain as we walked in.

I raised an eyebrow and opened my mouth to speak.

"No was the definitive answer, Detective Beech."

I shut my mouth, unsure of what to do next.

"We know him sir, all three of us. Better than anyone, better than the Force or the Van' Police. You need to let us go, they need us." Booth said eloquently.

"Mike's right," Grace chipped in. "Each of us has been attacked and lived to tell the tale. Each of us has found him once, we can find him again. Before anything else happens," she continued, her voice imploring the Captain to change his mind.

"That's exactly why you cannot go," he firmly replied, "he knows you too well, what makes you think you'd get anywhere near him? If you did, what makes you think it would be any different? You failed to catch him last time. That was okay because you rescued the girl. If it happened again all your careers would be over, done. Mine too, come to mention it."

"Sir?" I finally spoke, stepping forward. "This is my case, the last time I checked it was still assigned to me. The stabbings? The four stabbings in our Precinct? They're for me to investigate. I've a new lead in Vancouver, will you let me chase it?"

The Captain sat back in his chair and placed his hand on his chin. He made us wait, it was interminable. Eventually he leaned forwards, "you can go, Minty. Alone."

Booth and Grace both gasped. As they started to protest, the Captain held up his hand to stop them. "Detective Beech is correct, it's his case. He can legitimately chase any new lead. Van' PD should accept that and probably will. Also, it's his first case and he should see it through to the end. Maybe if you catch him we can roll free from the trouble that's coming our way over letting Id out of the province."

Grace went to protest but the Captain continued, ignoring her.

"You, CSI Bouchard, are not even police. I have no authority to even request that Vancouver take a Crime Scene Tech on a temporary assignment, so forget it. And last but not least, Booth. You're on sick leave, at least until you get your stitches removed. Then I have a pile of cases for you to work on, so you're going nowhere. Now all of you get out of here before I bench the lot of you. Bouchard, seeing how you think you are fit enough to race off to B.C. to chase criminals, I assume you're coming back to work tomorrow."

This last parting statement was to Grace's back as we left the office. Sighing, she agreed with the Captain, "yes, Sir." She closed his door and we all walked to the elevator together.

"That was harsh." I stated as we waited for it to arrive.

"No," she replied, "he knows that I would have gone with you, using my time off. He's keeping me here to prevent that. He'll let me take my time once you've caught him."

I looked at her. Her expression of total faith lifted me.

"Too right." Booth added, slapping me on the back. "Go get him, Ace."

Smiling at Booth, I put my hand on his shoulder, "you know, Mike. I quite like being Minty."

*

Booth drove us home, Grace squeezing into the cramped back-seat of the Mustang as he rumbled to her apartment. I exited the front seat and let her out of the back by tilting the seat forwards. She climbed out over the seat-back and gave me a kiss on the way out.

"Take care, Minty," were her parting words as she walked into her building.

I climbed back into the Mustang to be greeted by an inane grin from Booth, "Minty! I knew it, you old dog. You hound."

Jokingly, I gave a little howl in the confines of the car as he pulled down the road, heading to my place.

Four hours later and I was in the arrivals lounge of Vancouver airport. A grey duffle in one hand, phone in the other, I was trying to look up the name of the detective that was supposed to meet me. Faintly in the distance, I heard my name being called.

"Montgomery Beech."

Tracing the source of the sound, I spotted a young man with my name hand-written on a torn piece of card. Making my way to him, I pocketed my phone and waved. He took my bag and led me to his car which was parked in the no-waiting zone. He threw my bag in the back seat as I climbed in. Just as I buckled up my seatbelt he hit the gas on the running engine. We shot off, past the airport terminal and down a service road, signed no-entry.

"Don't worry..." he reassured me, noticing me grip the door handle in fear. "That sign's to stop people driving this way, official vehicles are permitted of course." He leaned down, turning on his lights, and sped up. "We're going straight to the scene, if that's okay?" He asked, barely looking at the road. I was petrified, rooted to the spot. I had never driven at such speed through such narrow roads.

"Sure, sure," I tried to sound calm despite my growing fear.

We arrived at the crime-scene tape, thirty, white-knuckled, minutes later. Exiting the car, I made my way there, leaving the young officer behind. Mostly to try to regain my composure, partly to assert some authority over the situation. He caught up with me at the tape and nodded to the guarding officer to let us through. As we ducked under, he held out his hand to introduce himself.

"I'm Detective Garibaldi, you can call me Henry though."

"Pleased to meet you, Henry. People call me Minty." I proudly told him as I shook his hand. "What do we have here then, Henry?"

"We were kind of hoping you could tell us, sir. The victim's a local homeless man, known to us unfortunately, as he causes all kinds of trouble amongst the tourists when he's had a few. Nothing serious; he shouts at people, demands money, that kind of thing. Anyway, yesterday morning his mates find him stuffed in this dumpster and cut open. His insides are someplace unknown. The medical examiner filed his report which flagged up the link to your guy because of the same type of knife, apparently. Does this look like his work?"

He handed me a folder containing photos and the medical report, and as he spoke I leafed through it. I closed it with a feeble waft of paper that did not match the severity of my conclusions.

"Yes. Id did this."

"Damn," was Henry's reply, taking the file back from me. "Our own serial killer comes to B.C., eh?"

"Yeah... did you contact the RCMP?"

"No choice, the computer did it for us. An officer Cote is waiting for us back at headquarters. She told me to take you there after you'd seen this."

I smiled, despite the carnage and death Id had now carried across the country to the coast; seeing Elisha again would be interesting. It felt good to be back on the case after a week off. I smiled even harder at the memory of that week's activities. Forcing a more serious face, I turned to address my new temporary partner.

"Let's go then, Henry." I commanded, starting the march back to his car. "And slower this time, Mario Andretti. I want to get there in one piece if possible." I was going to enjoy picking on the new guy, I thought, ironically.

A new crime, a new province, but it was the same case and the same procedure. Edward's face had been released to the media with a strongly-worded warning. Cards with his details and image were on the dashboard of every police car in the city. Elisha was not happy that the perpetrator of the crime had been leaked, but now the news was out she was determined to make the best use of it.

"Minty." Elisha called, beckoning me as I walked into Vancouver Police Headquarters. "Good to see you, though I wish it was under better circumstances."

"Yeah," I agreed, shaking her hand.

"We knew he would kill again, though." She grimly added.

I hadn't been so certain and had said so in my final report of our last encounter, "I was really hoping that Edward would have broken through, that he would hand himself in."

"Yeah, I read your report. You thought that he broke through Id's personality in the woods?" She asked me.

"That's how it seemed at the time. For a second it was like he was a different person, the Edward I'd met before this all happened." I commented, gesturing across the RCMP Operations Centre she had set up.

Elisha and I talked for a while, and she suggested I call Doctor Crown, the Force psychiatrist. Together maybe we could think of something that would help us connect to Edward, tease him away from Id and get him to turn himself in. With the Vancouver PD running the manhunt and Elisha coordinating, there wasn't much else I could do.

Chapter Fifty-one

I awoke suddenly from a deep sleep. I was in the driver's seat of an old truck. Memories came back to me; I had allowed Id to steal it. As I thought more about it, I remembered directing him to steal it. There was no violence, I was pleased about that and felt satisfied. I started the engine. It fired up with a single turn and quickly settled into a smooth beating rhythm. Turning the heater to warm me, I rested back in the reclined seat. I was in command. I searched my mind, looking for Id but I found that he was not there. I felt nothing, no emotion and I was in control. It was mentally disconcerting but emotionally, still nothing. Truly I was a man without id.

Recalling that I was heading to the city of Vancouver, I waited for the mist to clear from the screen and put the car in gear. Applying my mind to the simple act of driving was novel to me and resulted in an awkward forward lurch of the truck. I tapped the brakes and skidded to an abrupt stop, failing to apply any nuance to my movements. Trying again, pulling away slowly this time, I allowed my muscles to remember the actions required, leaving my mind out of it. Trusting in my legs and arms to convey me toward the highway, I allowed the truck to pick up speed. Soon I was moving on the smooth straight road, counting down the kilometres to my goal.

Still some way out of the city, I had filled up the tank and was walking through the shop to pay, when a sudden need overcame me. It was not a desire, it was a physical necessity. Unable to not comply, I asked the clerk for the item in the case. Adding it to the price of my full tank it depleted my funds to zero, yet somehow this did not worry me. Walking back to the truck, I admired my purchase as I rolled it over between my fingers. The filling station was also the local fishing and hunting store so had many different items for sale. What I was now the proud owner of was the strangest knife I had ever seen. It sat in a long rectangular plastic case. As I pressed a switch, a thin white blade protruded without a sound. I pondered the item, caressing and loving it as I did. I placed it carefully in the pocket of my coat and pulled away once more to the highway.

I drove as far as the needle on the petrol gauge allowed. Pulling into yet another gas station, I had four hundred kilometres yet to travel and no money remaining. Ignoring this fact, I placed the pump into the receptacle and clicked down the lever. Minutes later and I had another full tank. I drove away without experiencing any conflict, which in itself presented me with a strange feeling of freedom. I was a thief. I searched my mind for some feeling of guilt, hoping and expecting to find a complaint from the superego. I found none. I supposed that necessity causes the moral preclusion of theft; a starving person is justified in stealing a loaf of bread, so my need to get to Vancouver seemed to justify stealing petrol.

I drove in silence; the sound of the engine and the rumble of tyres on tarmac were the only noises accompanying my approach to the city. I drove straight and true, directly to downtown. The highest buildings guided my way as I arrived at a bustling intersection. I pulled the truck up against the curb and climbed down. Leaving the keys in the ignition and the engine still running, I walked away. Without turning around, I strolled down the street. Seeing a group of tourists consulting a map and pointing toward some distant sight of interest, I decided to follow them. They led me to Gastown and by the time we reached the main attraction, a steam-powered clock, I was tired. It was dark and the tourists were clearing out of the streets. Instead the homeless abounded. Smelling of marijuana, some shouted confusedly and aggressively, others sat unresponsive in doorways. I followed the general flow of movement to an area in which many were climbing under cardboard or into stained sleeping bags. I moved to a vacant corner by a large blue bin and pulled the rubbish that lay there over me.

*

I was ripped from my pleasant slumber by a beast of a man. He shouted while pulling me upright by the collar of my coat. He smelled terrible, the stench of drugs permeated his being. He screamed once more, no words, just a primal gargle of hatred. The composition of his breath made my mind stagger. My sleep-addled brain failed to comprehend what was happening. I felt a tickle at the back of my mind, a stirring of movement. An itch that could not be scratched. I shifted my focus from the strange assailant before me to concentrate on the feeling.

I studied the sensation in my mind and tried to feel the shape of it. I went from confused curiosity to understanding in the blink of an eye. It was fear. It was anger. It was hatred. The revelation caused a switch to be flipped. The bright world around me faded to grey as the fog encompassed and contained me.

I am here. I am Id and I am being attacked. I see the man before me, the animal barking in my face. Considering my position, I perform the most expedient action. I clench my hand into a fist and punch him. My hand is a hammer, rising from my waist, connecting to his jaw. His vocalisations cease as I make contact. His jaw snaps shut and his head flies back. I hear a click. He slumps to the ground as an empty bag of bones.

I look around, surveilling the area for danger. Seeing no immediate threat, I turn to face my erstwhile assailant. He is a pathetic sample of mankind. Frail, used and worn. He is dead. I smile with the satisfaction of a job well done. Reaching into the pocket of my coat, I feel what is there. Pulling it out, extending the knife, I crouch beside him and begin my work.

Chapter Fifty-two

"How many is this, Henry?" I asked my new partner, his keenness showing in his eager smile and rapid footsteps that were taking us into the next shelter on his list.

"This will be the eighth," his keen reply reminding me of a puppy.

"How many homeless shelters are there in this city?" I questioned with a sigh.

"Officially thirty-two, unofficially maybe up to a hundred?"

"A hundred? How come? What's wrong with this place?" I said, gesturing to homeless people surrounding us.

"Nothing's wrong with it, sir. It's the weather. How many cities can you sleep rough in this country?" He asked rhetorically.

"Well, Calgary is quite nice this time of year," I replied, being pedantic.

"And in the winter?" He asked pointedly.

We climbed the steps together and I considered his point. He was right of course; the winter snows would arrive in a few months. Living on the street would be a death sentence in most Canadian cities. Here in Vancouver, the 'rainforest micro-climate' kept things survivable at least.

"I see your point. So, if this one's official, what's an unofficial shelter?"

"Just hotels and doss-houses around here. They slide under the radar of health officials and other checks because they provide a service we sorely need. Cheap rooms that some people can afford with off-the-books jobs and begging. They're hovels really but better than nothing, better than queuing for this place every night, hoping and praying to get a bed."

We set about the routine we had established during our earlier visits to the other shelters. We wandered amongst the beds, showing and handing out the cards with Edward's details prominently displayed. We pasted posters around the food areas and bathrooms. As was becoming expected, no one had seen or heard anything. Neither staff nor residents had anything to add. Many of them were as high as kites and I had stopped bothering to ask these people anything at all. Some were docile enough for me to slip a card into their shirt pocket, but most I avoided completely. British Columbia was in the process of legalising marijuana and already it was everywhere; the smell of it hung thick in the air.

"Let's get out of here, shall we? No-one knows anything and it's as depressing as hell."

"I know what you mean," he agreed as we left. Jogging down the stairs together we hurried away from the smell, away from the sad sight of so many people in so much need.

"How about we go and get something to eat?" I suggested, trying to shake the depression off. "Eight visits for the day seems about all I can take without getting suicidal."

He smiled and nodded, walking me down the road a short distance to the tourist part of town. I was surprised at how close the tourists were to the homeless shelters we had been visiting. We were soon sat in the Old Spaghetti Factory with huge piles of pasta before us. I watched Henry spear another pile of spaghetti with his fork and roll it around a spoon. Creating a tangled ball that he could just about squeeze into his mouth, he proceeded to chomp it down. I was enjoying mine too, large quantities of good food was just what I needed. I pulled down another gulp of beer from the bottle and shook it at the waitress, signalling that I needed another.

She placed a new bottle on the table with a bang and took the old one away. Eventually, after we had mopped up the remaining sauce with slices of garlic bread, we both sat back with a bottle in our hands. Henry patted his stomach and belched, "I needed that."

"Yeah, I had no idea I was that hungry. I wasn't going to let it defeat me, though." I joked as he politely laughed.

"So, Minty. Can I ask you a personal question?" He asked after another pull on his beer.

"Sure." I agreed, feeling magnanimous. He had just fed me after all.

"Why are you here?"

"To catch Id of course." I was confused, it seemed obvious to me. His question didn't seem personal at all, so I looked at him quizzically.

"I know that, but he's in B.C. now, Van' police jurisdiction. Why are you here?"

"What, you don't appreciate my expertise on the matter?"

"No, it isn't that..." he backtracked, holding out placatory hands. I signalled that I was joking and asked him to carry on explaining. "You see, you've done all the investigating. We know who he is. We know what he looks like. Now we just have to look and soon we'll find him. Van' police are better at searching Vancouver, so why are you here?"

"Okay, I see your point. And it is personal," I replied.

"Never mind, I was just curious..."

"No, no. It's personal but not private." I took another gulp of beer and leaned forward, taking him into my confidence. With a conspiratorial whisper, I told him the simple truth. "If you want to know, it really bothers me that I interviewed the guy, talked to him, chatted with him, not once, but twice. I even called him Edward and asked him to call me Minty. All that and I didn't know he was the murderer I was chasing. The simple truth of the matter is that I feel stupid."

"But, Minty. It wasn't Edward who was the killer. It was Id..."

"I know, I know all that. But the fact is, I still feel stupid. Also, he attacked me, knocked me out. He sliced up a good friend of mine and tried to rape and kill my girlfriend."

"So it's personal then?" He summarised.

"Damn right it's personal. I'm going to catch him. Catch him and lock him up forever," I stated.

"Here's to catching a serial killer, then." Henry raised his bottle and I leaned back after touching the neck of mine to his. Together we drained them and slammed them down on the table.

Henry paid for the food and drinks, reminding me that hosting an officer from outside the province could be expensed to the

Department, and we parted ways. On my walk back to the hotel, I took the time to look at the people around me. Homeless figures were moving into various alleys and corners to sleep for the night. Any one of these could be Id's next victim. In fact, any one of them could be Id himself. Their shoulders were hunched over, faces drawn back under dark hoods and hats; no-one could see their anonymous faces. A shiver passed down my spine as I quickened my pace.

Chapter Fifty-three

I was not happy on the streets. I was not happy that Id had appeared. I was satisfied, however, that he had dealt with the crazy homeless man. I tried to put it behind me now I was, once more, in charge of our body. I did not know where he had gone. Presumably to a similar space to which I was banished when he was in control. I liked to think that whereas I was relegated to some place behind the eyes, in the higher portions of the brain, he was instead pushed down deep. Deep into the amygdala, the lizard brain, the basement of the mind. But this was just my petty way of feeling superior to him. He had the animal, the instinct, the emotion. I was reason, I was intelligence, I was Ego.

Shaking the thought from me, I exited the grimy back alley that was my home. This was not acceptable, this would have to change. I looked down the street; people were crossing to avoid me. I considered assaulting one of them, taking their money and their clothes. I could release Id, have him do it for me. I quickly banished that thought from my head. I did not need Id. I was better than he. I decided, standing there, to go and gain useful employment. Checking my reflection in a shop-front window, however, I realised that I did not look very employable. In fact, I looked homeless. The face before me had an impressive beard that was matted with dirt. My clothes were respectable but my nights in the gutter had left them damp, smelly and covered with a thin layer of grime. Pondering my situation, I realised that I was indeed homeless, I also remembered that I was a fugitive from the law.

Determining that a job in the software industry was impossible, I walked down the street. Walking away from the high-rise buildings and the respectable neighbourhoods, I wandered. Fate must have been looking kindly on me that day for I soon passed a small Chinese restaurant. Having crossed into Chinatown, it wasn't their choice of cuisine that attracted my attention. It was the small card in the window asking for a dishwasher. While seemingly beneath me, it would convenient to be hidden in the back corner of a small kitchen, away from enquiring eyes. I walked inside and asked for the proprietor. A short interview later and some negotiation about payment and I had a job, starting that same evening. During the interview, it had quickly become clear that he wanted to avoid paying tax by offering cash-in-hand. Happy that it would serve me to avoid police attention, I accepted the meagre wage without question or negotiation.

Satisfied, I went and sat in a park. The weather here on the west coast was decidedly more pleasant than Calgary and I basked in the feeling of early autumnal sunshine on my face. I passed the time watching people pass me by. They paid me little heed as I sat there, quietly observing them. The bench beside mine soon gave up its occupant, leaving a newspaper behind. Shifting across to the newly vacated seat, I picked up the local paper and read. I was taking in the words with little interest, when with a turn of the page, I saw myself. Not myself, I suppose, but Edward. He, I, Id, we were celebrated men. I smiled a little at the description. Strong and lean, six feet two inches in height, dark blonde hair. All these features were correct, yet they could describe any of the men I could see from where I was sat. I rubbed at my healthy growth of beard. True, I did have dark blond hair. But nowhere did it mention that my beard, when grown, became a rich deep red. Anyone looking for the man staring back blankly from the grainy photograph would never look twice at the man I was now.

I read the story about myself, about Id mostly, satisfied that there was nothing of interest or danger to me in it. It was true that the police might have more information than reported, but searching the memories of Id, I couldn't determine any risk in the things I had left behind. It was unfortunate that they had linked the killing of the homeless man to Id. Subsequently they would be looking for me but they were not so dangerous that I should leave. However, it did perplex me as to how they had managed to connect me to the man's death. I sat there for a time pondering the question when I happened to place my hands in my coat pockets. There, betraying me, was the knife I had purchased. It sat heavy in my hand, still calling to me seductively. Why did I love it so? I knew, looking at it, its special construction, its wondrous blade, that this is how they had attributed Id's work so consistently to us. I knew I should throw it away. Seeing a bin not three metres from where I sat, I knew what I had to do. Yet I could not. It was too beautiful to me, precious, I would keep it. *It was mine.*

*

My evening of work passed pleasantly enough. Dishes, pans and cutlery came to me in a steady flow of clattering deposits. I loaded them onto a metal tray that was protected with a white plastic coating. First hosing down any troublesome areas, I would push the tray along a track into a hot metal box. Activating the machine, I would prepare the next one. The noise of the device would finally abate, signalling that I empty it. Checking the cleanliness of each item, drying where required, I would stack them and resume the procedure. It was mindless, repetitive work. The machine heated the plates to a temperature rendering them almost untouchable, steam blasted from the doors as I opened them each time. Despite the hardships and mind-numbing nature of the work, I enjoyed it. It was satisfying. Things came in dirty and unusable. They left pristine, ready for new food.

I was focussed, I was engaged, I was good. The owner praised my work when he handed me the cash for the evening and asked that I come back tomorrow. Agreeing, I exited the restaurant from the rear clutching a gift of a meal in a cardboard box. Wolfing down the excellent noodles and vegetables with a pair of chopsticks, I walked back to the poor area of town. I had heard from another member of kitchen staff that there was an acceptable hotel in which men of my status could get a room by the night. I climbed the short steps to the establishment with a skip in my step and a new sense of purpose. It was good to contribute.

The manager of the hotel was less than pleasant but I handed over the cash for a night's accommodation and he handed me a key. The room was basic and dirty but infinitely better than a gutter. It was with a lightness of step and a happy heart that I visited the communal bathroom that night. I was cleaning my teeth with my new toothbrush when I looked up into the mirror. A sense of déjà vu passed over me as I did so. Looking back in the mirror I saw the face of Edward but with my own eyes, the eyes of Ego. I wondered out loud if Id could see me, was he looking out from inside? I searched for him, for the feeling of distant buried emotion within but could sense nothing. That did not mean he wasn't there.

Looking into my own eyes, encased in the face of Edward Gooch, I considered the problem before me. He was broken, fractured. I knew this because if he were not, I would not exist. For the majority of the time he had been Id. Id was in control, powerful and dominating and I was suppressed, caged by him. I knew not where he lay now, but for some unknown reason I, Ego was now in charge.

Suddenly, I felt an unexpected pang of guilt, a stirring of concern. From the feeling, I deduced that this must be the superego. I was pleased that it was still a part of me, for it said that I was a moral being. But what of Edward? The guilt I was feeling must be for his demise. I looked at him in the mirror, looking at me. This was his body, this was his life. I was he, he was not I. I belonged to him, not the other way around. I should not be enjoying my existence, my life. I should be giving it to him, I realised.

The problem resolved itself in my mind in an instant. I needed to be no more, I had to make Edward whole again. In doing so, I would release myself back into him. This was no noble sacrifice as I too would be solid again, complete. I realised, with a shudder, that I missed feeling. I missed Id. I needed him. The solution was clear, but it frightened me. I had to find Id, to release him; I needed to become one with him. I feared his power; I feared the absence of it more so.

Chapter Fifty-four

It was hard to find a specific person in a city of millions. That was my conclusion after another week of fruitless man hunting. I was doing less and less as we progressed. The daily tasks of the investigation transitioned to the local officers. As time wore on and no more victims appeared, the detectives assigned from Vancouver faded away, as did the RCMP presence. Priorities shifted; people forgot there was a serial killer on the loose.

I was being unfair, I knew that. I tried to look at it from their point of view. They couldn't assign everyone to a single case, especially when there was nothing sensible to do. They had other crimes, other murders even, to investigate. Eventually the conference room was vacated and the crime board moved to a small office on the fourth floor. I sat around, playing solitaire on the supplied computer, chatting to Henry who was the only remaining Vancouver detective on the case.

"So Henry, how do you find being a detective?" I enquired one morning, trying to make conversation to pass the time.

"Okay, I guess. I don't get any cases myself which is frustrating." I smiled empathically, knowing just how he felt.

"I know the feeling, stick with it. You'll get going soon enough."

"Yeah, how many big cases have you worked on before this?" He asked me.

I paused, knowing that the answer would probably shock him. "Actually... this is my first."

"What! You scored a serial killer the first time out?"

"Yeah, just luck really. A simple witness statement turned into this really big deal before I knew it... with me in the middle of it."

"Cool, that is so cool."

"Well... I did want this... I suppose. But it's starting to look like my first big case is going to be my last. If I don't get the guy it's going to hang over my career like a dark cloud."

"Surely not, we've done everything right. It isn't our fault we can't find him," he insisted.

"I know that, you know that. Everyone knows that. But the stigma sticks, you can't avoid it."

"That sucks."

"I know. But think about it... it goes the other way too. If we do get him, my career will take off. I'll be the guy who caught the Id Killer on his first solo run. I'll be golden. Why? Because some other officer saw him walking down the road or knocked on the right door. That's not fair either."

"I s'pose."

"Yeah... we solve cases as a team, we fail as a team. But the lead detective either gets the blame or the credit. That's the way it is. I'm just afraid that this one won't end well."

"We'll get him, we have to," he nodded keenly.

"I'm not so sure. He's just too good," I admitted.

"Hey, Minty. Let's cheer this up, why don't we go check some hotels again? Show that picture around some more. He must be staying somewhere. I can't see this guy sleeping rough, he'd just rob someone, eh?"

He was right, it was no good sitting around moping. I stood and walked to the RCMP Officer in charge, Elisha having left days ago to work another case. We informed him of our plan and he just waved us away to return to his deployment plan. They had changed tactics; now roaming the streets or sitting in cars, checking the faces of people passing by. Our plan wouldn't clash with theirs, so he didn't care what we did.

"Come on then. Let's go check out some exciting new slums," I called to the eager figure grabbing his coat from the rack against the wall.

*

We were at our third hotel, a grimy place called 'The Empire'. Its ancient sign was yellow and crusty, the glass in the doors opaque with dirt and age. We entered the lobby and could see at least five transient residents resting on benches against the walls. Extending our badges, we approached the cubicle in the corner. A modern addition, it was fairly standard in the hotels we had been visiting. Behind thick glass with a slot in it at counter level, sat the building manager. An emaciated man with sunken cheeks; he sat puffing smoke from the slot as we approached.

"What d'you want?" He resignedly sighed at us. Henry pulled the picture from his inside jacket pocket and pressed it against the glass. "Have you seen this man?" He asked, pointing to the image. The man behind the counter sighed and lifted a matching card from beneath his pack of cigarettes.

"You guys have been here three times already, and again no. I ain't seen this man."

"It's important sir, he's extremely dangerous. Can you look again?" Henry asked, our routine well established now. He signalled that the manager look at his own picture. "Please, look closely and think. He may have changed his appearance, he would be dirtier, he might have let his hair grow, he would look more like a transient now."

The manager looked cursorily at the picture. "Nope, still not seen him."

"Sir," I chipped in, stepping forward, "are you aware that since that release there has been a reward added? For information leading to his capture..."

"A reward?" His eyes lit up and he lifted the picture higher. He turned on his chair to move into the light as Henry turned to me.

"A reward?" He muttered from the side of his mouth.

"Yeah, I was thinking fifty cents," I whispered back with a wink. Smiling, Henry turned to him.

"Sir, please. He must be caught, he's a multiple murderer and very dangerous to yourself and your residents." Henry waved expansively at the people behind us, taking them in with the movement of his arm, "this is far more important than usual, hence the reward."

He was catching on to the trick, building the importance of the case, increasing the 'reward' amount in the man's mind.

"Well..." he finally spoke, a non-committal noise.

"Sir?" I asked, coaxing the information from him.

"There is this guy. Recent arrival, fifth floor…"

"Oh yeah?" Henry gently queried. Despite his attempt to seem nonchalant, I could sense his excitement building. The manager looked up, sensing it too.

"Just how much reward?"

Henry cut me off as I was about to say something, his voice more commanding now, "the information please, sir. I should also add that withholding information from the police is a serious offence. Particularly in cases such as this."

"But the reward…" he persisted.

"Any reward will be made available upon arrest of the individual."

"Well, I don't know if it's your guy… he's got this big new beard."

"New?"

"Yeah, new. Clean. All the other guys here, their beards, well they've had them for years. Under the beard you can see the dirt. This guy, his beard's new, cleaner, you can see his skin underneath. The grime's not ground in yet."

"That's observant of you."

"Not really, place like this, it really stands out. Also, he doesn't smell as bad, his clothes are newer, ya know?"

"Not really…" Henry admitted.

"Well I know, I know these tramps. I know a tramp inside out. This guy ain't one, not yet, anyway. And he's too old to be a runaway."

"Forty, six feet two inches, one-hundred and eighty pounds?" I blurted at him.

"Maybe, I don't know, do I?" Was the manager's response as Henry and I pulled our guns.

"Is he in by any chance?" I asked him, looking to the stairs.

"Yeah, go look for yourselves. Room five oh-three," he said, sliding a key through the slot in the glass.

Henry grabbed the key with his free hand, looked to me and nodded. I returned the gesture and we started to the stairs. The sweat was already building in my hand, slippery against the butt of my gun as I put my foot on the threadbare stair carpet.

"Remember, Henry. Carefully and by the book. This is Id."

Chapter Fifty-five

I liked washing up, it was a simple activity in a world of complexity. I had been performing the same task now for a week and I had not tired of it. It satisfied my need for physical involvement while giving me time to think. Outside of work I was tired. I ate and slept mostly. My life had become a pleasant routine of washing-up, eating, sleeping and little else. All the while I worked, however, I thought. My goal was clear, I needed to merge myself with Id. I needed to save Edward. As I performed the essential physical tasks at work, I let the heat and the water wash me, to cleanse my soul. I tried to merge myself with Id.

I came close many times. I would allow my hands to perform the job whilst my brain went elsewhere. I would find him invariably hiding in some recess of our psyche. It was like trying to find the location of an awkward itch. I could feel the sensation, but the source somehow consistently eluded me. I discovered, after two fruitless days of attempts, that the key was to feel the emotion he was currently feeling. As an emotional entity, he hid within those parts of Edward's mind. Parts that I had no access to. However, I found that if I recalled some past event in Edward's life that had elicited the same emotion, the memory would flare inside of me.

One by one, I would consider an emotion. Recalling a memory that would elicit it, I would concentrate on it. If Id was not there then the action would be a dry, emotionless recollection of the facts. If Id were there, it would light up and flow from my mind. Like a wave of heat, it would emanate from me. I would feel Id coming forward, merging with me. Yet, each time I attempted it, the flow would stop. Id did not want to come forward, it seemed. He hid still, deep in the mind of Edward. He was out of reach, unable or unwilling to combine with me.

It was frustrating but expected. If it were easy, it would have happened already. Thankfully it did get easier, however. As I practised, I found that I didn't have to go through every emotion. I started to get an intuition about where he was. After a week, I could tell approximately where he was hiding and quickly coax him from his corner. The progress buoyed me; I would get him.

It was with this feeling that I left work on my seventh day of gainful employment. I was finishing up my complementary meal from

Ben, the restaurant owner, when I heard a noise. Turning to look deeper into the alley where I was leaning against a dumpster, I saw three boys playing. Ignoring them, I turned to walk the other way, back home. I stopped. I had heard something out of place, a whine. Holding my breath, listening hard, I heard it again. A definitive whine of an animal. I turned, striding to the boys.

As I approached I could see they were in their mid-teens and all wore the same matching coats. A stylised crest was stitched into the left breast of each one. No doubt the badge of a school or sports team, I decided.

"Hey!" I called out from a distance, causing them to stop and turn around. As they did so I saw the shape of an animal cowering in the corner.

"Stop that!" I commanded as I walked to them. They were still holding some of the stones in their hands that they had been throwing at the poor defenceless creature. It sat shaking in the corner, trapped; tail between its legs, head down, eyes up. It was looking past them to me, its eyes seemingly pleading me for help.

"Leave that dog alone!" My third command echoed through the alley as I reached them.

"What's it to you, old man?" One of them asked me in the quavering unbroken voice of a boy. It was an unexpected sound from one so large. He was almost as tall as I, and far more muscular. As I reached them I could see they were indeed in a sports team, most likely football considering their sizes.

"I don't like seeing defenceless animals being tortured by idiots," I simply stated, standing tall and unafraid.

"Yeah, are you defenceless, asshole?" Another boy queried of me in a deeper voice.

"No, I most certainly am not."

"Euh, Jake. This guy stinks." The third one interjected. "I don't wanna touch him, he's gross."

Just as I thought that the incident would be resolved easily, that they would leave, the first one to speak stepped forward and punched me in the stomach.

Fighting the urge to vomit, I collapsed to the ground and dropped my unfinished supper. I was finding it hard to breathe and I curled up on the ground, fighting to suck in air as I clutched at the pain. I felt an impact on my back, not painful but uncomfortable, as one of them kicked me. Then another kick, this time to my shins; that one hurt a lot. I put my hand to it, only to be punished by another. I curled up tighter, trying to roll myself into a ball. They kicked me all over. I didn't feel most of them, their soft trainers failing to strike me with enough force. However, each third or fourth strike would be to a sensitive area. On these strikes, I would grunt with pain. Doing nothing, simply willing it to stop, I lay on the ground trying to protect myself. Luckily for me they seemed practised in giving a beating and avoided my head, focussing instead on my back and legs.

Eventually they stopped. They backed away, shouting insults as I rose to my feet, "that'll teach you, asshole," the unbroken-voiced teen informed me. He spat in my direction but missed by metres. I was just about to turn, to tend to the dog behind me, when one of the boys made a mistake for all of them. He was still holding a single stone and, instead of discarding it, whipped it at the dog. The stone hit the animal on the back of its curled-up body and caused it to yelp in surprise and pain.

I quickly marched to the youth. Powerful and confident strides drove me forward.

"What? You want more?" One of them called out. All three started laughing. They were being over-confident and their laughter was ill-advised as I approached. For as I strode, a powerful memory had come to mind. The memory of a bully whipping a teenaged Edward with a fern. The memory flooded me, how upon striking, he had laughed at the pain it caused. At the time, as a young child, it had enraged Edward, but he had done nothing about it. Now however, at this time, in this place, it had enraged Id. He rose to the forefront of my mind with a heat I had not yet experienced. I revelled in the sensation as one would on a cold winter night around a fire. I allowed him to take me forward. Yet I did not retreat, I did not hide. I let Id take me, take us, to them.

The first target, the one who had launched the stone, received a sweeping punch to the face. This was not the fight of a playground, nor the impact on a sports field. This was a strike from the heart of an animal. He instantly fell to the ground, clutching at his face with both hands. The second boy was struck with the other fist, directly to the nose. Driving from the legs, through the hips in a rapid twist, my arm stretched out. It impacted him in a direct line and piled through his face; he too went down amidst an explosion of blood and snot. The third was a little further away so I stepped back and launched a kick. Coming from behind me, it swept up and impacted between his legs. He hands shot to his groin in a flash as he doubled over with a long painful groan.

I stepped back and checked the situation. All three boys were on the floor, essentially undamaged. With the lack of danger and rage, Id disappointingly faded away. I was hoping that the stimulation might have blended us for longer, but I knew it was not to be as he slipped back into some dark emotional corner. Turning to check on the dog, I found it next to my legs. It was up on all fours now, tail wagging cautiously, looking at me with wide brown eyes. A medium-sized mongrel of some kind, white with a large brown patch. I stroked its offered head and it was suddenly transformed to being ecstatically happy in the way only dogs can manage. Considering its white colouring with the chocolate patch on its back, I decided to call it 'Kendal' after Kendal mint-cake.

"You are welcome, Kendal," I informed the dog with a smile.

"Woof."

Which I took for 'thank you'.

I went to leave and was not surprised that the dog followed. Having stroked him, I could tell from his lack of a collar and the matted texture of his fur that he was a stray. I let him follow me, showing him that I was permitting it by stroking him some more.

"Come on, Kendal. Come with me and I'll get you some food and give you a bath." I informed my new friend.

Arriving back at my hotel with supplies for Kendal in hand, the Manger called me over to his booth, "hey!" He called out, rudely. "No dogs, asshole."

I stepped to his glass box, his transparent cell protecting him from attack. I smiled. Suddenly reaching through the slot in the glass like a snake striking a mouse I grabbed him by his shirt. I pulled him toward me violently, causing him to bang his head against the glass.

"This is my brother," I informed him, "he will be staying with me." He simply nodded in surrender and I released him. I slid some money through the slot, "his rent."

He accepted the bribe and turned back to watch his small television, rubbing his forehead. Looking back to Kendal, I went to the stairs, he running eagerly in front of me.

Back in the room, Kendal had been washed and fed and was sleeping against the heating vent. I was lying on the bed, conflicted. I had found Id combined with him to punish those boys. This was a promising sign that again we could become one. His unannounced appearance with the hotel manager, however, was less reassuring. He hadn't taken control, but the actions were his. I hadn't fought them. I couldn't have because I wasn't even aware of them at the time. I was concerned that he might take control completely again, banish me as before. As I lay there worrying, Kendal stirred. Cautiously he moved to the door, sniffing. Looking back to me, he slowly raised one paw off the ground. He could smell something from under the gap of the door.

Chapter Fifty-six

Henry and I arrived at the door to room five oh-three; the tarnished brass number testifying to the fact. There was a light on inside which spilled into the dark hallway where we stood. Henry nodded to me, leaning forward to insert the master key into the lock. He paused, and I jumped as the light under the door flickered. There was movement inside. I held up a hand for Henry to stop and he immediately obeyed, stepping back and pointing his gun at the closed door.

I counted to ten and there was no more movement. I beckoned him forward, miming that he should try again to insert the key. He slipped it into the lock a millimetre at a time until a soft click signalled that it was in. Placing his fingers around the key and gripping his gun tightly, he nodded to me. I banged three times on the door.

"Police! We're coming in!"

Henry turned the key and immediately put his shoulder to the door, smashing it open. Holding onto the handle he ran with it, opening it the full one hundred and eighty degrees, slamming it back against the wall. This left me with a fully empty doorway into which I stepped, gun forward, stance wide.

"Freeze! Don't move! Police!"

From the corner of my eye I saw Henry spin around and drop to one knee, his own gun extended.

"Everybody down! Police!" He yelled.

We both started sweeping the room for Id, fingers on triggers. Sweat dripped from my brow to the floor. I held the grip of my gun with both hands as I allowed my brain to take in the situation.

There was a bearded man on the bed.

I pointed my gun at his chest and tightened my finger.

"Freeze! Don't move, Id. Don't you dare move!"

I smiled, we had him. Henry's gun was pointed at the man on the bed too. "Stay right there, asshole!" He shouted, turning to me with a grin on his face. I smiled back, this was the moment, the moment of triumph. Seeing no movement, confident that between Henry and I we had him, I reached to my belt for my handcuffs. As I did so, I saw movement in the corner of the room. I slapped my hand back to the gun.

"Don't move! Henry, we've got another one!"

"One here too, Minty," he called back. My brain was finally catching up with my adrenalin fuelled body. This wasn't right. I looked closer at the man on the bed.

He was holding his arms out wide, surrendering. I looked harder. No, he was chained to the headboard. He was gagged, naked, spread out on the bed. I looked to my right; there was a woman in lingerie with a whip. Her hands were in the air and she was shaking like a leaf. I looked to my left, beyond Henry. There was another woman in lingerie, another whip. Beside her was a video camera on a tripod. Looking back to the man I could see red welts across his chest. I looked to a confused Henry, still kneeling on the floor.

"Okay, everyone stay where they are," I commanded in a more reasonable tone. I clicked the safety back on my gun and slid it into my hip holster. The slide of metal into plastic seemed to calm the situation in the room and the women lowered their hands a fraction. I was holding out my hand, palm out, signalling everyone to be still. Henry rose and holstered his gun. He moved to the chained man as I pushed the door closed with the heel of my foot.

"What the hell?" The man asked, voice shaking as Henry removed the gag.

"Sir, are you here by your own volition?" He asked him.

"What the...? Of course, are you stupid?"

"Just checking sir, just doing our jobs." Henry stated dryly, looking around him at the scene. He looked back at me and pulled a face, shrugging.

213

"Sorry to disturb you, sir. Ladies…" I said with as straight a face as I could manage and turned to open the door. I heard Henry scamper after me as we both left the room and the building in a giggling dash.

Chapter Fifty-seven

Kendal was staring at the door, expectantly. I waited, waited for movement, a knock, something. Nothing happened. Eventually I rose and opened it, looking outside. It was nothing; just a woman shuffling down the corridor to the elevator. Softly closing the door, I turned to Kendal.

"What is it, pup?" He looked at me and then sat down, staring. He was looking at me so intently, with such concentration, I wondered what it was he was seeing. "Can you see me? Can you see Id?"

This was an interesting development, I thought. I was asking a dog for answers now. I sat back down on the bed and placed my head in my hands. This was bad, I was losing touch with reality. I had known this for a long time now, but I had thought I could fix it, repair myself. This was a fantasy. I couldn't fix myself. Edward had fractured, he was broken, and I was a part of the damage. How could I possibly repair him?

"Hmmf," Kendal exclaimed in an exhalation of breath. He didn't agree.

"What, you think I can? You think I can find Edward?"

"Hmmf." Maybe he did think so. "Arf," he snorted through his nose, looking around.

"Edward's here?"

He looked at me, his deep brown eyes communicating the truth. Edward was indeed here. I was Edward.

"Is that it? Am I really Edward? I am still in control?"

He spun around, a single loop chasing his tail before sitting back down with a bang.

"You're right, of course. But I need to feel whole again. I need Id, I need to be Edward." I started to cry, a slow tear forming in my eye. Kendal came closer, nuzzling his nose into me. I reached around him, hugging him as I cried into his now soft fur, "oh Kendal, maybe I should just turn myself in. Get some real help." Still hugging me, pressing his nose to me. I heard him growl in disapproval. "No?"

"Grrrr."

I agreed with him, I was better off out of prison than in. I seemed to have control of Id now. He emerged when we were threatened but I still had power over him. There would be no more killing. He and I were still split but I was in control, just as I had been when we were Edward.

"You're right. Soon we'll be Edward, soon everything will be okay again."

Kendal responded by wagging his tail, thumping it against the wooden floor.

Chapter Fifty-eight

"What on earth?"

The shout echoed around the open-plan office of Vancouver Police Headquarters amidst a wave of laughter. Someone had just shown the RCMP agent in charge of the manhunt, a video of our raid on the hotel room. Sighing, closing my eyes, I pictured the scene again. Someone had already shown me the YouTube video with much delight. As Henry had smashed in the door, the woman operating the camera had spun it around in surprise, hiding behind it. There was a perfect high-definition recording of me standing in the doorway, shouting for the man in chains to freeze. To my right, obvious to the camera but not to my yelling figure, there was the woman in lingerie with the whip. If it were not me, I would had found it very funny. As it was I saw it for what it truly meant, the death of my career.

"Detective Montgomery Beech," Officer Butcher called out to me. He was the RCMP officer in charge now Elisha had left, and he didn't like me at all. "No, don't come here," he shouted across the room as I started to walk towards him. "Just leave! Just leave and never come back. You are off this case, go home to where you belong, Detective."

I could see that there would be no arguing by the look on his bright-red face. I turned, smiled apologetically to Henry, and walked away. A large round of applause and laughter accompanied my exit. A few people shouted, "freeze, don't move," mocking my voice. I left with head hung low, embarrassed and defeated.

*

Returning to my hotel room, I was surprised when the door swung open before I had chance to open it. It was Grace, but I had already instinctively reached for my gun before registering that it was her.

"I wanted to surprise you," she said as I regained my composure. "Looks like it worked," she nodded to my hand as I removed it from my gun. I smiled, kissing her on the lips.

"Sorry, weird night," I explained.

"I saw. You're an internet sensation..."

I groaned as she gave me an sympathetic smile and a pat on the back. "They kicked me off the hunt, so I have to leave. I was going to come home to you," I moaned to her.

She moved to the counter in my room and started making two cups of tea from the tiny kettle there. As she did, I studied her from behind. She had a short black woollen skirt on and a silk blouse. I hadn't noticed at first, but she was wearing high black heels. Very high in fact.

"Grace?" I asked suspiciously, "why are you wearing such high shoes?"

She turned to smile at me, then resumed making the tea. "It doesn't matter now, Minty." She kicked off her shoes and stepped down from them. Her feet on the floor were clad, I noticed, in black hose. Around the toes they were thicker in a triangle. I recognised those black clad toes.

"You're wearing stockings, aren't you?" She didn't turn but I could feel her smile somehow by inspecting the back of her head. "I'm sorry, Grace. Really I am, I ruined your surprise by trying to shoot you."

"Don't worry, seriously. Let's have a cup of tea and you can tell me all about it."

I told her the whole sorry story. My gradual decline to the back of the task-force. My attempt to find Id with Henry and the subsequent ill-advised raid. I was ashamed of my naivety, and embarrassed. I was annoyed that my career was over. She was sympathetic but didn't disagree. It certainly looked bad and we hugged for a long time, sitting on the single bed of my compact hotel room. Finally, lying back on the bed, she showed me the surprise she had bought for me. She looked amazing and it did lift my spirits. Looking at her, however, I couldn't help but think of the similarly clad women in the hotel room the night before. In the end, I removed my shirt and we lay hugging on the bed. Holding her tight, I was too worried about my future to appreciate her as I should have.

They wouldn't fire me. I hadn't actually done anything too wrong, just embarrassing. The raid on the hotel room was legal and justified given the information provided by the Manager. I had even informed the RCMP lead that we were going and the video actually showed that we followed correct procedure in the event. There would be some comments about how I hadn't noticed the barely clothed woman standing right next to me, perhaps some retraining about sweeping the room and avoiding tunnel vision. What was certain, however, was that from now on I would be back on the rubbish cases again. Seeming to sense my thoughts, Grace spoke up.

"Minty, you're a good detective. You fought your way on to a big case once, you'll do it again."

"I'm not sure I can do another two years," I was being petulant and I knew it. I didn't care though. "All that rubbish again, being 'Minty-fresh' again. I might just quit."

"You aren't going to quit," she said.

"What do you know? You don't understand." I raised my voice; I wasn't angry at her, just angry.

"Don't shout at me."

"Why not, you aren't helping any. This was my case, not yours. You're fine, what do you know?"

"What do I know? I understand more than you!" I went to hold her, to hug, but I had made her angry now and she pulled away. "I've been listening to you complain for two years now. Why can't I do this? Why can't I do that? All the while I have been standing around patiently, a second-class citizen. Just a woman, how could I understand? Not just a woman, but only a CSI too. Nothing to anyone..."

"I didn't mean that. I never said that."

"No, you didn't have to. Detectives, you're all the same. You all think you do it all. Do you know how many cases I've solved?"

"Well, I..."

"Hundreds, that's how many. And who says, 'thank you', who says, 'well done'? No one, that's who. You included!" She was up from the bed now, dressing angrily. "Screw you, Detective. I came here for you, like I always do. I should have listened to myself. I told myself over and over, don't date a detective. Yet I did. Like an idiot, I did. I should have listened."

"Please, Grace. Don't go. We can sort this out. I didn't mean--"

"I know that. I am leaving though..." she opened the door, case in hand, tottering on her heels. "You know what a real detective would do now?"

"No, what?" I asked quietly, afraid of her response.

"Solve the case, stupid!"

Chapter Fifty-nine

I was happy again, my bout of depression banished by the happy company of Kendal at my side. Having ridden out on the bus, we were walking through a large park by the University. Kendal refused to run, electing to permanently stay beside me with his tail periodically slapping my leg. Knowing that he needed to run, I searched my mind for a memory of that feeling. Concentrating on the memory of rushing through trees from Edward's past, I happened across Id. He easily flowed into me and we quickened our pace. We jumped from the path and into the trees, bounding across the large roots of the redwoods.

Kendal ran with us as we flowed through the landscape. We wove around trees, our arm wrapping around them, swinging us around. Kendal jumped and scampered beside us, swapping sides, coming close but never in the way. He yipped and barked in excitement as we began to chase each other. He would dart ahead of us and we would run after him, increasing our speed until within touching distance of his tail. Then with a spin, Kendal would flip the chase and run after us as we darted in a different direction. Id and I rolled on the soft ground, bouncing into a low crouch as Kendal intercepted us. We wrapped him in a hug and we all rolled around together. Three best friends playing in the woods; I laughed, Id whooped and shouted, Kendal barked.

Eventually we came to a small pond and paused our playtime. Kendal raised his paw; he had smelled something on the other side of the lake and I lay on the floor, silent. Id was gone. Just as he had arrived to play, as things got serious, he was once more absent.

"What is it, Kendal?"

He sniffed, pointing his nose across the lake. I crept forward on my belly, staring hard at the point he was signalling towards. I saw the ferns move. Listening hard, I thought I heard men talking. I rose to my feet, crouching low, and quietly moved around the pond to the source of the commotion. It was louder now, the movement more violent and I could hear the voice of a man.

"Lie still or I'll cut you."

In response, I heard a woman make a whimpering noise. I leapt into action; I wasn't going to wait as Id had done before. Without thinking, I was on top of the man. Kendal was with me, behind me, barking and growling. The man had his jeans around his ankles which hobbled him as I held him tightly around his neck. I heard a noise and saw his knife fall to the ground. He grabbed my wrists and tried to pull me from him. He failed to do so but his actions scratched my hands with his nails and the pain made me release him.

I stood before him as he quickly recovered from my initial attack. He pulled up his jeans and I heard the woman move away from us into the undergrowth. Soon we could hear her feet making hollow sounds on the soft ground as she ran away.

"You'll pay for that," he threatened me.

I turned to depart, gesturing for Kendal to follow. But something stopped me.

I turn to face him. My hand in my coat pocket. "You chose this place poorly," I explain to the man, "for you chose a place in which a predator resides."

"Screw you, buddy. You've got no idea. D'you wanna to get cut?"

Seeing his knife on the ground, he retrieves it.

"You know not what you invoke, pretender."

He darts at me with knife extended, arm outstretched. I grab him by the elbow and roll into his body. My back slams against him and I allow the back of my head to smack his nose. I am holding his arm across me as I force him to embrace me from behind. He attempts to bring the knife in, toward my throat. I duck down and under his arm, twisting it to his side. Placing my hand in the crook of his elbow I bend his arm and force him to stab himself in the kidney.

"I warned you. You confronted a real animal and you are defeated. It is the way of nature." He is on the floor, making pathetic sounds. I pull my knife from my pocket. "I wonder. Do you know what your insides look like?" I ask him, rhetorically.

Two quick cuts later and I am reaching inside of him, I pull something out. It is dark purple, filled with something soft.

"What is this, do you think?" I ask, showing it to him. "It's attached to this stuff." I explain as I pull a length of spongy pipe from his open belly. "I mean, all these bags and pipes inside of us. It's quite interesting really."

He is just making noises now, spittle bubbling from his lips.

"Pull yourself together. I left the knife in, you aren't even losing much blood." He looks down at the knife in his side; disappointingly he starts to cry. "Come now, you are a man, are you not? Pull it out. Stab me with it. Defeat me."

Pulling something else from him, I show it to him squishing it between my fingers. "I tell you what, if you can tell me what this is, I'll stop."

I smile, laughing, squeezing the soft sack still attached to him via a tightly pulled mass of fibrous material. He looks at me grinning back at him. I watch as his eyelids flutter and his eyes roll up into his head into unconsciousness. Dropping the offending item back into him, I arch my back. Staring into the canopy of trees, I scream my name.

Chapter Sixty

"Who are you again?" She asked me for the fifth time. The drugs the nurse had given her were affecting her ability to concentrate.

"Police, miss." I said with confidence. True but untrue, I thought. Knowing I had no right to be questioning her, I repeated my question, "you said in your report that your rescuer shouted out, 'Id'?"

"Did I?" She mumbled.

"Yes miss, please. Try to remember. It's important."

"Montgomery." A voice I recognised called me from the door.

"Hello, Elisha," I replied without turning around.

"Out.' A simple command, one word, lots of meaning. I trudged out of the room as the young lady fell asleep again. "She has nothing to tell us, Minty." Elisha informed me as she marched me out of the hospital. By the time we were both in her car I had learned that Id had saved her. They knew this because he had used his knife to cut open her attacker. Miraculously the man was alive; the surgeons had put everything back inside and stitched him up. There was still the risk of blood poisoning, but they had high hopes that he would survive.

"Nice that he'll live to go to prison for attempted rape," Elisha commented as she started her car and pulled away from the hospital. "I was told that you were no longer working this case, Minty."

"I know, I was supposed to be going home but then I heard about this. I thought I could help," I said eagerly.

"Help how? Raid some more porn sets?" She looked across at me, smiling. "You might like to know that I charged the man and women you raided."

"Really?" I asked her, surprised.

"Yes. Of course. Didn't it occur to you that they might be committing a crime? The production of pornographic materials requires a licence. Production of sadomasochistic acts, more so."

"Oh, yeah," I remembered.

"If you'd just arrested them there and then, the video would have been evidence, and no one would have known or cared about your little raid," she added.

"Right, sorry," I apologised, embarrassed again at my stupidity.

"Look, I am going to reinstate you, Butcher shouldn't have dismissed you for just being stupid. He was covering his ass mostly. Just try to use your brain next time, yeah?"

"Sure, yes. I hope there won't be a next time."

"Me too, but knowing you, I feel like there will be. The unwritten rule of police work is..." she waited for dramatic effect and I knew not to respond. "Cover your own ass." I smiled as she added, "and don't you forget it."

As we arrived back at the Station, Elisha jumped to rallying the troops. The team had dramatically swollen again to our previous size now there was another lead. We had a new augmented image of Id based on the witness' description; it was still Edward but adjusted to include a newly grown, bushy red beard. Looking at it, I could see why we hadn't found him. He looked like a completely different person, damaged and frail, a true vagrant.

"This is what Id looks like now, people. We have new cards, one side with beard and one side without. We're hitting the hotels, hostels, anywhere he could be. This is not for the media, this is for us. We don't want him running again, we want to find him. Us, not the public, so show these around but do not hand them out, understood?"

*

Henry and I returned to trawling though the transient hotels we had become so familiar with. We *would* find Id, I knew it.

This time, we would take him.

Chapter Sixty-one

"Kendal, please help me." I implored to his brown eyes. We were back in our room and I was conflicted about how I had saved the woman in the woods. True I had helped her, but in letting Id cut her attacker open and show him his organs, I knew I had done wrong, we had done wrong. It felt like the actions of an evil maniac. "I don't want to be evil, I don't want to be an animal."

"What do you mean? We are all animals."

I looked to him, looked at Kendal. Had he spoken or was someone else near? I looked around the room, he and I were alone.

"Yes, I am talking to you, Ego. Please don't lose it." His tongue lolled out and he tilted his head inquisitively.

"So I'm talking to a dog now."

"You did name me, Ego. Please, my name is Kendal now."

I realised, that as he 'spoke', his mouth didn't move. I was talking to him, but in reality, I knew I was hearing voices. Somehow it worried me less than thinking that he was actually speaking. Still, I was interested that his name was Kendal *now*; I wondered what it had been. "Sorry, you had a name before?" I asked him.

"Yes, I had a name before. The man who gave me it was not very nice, so I would rather leave it behind. I prefer to be Kendal; I prefer you."

"Thank you." I said, appreciating the compliment.

"You're welcome. Why are you afraid to be an animal? I'm an animal."

"But you're good, you don't kill," I pointed out.

"I have killed, many mice, rats, a shrew one time. I am a dog, you know."

"But never another dog."

"No, of course not. I'm a dog, not a human. But humans kill humans, don't they?"

"Yes they do, but that's either war, or it's wrong."

"Hmmf." He snorted, which in both dog and human terms seemed to sum up his scathing opinion of people killing people. "Personally, I don't see your problem. I like you. I like Id. I like you both when you are together or apart. That woman needed help; Id is better at that, so he did it."

"But to kill is bad, Kendal."

"Bad, good. I don't understand you humans. Why can't you just do what is right?"

"Right?"

"Yes, right. You are an animal, as am I. You are civilised, as am I. I don't kill unless I need to eat. That's what I have to do. Since you are feeding me, I don't kill. Id hurt that man, but that man needed hurting. It's wrong to attack the weak for fun, isn't it?"

"It is…" I conceded reluctantly. Kendal just looked at me, letting his argument settle in my mind. Finally, I reached the conclusion that he had a point. We all have an animal inside us. My relationship with mine is more complicated than others but I was as human, and as whole, as anyone else.

"Was it my fault, do you think?" I asked Kendal who responded with a tilt of his head. "The fracture of Edward. I think I did it," I elaborated.

Kendal didn't answer so I just lay back. Edward had locked his id away; all of his life he had given me the power. I had listened to the superego while completely suppressing Id, caging and trapping him. I gave him nothing with which he could sustain himself. Finally, something had snapped inside of Edward; he released Id and gave him free reign. Who can blame the animal for his reaction? Having been caged and mistreated his entire existence, Id had reacted as any animal would; with rage.

Once free, Id had rampaged against his oppressor. However, he seemed to be more tame now. Had he exorcised his need for violence, for control? Was he hiding in order to be assimilated back into Edward? Perhaps Id was no longer the problem, perhaps it was me who was fighting the integration.

"Kendal, what should I do?" I asked the slow breathing form, lying in front of the heating vent.

"Let your Id out, Ego. Let it out for a run, let it play."

Lying back down to sleep, I decided that I would consider his sage words.

Chapter Sixty-two

I pulled a face as I sipped the last cold dregs of coffee from the cardboard cup I had been nursing. Between coffee and scanning the faces of transients in the street, I was still apologising to Henry about our ill-fated raid.

"Don't worry about it, I didn't feature too much in the video anyway," he pointed out.

"Yeah, I was the real star of that one, wasn't I."

"I thought it was cool though, you standing in the doorway like that, very Dirty Harry." He laughed, pulling the car to the curb in front of another hotel. I laughed too, enjoying the rapport we had built over our time together.

"Right then, Detective Garibaldi. Shall we see if there's a serial killer in?"

"By all means, Detective Beech." He said with a slight bow from the waist, leading me up the steps to the hotel. This one didn't have a reception but the first door beyond the steps was signed 'supervisor', so we knocked on it. We were met by a very large man in a stained white vest and tight shorts. I took a step back at the sight, gathering myself for a second. Henry, seemingly unfazed, stepped forward.

"Evening sir, could you please look at this picture and tell us if you have any tenants resembling this man?"

He took the picture and studied it intently as I studied him. He was as wide as he was tall and the flesh on display rolled down him in a half-dozen folds. There was a large, unidentifiable stain on the strings of his vest. He handed the card back to Henry and his chest swayed with the movement.

"Got enough of a look?" He barked at me as I continued to stare. I spluttered something, but he quickly interrupted me, "haven't seen him, but feel free to take a look." He gestured at the stairs and slammed the door closed on us.

"Smooth, Minty. Upset by the naked male form?" Henry asked, grinning.

"Specimens like that… honestly, yes," I joked with a smile.

"Come on, let's do the door-to-door, shall we?"

I followed him up the stairs, continuing our ritual of taking the picture to each door in the building, asking the same questions to everyone who answered. It was monotonous work, but vital. We needed to ask everyone in order to find that one person who knew something. It was exactly the kind of work that caught a fugitive and we needed to catch this one.

"Married then, Minty?"

"No, but I have a girlfriend," then, thinking about it, I added, "I hope."

"Cool, police?"

"No, CSI. She's called Grace."

"Pretty?"

We asked our questions of an elderly man who walked to the door with an oxygen bottle in tow, I took the enforced pause in the conversation to consider his question.

"I think so. I think she's beautiful."

At the next apartment there was a delay trying to get someone to answer their door. Henry got nervous, fingering his gun, anticipating the appearance of Id. I must admit I did too as we waited, hearing the movements from within. Eventually someone did arrive, drug addled and barely conscious. We asked our questions but, as expected, no information was forthcoming.

"We had a fight, actually. She was here, but she left," I opened up to Henry.

"Sorry to hear that," he said sympathetically.

"Yeah, it was my fault. I've been too focussed on work."

"Tell me about it, I haven't had a date in almost a year."

As he said it, an attractive young lady answered the door. She wasn't wearing very much and upon seeing us and registering our badges, quickly pulled her robe closed. Apologising, she said she had been expecting someone else. She was the last tenant so we made for the stairs.

"Just my luck." Henry commented. "I meet the woman of my dreams and she's waiting for someone else."

I laughed with the release of tension and slapped him on his back. "Just you wait, Henry. We'll find you another one in an even worse part of town. How's about that?"

"Yeah, of course. Plenty more fish in the sea, or looking at her, prostitutes on skid-row."

We left the building happy, laughing despite the grim monotony of our task. It was either laugh or cry, I lamented as Henry consulted the map to find the next building on our list.

Chapter Sixty-three

Kendal's argument had swayed me. It hadn't taken much, I knew. The fear of prison so horrified me, I had quickly decided not to hand myself in. But I had done something very wrong and could not escape that. I looked at myself in the small grimy mirror in the corner of my room. Life had taken a distinct downturn. I was hiding in a hovel; filthy, a murderer. Hearing a sniff behind me, a small smile started to form; maybe it wasn't all bad. Slapping my hands against the wall, I made a decision. I wouldn't turn myself in; I couldn't face prison, but I could repair myself. Starting now, there would be no more acts of violence. Resolution made, I looked again in the mirror and felt an overwhelming need to cleanse my appearance and physically wash the evil from me.

The communal bathroom in my accommodation would not do, so I quickly made my way to Ben's restaurant instead. It was still open; he was hosting a private party that night and hadn't required my skills. After a short detour to the adjacent shop to buy shaving cream, shampoo and a razor, I crept into Ben's kitchen. Stripping, I used the powerful spray that hung from a high pipe to hose myself. The water stung, sluicing grime from my body into the floor drain. I turned it to my face and the heat and steam boiled at my beard. Using the reflection in the dishwasher, I shaved my face and washed my hair. Blasting my body again, I let the needles of water refresh me.

I am renewed. I am refreshed. I see myself standing tall, naked and powerful. I walk to the lockers where my fellow kitchen workers keep their belongings. None are locked, and I take my time to explore my options. I hear movement. I hear footsteps. Soft, light and gentle, they slap the ground on their approach but I do not turn. Two more steps. They are the padded footfalls of a small person, a woman. It is Chenguang, I confirm, as I glimpse her reflection in a mirror mounted on the inside of an open locker door.

"Good evening, Chen," I say without turning. She gasps, caught in the locker room with a naked man. I turn to face her, proudly showing myself to her.

"You have shaved, Mr Sigmund."

I smile at her use of Ego's pseudonym, "call me Id, please Chen."

Chen is a waitress in the restaurant and also Ben's niece. I have looked at her often, she is small and slight. She is a woman, but young and naive. She would be delightful to bed, I think.

"Yes, Id, okay," she stammers, "you're getting dressed?"

"Yes, Chen. I will... Do you like?" I ask her, gesturing to my erect form.

"I, I..."

"It's alright, I know that you do."

I slide across the floor in bare feet. I arrive at her with one fluid movement, wrapping one arm around her waist. She gasps, and I lift her from the floor with one arm, my other hand caressing the back of her neck. I pull her face to mine, breathing in a long drag of air through my nose.

"I smell you Chenguang. Tell me, what does it mean, your name?"

"It means 'morning glory', Mr Id."

"And are you?"

"What?"

"Glorious in the morning, Chenguang." I breathe her in again. "Do not answer that. I think I would like to find out myself."

She moves to speak, to complain no doubt.

"Do not deny it. I can smell you, I can smell your need. My naked body has aroused you. You might well be glorious in the morning but in the night, I will fulfil your need."

I put her down and return to the locker. She remains where I placed her, still as a statue, watching me dress. Turning I see that Kendal too is waiting for me.

"Come," I command both of them, "let us retire."

I take her hand and lead her to my accommodation. Kendal dutifully follows suit, walking by my side.

Chapter Sixty-four

She stands before me, her little body wrapped in a red patterned dress. A gold thread wraps around her in an asymmetric path; suggesting dragons and demons. I consider her as she stands before me. Her short black hair is pinned up with a large clip, face unadorned except for two swipes of red across her eyelids. Kendal has taken up his usual place on the heater and fallen asleep. For a moment, I marvel at how he can be so disinterested in this delicate creature. I turn my attentions back to her. She is standing, uncertain, close to the door, contemplating retreat. I remove my clothes under her gaze.

"It's okay to look," I tell her, as her eyes fall to the ground. She looks up and I smile. She is interested in the man that I am. "You want this. You want me to use you, to take you." Detecting fear in her, I add, "don't worry, Chen. You will not hurt. You will achieve the same level of pleasure as I."

I close my eyes and touch myself. She moves on her small feet, rising on her toes. Opening my eyes, I see her watching my actions. She licks her lips, replacing the dryness her breathing is causing.

"Remove your clothes please, Chen." I ask, sitting down on the end of the bed. The door is behind her, locked but not chained. I have left her the opportunity to escape. She does not take it.

"Chen. Your shoes."

She raises her heels and slides the thin slippers from her feet, revealing red painted toenails.

"Now your trousers."

She pauses a second. Placing her hands under her dress, she unfastens a clasp.

"Along with your underwear."

There is no pause this time as she pushes her underwear and trousers down her short legs. She steps from the gathered pile and kicks it away.

Shaking with anticipation, she stands before me wearing only the dress.

"Buttons."

She releases the large black buttons, slowly. She opens it to me. She is unclothed under the final garment and her body is revealed to me in its entirety. I take a moment to admire her as, without further command, she removes the dress and drops it to the floor.

She steps towards me, releasing her hair from its clip as she does so. It falls into straight lines ending just above her shoulders. Her body is tiny, petite, delicate. But the look in her eyes is not so delicate. It is filled with need. I will fulfil it tonight; I will complete her need as I complete my own. She climbs on to me, wraps her legs around me and embraces me. I fall back to the bed taking her down with me.

She whispers my name.

Chapter Sixty-five

"Hotel eighty-four," Henry said as we climbed from his car.

"What?"

"This is the eighty-fourth visit we've made in this man-hunt."

I thought about that for a second, "there can't be eighty-four hotels."

"No, but we've made eighty-four visits. Well, we will have once we do this one."

"Eighty-four's the charm?"

"Let's hope so, I'm getting really tired of this. This is what I got out of uniform to avoid."

I had to agree with him, it was both frustrating and boring. At the same time, it was occasionally terrifying, waiting for someone to come to the door, knowing that they could well be a dangerous killer.

"D'you want to do the landlord this time?" I asked him.

"Sure, why not? Variety is the spice of life." He replied with more energy in his voice and a forced spring in his step. We pushed the door and stepped into the familiar lobby. At the landlord's booth, there was a young man instead of the manager we had interviewed the last time we were here.

"You seen this guy?" Henry asked hurriedly, eager to get the visit over with and go home for the night.

"Sure, room three-thirty."

Henry looked at me and I at him. Our mouths open.

"This man? This man here?" Henry repeated, pointing to the image.

"Sure, Sigmund I think he calls himself."

Henry retreated from the booth, back to the entrance. His phone was out and he was calling in the task-force, requesting armed response and breaching teams.

"Describe him to me," I commanded the young man. Despite his growing anxiety he proceeded to describe Edward Gooch perfectly. Weight, height, hair colour, everything matched. I quickly asked if he was currently in and he added the information I did not want to hear.

"Sure, he went up with some hot young Chinese girl a few hours ago."

I did another double-take. There was a girl in his room with him. This was not good.

"Henry!" I called. He ran back to me, shoving his phone back into his pocket and taking out his gun.

"Backup will be here in ten minutes." He informed me breathlessly.

"I don't think we can wait." He looked to me with fear in his eyes. "Sorry, Henry. There's a girl with him. I don't think we should wait."

"They'll only be ten minutes."

"Ten minutes with Id?" I asked.

He furrowed his brow, concentrating. He looked to the door, he looked at his watch, he looked to the stairs. "You think?"

"I think..."

"Okay, then. Let's do it." He simply stated, darting to the stairs.

"Is this the only way up or down?" I demanded of the young man in the glass booth.

"Yeah, fire-escape doesn't run to third. Straight up the stairs, turn left, four doors down on the left."

"You stay there. When the rest of the police arrive, send them up. Tell them two officers already went up. Understand?"

He nodded confidently, and I nodded to Henry. We quickly ran up the stairs. Running to our fate, running to room three, three, zero.

Chapter Sixty-six

I woke up with the feeling of naked flesh against my own. Opening my eyes, I looked down. There was a small Asian girl lying across me. Her head was on my chest, arm over my shoulder. Her bare breast rested against my ribs and one leg was bent, straddling my hip. I felt the roughness of her pubic hair against my thigh. I was soft but there was moisture there, a gentle numbness. Panic overcame me; she was tiny. Had I bedded a child? I looked down and she moved slightly, dragging her short black hair from her face. I sighed, relieved. Instantly I recognised her as a waitress from the restaurant.

It was Chenguang Lin, Ben's niece. She was at least twenty, I knew, so I relaxed once more. A pang of guilt, however, caused my stomach to squirm. Taking advantage of his niece was not the best way to return the many favours Ben had bestowed upon me. However, from her position, it seemed clear that whatever had transpired had been pleasurable.

I heard Kendal move, repositioning himself under the grate. "Kendal?" I asked, "was I gentle with her? Did Id mistreat her?"

He just snorted derisively and I understood. Id would not have hurt her, and if he had started, Kendal would not have allowed it. I smiled, the memory of last night finally arriving in my mind. Our lovemaking had been sweet and tender. Suddenly, accompanying the memory, the feel of her skin against mine invoked a wave of emotional and physical pleasure. This was Id, I understood. This was emotion I was feeling. It was raw, powerful and majestic.

With the wave of emotion, instantly I understood his desires. Their purity could not be reasoned or understood, only felt. Power, love, and warmth flowed within me. It was beauty. I felt her stir as she started kissing my chest, and the feeling intensified. I, Ego, had to have this woman. I pulled her further onto me and kissed her hard on the mouth. She moved slowly, rubbing her hands on my chest. The top of her head only came to my chin as her smooth body rubbed against me. I wrapped my arms around her, squeezing her tightly.

I swam in the physical and emotional waters that flooded through me. As her body wrapped around mine so did the emotions she was generating. We lay there a time, both of us enjoying the feelings of warmth and comfort our connection had created. I tried to hold on to the pleasure, but eventually it slipped from my body and mind. I left her there, however, enjoying the contact. I, Ego, was enjoying feeling. It was truly awesome in its most literal sense and a tear traced a path down my cheek at the realisation.

Eventually she rose, sliding from the bed. I sat up, so I could watch her in the light that spilled through the cheap curtains at the window behind us. Moving to the bowl of water I kept in the corner, she collected up the towel there. Wetting it, she began to wash herself as she turned to face me. As she started to wipe her belly, an older memory came to the fore of my mind.

I remembered me, cutting flesh from a figure in an alleyway. How could my love of Chen come from the same place? Was it yin, yang; two sides of the same coin? Pain and pleasure the same thing, just opposite physical actions?

"No, it is not." That was Kendal, informing me of my error with a snort. He was right, of course; violence and sex are different. They are both intense and emotional, but opposite. One fills us with fear and anticipation, the other tingles with passionate love.

"Someone could mistake one for the other," I told Kendal, now sitting beside me. He barked in agreement and understanding. Someone else could, but we did not. We saw them as different, for we had fully explored them. Id understood what Edward had not. Edward had suppressed his sexual desires. He had feared them.

"I think I finally understand," I informed Kendal, who wagged his tail at my realisation.

Not all sexual urges have to be fulfilled. Thought is not action; immoral action remains the thing to suppress, not feeling. Feeling and thought can never be morally wrong, so we need not fear them.

That was the key to the split of Edward. He had feared the consequences of releasing his id. He had suppressed it, not understanding it. He believed that what he felt, what he desired, would lead to immoral acts. He underestimated the power of his ego. For I, Ego, could have easily controlled Id, prior to our split.

Jumping from the bed with a cry, I leaped to my feet at the

realisation. Chenguang was fully dressed and looking at me in confusion.

"Id... I should go now... my uncle will wonder about me."

"Of course, Chen."

I kissed her on the forehead, thanking her for the evening. Standing on the tips of her toes she stretched up to kiss me on the lips as I bent down to reciprocate. Slipping my arms around her tiny waist I lifted her from the floor and we kissed deeply and passionately.

"Thank you, Id."

I considered her thanks, realising that it was I who should thank her; she had turned on the light, the dawn had risen.

"Thank you, Chen, but I am remade. For my name is Ed."

Chapter Sixty-seven

Henry and I had reached the door to room three-thirty. We were stood each side, preparing to breech when a small Asian girl opened it. Standing before us, she slowly opened her mouth, preparing to scream. I saw Id behind her, naked. The girl quickly found her voice, her piercing wail hurting my ears. I wrapped my arm around her and pulled her toward me. Henry slipped though the gap, his gun pointing up in the safe position as he entered. Id instantly lunged forward as Henry tried to bring his gun to bear.

In an instant Id is here, taking control. I reach the first man in the doorway. Concentrating on his weapon he leaves no space in his mind to defend himself. I ignore the gun; it is useless in such tight confines. I clench my fist and bring it down hard on the top of his skull. Detective Beech is still fumbling with Chenguang, he is no immediate threat. I take his colleague's gun from him. He is dazed and confused from my first strike and I smile. I do not shoot, he will not die today. Instead I raise the gun high and bring it down hard on his temple.

Henry went down, the second blow to his head with his own gun knocking him cold. Finally, I managed to extract myself from the girl by unceremoniously dropping her. I stepped back and raised my gun. I had finally done it. For the first time, I had a loaded weapon pointing at his chest. "Id, I have you. Stand still!" I commanded. Taking a breath, I looked at him more closely; he seemed different to the last time I had seen him. His nudity was putting me off; he was aroused and it was very unsettling.

"Minty, isn't it? Minty, shall we withdraw to my room. My nudity seems inappropriate in such a public setting."

Id gestured to unseen people moving in the corridor, but I did not waiver from our eye contact, my gun tracking him. I could hear doors banging behind me, the footsteps of people leaving the building. He stepped backwards. "Stay still, Id!" I commanded, but he stepped back again anyway. I shuffled forward, not letting my gun waiver from his centre-mass. Suddenly I felt something on my leg. An intense pain; it was the girl, I realised too late.

I back up and the policeman predictably follows. His focus is on me. His tunnel vision causes him to forget Chenguang on the floor between us. Snake-like she strikes, gripping his sensitive area with the fangs of her sharpened nails. His eyes close and I lunge forwards. With fluid motion, I place my hand on top of his gun and, sliding back the mechanism, render it useless. My other hand grabs at the badge hanging from his neck and pulls him into the room. As I throw him past me, I hear Chen flee. Closing the door with my foot, I release the clip of bullets from his gun and let it clatter to the floor. Next, I slide the top back completely and let the bullet in the chamber fly out. Its metal shine glints in the light from the street.

Id disarmed me with ease; the round I had chambered flew through the air; it was now rolling around in a circle on the floor between us. "Id…" I said, desperately thinking how best to delay him until backup arrived.

"My name is Ed, Minty. You know that," he said to me. That was the difference. That was the change. It was in his eyes, he was Edward again, not Id. My heart lifted as I realised I had a chance. Edward was not a cold-blooded murderer, he was a man. He could be reasoned with.

I see the policeman's expression change. He has hope, he thinks he can negotiate. He looks to his watch; a subtle movement of his head that he does not complete and I realise that there are more police coming. "You found me, Detective. But I am more than just Id now, I am three again; Id, Ego and once more Ed. My id and ego are pure now, deconflicted. As you can see from your predicament, I can be as effective as Id was alone. But I am everything now. You might call yourself hunter, hunter of me. But I am the hunter of hunters, you cannot defeat me."

My heart deflated again. This was Edward, I could see that, but I could also see Id. He was as dangerous in this state as before, maybe more so. While I was glad for the time it had taken him to dress, it worried me that I could see that he was preparing to leave. I had to delay him and keep him here. "Edward, it's over. The RCMP are downstairs, let's just end this. Come with me peacefully."

I smile, he is lying, it is so clear to my eyes it is almost insulting. I need to leave but not before I defeat him and prevent him from tracking me down again.

Id lunged at me, arms outstretched. I managed to knock one of his arms away with both of my forearms but the other smashed against the side of my head. Failing to recover, I wobbled to one side as a fist connected with my abdomen, sending a wave of nausea through me.

Detective Beech is against the wall, his leg presented to me is too tempting a target to ignore. I smash my foot down on his knee with a loud crack. He slides to the ground, screaming, clutching at his leg. I take his compliant wrist and hold his arm out, quickly breaking his arm to match his smashed knee. Stepping away from him, I check his position on the floor. His right leg and left arm lie in painful shapes, broken. His hunting days are over.

Kendal barks; he hears people coming. "I must leave you now." I inform Detective Beech as he starts to fall into unconsciousness. "You will not see me again, you will not find me. Ed is in control now. We listen to Ego now, so we will no longer kill. We will defend ourselves, however, if attacked. My advice to you Detective is to go home. See your woman, show her your id, let it out to play. She will like it, I assure you."

Chapter Sixty-eight

We ran, we do not recall for how long but soon we were far from the places we knew.

I needed to flee.

I needed to fight.

I needed to turn myself in.

The fractured nature of my mind was hindering our escape. Finally, reluctantly, Id retired to sleep, resting in an emotional puddle of our psyche. Ego went willingly, accepting that I, Ed was more entitled to our body. Upon their departure from my mind I fell to the floor in confusion, landing on one knee splashing into a pool of cold water. I coughed, hacked at a tickle in my throat, spitting it from me. I had escaped, temporarily free of the police, but now I was lost and alone.

Hearing a whine behind me, I turned to look into the soft brown eyes of Kendal. I was not alone, I had Kendal and together we would escape. Looking up, I could see that I had come to rest in front of a small wooden house. It was covered with dirt and boarded up. Taking the sale sign from the yard, I used it to lever away a board, which, already curling with age, quickly acquiesced to my efforts. Climbing through the opening, I surveyed the inside of the house. It was rotten; I could smell the damp permeating every surface and item of furniture. I stepped forward and one foot went through the floor. Extracting it with a grunt, I saw Kendal leap through the entrance I had made and dart past me. His agile paws scratched and tapped on the wooden flooring as he scampered through the house.

I curled up in a corner, tired. Kendal returned and gently nuzzled into me. Soon we fell asleep.

*

When I awoke I was determined to leave this place. I would leave the city, get away. I was in danger. I would escape the curse of people, take Kendal and go to the woods, for there was peace. Id was awake within me and he agreed that we should leave, he wanted to take, to take what we needed. One last time, I agreed. Leaving the rotten house behind, leaving the rotting human race behind, I climbed out of the window. I walked to the first house that had a car outside and knocked loudly on the door.

There was no one home so we broke down the door. The keys to the car were in a bowl just inside. Soon we were driving; Ego guided us to the port of Vancouver where we took a ferry to Vancouver Island and started heading north. It was a long journey, risky in a stolen car. However, we managed to reach the coast without incident and, finding an isolated stretch, disposed of the car in the sea. We walked a short distance until we came across a small metal flat-bottomed boat. We hastily pushed it down to the shoreline and climbed in. Pointing out to sea, I twisted the throttle and powered the little craft away from land as fast as it could manage. Finally, I was away from people, finally I had left civilisation behind.

We were soon navigating the wide waters and small islands off the west coast of British Columbia, alone and free. Kendal sat proudly at the prow, sniffing all the exciting scents as the little motor at the back powered us along. He let out a bark as a dark form slowly emerged from the water. With delight, I realised that it was a humpback whale surfacing. Back down it went after it blasted a puff of air and water high above us. It came back up twice more, the final time raising its tail in salute to my escape. Taking the appearance of the whale as a sign, I turned the little boat to match its course.

We followed it for a while, with the whale appearing periodically to blast us with air before diving back down. After several miles, the fuel in the small engine was almost depleted and it started to cough. Kendal turned back to me and let out a single bark. It was his first sound since sighting the whale. He lifted one paw and pointed with his nose to an island just off to our right. I slewed the boat over and spent the last of the fuel as we beached on a small pebble beach.

Shakily climbing from the small craft, I sat on the beach just above the waterline. Kendal had departed as soon as we had arrived, away to sniff and explore the island. I sat in silence, listening for the sounds of human occupation. I heard nothing, but it felt like a large island and I could not be sure. I had been there, silently waiting, for two hours when Kendal returned. Walking around in two tight circles he settled on my feet. He was satisfied, this was our home. Gently manoeuvring myself free, I left him there to rest as I returned to the boat. I carefully removed the motor and, carrying it into the woods, dug a hole in the soft ground and buried it.

Moving back to the metal boat, lightened significantly now, I dragged it up the beach. I heaved it over a log at the high watermark and pulled it deeper, its tin bottom scraping against the undergrowth. Tilting it sideways to get it between trees, I heaved it over logs and ancient stumps. Eventually I collapsed to the ground over a hundred metres from the sea. There I lay it to rest behind a large fallen log. Ripping ferns from the ground and snapping branches from the trees, I proceeded to cover it. Then, collecting rocks from the beach and driftwood from the sea, bit by bit I filled the boat with rubble and covered it with anything I could find. Finally, I returned to the beach and brushed away the evidence of my work. I looked to Kendal who breathed out a snort of satisfaction.

We circumnavigated the island shore. As we came back to the point of our arrival I was pleased to note that no manmade structures existed anywhere. There was no sign of any dock past or present; there were no people here. The route had taken what remained of the day from us and I estimated the island to have a circumference of twenty miles. Scratching numbers in the dirt, I calculated that it was approximately six miles across and had an area in excess of thirty square miles. Plenty for a man and a dog to live undisturbed, but not so large to be of interest to anyone else.

Together, as the light faded, we moved inland. I let Kendal lead; he was better in the fading light and seemed to know where he was going.

I run through the trees, chasing my friend. We run together as animal brothers. He uses all of his limbs as do I. My hands seek out a fallen log and I vault it. Feet on the ground, I bound forward. He scampers and darts, dips through undergrowth and jumps over rocks. He barks in delight and I shout in response. I whoop and yell as we run unfettered about our new home. I scream my name.

Id slipped away, and I found myself taking in a magnificent view, massive redwoods reached high into the darkening sky. A star emerged in the deep blue expanse, winking to me. This was the place of my salvation, my home. I smiled. Kendal ran around me, yipping in delight and I stooped to stroke him. He paused and looked up at me, so I scratched behind his ear just as he liked and he ran back into the woods. I heard him bound and crash about, as delighted with his new home as I was. I looked back to the star above me. I murmured my name.

Ego joined Id to leave me standing alone in the woods. Listening to Kendal dart about, I was instantly concerned about my new situation. I had no food, no water, no means of remaining dry and warm apart from the clothes I wore and the boots on my feet. The sky was darkening and a chill was permeating the woods. Noises of animals found my ears and I shivered. I was not sure what was causing me to quake; it could have been the cold but I thought it more likely that it was fear. Fighting the terror that could have taken me and overwhelmed me, I moved in the direction of Kendal. He was going somewhere, I would place my trust in him, he would take me to safety. I shouted his name.

Chapter Sixty-nine

I needn't have feared, for Kendal did indeed lead me to salvation. We emerged from a deep patch of undergrowth to discover a cabin. It was hidden from view in the poor light as the woods had almost entirely reclaimed it. Small trees, ferns and bushes grew right up to the edge of what was once a small clearing. However, I could see the sky once again through the diminished covering of the trees above me and the improved light showed me my new home. It was made by hand decades ago, cut logs lay on their side forming each wall. Joined with strategic cuts at the corners they had settled together over the years to form a solid box of wood. The roof was similarly constructed from fallen trees, and together they made a sturdy structure. It had many holes and gaps from years of neglect but the forest had filled these with fallen leaves and branches. This had rotted to mulch and given the cabin an earthen hat of green moss and grasses.

I forced the door open with a heave and stepped inside. There was the frame of a metal bed against one wall and I collapsed onto the bare wire structure. Soon I slept as Kendal lay in the doorway, guarding his new castle.

*

I awoke the next morning; the sun shining through the open door was my alarm clock. I dragged myself from the wire upon which I lay. Stepping outside I stretched and rubbed my aching bones. Kendal ran out into the woods, no doubt to explore as I looked back to the inside of my new home.

I spent the first hour clearing nature from the inside. Sweeping with the leafy branch of a small tree, I cleared the dirt from the floor. I discovered that there were windows in the walls and, pulling away the wooden shutters, I was delighted to find that the glass remained intact. I was even happier when I had cleaned them with the sleeve of my coat. The light in the cabin and the cleaned floor revealed to me a hatch beside the bed. Pulling it open, breaking the seal of dirt that had held it closed for many years, I peered into the pit beneath the cabin. It had been a natural cave at one time, cut into the rock on which the cabin had been built. I saw that the walls had been straightened and smoothed with a pick. I used my finger to trace the outlines of some of the thousands of marks against the grey stone. Stepping down into the ground, I carefully picked out the shapes of the steps in the smooth floor. When I reached the bottom, there was little light filtering down from above, so I took a moment to allow my eyes to adjust to the gloom.

I could feel the space extending beyond me, and called out to detect the return of my voice from the depths. There was no echo, but from the sound I could sense that it extended some distance. As my eyes slowly adjusted, I still could not see an end to the tunnel. There was, however, an oil lamp resting in a niche cut into the wall. I retrieved it and, turning the dial over, smiled as the oil inside ignited as the flint sparked. As the lamp burned it illuminated a scene of wonderment. The tunnel was indeed long, stretching away into the hill, travelling downwards. It looked like an abandoned mine of some kind, held up with ancient timbers and the marks of hand tools covering every wall. It was now, however, a storage room for the cabin's previous owner.

The old owner was not coming back. This I knew because I was staring directly at him. A skeleton covered in tattered rags was sat in a plastic chair. Ignoring him, I walked the length of the mine. There were shelves cut into the side of the rock and on each of them sat everything I would need to live many months here in comfort. Cans of food, tools, medical equipment. Most importantly I found a small well in an offshoot of the mine. There were even some clothes, protected from the elements in yellowing plastic.

I carried the skeleton from its resting place and dug a hole using a folding spade I had found in the store. Laying him carefully in the shallow grave, I slowly filled it in, all the time staring at his now hollow eye sockets. I knew as I looked at him that this was the place in which I too would die. Returning to the cabin porch, I saw that Kendal had returned. Sitting beside him on the plastic chair I had kept for myself. Finally succumbing to his longing stare, I went to the store and retrieved some food for us. He wolfed his down in frantic gasps, inhaling the canned meat as if I would take it from him given a chance. I savoured mine as he looked expectantly at me, wanting mine as much as he had wanted his.

I tried to be strong, giving him none. But the way he was looking at me was melting my resolve.

"Fine, but only a bit," I told him, handing him a piece of my packaged meal. This had been a place of refuge for the previous owner, I thought. He had built this cabin and stocked it well before hiding it from discovery and waiting for some imagined end of civilisation. An end that did not come, except to himself. His cabin of military ready-to-eat meals, canned food and water hadn't served him any purpose. His preparation was ultimately unnecessary but fortuitous for me. I considered myself the luckiest man alive as I sat on my porch, faithful friend by my side.

As night fell, the woods became more alive as the evening animals started to move. A nearby rustle caught our attention and we watched with fascination as a porcupine briefly emerged. As it waddled back into the woods, I looked up to the stars and started to plan a delicate pruning of the trees overhead. I could cut them back to see more of the night sky, and maybe even cut back some of the larger growth in front of the cabin; it would be nice to look out over the water. It wouldn't take much, and strategically done the cabin would remain hidden from view. Lost in my thoughts I didn't pay attention to the noises behind me; when I finally did turn to investigate, I was confronted with the uncomfortable sight of a large grizzly bear three metres from where we sat.

She looked at me and I at her. She rose up on her hind legs and sniffed at the air. Kendal's ears went flat against his head and he crouched low. Slowly, my eyes on the bear, I bent down and scooped him up. I held him close to me and hugged him tight as we sat together in the chair. The bear showed us her teeth as she snorted in more of our scent. Carefully I spoke to her.

"Hello..." I said, speaking softly and slowly. "We mean you no harm..."

I repeated this mantra in what I hoped were calming tones. She dropped down to all fours and darted at us. She stopped again after just a single movement and stepped back a fraction. Forward she darted again, again stopping and moving backwards. Once more, and this time I could feel the blast of air from her mouth as she barked in our faces. Kendal squirmed in my grasp, wanting to run, but I held him close. We did not need to run, she was testing us, we would not fail.

She rose up, towering high above us. She barked into the sky and I rose from the chair. I released Kendal down to the ground and let him go. He scuttled into the cabin and under the bed inside, only his nose remaining visible from the cascading covers. I stood before the mighty bear towering high above me. Her massive clawed paws waved from side to side as she balanced herself, barking into the night. I joined her, shouting as loudly as I could.

"Ed..."

"Id..."

"Ego..."

We shouted our names as the bear barked hers high to the stars. She looked back down at me, and with a crash she fell backwards on her bottom. The whole cabin shook under the shock of her landing. She faced me now, about a metre distant, eye to eye, teeth to face. I nodded and smiled. Breaking eye contact with her, I looked to the ground.

These were her woods, this was her island. I felt as though I should ask permission to stay here. Still looking down I gestured to the cabin.

I continued to calmly talk, hoping that she at least understood my tone if not my words, "may I stay here, on your island? I will do no harm, cause no damage."

She barked at me, warming my face, covering me with damp spray.

"No one else will come. It's just me and Kendal." I softly informed her, gesturing inside to the cowering form under the bed. "I will keep others from here. If they come, I will send them away."

I looked up and she looked back at me. I felt as though she understood, but somewhere in her deep black eyes, her long snout smelling me, detecting the truth of me. She stretched her paws wide and barked again.

I made a decision, "all of these islands, I will keep people away from all of them." I confidently stated, waving my hands around as I did. Again, I looked her in the eye, hoping my confidence communicated something to her.

We stayed there for what felt like an eternity. My legs

complained at our stillness but I dared not move for I knew she was deciding. I would live free from this moment, accepted, or I would die in a second. The choice was hers, I would not attempt to defend myself. I just hoped that she spared Kendal; he meant no harm, he was no threat to her. I waited, waited for her choice. Slowly the light faded to the point I could no longer make out the details of her face before me. With the fading of the light came her decision. She fell back to all fours and backed away, grumbling at me, no doubt a threat that I should keep my word, and slipped into the woods.

With a sigh of relief, I sat back down into the chair. Kendal came outside and slid underneath, pressing his nose between my legs, looking out into the dark woods.

"You weren't much help," I chastised him playfully. He responded with a snort and I stroked his head.

"Why don't we light a fire?" I asked him, thinking the light and the warmth would calm us down after our experience. He agreed by making two tight circles under the chair and laying down underneath it as I fetched some wood.

Chapter Seventy

I sit on the porch of my cabin, watching the fire burn brightly in the small clearing I have made. I am animal, human animal, master of my fate and that of this island. I will protect the creatures of my new domain. I will hunt and destroy any man that comes here seeking to hurt or to take away the beauty of this place.

I sat on the porch of my cabin, watching the flames consume the wood. My life on these islands would be purposeful and noble; devoted to protecting this wilderness. People would come, and some would be permitted if their intentions were pure. Others, however, hunters and developers would be ejected. I would invoke Id to remove them.

I sat on the porch of my cabin, listening to Id and Ego think their evening away. They had the same idea, but each of them considered only themselves. As they rested their minds, I decided to finally speak.

"I am Ed." I simply informed them, the statement said it all.

"I know that, Ed. But I am Ego. I am reason, the reason you are free. I contained and overcame Id."

"Yes, but our mind is mine, not yours. I must have it back."

"You have it," growled Id, "you have it as much as we do, that is enough."

He stood us up, aggression building. Kendal scuttled away and lay down in range of the heat from the fire but far away from our argument. He stared back at us.

"See now," I chastised Id, "you've upset Kendal."

"No. He is just escaping what is about to come. We will decide now, who will win." Id challenged us, "I will win. For I am Id, I am more powerful than both of you combined."

"No, Id. I, Ego, will win for I have reason. You are powerful with emotion, but emotion is ruled by reason."

This was not something I would stand for, I decided. "You're both wrong! I have the intellect, I am Ed. I am the rightful man in charge of us. You two are just parts of the psyche of Edward, you have no rights here."

"The psyche of Edward?" Ego said.

Id joined him, "you said the psyche of Edward?"

"So?" I challenged them.

"You talk about Edward as if he is another person..." Ego tailed off, thinking. I could feel the scratching in my mind that was his process of deduction. Finally, he found it, the realisation he was searching for. "Ed is not the combined psyche of us, for if he were, we would no longer exist. He is still only a part of Edward; he has more of his personality, but he is not him."

"But I'm more him than you..." I insisted.

"No!" Id screamed, stopping me. "You are no more Edward than I am. Or, I must admit, Ego." He became calmer as he conceded that last part; was he admitting defeat? "No. I admit no defeat. I am the purest part of Edward but cannot exist alone. My drives are nothing without reason to guide them. I need Ego to help me fulfil the desires that would otherwise eventually be agony for me."

"I too need you, Id. I need passion, I need emotion. Without it I am a cold machine of reason that could just as soon end its life as take a step."

"Then it's settled, you two will concede defeat. I am Ed, the person that Edward was meant to be."

Following this statement there was silence. Both Id and Ego sat still to consider their position. We had to settle this, we were not normal, we were not functioning correctly. Our new task would take a properly formed personality, and that personality would be me, Ed.

Even as I thought the idea, I knew that it was wrong. I needed the emotion that was Id, just as I needed the reason that was Ego. None of us could exist without the others. I wanted them to surrender, for Ed to take control, but even if they chose to sit back, how long could they remain dormant? They couldn't will themselves, their existence, to nothing.

"He's right," Ego stated simply, calmly.

"We know..."

None of us dared to speak the truth, but I felt it. We knew the truth. "We must all depart, Edward must be reconstituted."

Slowly tears started to fall from our eyes at the realisation.

"I am Id. I am pure, I am animal. I will be strong again."

I wail my name.

"I am Ego. I am tough, I am responsible. I will control again."

I cry my name.

"I am Ed. I am a man, I am strong. I will be me again."

I speak my name.

We sit in silence.

*

In the fire, the last three logs are burning brightly. In their destruction, there is the formation of something new, something whole. The ash pile beneath them, glowing orange in the heat of its own creation. Id, Ego, Ed. Burning, destroying ourselves, and in doing so creating Edward, the phoenix.

First Ed fell away, collapsing into his own self, slipping into stillness. Then Ego, his talking abated, his thoughts first becoming confused, then incoherent, then silent. Finally, the feeling faded, Id was dying, slipping away. Fear, pain, love, anger all collapsing to nothing. Finally, only one sensation remained: peace. The death instinct called to my mind, letting all parts of it collapse into the black hole of my demise. We slipped in, willingly letting it welcome us into its cold embrace.

Chapter Seventy-one

I woke in the new dawn of a sunny morning. Sweat covered me from head to toe. My eyes took in the familiar surroundings, and sunlight slid through the canopy of trees above.

Sitting up next to the still smouldering embers of the fire, I remembered the feeling of the deaths inside of me. I shed a tear for Ed, his fractured mind filling him with doubt and fear. The ending of Ego, still calmly considering the sensations of consciousness as he slipped away. Finally Id, the raw feelings of this disappearance chilling me until I remembered his final, lasting, sense of peace. That same feeling now flooded my mind, rousing me, filling me with hope. I looked up to the clouds above me as they parted to reveal the blue of the sky. I was home, I was free, I was Edward. I could feel the construct of my soul within me, my desires, my logic, my mind once more a gestalt of all its components.

I stared into the morning sky, tears streaming down my smiling face and whispered my name.

Chapter Seventy-two

I was in pain. Everything hurt. My right leg had been fractured in three places and my knee was shattered. It had taken two separate surgeries and seven screws and other pieces of metal to put it back together. My left arm was not so bad. It was broken and painful but required no surgery, just a cast and a lot of painkillers. On top all that, I had four broken ribs and countless bruises making it hurt to even breathe. Trying my best to ignore the pain, I distracted myself by watching the television mounted on the wall high above my hospital bed. The character on the show said something funny and it made me chuckle. The pain washed through me from the movement of my chest and I reached out to press the morphine button. That's when I saw her, standing in the open doorway, looking at me. Grace was here, watching over me. She saw me looking and rushed over to my bed.

"Oh, Minty..." she started to cry. I wrapped my good arm around her as she rested her head on my shoulder.

"It's okay, Grace. I'm fine really." I wasn't, everything hurt like hell, but I was alive. "Just some broken bits. That's all. A couple of weeks and I'll be up and about again."

She just lay there. I managed to reach the button and the pain subsided again. I watched the television as she gently hugged me. Eventually she sat up, wiping her eyes with her sleeve. "I'm sorry, Minty."

"Sorry? Why?" I was confused, the drugs were making me groggy and I couldn't remember anything for her to be sorry for.

"Our argument."

"Oh, Grace. You have nothing to be sorry for, you were right. I was being stupid, I should have just come home with you."

"Well, that's clear..." she gestured to my casts and tried to smile.

"No, without that. I should have come anyway. You were right. I was obsessing."

"So you're stopping now?"

"Even if I could chase him. Yes, I'm done. He's the Force's

problem now." I was serious. Edward, as he was now, would be chased and apprehended by the RCMP. I was a police detective, solving crime was my job, catching fugitives theirs. "Besides, Id's gone. He told me that he was 'Ed' now. Then he proceeded to do this to me."

"Ed?"

"Yeah, he told me that he was in control, but clearly he wasn't. Edward wouldn't have done this, he couldn't have, for one thing."

"Yes, but Ed? Not Edward?"

"No, like I said. 'Ed', he shouted it quite a lot."

She was quiet for a time. I looked to the television again and chuckled at it some more, the drugs were making everything funnier than it should be.

"Minty, when did Edward ever call himself 'Ed'?"

I thought for a while, "never. In fact, he made a point of calling himself Edward." I said finally.

"Exactly, that's why he attacked you. Edward isn't back, Ed is out. Something new, someone new."

"It doesn't matter now. Maybe you should tell Elisha, she might be interested, but it's nothing to do with me anymore."

"Seriously?"

"Seriously, honestly. He hurt me to prevent me from chasing him, broke my leg to put me out of action. And I am. I'm out, S.E.P."

"S.E.P?"

"Someone else's problem. Someone else's problem..." I said with a smile, finally letting the drugs pull me into a painless stupor.

When I came to, she wasn't there. Bored and in pain again I just pressed the morphine button and went back to sleep. The next time she was there and I resolved to leave the button alone. This time Grace was holding a stiff piece of paper which she handed to me with a frown. It was the Precinct memo I had been dreading. As expected, I was suspended pending an investigation. Sighing, I put the note down, somewhat relieved that at least it was with pay.

"What d'you think, Grace? What's the gossip?"

"Sonny in internal affairs thinks that you'll be okay. He says that you didn't do anything wrong. In the end, it was the wrong decision to go up there without backup, but you didn't know the girl wasn't in danger. I think it was the prudent course of action. Henry's backing you up too, which helps."

"How bad was Henry hurt in the end? I heard he was okay but didn't get any details."

"He's fine, just one night in hospital 'cause he had been unconscious, but no lasting damage. He called by while you were under. He hasn't had any blowback, career-wise."

"That's a relief, he's a good cop."

"Yeah, he seems nice too."

"And what about you?"

"Me? I haven't done anything, no one's coming for me."

"Not that. I mean, what are you to me? Are we okay?"

"Oh, Minty," she responded by kissing me. It was long and deep. Despite the pain I was happy. I hoped my career would survive but as long as I had Grace I knew I would be just fine. Still kissing me, she reached between the sheets and took me in her hand. Hiding us from the door she gently massaged me while we explored each other with our mouths. I found a release from the pain that had nothing to do with medication as she whispered my name.

Chapter Seventy-three

My new home is a paradise, buried in the woods of my own private island. After some renovations, the cabin remains nestled against the hillside, the ancient wood of its construction hard and permanent. Every crack and dent has been filled with moss or grass, larger areas sprout leafy plants and the occasional flower nestles in the gaps between the fallen trees. It has become part of the landscape, effectively camouflaged by the decades of nature growing across its construction. Since arriving here, I have been busy improving my situation. I started by climbing the nearby trees and pruning the larger branches to provide a view of the stars at night and more heat from the sun during the day. I felled some more trees that were blocking my view of the ocean and now, sitting on the porch, I can watch the humpbacks pass through the channel beyond. Having extensively explored the island, I've discovered berries and plants that have expanded my diet to include fresh food. I have even located a nice rock on the east shore from where I can fish. The bear that lives on the island with me is making her own nest in another slope of the same hill. I leave her alone as much as I can. We seem to have a mutual agreement to keep away from each other and I am happy to honour it.

During a deeper search, I found a number of survival books in my stash and devoured them with haste. I have to prepare for the coming winter and my life may depend upon the knowledge within them. At their instruction, I insulated the cabin floor with dirt and fallen leaves, fished and dried my catch, and gathered and stored berries and root vegetables. To keep me warm at night, I unpacked the previous owner's clothes and wrapped them around me. There were also some skins to keep me warm and dry. I have no plans to kill any animals, except for fish, and did baulk at the use of the skins initially. They had already been killed, however, and my life probably depends upon them. Better that I use the mistakes of people in the past than ignore and dishonour the animals they used to be, I decided. I left the bear skin in its container, though, not wanting to offend the true owner of this island.

Having prepared as much as I could, I thought on my promise to the bear. I had sworn to protect all these islands but had no means to travel between them. I considered unearthing the metal boat but it seemed inappropriate to my new natural life and ill-suited for the growing waves of the rougher waters surrounding me. Finding a chapter in one of the books on creating dugout canoes, I sharpened the tools in the cabin and set to work. It took me three weeks of labour; sweat and cuts covered my body, but I persevered. Finally, I had a workable canoe that rode high and stable in the rough waters. I even made a sturdy paddle and could travel with good speed between the islands using it.

By the time I had finished, snow had started to fall and the temperature had fallen below freezing throughout the day. I gave up my plan to patrol the islands until spring, as it seemed unlikely that people would visit in such conditions. Besides, in the still winter air I was sure to hear their approach. I had also recently discovered that from my cluster of islands, there were some visible signs of civilisation. One night in my canoe I had noticed the unmistakable glimmer of electric lighting on another large island separate from my own archipelago. I calculated that this is where people would probably originate, so, noting its location, I decided to at least periodically check in its direction.

*

As I sat on my porch reviewing my progress in preparing for the winter, occasional flakes of snow fluttered to the ground through the trees. I had already lit the wood-burning stove in the cabin, warming it for the night, and I carried a stick from it to light one in the pit. I was determined to enjoy as much time outside while it was still possible; soon the snow would set in and trap us inside. Us. The word had a pleasant sound now that it no longer referred to minds inside of my own. I was certainly 'I' again. Kendal and I, made us. I reached down and scratched behind his ear. Satisfied, he wandered off for late-night explorations and I returned to my task.

I was halfway through making a basket in which Kendal could sleep. It was constructed from thick reeds cut from a pond on an adjacent island. Letting them dry over two days, leaning them against the stove, one by one I had woven them in to a wide oval. I whistled a tune, happy in my work, happy that I was making Kendal warm and comfortable for the winter. He returned, a fat rat in his mouth. He deposited it on the decking at my feet, proud of his kill. He pushed it towards me with his nose and I accepted the gift graciously. Rising, I walked to the fire and threw the carcass on the flames, not yet at the point where I would eat a rat. I could have chastised Kendal, but it was in his nature to hunt and I could not deny him that.

Watching the body of the rat flare in the fire and crackle to ash, I shed a tear for the creature. My mind naturally turned to my actions as Id and soon there were tears for my own victims. I decided to weigh the balance of my scales. One man dead in an alleyway; my first crime against the civilisation that had nurtured me to adult life. Second were three rapists in a dark place. They weighed on me less, but they only deserved punishment, not murder and disembowelment. Next was the driver of the pickup truck, he didn't deserve to be so brutally attacked, but thankfully I didn't think I had killed him. Jessica. The name was etched in my mind; I did not kill her, but I did torture her mind, restrain her and deny her freedom.

Then there were the hunters. Try as I might, I could not count them. I think there were probably five, the hunt of each one was a blur of motion, action, camouflage fabrics and guns. Morally, mentally, I knew they did not deserve to die but I was remembering the peaceful deer nuzzling the ground; innocent and gentle in the sights of their guns. I remembered finding a bloodied corpse of a deer one evening, its head cut from his shoulders, trophy gathered, remains left to rot. Anger bubbled up inside of me. I should not have killed these men, these monsters, but of all of my victims they maybe deserved it most. They were at least on par with the alley rapists. Finally came the homeless man, shouting at me. Again, I felt guilty about him, but it had been accidental; I had meant to send him away, to stop him attacking me. I hadn't meant to kill, but still I had.

The balance was tipping heavily to one side. I had let people live but they were grains of sand on one side weighted against boulders of shame on the other. Looking down to Kendal who was positioning himself closer to the fire, I mentally added a stone to the positive side. I had saved him, he was worthy of it, he needed me and I had been there for him. I heard a sound in the woods outside the ring of light cast by the fire, a skunk probably, or a racoon. I would save these animals from the influence of man. In this way, maybe at the end of my life my scales would balance. At least I would have tried.

Chapter Seventy-four

In total, I'd spent over a month in hospital. By the time they finally released me there was snow on the ground. I was walking now, albeit with a cane, and the icy ground made it hard for me to get around. I was determined to maintain my independence, however, and smiled triumphantly as I finally crossed the threshold of my apartment building, having taken a cab home from the hospital. Riding the elevator up, I breathed deeply from the effort of the short walk across the lobby. The physical therapy had restored my mobility, but it would be some time yet before I regained my full strength after the prolonged bed rest. I had insisted that Grace let me leave the hospital on my own and return to my own apartment. I needed my independence regardless of how much I wanted her by my side, knowing that if I opened the door to reliance on her I could happily never close it again.

The apartment was clean, spotless in fact. Dropping my bag to the ground, I sighed with a smile. Grace had obviously cleaned it and there was a vase of flowers on the kitchen counter. Next to it was a card from the Precinct. Lifting it, I saw that everyone had signed it. It had been propped up by a small stuffed dog, white with brown ears. The note on his lap read that his name was 'Minty', a gift from Booth. Below the introduction to my new pet was an invitation for a drink when I started work again. The efforts of my journey home had drained me and I stumbled to the sofa, collapsing onto it with a deep groan. Massaging my knee, I cursed Edward and his overzealous attack.

I heard the door open. I knew it was Grace, as she was the only one who had a key.

"Hello?" She called.

"Hey, Grace. Come on in..."

Walking though the hallway, she kicked her shoes into the corner. She shook her coat from her, the melting snow falling to the floor.

"It's really coming down now," she commented as she tidied, "shouldn't wonder if we needed the chains soon."

She was right, soon enough I would have to get the chains out of storage and wrap them around the tyres of my old Toyota.

"I'm not sure how I'll manage that..." I gestured to my aching and damaged knee.

"I'll do it, dummy," was her response.

"I know you're trying to help, but I have to do these things on own. I can't just have you do everything."

"Of course you can. I don't mind."

She started unloading a bag into the cupboards and refrigerator. She was stocking my kitchen now.

"Grace, you shouldn't have."

"Oh? What were you going to do? Walk a mile in the snow, or just live off takeaway. I left strict instructions with the concierge to call me on the third consecutive order of junk food."

I'd put on ten pounds in the hospital and was under strict instructions from the physical therapist to lose it or my mobility would take even longer to return. "Yes, boss," I replied, to which she rolled her eyes and continued unpacking the groceries. "Hey, can you stop that please. You only just got in."

"Almost finished," was her reply, head under the kitchen sink. I took a deep breath and waited; finally the banging finished and her head reappeared from the counter. "I thought you would be in a better mood, being home finally."

She was right, I should have been happy, but I wasn't. "I'm sorry. It's just that it was so hard getting here. The taxi was agony, I swear he hit every rut of ice he could find. Then the walk across the lobby was like a march across the country. I only just made it."

"I said I should have brought you home."

"It would have been just as bad, it just isn't getting any better. I can barely move, and I'm fed up with it." A tear formed in my eye and I blinked it away. "I'm gonna have this damn cane the rest of my life. Building strength to get from here to the bedroom is going to be my night's activity. It's rubbish!" I was shouting now, it was either that or cry, I thought as I banged the coffee table with my cane. "I'm an old man, tottering around on a stupid stick, it's pathetic!" Despite my anger, I was crying now.

"Minty..."

I looked to Grace, she was crying now too, tears falling down her cheek, sympathetic eyes looking at me.

"Grace, please. Don't look at me like that, I don't want to upset you too."

"Just let me help you, let me make things better."

"Can you fix my knee?" I asked her petulantly. My mouth seemed set in a downwards direction, chin crinkled with annoyance and depression. My arm was hurting too. That at least had healed but it refused to give up the dull ache it sported as a souvenir. "And my damn arm still hurts," I grumbled as she moved towards me, her soft socks padding with deep thuds on the hard wooden flooring. She placed two pills in my hand and a glass of water in the other. I knocked them back and waited for their effect to temporarily remove the ache. "I can't keep taking pills either."

"I know, but the doctor said it was okay for now. You can stop when you're better. He said the pain should mostly be gone by the summer."

"Yay, a winter of misery then. What a treat."

She cast me a disapproving look at that last comment and walked into the bedroom, no doubt to tidy that up too. I slumped back into the sofa and rested my leg on the coffee table, trying to get comfortable. Lifting the remote, I flicked the television on and browsed the channels. Settling on a comedy I had seen a hundred times before, I tried to relax. I called to her, still moving around in the bedroom.

"I'm sorry, Grace. I'm just a bit fed up. I am grateful for your help, honestly."

"Are those pills helping?"

They were not. I ached all over from my exertions and trip in the taxi. "Yeah, I feel a bit better sitting still, too."

"Good," she stated, stepping from the bedroom. She hadn't been tidying up, she had been changing. She was wearing black stockings held up with a suspender belt that I could see through her lacy black negligee. She had combed her hair and I noticed that she had make-up on. She stood by the side of the doorway with a hand on her hip and leg slightly bent toward me. I looked down her smooth legs and saw she was wearing very high, red heels.

"You look good," was my simple understatement.

"Thank you, Montgomery," she said as she tottered towards me unsteadily.

"Grace, I..."

"Shush, dummy," she said, continuing her show. She put some music on and started a slow dance for me. She bent over and ran her hands up the insides of her thighs, lifting the negligee. Drawing it from her, she cast it away. It flowed, changing shape as the light material twisted in the air. It took my attention with it as it came to rest across the lamp lighting the room, the light fading seductively as a consequence.

I turned back to her in the dimmed light of the living room of my apartment. She was on her knees on the rug in front of the sofa. She gently raised my bad leg from the coffee table and placed it on the floor.

"Remember, don't let your knee lock," she chastised me gently. I said nothing as she undid my fly. She removed my shirt and rubbed her hands across my chest. She kissed me on the mouth but quickly moved down, kissing my body. Her hands were on the top of my thighs. I went to touch her, to stroke her hair, but she batted me away.

"You just sit there. Let me do this..."

So I did, I lay back, my neck stretching as I placed the back of my head on the sofa. She murmured my name.

Chapter Seventy-five

Winter arrived on the island like a hammer on an anvil as I woke one morning unable to open the door. Eventually I levered a shutter from a window and climbed through. Looking at the pile of snow and ice against the door I could see why people build extensive porches on the front of their cabins. I spent the entire morning digging out the front door. The afternoon was dedicated to extending the roof over the porch using freshly cut logs. By evening I was exhausted. The snow had carried on falling throughout the day and I had to clear yet more from in front of the door. I was finally sweeping the last of it from the porch, looking back to see that no fresh snow had penetrated my new awning, when it happened. My foot fell from beneath me, through the floor on which I was standing. Without warning, half of me dropped down. I landed on my knee with one leg dangling in mid-air, having crashed through a rotten floorboard.

I tried to pull my leg out of the hole, but the wood had formed sharp edges when it had snapped and they cut into me. I could feel that I was bleeding, fluid escaping, running down my leg. It hurt, it hurt a lot and I cried out into the snowy sky. Kendal was immediately by my side barking in concern. He ran around me, back and forth to the cabin, unsure of what to do. Finally, he came close enough for me to grab him. I held him, comforted him.

"It's okay, Kendal. Just a fall, I'll be fine."

As I spoke the words, I started to calm down. I was still stuck, hurt and bleeding but my reassurances to Kendal also soothed me. It hadn't completely worked for him though. As I released him he refused to leave, sitting next to me, staring with worry. I had to get out of the hole, I knew that, despite the pain and damage it might cause. I gritted my teeth and pressed my hands to the floor. Heaving and pushing, I forced myself up, tearing more flesh in the process.

Finally my leg was free, trousers torn and bloodied. My foot was still in the hole, however. Lying down on the frozen wood, foot pointing down, I finally extracted myself completely. Still on my stomach, I dragged myself across the porch to the house with Kendal following and whining. Depositing myself by the stove, I pulled the ruined trousers from me; the pain was excruciating but finally they were off. I lit the oil lamp and inspected the damage. There were slivers of wood stuck inside my leg in various places. Managing to get myself upright again, I painfully moved to the store in search of a first-aid kit. Crawling back to the stove, I painstakingly extracted everything I could find, repeatedly mopping up the blood as it flowed.

Gradually my leg started to become numb in the cold, I knew this was a bad sign, but welcomed the pain relief it provided. Quickly I bandaged it and slid into bed. Pulling the covers over me, I added a deerskin to keep the cold away as I shivered violently. Kendal, still whining, pushed his nose under the covers and I felt his head come to rest on my stomach. His warmth was very welcome as I allowed the fatigue caused by my work and my injury to carry me into unconsciousness.

*

I awoke at dawn. The light from the sun rising through the trees sliced through the grey sky and illuminated the inside of the cabin with a harsh white light. Sitting up, I felt the pain of my leg; it was throbbing and stung like hell. As I pulled the deerskin from me, Kendal awoke with a start. He was still by my side and was looking concerned with his tail between his legs.

"Don't worry, Kendal," I said as I looked down to my leg. But he was right. The bandage was red with blood. The bed slick with it. The wounds had not closed at all and the pain was throbbing. I lay back, considering my problem. I was hurt, badly. I had no needle and thread, no sticky stitches, no glue. I looked down to Kendal.

"Bark," was his response and I agreed, "okay, I know. We have to go and find help, don't we?" He snorted, so I rose from bed, painfully pulling my tattered trousers back on and slipping into my boots.

Pushing the door open, I was pleased to find that at least the awning had worked and it was free from snow. The same could not be said for the ground outside. Carefully I made my way down to the water where the canoe was concealed, pressing on through the deep snow that made the going difficult. Kendal too was struggling. Unable to walk, he had to bound from place to place, barely keeping up with me. Finally we made it to the canoe. Rolling it upright we slid it into the water and climbed in. Kendal leapt in after me and lay down between my legs. His contact hurt, of course, but his comforting warmth was too welcome for me to move him.

Snow fell all around, immediately disappearing into the flowing water as it landed. I made my way around the island to the point from which I had seen the lights of civilisation. I could see nothing but a curtain of white falling in a grey fog over the water. Positioning the canoe carefully, pointing in line with the land that jutted out, I started to paddle. The sun was trying to penetrate the grey with a faint yellow glow. Using it as a guide by keeping it on my right, I paddled as strongly as I could manage into the mist. Kendal moved ahead, his nose pointing from the prow of the canoe, balancing out my weight at the back. When I felt myself veer left or right his nose moved in the opposite direction. I corrected it each time, with Kendal acting as a compass to guide me, pointing the way.

Eventually I felt the grind and scrape of pebbles against the bottom of the canoe as it struck land. Following Kendal's nose, the lights had emerged from the fog, faint at first but becoming brighter as we approached. I put them on our right as I did not want anyone to see me arrive from the water. Painfully I climbed from the canoe, soaking my boots in the process, and hobbled ashore. Wanting to approach the lights from inland, I made towards them in a lazy arc. Finally, as we neared, their source became clear through the fog. It was an ancient grocery store with a short dock floating on blue plastic barrels. The bright light was a large security spotlight on a high pole illuminating the dock and the front of the store. Dim orange-tinted lights lit the inside where there was a person moving around behind the condensation-coated glass. Taking a deep breath, I pushed open the door, causing a bell overhead to tinkle my approach. A wet Kendal followed me in, his tail whipping against my leg.

It was Kendal who introduced us by running to the person inside and immediately licking and sniffing them. I took this as a good sign, as, having been so mistreated in the past, he was not a trusting animal in general. If he liked this person, then probably they were a good person to like. Either that or he was so cold he would lick anyone for a stroke, I thought with a wry smile. I rounded the shelves behind which they were crouched.

"Hello," was my simple greeting. I was, in return, greeted with a wide, kind smile on the face of an angel. She had been crouching low to

269

restock the shelves and she was still on her knees, cuddling Kendal affectionately. She was about my age, I deduced, as her soft skin showed a few lines and the odd strand of grey shone in her dark hair. Her eyes penetrated me, seemingly accessing my soul with one look. I stepped back, shocked both at her beauty and its affect upon me. Doing so, however, I absentmindedly placed weight on my damaged leg. The pain shot up through my entire being, ending in a dark cloud forming behind my eyes. I fell to the ground with a scream and instantly blacked out.

Waking up exactly where I had fallen, I found my angel crouching down beside me. She was looking intently at me, gently tapping my face.

"Huh?" Was my eloquent opening.

"You're awake?" Her obvious question.

"Yeah," my quick riposte. Our initial conversation seemingly completed, she rose and walked away. I looked down at my leg. She had cut away and replaced my bandage with a far more professional arrangement; my trousers were totally destroyed now and lying beside me. It felt better already, although it was far too stiff and painful to bend, so no matter how hard I tried, I could not lever myself upright. She returned to my side and bent down to help me up. Eventually, between us and the shelves, with great effort I managed to pull myself upright. She handed me a silver crutch and I slipped it under my arm. She guided me to a room behind the shop and sat me down in a large comfortable chair.

"Thank you." My first proper words, a sentence. They felt inadequate. "You're a lifesaver."

"Not really. But these might just be." She said, handing me two pills and a glass of water. I swallowed them down with a questioning look.

"Antibiotics." Was her response. "Without them you would probably get a bad infection. There was a lot of wood in your leg, is your tetanus up to date?"

I had no idea but knew a hospital was a bad idea so replied, "yeah, I think so." She looked at me quizzically, assessing me. Kendal barked and she looked to him.

"Yeah, I didn't think it was..."

She left again. I looked around; if she had recognised me, called the authorities to help, I was finished. Hearing her return, I tensed but immediately relaxed again as I saw the needle she was holding.

"The doctor retired years ago, moved to the city. But he didn't take his supplies with him. I've got them all here, lucky for you." She sat beside me and swabbed an area with a cotton pad. Efficiently she injected me with the contents of the syringe.

Leaning against the wall, she surveyed me, as I too inspected her. She was little, maybe five-feet tall but still perfectly proportioned. I couldn't see her figure clearly beneath her thick woollen jumper and jeans but I had felt her strength as she had helped me. It was her face, however, that captivated me. She had soft features with a small nose and ears, brown eyes shining in the overhead light. Her openness pulled me in and drew me to her. I felt very exposed, sat in the chair opposite her in my underwear. She seemed to notice my discomfort and moved to gather and place a blanket over me. She sat back down, hands on her lap, legs crossed.

"So, I haven't seen you before. Where've you come from?" She asked.

"Oh, I've got a cabin in the woods."

"Oh, which one?"

I tried to think of a convincing lie.

"You're over on the islands, aren't you? Up past the Devil's Chute," she said.

I looked at her, knowing she knew exactly where I had come from, "I don't know the name."

"Okay, but that's what it's called. They're the Devil's Chute Islands, for your information. I saw you motor over there months ago in that little tin boat. It was a good idea to replace it with a canoe, that thing would never have managed the channel in full flow."

"You've seen me?"

"Yeah, don't worry though. I know that people like their privacy round here. I know everything that goes on in these islands, but I keep it to myself. Discretion's good business, you know?"

I did. She knew I was on the run or running away. Why else would anyone live out this far from civilisation? But I had thought I was hidden, out of sight from everyone, including her.

"So how did you see me? How did you know I've got a canoe?"

"It's pretty boring 'round here," she explained, "no entertainment to speak of. Only a hundred or so other people live here, fewer in wintertime. So, I've got nothing better to do than watch the wildlife." She paused, looking up to the ceiling, "I've got a pretty powerful telescope upstairs. You were the most interesting thing to float into view in months. You're staying in Joe's cabin then. He's dead?" She asked, calmly.

"Yes, sorry. I found his body," I admitted, assuming she was talking about the skeleton I had found.

"Yeah, he was a bit of a legend around here, Old Joe. He wanted everyone to stay away so bad they just left him there. I heard they even left his body where it was. That right?"

"Yes, but I buried him."

"That's okay. I never knew him. My daddy did though, this was his shop before mine. When he died five years ago, I moved here to take over. Locals told me all about Joe. Probably time someone buried him properly."

"Will you tell people?" I was worried, "about me, I mean."

"No, don't worry. I like the legend. Stay away from Joe's island or he'll chase you off with a shotgun... that's the story. People like it. I like it. You obviously like your privacy the same, you can be the new Joe is all."

She stood up, walked over to me and pressed a lever on the side of the chair. It collapsed backwards and a footrest extended, lifting my damaged leg.

"You can sleep there, I don't think I can get you up the stairs. You warm enough?"

"Yes, very. Thank you." Was my feeble response as she climbed the stairs.

"Why are you doing this?" I called after her.

"We all help each other around here, have to. Who else is there? Besides, I like your dog."

*

The pain in my leg finally started to dull again as Kendal curled up next to me and quickly fell asleep. I listened to my saviour moving around for a while, picturing her climbing into bed, slipping between the sheets. Soon the sounds faded away and finally with her stillness, I too found sleep.

Chapter Seventy-six

Slap. That was the sound of another file hitting the completed pile. I reached over and pulled the next one from the inbox. I sighed; this was my job now. Opening the file and beginning to read, not looking up when I heard another hit the inbox. It was constantly growing against my futile efforts to stem the flow. I was the Precinct paperwork detective. Other people's cases fell on my desk for me to check them, correct and complete them. My job was to digitise the investigations and results, search for errors, create the summaries and prepare them for prosecution or filing. It was important work, I knew, but work that was usually the job of the investigating detectives themselves. With me only able to perform desk duties, however, the Captain had come up with this new system whereby I could close out cases while the others moved on to new things. As expected, it was popular amongst the team, it being the most boring part of an investigation. They were as happy with the situation as I was miserable, I suspected.

This was my job, only in part because of my inability to work cases. It was also my punishment. The review board had found me not culpable for the escape of Edward and ruled that I had acted properly and within the bounds of procedure. However, I was the man to have let him escape twice, and mud stuck. I had been back at work for a month now as the paperwork lackey and hated every second of it. Without warning, the alarm on my watch went off and I rose to take my recommended exercise. I was finally moving about more normally, albeit with a cane, but if I sat still for too long my leg would stiffen painfully. So, every twenty minutes, I would take a lap of the Precinct, wander between the desks and over to the break area, only to return to the pain of the paperwork.

The click of the cane on the floor grated at my patience. I looked down at it; at least it wasn't entirely an old-man stick. Grace had bought me a modern one, made with black plastic and metal. I suspected mostly so I would stop complaining about it. Trying to cheer up, I looked ahead; moving to the break area, I decided that I could afford half a doughnut and still be within the limits of my diet. I was just breaking off a part, having poured a coffee, when Grace walked in.

"I was just going to have half a plain ring," I said, defending myself in preparation.

"I didn't say anything. Go ahead, you deserve it," was her loving response as she kissed me on the cheek. "How's work?"

"Oh, fine..." I lied, "how's yours?"

She proceeded to tell me all about the interesting case she was working on with Detective Booth. It was a string of robberies that had just escalated to murder. Because of the escalation, Grace had been tasked with going back over all the physical trace evidence.

"Mike says that if we can find some DNA, now it's a murder they'll pay for the testing."

This was an ongoing battle for all our cases. We wanted DNA and trace evidence analysed for every investigation, but the lab was overworked and understaffed. Therefore, crimes were prioritised, and burglary rarely got any testing beyond a few fingerprints if the perpetrator was naive enough to leave any.

"Sounds good, you think you'll find him?"

"It's early days yet but I think we will. These guys always leave something when they're rooting around for things to take. I'll find it, I just have to keep looking."

She was smiling, sipping her coffee. I was glad she was happy in her work. At least one of us was. I took a bite of the doughnut. Looking at it, I dropped it in the bin.

"You don't want it?"

"Stale. Not worth it," was my miserable response. I was being grumpy and I knew it. I tried to smile, "sorry, it's only worth the calories if it's tasty. I'll save them for something later." My diet was working, I was losing weight, but it was slow progress and another thing that was depressing me. "Maybe I'll go for a swim again tonight, try to get some exercise."

She started to speak but her response was curtailed by the entrance of Booth.

"Hey, Grace. Sorry to bother you, but I put some new things to test on your desk. The second victim thought our guy had searched her underwear drawer. She didn't want to wear anything he touched so hasn't been in there since. Good idea?"

"Great idea," she bolted from the room, excited to be on her way to the lab to test some woman's pile of knickers for foreign DNA. I went to leave too but Booth placed his hand on my shoulder.

"Hey, Minty."

"What's up, Mike?"

"I just wondered if you wanted to grab a beer after work. You seem down."

That was an understatement. As I glanced across to my desk, I could have sworn the inbox had gotten taller in my absence.

"That actually sounds great. Sounds like Grace will be busy testing knickers anyway."

"It's the life of the modern woman, Minty..." he chuckled, as I hobbled back to my desk.

*

After a dozen more processed files and a painful walk to town I was finally sitting with Booth in a sports bar downtown. The hockey was playing and we were half watching while chatting about work.

"It isn't forever," he reassured me, sipping his beer. "Once you're fit again you'll get cases to work. They can't afford to just have you sit there all day. Time heals all wounds, and memories fade."

"Yeah," I responded reluctantly, "it would help if they caught him," I commented, as the Flames failed to score once again.

"Yeah, I know. No more murders either. You really think he isn't Id anymore?"

"Yes, I do. Although, he's not just Edward either. I don't understand why he hasn't killed again."

"I know, that guy. He's nuts. He wants something, he's going to just take it, right?"

"Right."

"So, someone won't want to give it. That's murder right there, or at least aggravated assault, that's a crime reported, and we got him."

Booth's summary was succinct and correct. It was something I had been pondering since Vancouver. In that time, I had only thought of one sensible theory. "I wonder if he's better now," I said to Booth, finally voicing it to someone. "I think he might have fixed himself partly into Ed when I saw him last. By now his mind could be complete, he could be Edward again. Which would explain why he hasn't killed again. Edward's not a murderer."

"But he hasn't handed himself in either."

"No, but would you? I think that if he knows he won't kill again he'll just go off and hide somewhere. Imprison himself, punish himself maybe. Better than what would wait for him back here, don't you think?"

"Yeah, maybe. I like it..."

"But?"

"Oh nothing... I was just wondering how you felt about that?"

"Fine actually..." I said, surprising myself. "I've thought about it a lot and I've decided to be satisfied with a self-imposed exile. As long as he doesn't kill again, it's better than nothing. As long as Id's gone, right? If Edward's back, hopefully he doesn't even exist anymore."

"But he's a killer, a murderer, a kidnapper and not forgetting how he assaulted you..."

"I know, and I did want to catch him, even kill him if I'm being honest. But I've had a lot of time to think about it" I said, gesturing to my leg, "and I think maybe I'm finally willing to let it go."

"It seems a bit much to forgive him..." Booth said, sucking on his bottle of beer.

"Well, I don't think I have, not really. But I have decided that it was Id, and not Edward. I read a lot about it, and when you have a split personality, it really is split. One part doesn't have a clue what the other is doing, they are totally separate people."

"Still--"

I interrupted him, "when Edward came back, well Ed anyway, he broke my leg, sure, but he didn't kill me. He could easily have killed me, he even had a loaded gun in his hand at one point."

"I s'ppose," conceded Booth, "so you think that it was Id killing, not Edward."

"Yeah," I confirmed, "and honestly, I think Id is dead. I think Edward killed him."

We sat drinking our beers, letting that settle in our minds. Booth raised his bottle to mine and we clinked them together.

"To the death of Id. Good riddance," he toasted.

"Good riddance," I responded with a confidence I had not felt in a while. It was a good feeling, to let him go, to let the past go. I felt a weight lifting from me that was only partially down to the effects of the beer.

Chapter Seventy-seven

My saviour was named Star; her parents were hippies, she explained. She cared for me, fed me and Kendal, and we talked. Only one person visited the store during my two weeks of recuperation there, for matches. Star closed the door when he came in, hiding me while she served him. They chatted for a long while, passing the time, and he bought a lot more besides the matches he actually came for. She seemed to make a fairly good living; being the only store for hundreds of miles in all directions gave her a steady flow of people needing supplies and wanting company. She said that it was better in the spring and summer when the hunters came through. The mention of hunters made me wince.

"You don't approve?" She asked, detecting my discomfort.

I didn't want to offend her, but I didn't want to lie either. We had established a close relationship over the weeks and I liked her a lot. "No, I don't," I stated firmly.

"Nor do I," was her response, which was very welcome. The hunting of animals had become more important to me the more I had thought about it, and if she had been a hunter it would have ruined our relationship. "Macho nonsense," she stated, "I'm glad you don't."

"It's disgusting," I agreed, "they do it to prove something, but it proves nothing. So, someone can point a gun at a defenceless creature and pull a trigger, does that make them a man?" I added.

She shook her head, agreeing that it didn't, and then went one step further, "I'd like to see them actually face down a bear. With nothing but their hands. That would be nature against nature, let's see them deal with that."

"I like it." I told her, as she smiled.

"Sorry, I like animals. Probably more than people. I guess that's why I'm out here, running this place," she said, gesturing to the store.

"Nothing to be sorry about, and don't you worry. No one will be hunting on my islands as long as I'm there."

"Your islands, are they now?"

"Well, you know what I mean."

Star laughed, a free, open and happy sound that I had heard often. She bent down to where I was sitting and suddenly kissed me on the cheek. It was the first time I had felt the softness of her lips on my skin and the feeling ignited something in me. I felt a surge of passion from a well deep inside of me. It grew from the pit of my stomach and rose up to my throat. My heart thumped as I grabbed the back of her head. Pausing, I stared into her eyes, quickly launching into a kiss. I pulled her tight to me, strongly pressing my mouth to hers. She reciprocated and collapsed to sit on my lap.

Wrapping her arms around my head, she kissed me as I kissed her. I felt the power inside of me grow as a building heat. With the heat came the memory, the memory of Id. Abruptly, I stopped, pushing her away from me. I wanted with every part of me to take her and make her mine. She tried to pull herself to me, to continue. It took every molecule of willpower I had to resist. Bunching her hair in my fist, I clutched it and held her away from me by the back of her head. She winced with pain but I dared not release her. I breathed deeply, slowing my heartbeat, calming my passion and let out a long sigh.

"I'm a bad man, Star... I've done terrible things."

"I don't care about that. I know you, you aren't doing anything bad now."

"No... now I'm trying to make amends, but I don't deserve this. I don't deserve you. I don't deserve to be happy."

"What about me?"

"You deserve someone better than me, Star."

She stared intently at me, frowning. "You can let me go now," she said and I released her. "That's not your choice to make, Edward." She stated, with no room left for argument. "When you realise that, you can come back. Until then, I would like you to leave."

I rose, saddened but knowing it was right for me to do so.

"Come back if you want to use the store, of course," she added more softly. I gathered my things, including the clothes and other items she had given me during my stay, and moved to the door. She followed me out. "Of course, and to pay for all that."

She gestured to my belongings and smiled. I smiled back, glad to see that we could at least be friends. I stepped down from the porch and she followed. She took the opportunity to kiss me again, a quick peck on the lips.

"Come back soon, Edward," she said coyly and walked back to the store. I watched her leave, her pert bottom swaying from side to side in her jeans. I trudged to the canoe, a downtrodden Kendal following behind.

"I know, Kendal. I like her too. I can't let Id out though, you know that." He whined and reluctantly climbed into the canoe as I pushed us away from the dock with a sigh.

*

I didn't go straight back to our cabin, I wanted to get out, to stretch my healing leg and feel the cold of the winter air. I had been immobile for two weeks and while I enjoyed my time with Star I had been feeling cooped up in her store. Feeling her eyes on me from afar, I paddled hard to the other side of my island. I pulled the canoe high on a beach and walked into the woods. Kendal, objecting to my decision to leave Star behind, lay down in the canoe and stayed there.

"Fine," I said petulantly. "I'll go for a walk on my own, you wait here."

He snorted at me, confirming that was his intent all along. Annoyed, I trudged away through the deep snow into the woods and started up the hill. I just wanted to walk, not minding where I was going, I walked up and away from the water.

Without thinking, I had accidentally climbed the northern side of the hill, stupidly close to the bear that was denning there. I stopped dead when I saw the branches at the entrance to the den, they had been pushed aside. She was out. I recognised the signs of movement, her recent footprints wide and deep in the snow. Hearing a noise, I turned to discover that the she was walking through the trees just behind me. Now thinner, she had not yet seen or smelled me, and I carefully dropped to the ground. She was moving around, snorting in great pulls of air, searching for food having come out of hibernation prematurely. I knew that soon she would return to her den but in the meantime, she was dangerous. She would be even more threatening to me as I was freshly bathed and scented with Star's shampoo. I wouldn't be a pleasant experience for her delicate nostrils.

Just as I was considering backing away and looping around the hill, I detected that she had smelled me. She rose up and snorted in more air. Following her scan of the air around, she turned to face me. She saw me now, I was a dark shape against white snow and she would be wondering what I was. She would be calculating if I were food, foe or friend. Not wanting to be around to see what the decision was, I tried to crawl backwards away from the beast. She charged me. She bounded through the deep snow as if it were not there and quickly I decided that I had to change tactic. Rising high on my feet, I opened my coat. Spreading it wide, I made myself as large as I could and screamed, roaring at her.

My roar tore at my throat as I bellowed as deep and as loud a sound as I could manage. It worked; I was temporarily reprieved, and her charge stopped. Instead, she rolled her head around in circles, trying to work out what I was and why I was making such a sound. I roared again, rising on my toes, getting as tall as I could. She rose on her hind legs, and towered above me, roaring in return. I attempted to match her mighty bellow. I increased my noise by shouting, screaming and clapping my hands together. I was succeeding in confusing her. She dropped back to her front feet and bared her teeth. With a feeling of dread building inside of me, I realised that this was not working. She would charge again and surely drop me to the ground. She might not kill me, but it would be a devastating attack.

I steeled myself for the move, preparing to drop into a ball to weather what was about to come. Instead, I heard a rapid movement behind me and something leapt from the trees. I dared not turn, not wanting to break eye contact with the great bear before me. I hoped beyond hope that it was not some other dangerous animal come to join the feast. It was not. It was Kendal. I heard him start to bark ferociously, running all around, back and forth to either side of me. He alternated between growling and barking as he darted all around. It was causing the bear to pause, confused as to how many he was. I joined in, yelling and barking, flapping my coat.

The bear roared back at us and I started to back away. Kendal joined me as we gradually distanced ourselves from her. These were her woods, her hill, her den. We carried on signalling our willingness to fight, our ability to defend ourselves, while retreating with honour. It worked; the bear stayed where she was as we returned to the woods. Finally, Kendal stopped barking and came to me; I crouched down low and held his face in my hands.

"Thank you, friend, you saved me again."

He barked in appreciation and wagged his tail ferociously as I stroked and petted him. We circled around the hill and found the canoe where I had left it. Climbing inside I paddled back to the cabin, planning to treat Kendal to a fresh steak that Star had included in our provisions.

Cooking the steak over the fire, passing chunks to Kendal before they were fully cooked through, I pondered the bear. She was mighty, she would have killed me if it were not for Kendal. Thinking about it, I was fine with that. Her instinct was to kill and that was natural for her. It made me think of Id, of his behaviour. I had repressed him for too long, I knew. My whole life I had held him down. His late release had led to the extreme behaviour that Ego could not control.

Remembering how I had rejected Star earlier, I thought that maybe I had made a mistake. Suppressing my id could lead to me fracturing again. I looked down to Kendal chomping on his steak.

"You exercise your id, don't you, boy?"

He looked at me for a second then went back to his meal.

"Yes, I know you tried to tell me that already. I'm slower than you, sorry."

He wagged his tail in agreement but didn't allow me to distract him from his dinner. I wanted to be with Star, to chase her and free my id. It was frightening but I had to trust myself, trust my ego to constrain him. I must revel in my id, feed him, take him for a run. He will not rebel and take control if I give him what he wants. Moreover, I might enjoy it, I thought, starting to chomp down on my own slab of red meat.

Chapter Seventy-eight

Spring is here and I am healed. I run through the woods with Kendal, chasing nothing and everything. He bounds from a root and splashes through a stream of melt water. I laugh and follow him through the icy waters. It is a warm morning and I am wearing nothing at all, revelling in the feel of the air on my body, the soft ground on the soles of my feet. I am free and I am raw, at one with my world. He barks, stopping on top of a fallen tree and I race to him.

"What is it, Kendal? Have you seen something?" I ask him as I meet him there. He is alert, ears back, paw raised. He is looking out to the ocean below us. I drop down low and, hiding behind the log, I draw Kendal down with me.

"Hush now, they'll hear us."

There are two men below, pulling their boat up the pebble beach. They are not far from where I hide my canoe and I raise myself to check on it. I can see its location but it is well hidden. Being made from a log in the first place, that is all it looks like now that it is camouflaged. It and I remain hidden from them for the time being.

Kendal stays behind the log, looking at them. I pull back to the stream that we just both crashed through. Sitting on the banks of the fast-flowing water I gather handfuls of mud from the ground. Soon I am covered from head to toe with the dark brown sticky substance. I return to the log and look down at myself. If I remain motionless I am indistinguishable from the loamy ground. Pleased with my ability to remain unseen I start my approach of them. Inch by inch I move closer, sliding when there is line of sight, staying low to the ground. When there are trees between us I take the opportunity to scuttle, moving as quickly as I dare as they move around on the beach.

Pulling myself over the remains of a rotting tree, I crawl under a fallen log. Temporarily hidden from view I calm my breathing and collect my thoughts. I need to know why they are here and how long they might stay. I slowly raise myself up over the back of the log. I see them. They have moved away from the shore to a flat area of land that is relatively clear of trees. They have constructed a large bivouac and are starting a fire. Looking to their boat, I see large rucksacks. No doubt they contain food, camping equipment, things of that sort. They look prepared for a stay of maybe a week, no more. Inside the boat, behind one of the bags I see a large hard case protruding. A rifle case.

I lie there, still as a rock, hidden from view, covered with mud, invisible. Their loud voices carry easily on the still air and I wait. I wait for information, wait to hear their plans. Kendal is nowhere to be seen. I am pleased to see that he has the sense to avoid them. Worried for a second, I shake it from my mind. He will either be where we first stopped, watching us, or more likely he will have returned to the cabin. He will be more comfortable than me, I know, as I lie still, naked on the rough bark of a Douglas Fir.

I stayed there for an hour or more, listening to their conversation. I was disgusted to learn that they had purchased a licence to kill a grizzly bear on these islands and intended to do so in the following few days. Once they had their prize they also hoped to murder a deer or two to cook and eat, taking the antlers as souvenirs. I considered attacking them there and then, launching myself from my place of concealment, clawing at them with my bare hands. However, calmer plans settled inside my mind. A more permanent solution was required. If I attacked them as a man, they would surely return with the authorities. I would be apprehended and subsequently a bear would be murdered. That was not an outcome I would entertain; a cooler head was required to deal with these would-be murderers.

I slid from them as the sun started to set, knowing that they planned to hunt at dawn. I had my own plans for tonight that suggested otherwise. Once I was out of sight and sound of their camp, Kendal found me and together we ran back to our cabin. I made my way inside and, without removing the mud that was now dried on my skin, I went to my storage cave. Recovering the old bear-skin, I draped it over me. Taking another animal skin, I cut a number of strips of leather. Using these I bound the bear-skin to my body. It was so large it easily wrapped around me, covering me in coarse fur from head to toe. I tied the feet and hands around mine and placed the head on top of my own. I was looking out from under the jaw of the giant beast, once proud owner of this island. I emerged and found Kendal staring at me; it hadn't fooled him of course but I thought it would convince the hunters. It was still early evening so, wearing the costume in order to become accustomed to it, I created new bear-claw weapons as Id had once done.

I took my time, allowing the hunters to get nicely drunk and tired. As I sat with Kendal, a dark cloud came over the moon, blacking out our view. It was time; I stood. Instructing Kendal to stay at the cabin, I slipped into the void of the woods. Time to hunt. Time to hunt the hunters. I moved as Id, slipping through the undergrowth on bent knees, silent and deadly. I avoided thin twigs, staying on soft ground and muddy slopes. I travelled the woods slower than he, but just as proficiently. Soon I was near them and could see their fire through the woods. I would have to avoid getting too close to the light, I knew, as I considered my options.

I come at them the other side of their fire. In my hands are a large pile of leaves and dirt. I crawl closer to them, shielded from discovery behind a large Ponderosa Pine. They are resting, but not asleep. I can tell from their breathing, it is too shallow for sleep but too regular to be alert. They are trying to rest for morning but are excited to kill. I prepare myself, lowering myself down and stretching my legs.

Then, like lightning I rise, striking like a serpent from a rock. I leap from behind the tree and sprint for the fire. They both sit bolt upright at the sudden noise. Quickly reaching the fire, I spring over the dying flames, depositing handfuls of undergrowth on the burning logs. As planned, the fresh green leaves immediately start to sizzle and smoke, the accompanying dirt extinguishing any flames that had been providing light. My passage over the fire had been made with screwed up eyes lest I spoil my night vision. They are now wide open, and I can clearly see the fear on their faces as the dark fire crackles under the dirt with a hissing roar. A smile grows, revealing my white teeth to the darkness.

My coat of bear flashes over the sitting form of the first man with a whoosh as I land on the second. I smash him in the head with a rock, not so hard as to knock him out but hard enough to daze and confuse him. Turning quickly to maximise the movement and fluidity of my actions, I spin and strike the one I had flown over. With a guttural roar, I slash at the face of the man before me. I cut his forehead, causing blood to flow thickly over his eyes. His comprehension of the situation now truly compromised, I turn to his compatriot. He is on the ground, covering his head with his arms, blubbering. I set about slashing his body, drawing blood with each pass of my claws. He tries to crawl away, and I proceed to hack at his legs and posterior.

In his haste to escape he stumbles forward and hits his head, further incapacitating him. I turn back to the other man, struggling to clear the blood from his eyes. Him too, I cut from head to toe, frantically darting back and forth to make the attack as vicious and confusing as possible. Eventually satisfied with the damage I have done them, I leap to their camp and cut it to shreds, finally sprinting into the woods on all fours.

Once clear of their camp, I changed my movements to hide any trail of my departure. I carefully made my way back to the cabin and changed, hiding the bear outfit in the store. Slowly, with Kendal behind me, I returned to our viewpoint of their camp. I half expected them to be collecting themselves, repairing their camp, and maybe tracking their attacker. I was mistaken; they were throwing their belongings haphazardly into the boat, which was already in the water. They had spent the time I had been fleeing to tend their wounds and were covered with bandages and plasters. Now, shaking with fear, they were leaving as quickly as they possibly could. I roared into the woods and they almost jumped out of their skins. The rest of their belongings were hurled into the bottom of the boat and they fell in and started the small engine. It whined and thrashed at the water as one of them helped it along with his hands. Pleased beyond measure, stifling my laughter lest it reach their ears, I celebrated their departure. Kendal and I watched their small boat until we could no longer see it, their meagre lights finally overwhelmed by the rising power of the sun.

On the walk back home, I spoke my mind to a receptive Kendal.

"I felt Id tonight, Kendal. I felt him inside of me. He wasn't trying to escape or vying for control. He was I and I he. It was good, I felt pure. Ego was there too, overseeing our activities. He approved, he allowed it. I feel good, Kendal."

Kendal barked in approval. We looked to the sky; there was a single star remaining in the morning light, so together we howled our names.

Chapter Seventy-nine

As spring arrived, I moved in with Grace and my mood dramatically improved. I had thrown myself into the paperwork the Captain assigned me, and he frequently told me how impressed he was with my commitment, my new attention to detail. Grace noticed my improvement in attitude too and, as we grew closer, she suggested that we live together. I jumped at the opportunity, and we decided that I would move into her apartment as it was far nicer than mine.

It was not long before spring arrived and the city started to warm. As the city emerged from its hibernation, I became restless, feeling a growing need for action. The Captain, I think, noticed my urgency for life to move on and placed me back on active duty. I was partnered with Booth and together we started working real cases again. Life was good and getting better. This, I decided, was the best time of my life and I soaked it up. One evening, after finishing early so Booth could go and watch the hockey, I found myself home before Grace. This was a rare occurrence and as I sat on the sofa, thinking of something to do, a plan formed in my mind; an opportunity to grab life again.

Having visited the local shop, I transformed her apartment. I placed candles all around and drew the blinds, I lit some incense and put on some soft music. My diet had been working and so, sliding on a new pair of silk underwear, I didn't feel too self-conscious about my stomach. Checking my preparations, I lay down in the middle of the lounge on a large furry rug I had purchased especially for the night. Annoyingly, I ended up waiting quite a long time and eventually succumbed to boredom by watching television. It was less than romantic, therefore, when she entered to find me darting for the remote as she stepped into the apartment. Flipping off the television and returning to my well-planned pose on the floor, I saw her smile at me.

Dropping her things on the floor, she got down on to her knees. Creeping forward she slinked towards me. She was wearing sensible work attire but the way she moved made me think that she too was prepared for a night of passion. She crawled right to me and kissed me softly on the mouth. Breaking from the kiss, she moved forward again, climbing over me. I felt the soft material of her shirt on my stomach as she lowered herself onto my lap. She was wearing a knee-length woollen skirt that had transformed to a sexy outfit with her new position on me as I slid it up her legs.

A thought entered my mind and, in a move very unlike me, I slapped my hand down on her buttocks. She did nothing; no noise, no complaint. I did it again. Still no reaction. Enjoying the action, I carried on. She was moving on me now, starting to enjoy the sensation, enjoying my attentions. I rolled her over. She was smiling as she looked deep into my eyes. I bent down and kissed her. The passion was intense, the need was great. I tore her remaining clothes from her as she pulled urgently at my underwear.

We made love there and then on the furry rug. It was not gentle. It was raw, passionate and primal. She screamed and I cried out. Afterwards we lay on the floor, our hot sweaty bodies pressing together. She started to laugh and I quickly joined in. Laughing turned to kissing and we made love again. Finally, finished, she rolled away. This time we lay apart, our hot bodies too sticky to touch. My knee was screaming at me in pain but I didn't listen. Instead I lay on my back, smiling.

After a short delay, she rose to walk to the bathroom. I tried to stretch as the doctors had taught me, to no avail. I towelled myself dry instead, unable to stand and then crawled painfully across the apartment. We climbed into bed together and fell asleep, naked and entwined, in love.

*

I woke two hours later, my knee screaming at me again. I needed to move it, to relieve the pain. Gently I shifted my leg and, in doing so, accidentally woke Grace.

"That was interesting," she murmured softly.

"Interesting good?" I asked insecurely.

"Very good, silly."

I smiled in the dark and shifted my leg to a more comfortable position.

"What made you think of that, then?"

"Which bit?"

"All of it really, so passionate, so rough."

"Not too rough, I hope."

"Not at all. In the right situation, rough can be good. That was good rough," she reassured me. I enjoyed it immensely but considered myself a modern man. Spanking your girlfriend was not a liberal action, I worried.

"Was the spanking okay? I mean, I didn't mean to demean you or anything."

"I know that, silly. It was good, it didn't hurt. I liked it..."

"I could tell..."

"I liked that you wanted to. I liked that you wanted to pay attention to me, take me."

"I guess I let my id out..."

"We both did, it's good to let it out from time to time."

It was good to feel that raw. Lying there, I think I understood Edward a little better. He had not paid his desires enough attention and it had hurt him. It felt good to let loose, it felt healthy. It was strange to think of him; I hadn't given him a second thought since moving in with Grace, I realised. It made my stomach churn; ideas of catching him flashed in my mind along with a feeling of unfinished business. With some effort, I pushed him from my mind and instead focussed on the naked beauty nuzzling into my chest as she tried to sleep.

*

I woke early with another stabbing pain in my knee, so moved to the living room in a fog of pain and memories of pleasure. I flipped the television on and started to make breakfast. Slowly, word by word, the television penetrated my mind. Without truly hearing the words I listened to the story about an island. They were saying how it was haunted by a Spirit Bear who attacked any hunters who strayed into the area. The locals believed the ghost of an old prospector lived on one of the islands. When he died, the man had taken on the body of a bear and was now apparently a deadly hunter of hunters. The islands were considered off-limits by all and the local tribe had declared their interest in designating the area an official game reserve, out of respect for the Spirit Bear that lived there. They switched to their spokesman who was talking about the Spirit Bear and how hunting licences were destroying their culture and the local wildlife.

I stopped listening; one phrase stuck in my mind. Playing over and over again.

Hunter of hunters.

Hunter of hunters.

Hunter of hunters.

Chapter Eighty

I climb the stairs to her bedroom, gently placing my bare foot on each stair as I do. Silently I rise higher and higher, approaching my goal. I am naked, aroused, excited. I slip my foot across the next stair, placing it to the side to avoid making any creaking noises on the aged wood. I hear movement from above, a gentle rustle of bed linen. I pause, holding my breath, have I alerted her?

Breathing shallowly, trying to remain still and silent, I wait on the stair a full minute before proceeding. There is no follow-up sound to her movement. I deduce that she is sleeping as I creep towards her. Finally, I reach the last step and slip to the carpeted hallway. Her door is open and I peer inside, there is a shape beneath the covers rising and falling gently. She is there, in slumber, unsuspecting. I creep through the door.

I had woken an hour ago in my own cabin with a single thought in my mind. I wanted her, therefore I had to have her. I dressed and walked to my canoe, leaving Kendal sleeping in his basket. Paddling swiftly and powerfully across the wide waters, I made my way directly to the dock of her store. Gently I opened the door and silenced the bell, reaching up and holding it steady between two fingers. I made my way to the back room and stripped. Naked, prepared, I climbed the stairs to her private sanctuary.

The moon outside her bedroom casts a pale light across her. Star's sleeping face is an image of peace and contentment. The sight of her beauty excites me and after just a moment of looking at her I am unable to contain myself further. I slide to the foot of her bed and place my hands on the sheet that covers her. Slowly but inexorably I pull it from her body. First revealing her neckline, I pause to admire the colour of her soft skin, white in the lucent moonlight. Unable to stop, I reveal her breasts, pointing to the ceiling, their smooth curves delight me. She sleeps naked, I realise with a gasp.

"You are naughty, sleeping nude," I softly murmur to no one in particular as I proceed to pull the sheet. She is revealed to me; a target for my passion. I lick my lips as I approach the bed. I will take her now.

I stop moving, standing stock-still. Her eyes fluttered, she is awake.

"You took your time," she spoke without opening her eyes. Talking with a perfectly lucid voice, she had been awake the whole time.

"When did you detect my approach?" I softly enquired, moving to her side and sitting on the bed.

"I saw you in your canoe about half an hour ago, I've been waiting."

I smiled and placed my hand on her bare breast as she finally opened her eyes. Smiling at me, she placed a hand on my naked body.

"It was like I was calling you here," she said, "am I naughty?" She asked, referring to my previous statement.

"You are," I confirmed, "sleeping naked, with the door open. Anyone could enter."

She slipped onto my lap. In the moonlight, her buttocks seemed to be lit from within, calling to me. "I am a naughty girl," she whispered. I slapped her bare cheek and she gasped. The sex was passionate and raw. I cried out into the night as we ended together. Our screams combined into one long primal call to pleasure. We collapsed to the bed as I hugged her close. She reached down and covered us with the discarded sheet. There we lay, one entity, together. Falling asleep, contented, happy.

As I drifted into blissful oblivion, memories of the last three months filled my mind. I had returned to see Star just two days after I had refused her and confessed everything. I explained that I had been sick, damaged, deranged and was afraid of returning to that state. My greatest fear was that I would endanger her. She had understood, asking no detailed questions, saying she didn't need to know.

Our encounters had started gently but had slowly grown more intense and passionate. Gradually, I had cast aside my fears of accidentally releasing Id. Concurrently we had grown accustomed to each other's desires and needs. Our relationship was strong, and our sexual experiences were sensational. Through her passions, the way she listened to her own id, I had successfully and safely tapped into mine.

Morning rose, and we woke together to the sound of the bell over the shop door. She slid from under the sheet and I admired the view as she slipped into jeans and a flannel shirt.

"You stay here, I'll handle this and come back. I want another go..." she sexily whispered to me, skipping from the bedroom. I was going nowhere, I had found my nirvana and I wasn't going to willingly depart from it. Also, I was still hiding. Star had accepted me but I worried about the rest of the island on which she lived. Better that I remain anonymous and hidden from anyone else's eyes. Again, I considered telling her the details of my past, of Id's crimes. Again, I decided against it. They horrified me. They would forever taint her view of me, I knew. She also knew this and each time I suggested that she might want to know what I had done, she had declined. She was right, of course. My desire to tell her was my need to confess, to remove some of the guilt I felt by placing it on her. It was my guilt to feel, my punishment, and I had to bear it alone.

Hearing footsteps on the stairs, I prepared myself for some new experience.

"Get dressed," she hissed to me, entering, quickly stepping to the bathroom and flushing the toilet. "I said I had to go to the bathroom," she cryptically explained as I hurriedly dressed. Her urgency and panic was quickly spreading to me.

"What is it? Who is it?"

"Police," she responded. I relaxed, of course there would be police here. Such things would be normal, standard. She was overreacting.

"They don't know I'm here, Star. Relax, they're here for something else."

"Yes, he is, he's here for camping equipment."

I looked at her, confused, "well that's okay, then."

"No, no it's not," was her worried reply as she threw me my shirt. "He's going camping on the Devil's Chute Islands. Your islands, Edward."

"Coincidence?" I asked, not believing it could be, but hoping nonetheless. She shook her head.

"No, he showed me your picture. He's here for you. Now get

dressed!"

I pulled my shirt on and looked for my shoes, "where are my shoes?"

"Downstairs. I'll go and distract him, sell him his equipment. I'll close the door, so you can slip out the back. Get back to your cabin, pack your things."

"No. I can't do that," I stated firmly.

She looked at me incredulously, "you can't stay there, he'll find you."

"Be that as it may. Those islands are my home now. I can't let them drive me away."

"Yes, but..."

"Besides, Kendal's there."

She swore, standing with her hands on her hips.

"Star?" I asked her, as she looked at me sternly, "what's his name?"

"Detective Montgomery Beech," she said, confirming my suspicions.

"Don't worry. He might find the island, he might find the cabin. He will not find me. He's hunting a killer called Id. There's no such person anymore. He can't find a man who doesn't exist."

I kissed her on the forehead and together we descended the stairs to mask any noise I might make. Gathering my boots, I slipped from the back of the store and circled around to the canoe. Slipping gently down to it, I paddled hard across the water, fully aware that a casual glance through the window of the store from Minty would reveal me. Hopefully Star was keeping him occupied, making her money for the month.

He would not see me, he would not catch me. He was the hunter of Id, but I was still the hunter of hunters. To remind myself that I was Id no longer, rather an improved Edward, I slowly breathed my name.

Chapter Eighty-one

The woman at the store claimed she had not seen Edward, but I knew he was here, on these islands. I felt it as soon as I had seen the news that morning. I grit my teeth and goosed the throttle on my rented boat as I pointed it towards the larger of the islands ahead of me. Consulting my map once again, I checked that I was heading to the correct location. My destination was the forbidden islands of the Spirit Bear, the Devil's Chute. It sounded frightening, but I knew there was no spirit. It was, however, the hiding place of Id, which was a far greater danger to fear. I felt guilty about leaving the people I loved behind with a series of lies, telling everyone that I was working a case in Vancouver with Henry. However, I had to lie as the truth would have led either to Grace coming with me or forbidding that I come. But I had to come, I had to apprehend Id, it was my duty. Not to save my career but to rescue my pride. I was a detective who had sworn to apprehend criminals and protect the public. Id was a dangerous man and I had to stop him from hurting again.

My determination had been renewed as I'd listened to that news report. I had wanted to let it go, to leave the past behind me. But I couldn't escape the simple fact that there was still no resolution. I needed a full-stop to the story, to know what had happened to Id. Had Edward defeated him or was the Id killer still on the loose? I needed to know.

I was coming from Morgan's Island, where I had spent a week mixing with and interrogating the hunters there. Many of them had warned me about visiting these islands because of the Spirit Bear, a legend I was not prepared to believe. One of them finally told me of the story of Joe's cabin; the remains of a prospector's home. I knew that if Id were anywhere, he would be there. All his past movements had resulted in him setting up home comfortably; this time would be no different.

Driving the boat up on to the beach, I jumped out and pulled it ashore. I had been warned of the powerful currents, so I tied it to a large tree. Leaving my new belongings in the boat, I checked my firearms. I had come prepared with a shotgun and a pistol. Swallowing my apprehension, I stepped into the woods to start my hunt. I spent all day searching that island but discovered nothing. A person, regardless of how in touch with his animal, could not survive a north Canadian winter without some kind of shelter. Disappointed, I made my way back to my boat, cursing the thorns and branches that scraped and scratched at me the whole time. I waved another mosquito away, frustrated that the bug repellent didn't deter them completely. I hated this place, but I was determined to end this. I wondered again; would I find Id, hunting, chasing, living raw? Or would I find Edward? I hoped that it would be Edward. Meeting the woman in the store on Morgan's island had supported my hope. Id, if he were loose, would not have been able to resist the beauty at the store.

She reminded me of Grace in many ways. She was strong and short, pretty and feisty. Just as Id had wanted Grace, he would have wanted Star. He would, therefore, have taken her. She would not be walking around her store free and happy just a twenty-minute boat ride from the animal that was Id. No, Edward was here, and he had learned how to control Id. I gripped the stock of my shotgun, as Edward I could take him, I told myself. Checking that my handgun in the holster was loaded and cocked ready, I climbed into my boat. It was against every regulation and safety standard in the book to walk with a primed handgun. But, as I patted the loaded gun, I found it reassured me more than the fear of an accidental misfire.

The sun was starting to set as I pulled the boat up onto the beach of another island. Just above the waterline, there was an old campsite. I quickly cut some wood and set about lighting a large fire in a prepared circle of stones. As the logs caught from the fire-starter I had bought, I started to relax. It would keep the mosquitoes away, and hopefully the larger animals that roamed these islands.

I pitched my tent, it took me three attempts to get the poles and guide-wires right, but finally I stood back to admire my temporary new home. Feeling more comfortable, I found my gas stove and started cooking chilli and beans from a can. The sun was down by the time my dinner was ready and the stars were coming out over the water. I dipped a slice of bread into the pot and started to eat directly from the pan. As I blew on the hot chilli, I looked out over the expanse before me, admiring the view. Suddenly I fell back from my seat in surprise. Just off the coast, a humpback whale crested the water in a graceful silent arch. Blasting water and air from its blowhole it dove back down to the deep with a wave of its tail. Following the sudden loud burst of noise and water, it disappeared again into the dark waters without a sound. Eerily it was almost immediately replaced with a distant howl behind me from the island's interior.

I swallowed the fear that was building in the pit of my stomach. Either that was a coyote or a wolf. I wasn't sure if I should be afraid of a coyote, but I was definitely afraid of a wolf investigating my dinner. I stirred the pot with one hand and gripped the stock of my handgun with the other.

As I finished my meal, I finally calmed down again. The noises in the woods had settled into a reassuring rhythm. The stars twinkling over the lapping waves of water were soothing my nerves. Just as I was looking to the sky, studying the points of light, I jumped as I heard something large moving in the undergrowth. Snatching up my shotgun and pointing it towards the sound, I moved position, creeping towards the noise, crouching on one knee. In the dark, the ferns before me rustled and swayed from side to side. Something was trying to skirt the light of the fire, using the dark undergrowth to hide themselves from me. Sliding my left hand forward on the stock of the shotgun, I held tight to the grip and tensed my trigger finger. With my left thumb, I flicked on the torch that underslung the barrel of the powerful firearm.

With a click, the woods before me were illuminated in a powerful white light. Through blinking eyes, I saw another pair of smaller darker eyes looking back at me. It was a face wearing a mask, looking at me, hands in front preparing to attack. I pointed the shotgun directly between the eyes and pulled my finger tight on the trigger. At the very last second, however, I released the pressure, saving the life of an inquisitive racoon. It continued to look at me, flexing its fingers, hands together, grasping at the air. I guessed it had been attracted by my food and I spent a while returning its intelligent stare. It was not captivated by the light, it was interested in it. It didn't know the threat the hollow tube posed, and I moved the gun away from its gentle face. Satisfied that I was of no interest after all, the masked intruder slowly made its way back into the woods, disappointed that I had no food after all.

I sighed, laughing a little at my fear of such a gentle creature. It made me chuckle at my ineptitude as an outdoorsman. I looked across the waters. I could see that this was a magical place, a special place for sure. Even with the danger that I knew was nearby in the form of Edward, its reassuring sounds and views soothed me. As if to correct my perceptions and remind me of the true nature of the wild, I heard another howl echo across the island. Closer this time, it caused my heart to race as I threw more logs onto the fire and crawled into my tent. Zipping the tent shut, I climbed into my sleeping bag, tightly clutching a gun in each hand.

Chapter Eighty-two

"How dare he? How dare he come to this place to hunt me!" I shouted at Kendal. He didn't seem to take it personally, he knew it was not directed at him, so he simply sat there, wagging his tail. "Don't look at me like that. I told him what would happen if he chased me. I broke his leg and his arm to prevent this from happening."

"Woof!"

"I should have killed him, I shouldn't have let him live." Kendal growled, barking again, looking at me. "Fine, fine. You're right, he didn't deserve to die. He's a good man."

I sighed, collapsing into the chair on the porch of my cabin. It was hard to maintain my rage while looking at his soft brown eyes. Always happy, always accepting, despite his previous life of hardship and cruelty.

"It's okay for you, he isn't coming here for you. He hasn't got a cage to throw you in."

"Woof."

"Oh, don't. If I'm taken, you can go and live with Star and you know it."

The mention of her name increased the pace of his tail, now thumping on the wooden planks.

"I feel like you would like that more, living with her instead of me." I complained petulantly. He tilted his head in response. I signalled for him to come to me and he obliged. Stroking him behind the ears, I held his face close to mine and pressed my nose into the soft hair around his neck.

"Oh, Kendal. What I am supposed to do? I don't want to go to prison. I'm happy here, I won't hurt anyone. Id's gone, how can I live my life in peace? I want to make amends, I really do, but here in this place. Not stewing in some box surrounded by more monsters of men."

He nuzzled into me, comforting me as I started to cry. His fur soaked up my tears as I sobbed into him, crying that I wanted Star, that I wanted to be left alone, that I wished that Id had never appeared and done this to me.

"Life is so unfair!" I cried out into the night as rage replaced anguish. I flexed my fists and clenched my jaw tight, determination replacing sorrow. "No!" I commanded, "I will not go, I will act. It will not end this way." I stood and arched my back, looking to the moon. I howled my name.

Chapter Eighty-three

I slide through the undergrowth of the forest, slipping across the ground unseen and silent. I am the hunter of hunters in the skin of a bear, the anthropomorphic realisation of the beast. To his strength I add intellect, strategy and ruthlessness. I am a far worse creature than any in these islands, for I plan, acting according to perceived and anticipated threats.

I know where my prey resides, smelling the smoke on the air; his pollution offends me. He does not belong here, and will regret coming here. This island will be pure again, cleansed of his presence.

I slip to a fallen tree and lie behind it. Gently I raise my head to view my target. I see his camp, set up in the exact same place as the previous hunters. It was easy enough for me before, now it is more so. He is a lamb before the teeth of a tiger. He crawls from his tent. The sun has risen, lighting it, disturbing his sleep. I bare my teeth, hissing at the man who has hounded me.

He is holding a gun in his hands, sweeping the area and looking for me. Besides the shotgun, I see a pistol in a holster. He is prepared this time, cautious. I revise my plans, calming myself. I settle down behind the log to observe, confident that the dark bear fur atop my head will conceal me. The sun is behind me, blinding him further, and the wind is blowing in from the sea, masking my scent and preventing any sound from reaching him.

I watch as he coaxes his fire back to life, adding more wood, poking it. He announces his presence to all as the smoke climbs high. The wind changes and blows a cloud in his face, causing him to cough and splutter. He stretches and performs movements to bend and move himself in all directions. Recognising the movements as yoga positions, I am momentarily surprised. Then I remember the damage I caused him in my hotel room. He is repairing himself. A pang of guilt penetrates me, slicing down my chest to my stomach. I swallow the unpleasant feeling, preventing it distracting me from my actions.

I watch as he inexpertly makes breakfast. He prepares coffee on his gas stove and bagels toasted over the smoky fire. Despite the unappealing nature of his food, my stomach complains at being as empty as it is, and I hear a noise behind me. Without turning I know it is

Kendal. He drops to his belly and crawls alongside me, placing his long face on top of the log behind which we hide. He sniffs against the rough surface of the log. His tail starts to move, banging against my leg. I close my eyes and take a breath.

"Fine," I concede, backing away from the log. Returning to the cabin, I prepare us a breakfast of bacon and toasted bread. For me a coffee and for Kendal a bowl of water. He devours his food while I savour mine; still wearing the bearskin I sit looking out to the ocean. As I watch a sea lion playing in the rapid swells, hunting fish, I contemplate my next move.

Chapter Eighty-four

Making breakfast, toasting a bagel on the open fire revived me. My sleep had been fitful and worrisome. The tent had offered protection against curious animals and I had even taken the time to urinate all around it to ward off any passing bears. It provided very little protection against Edward, however, so I slept gripping a gun in each hand, nervously twitching at every sound. The sun rose, lighting the tent like a beacon and I was tired as I crawled from my cocoon. However, the sun on my face and the food in my stomach made me feel like a new man. The woods in the daylight were far less frightening. Musical birds sang their morning choruses and various unknown animals made gentle noises in the undergrowth. I did my morning stretches and felt renewed, looking to the rising sun, I greeted it out loud.

"Hello, Sun."

Smiling, I checked my guns again. Grabbing the toilet paper, I sat on a small fallen log and dealt with that morning chore. This place felt pure, natural and unspoiled. Looking around at my camp I immediately felt guilt about my presence. Wiping myself, I buried my waste and went to tidy the camp. No need to leave more mess than necessary, I thought as I busied myself.

The camp looking much nicer, I pulled my phone from my bag. I had charged it overnight from a large external battery and wanted to check that it was prepared. I brought up the navigation application on the phone and started it tracking me. My plan was simple, I was going to divide the island into a grid and walk across it row by row until I found the cabin that I knew was here. If Edward was here, he would have been here for months, surely he will have left a trace. Looking at the mess I had already made with my small camp over the course of one night confirmed this. I would find him and arrest him.

A small bird took flight from a tree above me and, taking this as a sign to move, I started my search.

Chapter Eighty-five

I move through the woods once more, Kendal's hunger satisfied along with my own. He remains at the cabin, disapproving of my actions. I reach the campsite and I see that it is tidier and less offensive to me. Slowly, silently, I approach. Moving in wide circles, narrowing in, lest he lay a trap for me, I stalk the camp. As I reach the tent, however, I see that he is gone. Looking around me, rising high and sensing the air, I wonder at his location, his destination. I see damage to the trees before me, broken twigs, compressed leaves underfoot. Because of his blundering movements, the direction of his travel is obvious. He has walked from the camp in a straight line, an arrow through the woods. Stepping into the undergrowth alongside his trail, I follow him.

I start to contemplate my foe, worrying that I am underestimating him and that his trail is a trap, a lure for me to follow. Just as I have decided to circle around, to come at him from another angle, I see him. I drop to the ground and lay still, ensuring that he does not see me. I needn't have worried. He is moving in a straight line across the island, ignoring streams and natural paths left by animals over decades of predictable movements. Periodically he looks to a device in his hand, correcting his movements according to some unknown plan.

His artificial line across the land is making his progress difficult. I laugh as a branch whips him in the face, causing him to curse. He is making a cacophonous sound, blundering through the woods. Amusingly, from time to time he pauses. He is stopping to listen for me, for my sounds. As if he could hear me over the noise he is making. He starts to walk again as I close in on him from the side.

I move silently through the undergrowth with ease, following the path of a stream. I needn't bother, truth be told, as the amount of noise my prey is making is masking any I might cause. However, I like to hunt properly, and I know that he could stop at any moment. I would not like to be detected, my pride prevents it as much as the guns he carries. They are the real threat. He might not be proficient in the woods, but he is a capable fighter. I have shadowed him as he has turned on himself twice, each time moving back on his previous path in a parallel line. I see his strategy now, he searches for my cabin, not me. He moves in a logical grid to cover the entire island. It is not a bad idea, as he will surely come across my home later today. From there I predict that he will wait for me. It is a sensible enough plan, but he fails to anticipate my reaction to his presence. I can take him here, before he reaches my home. An animal might retreat and run from the threat. But I am a man, I can see the future unfold, the danger of leaving him alone. A danger I can prevent by pre-empting the confrontation in a place of my choosing.

Moving ahead of his path, I find a suitable tree, a massive Ponderosa Pine that has been darkened by a previous forest fire. I pull myself up its bark and high into the canopy. I am still wearing the bearskin and the claws on my gloves. They help my ascent and as I come to rest on a large branch running across his path. I press myself to the wide dark wood, hidden from view, invisible from below. Ambush prepared, I wait for my prey to wander into it.

I hear his approach, like a freight train inexorably driving through the woods. I lie still, waiting. I roll my muscles around, barely moving but relaxing them for the forthcoming action. He is below me now, five metres away. Pausing, he scans the woods for movements, listening for sounds. I see the whites of his knuckles on the stock of the shotgun. He is scared and nervous. A bird moves in the bushes and he almost jumps out of his skin. He steps away, afraid of a ground bird. He wheels around as a squirrel jumps between branches in his field of view.

He continues on his path, checking his phone to ensure the correct direction. He steps below me, I prepare myself.

I stop. I cannot. I release the energy from me with a long gentle breath as he passes beneath me. The land whips and scratches at him but still he pushes ahead. He is afraid, incapable, yet he proceeds. I admire him. I like him. The realisation strikes me, he is more worthy of life than I. I cannot take his for mine, so I let him pass.

In front of him a dark figure moving through the ferns catches my eye. It is Kendal. He looks to me and I nod back to him. He has been watching and approves of my decision.

My heart leaps into my mouth as Kendal steps in front of the searching policeman. The shotgun swings up, pointing directly at him and my soul screams out a silent cry.

Chapter Eighty-six

I was on the third lane of my search, sweating with the effort and my fear of this place. Animals moved through the trees leaving no sign but their dark shadows and occasional sounds. I was on-edge and afraid. I was just checking my phone again as a large object suddenly appeared in front of me. Quickly I swung my gun around, finger tensing on the trigger, preparing to fire. At the last second, I relaxed. Looking at me quizzically was a medium-sized white and brown dog, its tail wagging furiously. He barked and ran to me as I lifted my gun away from him.

He reached me and pressed his head between my legs as I bent down to stroke him. Petting his head, I could feel that he was clean and soft. Clearly cared for. I dropped to one knee and swept my shotgun around the woods. This was Edward's dog. There was only one other person on this island who would care for and wash a dog. It ran around me in tight circles, barking happily but I remained vigilant, checking the woods.

Eventually it became clear that Edward was not coming and I relaxed again. Standing, I asked my new friend the question that burned inside.

"Where are you from then, boy? Where's your home?"

He barked and darted into the woods. Seconds later he reappeared and turned away again. He was leading me home, I thought. I abandoned my search grid to follow him instead. Keeping my gun high, my senses searched for danger as I followed the dog to a ramshackle cabin. The door was open and I could see that no one was inside. Cautiously stepping through the open doorway, I slowly closed the door. Sweat dripping from my brow, I dropped to the floor, checking under the bed. Relieved, I scanned the rest of the cabin, the dog and I were alone. Sitting on the bed, gun in hand, we would wait here together.

As I sat in safety for the first time since arriving in this wild place, the dog retired to his basket in the corner and lay down to rest. This was a frightening place, filled with danger. Id roamed wild beyond that door. My voice shook as I whispered to the closed door.

"Montgomery, let's end this..."

Chapter Eighty-seven

Kendal had shown me the truth, the truth I had already seen. The Detective was a good man. I slid down the trunk of the tree as he left with Kendal, moving toward my cabin. I unfastened the belts and slipped the bearskin from me. I walked to the stream and washed the dirt from me.

Calmly, soft-footed, I made my way back to the cabin. I would face my hunter and ask him to pass judgement upon me. I stepped to the porch. This was final move; I would open that door and something would happen. Rising to my full height, I prepared myself.

Chapter Eighty-eight

"You lay a terrible trap, Detective," he calls from the other side of the door. I stay silent, trying to call his bluff; he can't know I'm here. "You closed the door. How did Kendal get through a closed door, Minty?"

Looking at the closed door, I curse my stupidity, "fine, but I have a gun, Id."

"We both know, for Id, a gun would be no obstacle."

I shiver, clutching the handle of the gun tighter. He's right and I know it. He is the superior hunter, "I have to arrest you, Id. Arrest or kill. It's up to you."

The door opens and he appears, standing naked in the entranceway. He is glowing, lit from behind by the setting sun.

"Id is no more. I am Edward."

"Then, Edward, I'm here to arrest you."

"Are you? You alone?"

My gun waivers as he speaks again.

"Id is constrained, to kill me would be wrong. I have stopped him, I control my desires as well as you do yours."

"You killed people, Edward. Id killed people."

"True, but he's with Ego now and we're one. I allow Id his desires just as Ego keeps him in check. He is a beautiful part of me, giving me passion. We are the same now, you and I. I am not a murderer."

My gun droops as he steps into the room. I look into his eyes and see him, finally, Edward alone.

"Montgomery, please. Leave me be. I'm happy here. I'm needed here."

I pause to think about it, just as I have been thinking about it since I landed on this island, this wild place, filled with wild beasts. I know what I must do.

Chapter Eighty-nine

The Detective left, departing silently in the direction of his camp on the far shore. I sat in my chair on the porch. He was leaving it all behind, leaving me behind. I will not see him again.

"Will he be okay?" I wonder to Kendal.

"Woof."

Which I take to mean that he will be. I scratch behind his ear as he places his head on my knee.

I am Edward, I am whole, happy, and imbued with purpose. I lean back in my chair and look to the sky; the wind whispers my name.